The saga of death, treachery and redemption, the story of lovers torn apart and reunited, the myth of the restoration of a kingdom, all climax and conclude in

The Jewel of Fire

Prince Julian, hidden as an infant from the evil Caolin, Sorcerer and Seneschal, who killed his father, King Jehan, returns to combat Caloin's magical threat as a young man. But Julian was unable to prove his identity, so he was set a great test: only the true heir could recover and master the four hereditary Jewels of Power that protect Westria and confirm the bond between the powers of nature and humanity.

Three Jewels are in Julian's possession now. Now is the time for the final quest, and the final battle.

Tor books by Diana L. Paxson

The Westria Series

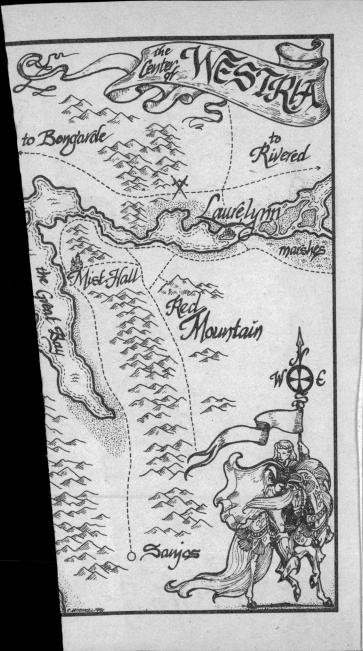

the Center of WESTRIA

to Bongarde

to Rivered

Laurelynn

marshes

Mist Hall

the Great Bay

Red Mountain

W E

Sanjos

DIANA L. PAXSON

THE SEVENTH BOOK OF WESTRIA

THE JEWEL OF FIRE

TOR
fantasy

A TOM DOHERTY ASSOCIATES BOOK
NEW YORK

THE JEWEL OF FIRE

Copyright © 1986 by Diana L. Paxson

A Tor Book
Published by Tom Doherty Associates, Inc.
175 Fifth Avenue
New York, N.Y. 10010

TOR® is a registered trademark of Tom Doherty Associates, Inc.

Cover art by Tom Canty
Maps by Ellisa Martin

ISBN: 0-312-51110-7

First Edition: March 1992

Printed in the United States of America

0 9 8 7 6 5 4 3 2 1

To Tracy,
who was there at the beginning—

"Lest we forget . . ."

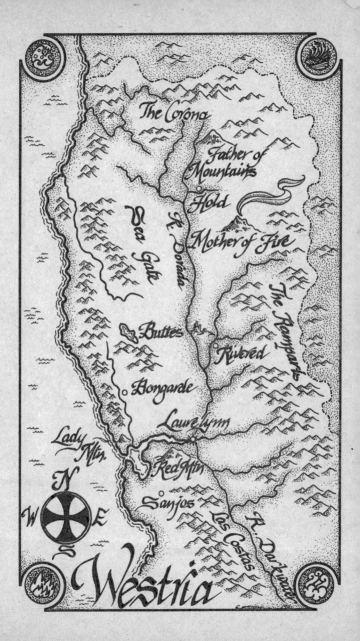

The Corona

Father of Mountains

Hold

R. Dorada

Mother of Fire

The Ramparts

Sea Gate

Buttes

Rivered

Bongarde

Laurelynn

Lady Mtn.

Red Mtn.

Sanjos

Las Costas

R. Darkwater

N
W E
S

Westria

ONE

"And now kill him!" The Blood Lord's voice broke the icy silence. He leaned on the cold stone arms of the high seat above the courtyard of his fortress as the new warrior flowed forward like some pale-haired beast of prey. Below, men drew breath in anticipation. The guards stationed along the walls of Blood Gard straightened, hands hovering above the hilts of their swords.

In the center of the yard, the prisoner strained at the rope that tethered him. Did he realize what was going to happen? Already, blood oozed sluggishly from the weals where he had been flogged, bright against the chilled gray of his bare skin. The other men who had been disciplined with him had already been carried away. The sky was gray too: Thick clouds hung low over the walls and towers of the fortress that encrusted the twinned peaks of the Red Mountain. Only the crimson robes of the sorcerer and the badges of his men strove with that cold light.

But the air was still. Caolin no longer went outside when there was a wind.

Perhaps the prisoner did understand—all of Caolin's men must know the penalty for trying to desert the Blood Lord's service by now. The sorcerer's gaze moved along their ranks, noting faces gone red or pale, eyes bright with fear or excitement. For those with doubts, this would be a deterrent; for those with none, a reward.

The prisoner glimpsed the movement and swung around to the opposite side of the post, the three-foot rope that held him to it vibrating as it snapped taut. The swordsman grinned and moved to the left, muscles sliding easily beneath bronzed skin. The victim's face grew a shade grayer as he realized that he was being driven in a circle that would leave him bound tight to the pole. Trembling, he held his ground.

Caolin blinked; for a moment the prisoner's sandy hair had seemed to darken, his shoulders grew broad, another man looked out of his eyes. An echo of laughter seared the sorcerer's soul. He closed his eyes, and the mist brushed damp fingers across his brow. When he opened them again, he saw only this poor wretch who had tried to run away. It was not Julian. *But it will be*, he promised himself silently. *One day* . . .

The warrior's blade was still in the sheath across his back, his hands open and ready at his sides, but his walk had become a prowl. Then he blurred forward. Steel blazed as the sword came out of its sheath. Blood sprayed as a two-handed stroke lopped off first the prisoner's right arm, then the other. Freed from the rope, the victim lurched away, screaming, but with another leap the swordsman was upon him. Again the blade blurred, taking out the man's legs.

"Now, kill *him*!" cried Caolin again as the warrior's blade whipped around to send head and torso tumbling in opposite directions. From each wall a man leaped out from among the guards. The Blood Lord's lips drew back in a snarling grin as four blades flickered free.

Suddenly the warrior was still. His dripping sword seemed to float in the air above him as his assailants crept forward. One of the guards hung back a little, and in that instant the warrior's blade sliced downward and around as the other three rushed him. Then the first guard's lifeblood was pumping out through a slashed chest, while the other three had fallen to the stroke that continued through the neck of one, the side of the next, and upward through the belly of the last.

For a moment there was silence. Slowly the warrior straightened. Crimson flicked from the sword at the bloodshake; then the weapon settled into its sheath again. The men were cheering, but the warrior's feral eyes were on Caolin.

"Oh, yes." The sorcerer laughed softly. "I will hire you. What is your name?"

"I am Konradin. And I am not an executioner." A disdainful shrug dismissed the men who were carrying the bodies away.

Silence spread around them. The men were watching the warrior as he had seen folk watch a captured wolf in a cage. Caolin smiled.

"You are whatever I will you to be." His gaze caught Konradin's. The man's eyes widened as he realized that he could not look away. *"Konradin, I know you,"* he spoke to the man's soul. *"I know who betrayed you, and whom you betrayed. But I will give you what you desire!"* He saw the hot light go out behind those pale eyes, knew the moment when Konradin believed in him.

The man brought one fist to his forehead in salute. The Blood Lord nodded, and Captain Esteban led him away. Caolin gazed after him, remembering how he had bound the great wolf Gerol to his service long ago.

Another nod sent the men marching back to their barracks. He heard the occasional sputter of suppressed laughter. They would have something to talk about tonight. Watching punishment was good for discipline. For those in barracks, it was a regular Saturday entertainment. When none of the men had merited the final chastisement, there were always prisoners.

The Blood Lord leaned back against the stone of his chair, surveying the graveled courtyard, where servants were already scraping the blood away, the walls of smoothly dressed stone. The dun-colored slopes of the mountain fell away below them, and the lands beyond were dim beneath close cloud-cover, bounded by the river's dull pewter gleam. From here, he could just see the jumbled roofs of Laurelynn—more jumbled now than they had been, for the destruction wrought by his whirlwind last fall was still being cleared away.

The work had been slowed by the need to build defenses between the city and Blood Gard. The Regent's blockade of the Red Mountain had ended as soon as Caolin's scattered allies had begun to respond to his summoning. On Samaine Eve they had swept down from the peak and burned the bridge into Laurelynn. Now the Westrian forces were spread perilously thin, and Caolin's fortress loomed unchallenged over Julian's tattered capital.

"Lord Sangrado, will you come in?"

Caolin roused. Captain Esteban stood before him, correct as always, from the sleek waves of his graying hair to the burnished rivets in his burgundy leather brigantine. Already winter dusk was shadowing the hills.

"I have tea ready for you, and some food."

The Blood Lord got to his feet, annoyed to realize that his muscles had stiffened from sitting so long in the chill.

Ordrey was waiting for him. Caolin went to stand before the brazier which was sending a welcome warmth through the little room. Thick curtains and hangings of heavy Elayan silk provided some insulation against the chill, but

Caolin was still cold. When Ordrey helped himself to another shot of hot rice wine, he took one of the shallow cups and downed it, felt the heat spread through him, and sighed.

Ordrey lifted one gingery eyebrow. "In Elaya, the geraniums are still blooming on the balconies."

"Yes." Caolin held out his cup for the little man to refill.

"Maybe we spent too many years in the south." Ordrey eyed his master, gauging how far he could push this moment of relaxation. "Our blood's grown thin. The way I see it, when we've got Westria, we shouldn't have any trouble with Elaya."

"Perhaps." The Blood Lord eased into the cushioned velvet embrace of his desk chair. "But this campaign is not yet won. If you feel sufficiently recovered, would you like to report to me?"

The tone had warned Ordrey before Caolin finished speaking. He set down his cup and moved the silver candelabrum between them out of the way.

"In Santibar the impis are drilling. The stages on the central route are stocked and the supply system in place. My recruiters at the high desert mines have been busy. Each month should bring you more."

"Axemen?"

Ordrey nodded. "The skills of a man who works with pick and shovel adapt well to war. And some of them are trained engineers."

"Our weakness is in heavy cavalry," said Caolin. "But there may be no one left on the other side who can field an army by spring."

Ordrey's lips pursed soundlessly. "It's been going well in the mountains, then?"

The Blood Lord smiled. "The new snow grows black with the smoke of their burning, and the streets of Rivered are choked with refugees. By spring there will be hunger.

But the merchants of the free cities have sold me their stockpiles already, and you've seen Laurelynn.''

Ordrey's balding head gleamed in the candlelight as he laughed. ''Oh yes—and to think that last fall they believed that they had won! I just came through Laurelynn,'' he explained. ''No challenges—no one left with the energy, I suppose! The repairs finished at sunset fall down by dawn, and they seem to be having some trouble getting supplies.''

''I promised him,'' whispered Caolin. ''I swore that this was how it would be.''

Ordrey gave him a narrow look, but did not ask who *he* might be.

''I must break him. He's been kept busy fighting since September. But I want to stop the attacks in the Ramparts for a time.''

''You're giving him time to rest?'' asked Ordrey.

''I'm giving him time to think. He's desperate. Even with three of the Jewels in his possession, all he can manage to do is defend. With a moment to catch his breath, what do you think he will do?'' Caolin's gaze rested on the flickering candle flames.

''Julian will go after the Jewel of Fire,'' Ordrey replied like a good student, but his face was still troubled. ''My lord, why let him? You can conquer Westria with the weapons you have. Why bring magic into it again?''

Caolin's gaze fixed him, and Ordrey's jowls quivered like those of an old dog.

''None of the rest of it matters, without the Jewels.'' The sorcerer's harsh whisper seared the air. ''If *he* masters them, though all Westria acclaim me, he can make a rebel of the land.'' Ordrey shuddered, remembering grasses that entangled men, waves that clutched greedily, mocking laughter on the wind. Caolin's long fingers caressed the dead wood of his desk, supported safely by lifeless stone. ''We will not underestimate him, Ordrey, not anymore.''

The candle flames sent light and shadow in swift pursuit around the room. On the river the wind would be rising, but only an occasional draft could stir the thick curtains that protected him.

"Do you know where it is?"

"I do," said the sorcerer. "But only Julian can pluck it free."

Ordrey shook his head. "That plan's failed once already, my lord!"

"Last time," Caolin cut him off, "a tool failed me. This time *I* will be there."

Caolin, this battle is between you and me. Why must other men be sacrificed? With a forced gentleness, Julian laid down the guardsman's hand.

It had been a long dying. The man had been burned when the raiders attacked the village that afternoon, and now it was midnight. The king remembered the brown face contorted in pain, and then, for a moment at the last, open in wonder. But the meaning was draining out of it already, as light fades at dusk from the sky.

"I don't understand," said Robert. His eyes were red-rimmed beneath the soot that smudged his skin. No one would call him Robert the Fair right now. "I've seen men survive with worse burns, even the loss of a limb. Why did he die?"

"Shock, maybe, or exhaustion," said Julian. "Cold saps a man's strength, and we were a long time getting him to shelter. Or maybe he didn't want to live, knowing he would be maimed."

He closed his eyes, shivering, and images of blood and burning rioted in his memory. In the past weeks there had been too many fights like this one. They had all been so proud to join him after he had been proclaimed king at the Autumn Sessions of the Council three months ago, and a quarter of those lives had been spent already, burnt out in a dozen inconclusive skirmishes in unimportant villages up and down the land.

"My lords, there's nothin' more ye can do for him." It was one of the new lads, a boy called Marcos, who had followed his brother into the guards.

"Nothing!" The chair rocked as Julian got to his feet. "That's all I did do!"

"Ye stayed with him, m'lord. It'll comfort his people t'know that ye stayed with him till th' end."

Julian nodded. The boy was so young . . . clear-skinned and bright of eye. He shouldered abruptly past him, afraid to shatter that innocence. The Wind Crystal was safe atop the Lady Mountain, but apparently he still spoke with its glamour. Why had he ever wanted to be eloquent? Why had he ever wanted to be king? At the door he turned, waiting for his cousin, who was saying something graceful and appropriate. The boy's face lit up as Robert smiled.

Julian staggered as the cold outside struck him. Stars glittered like chips of ice in the night sky. Pulling up his hood and striding toward the lights of the inn, he heard Robert crunching through the snow after him.

"Thank you. That lad would have found no cheer in anything I could say!"

"My pleasure," Robert said absently. "Young Marcos is the prettiest thing I've seen since I left Rivered!"

Julian stopped short. "Is that all you can think of? Best send him home then. How long do you think he'll keep his beauty here? Oh, Sweet Lady, let's send them all home before they grow stiff and cold!"

"Julian!"

Robert's hand was on his arm, but Julian could not feel it. He blinked, but the dead man's face floated before him—all those dead faces—he ground his palms against his closed eyes.

"Stop it!" Robert shook him hard, and the faces whirled

away. "Would you rather bury slaughtered children who had no chance or a man who died fighting?"

Julian's pent breath came out in a shuddering sigh. He let the other man hold him, warming his spirit at the fire of Robert's love.

"I'm sorry," he said finally. "I'm tired. I've been fighting too long."

Robert stroked the heavy hair back from his brow. "Julian, my Jewel-lord. In a week we'll be back in Rivered with good food and soft beds. A few days of that will restore you, and then we can go after them again. You'll win—you are the King!"

Julian straightened. "Will I? If we're winning, why did that poor bastard die?" Robert shook his head and put his arms back around him, but Julian remained stiff and still, looking at him helplessly.

"Go on inside—there's no need for both of us to freeze. I need to do some thinking."

I should call him back, thought Julian as Robert strode away, but what he had said was true. He sighed, and his breath puffed out in a frosty cloud.

It was very quiet. As Julian's own spirit stilled, he became aware of the small night sounds: the stifled bark of a dog, logs creaking as the temperature fell. Other senses stirred within him. He knew that an owl was quartering the wood behind the village, felt the trees draw inward as they endured the cold. In the frozen stream there was no motion, but he sensed warm-blooded life in the wood.

Somewhere in that wilderness, one of his men was struggling to carry warning of the raiders to the next village. Ignoring the cold, Julian took a deep breath of frosty air and held it, trying to free his spirit to follow him. He let his breath out in a slow stream of cloud and felt the world fall away. A tremor shook him; he swayed, twitching, controlling the urge to fight it. The wrench came then, and he was free, gazing down at the abandoned body that stood muscle-locked upright in the road below. Only the shimmering silver cord that swung downward connected self to the semblance that the world knew as the uncrowned King of Westria.

Julian's discouragement and fatigue had all been left behind with his body. How could he have forgotten what it was like to soar this way? Brighter than the fires that gleamed past closed shutters, the king saw the light of the lives within. And beneath the life-sparks of man and beast in the village he sensed a luminous thread that stretched toward the twin peaks they called the Shoulders of the Bear. He willed himself higher and saw the land laid out before him in lines of light. He had only to take one of those bright pathways to go where he would in Westria. He fought to remember his purpose. Once more awareness focused. Julian followed the path toward the mountain.

Light swirled inward in a dizzying spiral as he snapped back toward his body.

"Julian! *Julian!* Sweet Lady, can't I let you out of my sight for a moment without you doing some fool thing?"

Julian felt the jerk as something struck him, seized on the pain and settled back into his body again. He mumbled something, felt himself being carried, and then the blessed warmth of furs and heated stones.

"Checking on Loren," he mumbled. "He's almost there."

"Glad to hear it, but what would you do about if it he failed?" Robert had pulled off Julian's boots and was chafing numb feet. Julian felt the first stabbing pain as circulation started to return and moaned. "Serves you right! Maybe now you'll learn!"

Julian tried to answer him, but as the warmth began to drive the pain away, weariness closed around him. He was vaguely aware when the tugging and rubbing stopped, knew when the cozy comfort of the furs was reinforced by Robert's warm body holding his own. He felt his kiss, a hot warmth that might have been a tear, but when he tried to respond, exhaustion smothered him.

He roused a little in the still hour before dawn, murmuring Robert's name. But the other side of the bed was cold and empty. Julian fell back into sleep, still wondering where his lover had gone.

Cold weakens the hearth fire in her room in the palace, but in Rana's dream, the town is burning. She stumbles past the stark skeletons of homes . . . cabins . . . it's a village, not Laurelynn. She glances at a seared body folk have just pulled from the ashes—it was too small to be him—and hurries on, gagging at the smell of roast flesh.

"Julian! Julian!" Why did she ever let him go?

From the end of the street she hears shouting. Flames roar suddenly from a rooftop. Men are tossing buckets of snow in a vain attempt to douse them while others help people out of the building. She glimpses a familiar dark head and broad shoulders, slips in the mud, and falls. When she regains her footing, the man has disappeared.

Sparks explode upward as a roof beam gives way. Someone cries, "He's still in there," and she runs forward. Flames roar and the wall falls outward. Through a rippling barrier of light she sees someone moving. The form is Julian's, but his face glows like a god's. Now his clothing is blazing; it falls away to reveal the splendor of the body beneath. Through the flames their eyes meet, and he opens his arms.

She tries to go through the fire to him, but the heat blasts her backwards. The air sears her lungs; she is burned, she is blinded. The last thing she knows as the incandescence consumes her is her own voice screaming his name. . . .

TWO

Candle flame glittered on golden bracelets, firelight glimmered on garments bright with embroidery, and red torchlight gave a deeper color to the sweet-smelling swags of pine and juniper studded with the bright berries of the toyon trees. Outside, the foothills of the Ramparts shivered beneath the rain, but in Hightower, the Lord Commander's Great Hall on the heights above Rivered, light was everywhere.

The dance whirled a circle of girls outward, then in again, lifting linked hands high. Near the candle-decked hearth at the other end of the Hall, Silverhair was leading a group of young men in song.

"How can they laugh? Don't they know we're at war?" asked Julian. His strong fingers twitched uneasily at the fine red wool of his robe. They had managed to send one hamlet warning in time for it to be defended, but too many had had no warning, or failed.

Robert shook his head. "They know. Can't you feel the tension beneath that gaiety? It's not like other years."

The King sighed. "I'm sorry. I was here for Midwinter only once, my first year in the Borderers, and I was too self-conscious to notice anything!"

"You only stepped on the feet of six of your partners and spilled wine on one." Robert grinned. "I don't know why that should bother you!"

"I wanted to die," said Julian "I keep wondering if any of those girls are here!"

"So that's why you're so edgy. Cheer up—they'll be too dazzled by your present glory to say a word!" He surveyed the swirl of color on the dance floor, outshining everyone in an amber silk tunic, embroidered in a pattern of sunbursts in gold.

"You're the one who's glorious," said Julian softly. "Stop preening. It's not fair to make all the girls fall in love with you!"

A faint flush colored Robert's smooth skin. "If I am preening, you know who it is for." He reached out to touch Julian's hand.

Julian heard the unspoken plea, and his grip tightened. Last spring Robert's love had probably saved his sanity. Did some flaw in himself keep him from giving Robert the certainty he needed, or did Robert want more than human love could give?

"And what about *him*?" Trying to smile, Julian nodded toward the other side of the room, where the pristine white of a priest's robe reproached the exuberant colors of the crowd. Robert raised one eyebrow appreciatively.

"You're right, Frederic *is* beautiful, and he's so clearly trying to be plain!"

Frederic of Seagate had renounced his inheritance in order to study at the College of the Wise, but somehow the rigorous austerity of his garb only emphasized the lean grace of his walk and the shining gold of his hair.

"But the answer to your question should be obvious," Robert went on. Now Julian could see where Frederic was headed. The tall, amber-skinned woman who waited for him was gowned in flame-colored Elayan brocade, in clear defiance to any who might still blame her for the havoc her reivers had wreaked upon the coasts of Westria two summers before. But these days everyone recognized that Ardra had been Caolin's victim, too.

"She doesn't look very happy to see him," said Robert. Frederic had reached his lady, but she turned away disdainfully as he began his bow.

Julian sighted. "The Master of the Junipers is still at the Father of Mountains. I've made him Acting Master there now that the Mistress of the College has resigned. But Frederic has finished his studies. To become an adept, he must make the journey to Awahna, and Ardra doesn't want him to go. I understand. In the past ten years only half of those who tried to find the way to the Sacred Valley have returned. Even if Frederic does succeed, he will be changed."

"But you're not trying to stop him," Robert said quietly.

Julian found his throat dry, and swallowed. "When we camped at Tenaia Lake, I glimpsed Awahna. I almost didn't come back to you, but that was not my Path. It *is* Frederic's destiny, and no matter how much he loves Ardra, he will follow it."

"As you will follow yours."

Julian looked at Robert quickly, but his lover was smiling.

"Oh, damn, my brother is calling me," Robert said then. "I wish it was some disaster, but from the look on his face, I fear he needs me to charm one of our more belligerent landholders. Will you excuse me?"

Julian thought the Lord Commander's gesture seemed more like a greeting than a command, and his wife, Lady Elen, was smiling. Yet he did not try to keep Robert beside him. He had heard the words that his lover did not say: *"As you will follow your fate, no matter how much you love me."*

He watched blind-eyed as a circle of dancers parted and met and leaped away once more, but reason had no arguments to soothe the sudden pain. He did not know how to be the king that Westria needed and still love Robert as he deserved, not while they were at war. This war with the Blood Lord was like the dance before him—no matter how many times he came to grips with his enemies, they always melted away into darkness again. Swearing softly, Julian started toward the group that was laughing with Silverhair beside the fire.

For once Silverhair looked happy, thought Rana as she threaded her way among the dancers toward the hearth. Perhaps it was because of Piper, whose clear voice rose above those of the others as if it had never been bound.

"Lord Robert says after the feast I can sing in the small hearth room," said the boy. "Will ye come hear?"

Rana dodged as the viol players caught fire suddenly and the dancers skipped around the room.

"You know I will," said the harper, and his gaze kindled with unexpected joy.

"I'll come too." She grinned as she joined them. "My brother will want to hear all about it. He was hoping you could spend the festival with him at Registhorpe."

"I—I'd like that . . . maybe next year," said the boy, with a quick glance at Silverhair.

"I thought you would be going home for the feast," said the harper to Rana. Up close, she could see the same strain in his eyes that she knew must shadow her own, but the content that she saw there also was a thing she had not known in him before.

She shook her head. "No time. I've been working in the herb rooms with Lady Rosemary, preparing salves and remedies. Now that the fighting has eased, we're catching up a little, but Lord Eric is off so much with his soldiers, much of his work falls to the Lady, and so a lot of hers falls to me. She came here to see Frederic. Thank the Lady for a mother's love, or I'd have had no holiday at all!''

"*You're* mixing medicines? Aagh!" Piper made a face.

Rana punched him. "My brews haven't killed anyone yet! But I might as well have brought Cub—that's just the sort of thing *he* would say!"

"Guardians grant there will be no need for medicines soon," Mistress Siaran sighed.

"If this respite lasts . . ." Silverhair began. "Perhaps the King can say." Julian was coming toward them, dodging as the line of dancers curved. The last girl, miscalculating her turn, swung into him. He staggered, then smiled and shook his head, but when he continued on, he was holding his arm.

Rana watched him with narrowed eyes.

"What's wrong with your shoulder?" she asked calmly, but her heart had begun to gallop painfully.

"It's nothing. Somebody hit me wrong, and the blow burst a few links on my mail." He started to shrug, thought better of it, and grinned.

"Oh. And is there a *right* way to be hit by a sword?" She reached for the lacing at the neck of his gown. Beneath the heavy cloth his skin was surprisingly smooth.

"For the Guardians' sake, Rana, this is a revel. You can't just—" Julian stopped, because she had pulled the cloth away to expose the bandaging and was staring at the new red stain. "Silverhair!" He looked at the older man in appeal.

The harper lifted one eyebrow. The young King's face was almost as red as his robe, but Rana felt the blood leaving her own.

"Rana, please." Julian's brown hand closed around the

girl's. She looked up at him and blinked, remembering her dream, seeing him crowned with flame.

"I've been nursing wounded men since autumn." She tried to speak strongly, but her voice was a thread of sound. "I am qualified. Let me see."

"But it's been tended. There's just one place . . ." He let go of her. Carefully she lifted the bandage, looked, and smoothed it down again. "Yes," she whispered. "It has stopped bleeding now. But you'll need a new dressing tonight, and you could use some aloe vera to speed the healing."

"Don't worry!" Julian began to tug the laces tight. "This was nothing!"

"I know that." Rana repressed a sudden urge to smack him. "I've been dealing with wounds, I told you. But it *could* have been."

"We're all on edge," Silverhair put in, and Rana glanced at him gratefully. "The weather is lousy and so is the war. And for Caolin to give us peace as a present for Sunreturn seems out of character."

"It bothers me, too," said Julian. "He's up to something. It makes me twitchy to stand here doing nothing, even at a festival!"

Rana took a deep breath. How did she expect him to believe she was competent if she fell apart at first sight of blood? But it was *his* blood. Resolutely she focused on Silverhair's words.

"Dance, then," the harper was telling Julian. "Do you think this revelry is for entertainment only?" He gestured around them. "The fires that are lit in this hall kindle the heart as well as the hearth, and it is the heart fire that folk will carry with them when they go out into the dark. Every glowing candle, every note of music, every figure in the dance is an affirmation of life." He broke off. "I'm sorry. I should leave preaching to the Master of the Junipers!"

"You spoke truth." The light had come back into Ju-

lian's eyes, but as she looked at him, Rana's sight blurred.
"And it is the business of the King to remember it. Every
man who laughs is striking a blow against the Blood Lord.
It was because I finally learned how to laugh at myself
that Coyote chose me over Caolin."

"Did you invite *him* to the festival?" asked Mistress
Siaran apprehensively.

The thought of Coyote's laughter set Rana's teeth on
edge. *I've got to get out of here,* she thought, beginning
to edge away from them.

"What, are you afraid he'll run off with the roast boar?"
Julian grinned. "Of course he's invited—when they lighted
the Yule fire he was invoked with the other Guardians—
but I expect that he is reveling with his own kind today."

"I wonder if Caolin is celebrating Sunreturn," said Silverhair reflectively.

"I can't afford to pity him!" Julian answered. "If this
respite is a sign of weakness, I must use it any way I can!"

Rana cleared her throat abruptly. "I must go. I promised to help garland the roast boar, and they'll be taking
it from the ovens now." At least her voice was working
again. Her skirts flared emerald around her as she moved
away. The music blazed up in conclusion; then players and
dancers were suddenly still.

"Well, it *was* nothing—only a scratch! What's wrong
with her?" She could hear Julian's voice behind her, but
not Silverhair's murmured reply.

She did not stop until she reached the kitchens. As the
door opened, she gasped at the blast of heated air. The
pig was still turning on its spit in the great hearth. She
drew in a deep breath of richly scented air, striving for
calm. Music swelled and faded again as the swinging door
closed behind her.

"Rana! Good, we're almost ready for the herbs!" The
Mistress of Lord Philip's kitchens saw her and waved.
"Will you get them now?"

Rana passed through the kitchen and out into the sudden chill of the shed, wondering why it felt like a refuge. Lord Philip's hall was set in a fold in the foothills above Rivered. Dim in the fading light, the hill curved above them, studded with rain-dark oak trees and an occasional pine. The Ramparts were a presence more sensed than seen beyond. She wished she could escape to their empty silences, but the cooks were waiting. She gathered up the coarse sack, dampened to keep the herbs fresh and cold enough so that even a touch set her shivering, and hurried back into the kitchen.

I was running, Rana decided as she dropped the sack on one of the scrubbed tables. Her heart was leaping in her chest from fear. Julian's gash had been nothing indeed, compared with some of the damage she had seen. *What's wrong with me?* The whisper of music from the hall sounded faint as memory. Julian's physical presence had not affected her this way on last summer's journey through the Ramparts, she thought as she began to twine the slender branches of bay laurel into a garland with the prickly twists of rosemary and the sweet-scented basil and thyme.

She had not seen the King since autumn. Had Julian's formal election to the throne of Westria made a difference somehow? But he had been the King for her when she had found him walking in the Sacred Wood on Midwinter Day, and when he commanded the storm from the deck of *Sea Brother*, and when he stood atop the Wind Lord's Throne and claimed the power of the winds. The Council could only ratify that sovereignty.

"Hoorah, done to a turn! You timed it perfectly."

The cheering jerked Rana back to present awareness. They had gotten the roasted boar off its spit and onto a wooden platter. She gathered the garland into her arms, and the spicy scent of the herbs battled the rich smell of roast flesh in the air.

"Surely this is the king of boars—just look at him!"

Rana draped the interlace of greenery around the carcass and reached for a pickled apple to set among the leaves. And stopped, hand still poised in the air, gazing at the stiff limbs and juices oozing from cracked skin . . .

Not long ago, a wounded man had told Lady Rosemary how the villages of the Ramparts were burning . . . and that night she had dreamed she was searching through the ashes for a seared body that she would recognize only by the golden circlet it wore.

She let the apple fall.

"Rana, what's the matter? Are you ill?"

Once more she was running, her belly in turmoil as it had been the day that she realized that Julian wanted her.

It was better outside, away from the dreadful smell. Rana set her palms on the cold stone of the wall, then pressed them to her burning brow.

Last summer, she thought, *we were as unaware of our bodies as spirits of the air!*

But even in Laurelynn she had not been shielded from the physical realities of war. The wounded fighters who were brought to Lady Rosemary told their tales. Rana had heard them babble as she helped with the nursing, heard them wake screaming when her medicines could not conquer mind or body's pain, and gone to her own bed to dream their dreams all over again. But in her visions, the face on every corpse was Julian's.

And now she had smelled his blood, she had felt the smooth warmth of his skin. The King's body was as mortal as any other man's. *Julian's body* . . . Rana shivered suddenly. She ought to go inside. But not into the hall! They would be bringing the boar now, garlanded with greenery and song.

I will never eat roast pig again!

Rana splashed across the kitchen yard and up the steps to the end of the hall. The room there was used for board games or music, a refuge from the hurly-burly of the hall.

She crouched by the fireplace for several minutes, holding her hands over the coals, before she realized that she was not alone.

It was not because he had made any sound or motion, she thought, looking at the carven ivory folds of his priest's gown and the haze of gold the firelight laid across his fair hair. Frederic seemed to have acquired the Master of the Junipers' gift for stillness. He saw that she had noticed him, and sighed.

"Your hair is wet."

Now that he mentioned it, Rana could feel the damp trickle down her back. She began to fluff strands darkened to the color of carnelian toward the blaze. A ginger cat that had been draped across one of the benches jumped into her lap and curled itself into sleep again.

"Ardra looks magnificent tonight," Rana began conversationally, and saw him twitch. "Don't you think so?"

"Yes," he answered harshly. A tinge of color stained his smooth skin. Abruptly her numbed mind began working again.

"Oh, Frederic! Have you two quarreled again?"

"*She* has," he said bitterly.

"But she loves you!" Rana exclaimed. "When we were dressing she was talking about how much she was looking forward—" She broke off, blushing, for Ardra had been explicit about just what it was that she missed when she and Frederic were apart. She began to stroke the cat's soft fur mechanically.

"Oh, if we could spend our lives making love there'd be no problem!"

Rana's hand stilled as she stared at him, visualizing him and Ardra, smooth bodies interlaced in ecstasy . . . smooth, naked bodies . . . Julian.

But she had seen Julian with his clothes off many times! *That was before I learned the difference between dead flesh and live*. She imagined embracing him, and a tremor ran through her belly. Her mind had long ago forgiven the reivers who had assaulted her, but her flesh still feared. Or did it?

"If humans never made love, *I'd* have no problem!" Her voice was as harsh as Frederic's had been.

"You're beginning to feel again, aren't you?" Frederic said softly. "Does Julian know?"

"Of course not!" The cat glared at her indignantly as she moved. "He's Robert's lover. And I don't want—" She broke off. "I want to, but I can't—" She shook her head.

Frederic's smile had almost its old sweetness. "And I want to love Ardra, but I can't stay with her. We *are* a fine pair! Still, even if I never come back from Awahna, she'll remember what we shared. Julian is risking so much."

"Do you think I don't understand that?" Rana cried. "I dream of him broken, bleeding, and he was wounded in the mountains—only a scratch, I know it, but his blood burned my hand!"

"Then tell him," said Frederic. "Even if he remains faithful to Robert, it may ease his spirit. But in the Lady's name, don't run away from him again!"

Rana clutched the cat, waiting for the pounding of her heart to slow. "And what will you tell Ardra?" The cat growled softly, and she let it go, waiting for Frederic to reply. The ginger cat jumped to the rug and began to wash.

"I will tell her that though I pass through the gates of death, my love will stay with her, and she will be with me even if I enter paradise."

Rana heard a boy's laughter, and footsteps at the door. "I don't know what I will say to Julian, or what I will do. But I will try. Lady of Fire, I will try!"

As Silverhair and Piper came through the door she stood up, tossing her hair back over her shoulders. Before the fire, the tawny cat continued its own grooming with untroubled serenity.

* * *

"If I could second-guess Caolin, I might have let them elect *me* king," said Lord Philip.

"It's like trying to douse a brush fire with a thimble!" Julian exclaimed.

The Lord Commander of the Ramparts nodded, and Julian realized that his old master was getting bald. Would Robert's brown curls one day grow thin? It was hard to imagine. It was hard to imagine any of them living long enough to grow old.

The feasting had ended. Folk moved among the tables snuffing out candles, and shadows gathered in the hall.

"So what are you going to do?" asked the Lord Commander.

"We have as many men as the Blood Lord, but our defenders must be everywhere, while he concentrates his strength. Our people are dying to no purpose, Philip. This battle is really between Caolin and me, and it's time I challenged him!"

"With magic? Julian, he nearly killed you last time!"

The music strengthened. Girls pushed through the throng distributing candles. Light sparked suddenly as four dancers moved out onto the floor. For a few beats they circled, right wrists crossed as they held the candles together to form a single blaze. Then the melody shifted. The light separated into four flames.

> *"Slowly the year-wheel continues to turn,*
> *Brave in the darkness midwinter fires burn.*
> *Lonely my candle traverses the night,*
> *Seeking its kindred to kindle alight."*

"He nearly kills me *every* time." Julian laughed harshly. "But I'm like Coyote. When I die, I come back again!"

Lord Philip blinked, and Julian knew that he had suddenly remembered how the King had acquired the tracery of silver scars that ran from temple to cheekbone beside his left eye. A knowledge for which there was no words separated them. *Earth and air and water have destroyed me . . . will I return from my death by fire?*

Again the music changed. The points of light paused, then twinned suddenly as the first four dancers chose partners. Coupled, they formed a larger circle, moving sunwise in the graceful lift and dip of the dance.

> *"Outside, the storm strikes at shutters and panes.*
> *Here we are safe from the wind and the rains,*
> *Here by the fire we are sheltered from harm,*
> *But where is the love that will keep my heart warm?"*

Julian blinked, seeing the sunwheel itself in the movement of the dancers. *It's dark now, but this is the longest night. The sunwheel whirls the world toward spring. Every step the dancers take is an affirmation that we will defeat Caolin and the light will come again.* The circle dislimned; sparks radiated into the crowd as the music moved into the search-music once more.

"You will do what you must," said Philip heavily. "But for Westria's sake, boy, take care!" He squeezed Julian's arm, then glared resolutely across the room. The King glimpsed a flash of gold and saw Robert talking to the beautiful boy whose brother had died after that last fight.

> *"Into the darkness the radiance flows,*
> *Dividing and joining, see how the light grows—*
> *Parting and meeting, the many are one*
> *The love that is shared is no longer alone."*

Julian blinked as the circle began to re-form, and remembered the land of Westria laid out in lines of light. But the candle flames made a pattern that all could see.

He swayed to the music, forgetting his fears as he forgot muscles still strained and skin tight with healing wounds.

> *"Many the hands that love links with mine,*
> *Joined as our voices in sweet singing twine.*
> *My loves have been many, and all of them true,*
> *But to none have I given the love I give you."*

Julian watched the dancers through a haze of light that grew as the circle drew inward and sparkled outward again and again. His gaze followed one blaze of emerald around the floor—deep green embroidered with pearls and silver in vibrant contrast to the dancer's flame of red hair. Once more the circle shimmered into separate motes of light. The figure came toward him.

> *"This is the center, the heart of the sun,*
> *This is the place where the many are one."*

It was Rana. Of course it was Rana. Dazed by the light, Julian was not surprised when she offered him her candle. Her eyes met his, then flicked away. Was she still worrying about his wound? He felt Philip's hand pushing him forward. Rana licked her lips nervously, and Julian saw, without comprehension, that she was afraid. But she was still standing there, and her wide eyes were full of light.

Julian held out his candle.

> *"Separate spirits in love are the same,*
> *Joining my fire and yours into one flame."*

Light blazed suddenly between them, and for a moment he thought that she was offering him the Jewel of Fire. Dazzled, he let her lead him into the dance.

THREE

The air is acrid with the smell of burning. Caolin picks his way around a dead horse, jumps as a raven jeers at him without pausing to interrupt its meal. Where is the King?

"Jehan! Jehan!" He stumbles over an abandoned shield. If only the King would listen to his warnings! "Jehan!" he cries once more, hears distant shouting, and hurries toward the sound.

A familiar blue shield with a silver star blazes suddenly through the struggle, and Caolin begins to run. The King is battling against a horde of faceless men who wear as a badge a wolf's head affronté upon a crimson field. The Seneschal clings to a half-burnt wagon. He ought to know that badge.

The King's horse falls, screaming. Caolin plunges into the carnage, expecting from one instant to the next the blow that will take him down into the dark. But the enemy warriors draw away. He can see the King's body now—

*red blood soaking the blue surcoat, dabbling the dark
beard. He struggles to remove the heavy helm.*

*"Jehan, Jehan, what have they done to you?" He gets
the helm off finally, cradles the King's head in his lap and
begins to wipe the blood away—and stills. The face he is
gazing at is young, with a strong nose beneath the straight
line of the brows. He has seen this face before, white and
defenseless while the heavens raged. Then the eyes open—
dark eyes, not blue, like those of an animal in pain.*

*"No." Caolin starts to thrust him away. A voice shakes
the air:*

"As I served your father, so I shall serve you!"

*The boy's eyes roll upward. Caolin can see the life ebb-
ing out of him, as he watched it fade from Jehan's face
upon Midwinter Day.*

*"No!" His hands close on broad shoulders; he shakes
them and shouts, he is shaking . . . being shaken . . .*

Caolin opened his eyes and saw Ordrey, white and
sweating, and behind him Captain Esteban.

"You dared—" he began. His throat hurt, but he did
not need words. He reached within for the hot pulse of
power.

"You were crying out and thrashing," cried Ordrey as
the captain edged backward. "I didn't know what was
wrong!"

The air thickened, and Ordrey's eyes began to bulge.
Then the sense of what Ordrey had been saying reached
the sorcerer, and with an effort that frightened him, Caolin
clamped down.

"Leave me!"

"Yes, my lord." Ordrey was still babbling. "But I have
hot tea ready."

Caolin felt the pounding of his heart begin to ease. He
nodded, and his servant scurried from the room. The last
echoes of the screaming still reverberated within. He let
his head fall back against the pillow and took one deep

breath, then another, controlling his body's responses in a pattern learned a very long time ago.

Pale light was filtering around the edges of the heavy curtains. He could hear the faint sounds of the fortress awakening below. Midwinter morning . . . He winced, remembering. But Jehan had rotted in his grave for twenty years, while the trees of the Sacred Wood fed on his bones. The images that haunted the sorcerer now were only a dream.

Only! Caolin shuddered, remembering. Did Julian have enough power to send him these nightmares? For two weeks there had been no fighting—time enough for Julian to begin thinking about the Jewel of Fire. But what if the upstart was using that time to do magic? Perhaps he should send someone to distract him.

Ordrey pushed carefully through the door, carrying a tray, and Caolin got himself upright while the little man set it on the polished table and opened the curtains.

"A fine, bright day, my lord." Ordrey lowered his voice as Caolin grimaced. He poured tea, and the sorcerer drank, sighing as healing warmth radiated through flesh and bone.

Now that the hot liquid was easing his throat, he could feel the stiffness in his neck and a dull ache in his back muscles. He drained the mug and thrust it at Ordrey, swung his legs over the side of the bed and stood, controlling his features so that the other man would not suspect how much will it took to stay upright until the dizziness passed.

"Bring my breakfast." He needed food, though the thought made his belly clench. For so long this machine of flesh in which he lived had served him uncomplainingly, it was hard to remember that it, too, had needs. He reached for the heavy red wool of his gown.

Still belting the garment, the Blood Lord paused. He had heard something . . . He glared at Ordrey, who looked back in anxious incomprehension. Reluctant to believe his own senses, for his orders had been unequivocal, Caolin swept from the room.

It could not be birdsong. The sorcerer's warnings were very precise, and birds, even the scavengers, avoided Blood Gard now. But it was *music*. The door to the common room smashed against the wall as Caolin burst through.

The men who were eating at the long tables whirled. The whistler looked up expectantly. The mop with which had been swabbing the floor was still in his hands, his lips still pursed on a last thread of sound. The sorcerer lifted his hands, and the energy he had forced inward blasted free.

The fellow seemed to fall in pieces. The mop clattered to the floor and the bucket went over after it. The man's throat muscles contracted futilely. One of the men swore. The victim voided his bowels and someone giggled shrilly. Only the swordsman, Konradin, kept his eyes on the sorcerer.

It was crude—Caolin knew that even as the fury flared through him, but the relief as his rage found an outlet was exquisite. At the College of the Wise they manipulated the energy currents in the body in order to heal. Caolin had learned to use them to kill. He grinned, and the power that he was projecting began to dim. Ordrey stood in the doorway behind him, apparently overcome with awe.

"Is he still alive?"

"I doubt that his mind—if he had one—survived," said Caolin, "but his body is alive." The victim lay in an untidy heap, but his limbs were twitching.

Captain Esteban stepped forward, unsheathing his dagger.

"No!" exclaimed Ordrey. "Give him to me!" Everyone was looking at the little man now. "Creating pain is an art, you know, but it's hard to tell how much the body's endurance aids survival, and what part is played by the mind. If I can use a man with no mind for my experiments, perhaps I can find out how the body alone reacts to pain!''

A man who had not been sick before began to retch quietly.

''An artist.'' The Blood Lord raised one eyebrow, and Ordrey shrugged in self-deprecation. ''Very well, you may have him.'' He pointed at two of the men who were sitting down. ''Take this . . . raw material . . . to Master Ordrey's workroom.''

''My lord—'' Captain Esteban began.

''He disobeyed. You know the rule. He was worth very little before. At least now he may be useful.''

''But he was only whistling!'' came a whisper from the back of the room.

''You know the rule!'' Caolin pitched his voice to reach the mind's deeper level and saw them tremble.

''Even on Sunreturn?''

The Blood Lord's eyes narrowed. Who was it? Ah, that one . . . The man blanched as the sorcerer caught his eye, but Caolin restrained himself.

''What are you?'' he growled, fixing the gaze of each of them in turn.

''We are wolves!'' said a big man from the Corona. Konradin remained silent, but his pale eyes glowed.

''You are wolves,'' the sorcerer agreed. ''You are *my* wolves, and as wolves you shall sing. If you want to celebrate, there will be brandy later, and plenty of wine and beer. You'll have a chance at the whores. So what are you?'' he demanded once more.

''We are wolves,'' said Captain Esteban quickly. ''Wolves!'' added the beefy man, whose eyes had brightened perceptibly at the mention of booze.

''Then howl!'' cried the Blood Lord, and his tone tore sense from sound. ''Howl down heaven—howl, howl!''

* * *

Overhead, the infant sun of Midwinter burned silver. Julian watched the folk of Hightower moving toward the altar in the garden through a haze of light, their voices stilled, their faces shadowless. Even the children clutched their new toys in hushed anticipation. The tables in the hall bore platters of leftovers and cooling pots of tea, but in all of the keep no flame now burned. Bundled up against the damp chill of the valley, the people had come to pray to the newborn sun to give them fire.

With a glance Julian gathered those he loved most into his awareness—Silverhair and Piper, Frederic, Robert, and Rana, who was still carrying the prayer fan he had given her that morning. His Companions . . . He had realized some time ago that he always knew when one of them was near. He smiled in brief greeting but did not join them. There was a dull ache in his forehead that he wished he could blame on last night's wine, but his dreams had been evil. Why should his bad temper spoil their joy in the holiday?

He let out his breath in a puff of cloud. This feeling of mingled anxiety and excitement brought back his childhood. To put out the fire in Midwinter seemed madness. The sun was so pale—how could it restore warmth to the world?

The crowd parted to let Lady Elen through, Lord Philip behind her. In the stillness, their steps crunched on frost-rimed stones. Paths radiated to the four directions from the circle of flagged paving in the middle of the garden. In the summertime the pedestal in its center supported a birdbath. Now, at the hub of winter, all that remained was bare earth, skeletal foliage, and frost-browned perennials, and on the pedestal a nest of dry sticks that would cradle the new fire.

The Lord and Lady of Rivered took their places. Philip lifted his hands, facing northward. "Too long have we longed for light to free us, too long have we shivered with

winter's weather. When will the sun return from the south-
lands?''

As he spoke, Lady Elen had moved to the other side of
the altar. ''This is the brightness of a new dawning; now
the white world to her lover will waken. Behold, the newborn sun renews and revives us!''

Perhaps the sun was burning through the mists, for
surely the day had grown brighter. All around Julian, people were beginning to sing.

> *"Hail, Holy Light! Now ends Thy long retreat;*
> *The darkness fails, and with Thy quickening heat*
> *Life wakes again; upon this holy morn,*
> *The hope of all the world has been reborn!"*

They sang briskly, but he thought there was a touch of
sadness in the melody. Julian had sung this song every
year at the lighting of the new fire—why was he hearing
that sorrow for the first time now?

> *"Yet still we wait, enthralled by winter's might,*
> *Too frozen to receive the Gift of Light.*
> *Dare we believe that darkness will retire?*
> *Give us a Sign! Send down Thy holy Fire!"*

Dare I believe? Julian asked himself. He had never been
so aware of the surrounding darkness. For him, Midwinter
Night's Eve had been long indeed, haunted by dreams in
which he was separated from those he loved by a barrier
of fire, and burned, and could not reach them. Somewhere
during those wakeful hours one piece of knowledge had
come to him: this time it was not ignorance that was keeping him from finding the Jewel, but fear.

If I am burning anyway, he thought, *why should the
Jewel make me afraid?*

Lady Elen glanced at the sun, and extended her hands

above the carefully constructed cone of kindling, murmuring her own prayer. Philip stood close behind her, ready to shield with his cloak if there should be a wind. Brightness sparkled between her fingers as she positioned the crystal lens, and the singing sank to a hum.

Julian saw a point of white light glow in the wood shavings, held his breath as the first pale curl of smoke twisted into the air. *Oh, let there be Light!* he prayed with the others. But Julian desired a greater illumination. *Hail Holy Light! Send me Thy servant—give me the Jewel of Fire!*

The humming of the crowd vibrated through him. Was it because there were so many? Or was the power of the Wind Crystal within him resonating to the sound? Julian stiffened, then realized that perhaps this was his answer. What better time than the moment when the solar energies began to grow again to seek help from the elemental powers?

He let his breath out slowly and felt the buzz in his bones. He was halfway into trance already, it would be easy now! Julian sank onto a weathered wooden bench surrounded by pruned stumps where six months ago roses had bloomed.

As he settled, he sensed movement. Rana was pushing her way through the crowd toward him. It had not occurred to Julian that perhaps the others were as aware of him as he was of them. Her outlines wavered as she came to him, as though she moved through a shimmer of heated air.

He strove to regain control, but it had gone too far. The point of light beneath the burning glass captured the King's gaze. Consciousness contracted; then suddenly the wood caught and his spirit flared upward through the top of his skull on a gout of flame that blazed like Rana's hair.

He is a bright quick flicker that spurts upward, expanding, extending, settling at last into a pulsing mote of awareness, aware once more of its own identity.

Julian perceives the world as pattern in constant flux, a succession of forms that tantalize with familiarity. But this is not the Adept's Road. He has never experienced anything like this before.

He is faintly aware that the shell of flesh he left behind him is twitching. Someone is holding it, calling his name. He tries to answer, but the play of shape and color around him is too distracting.

For a moment he sees flames; then he is the flame—a ravenous, raging hunger that cannot be appeased. He seeks for some certainty to cling to, but everything is changing. A familiar flicker of laughter sparks his attention.

"Changer!" he cries. "I summon you!"

Instantly another point of light is dancing around him. It has no recognizable form, but it seems to Julian that he has encountered this particular energy before, in the shape of a man called Mañero.

"Fire-bringer, is that you?"

For a moment the light traces a coyote-shape around him, then contracts again.

"What you doin' here?"

"I wanted . . . knowledge . . . about the Jewel of Fire—" As Julian names it, heat explodes around them in crimson madness, golden pain.

"Fire, you wanted? Where d' you think you are?" says Coyote. "Watch your speech, cub. Here, names are Real." Coyote gestures, and Julian can think once more.

"The stone, then." Julian is still shaken. "I have to find it."

"Well, at least he's asking." Coyote is talking to someone else, but all Julian can see is a shimmer of emerald and gold. "Why not tell him?" the Guardian goes on. "Even a dumb human could guess where it fell. An' it's not finding, but keeping that matters with this one, anyhow."

There is an answer, and though Julian cannot quite hear

words, it seems to him that he should recognize the sweet-
ness he senses now, but a swirl of green and scarlet energy
pulses around him and he forgets again.

"Great One, where is it?" he asks.

"In th' womb of th' mountain humans call Mother of
Fire." In those words there is darkness shot with flashes
of flame.

"Will you show me?"

"Oh, I'll be around. But you can find it without me.
Feel th' other three Jewels, and reach out for th' balance.
'Twill call to you."

Julian senses the Guardian retreating. "When will I see
you again?"

"When you have faced the fire," comes the reply. Then
the world whirls around him, and Julian becomes a crea-
ture of flesh once more.

Julian opened his eyes, blinking as if he had come into
a dark room from the full light of day. He sensed Rana
near him, and Robert and the others as shadows. Perspiration was pouring off him as if he had just come out of
the sweat lodge.

"Listen to me, Julian—you're almost home now." A
quiet voice filtered through his confusion. "Breathe in . . .
and out . . . feel the solid bench beneath you, your body's
weight."

Julian forced rigid muscles to relax and gulped cold air
until the noon sunlight began to seem bright to him once
more.

"You are in the garden—we're all here with you. Look
at me, Julian. Can you feel my hand?"

The voice was Frederic's. Julian blinked once more and
focused on his friend. All around them Hightower folk
were embracing and sharing wishes for the new year. Others were already moving back toward the hall, torches held
high.

"Oh, let the hearth fire hallow friend and kin;
Touch every heart, light love anew within.
And kindle joy in those who gather here
As Thy flame blooms upon our hearths this year."

On the altar, the sticks from which those flames had been kindled were falling into ash that wisped away on the wind.

"You see!" said Robert in exasperation. "He did it again, just like I told you!"

Julian turned his head, and saw that it was Robert, not Rana, who was holding his other hand. Rana stood at his feet, but her face was hidden by the red gold of her hair. Something was wrong—he could feel her going away from him—but his question was lost as he met the radiance of Frederic's smile.

"It's all right," said Frederic. "This sort of thing happens all the time at the College of the Wise. What did you see?"

Robert looked up at Julian like a good dog who does not understand why it is being sent from the room. Julian met his gaze unsmiling. His heart ached for his lover's hurt, but there was too much at stake for anyone's pain to matter now.

"I'm not sure," he answered Frederic. "It was all . . . lines, and patterns of light." He gestured helplessly. Human beings did not have words for what he had seen. "It might have been one of the elemental realms. I was looking for the Jewel of Fire."

"On the astral?" Frederic raised one eyebrow.

"Would I have done better to ask at the College of the Wise?" A flush of embarrassment stained Frederic's smooth skin and Julian gave a short laugh. "It worked, anyhow."

Rana turned suddenly. "You *found* it?" Julian saw light glow between her fingers as it had when she offered him the candle in the dance. Vision blurred. The light flared and he knew it was the Jewel of Fire. But how could Rana give it to him? He blinked, and it was only sunlight once more.

"I *will* find it," he said softly. "I know where to look for it now." He bit back the rest of what Coyote had told him. Mysterious dangers were his own problem. Their expressions continued to change. Julian stood up suddenly, remembering what had happened the last time he set out to seek one of the Jewels.

"And I *am* the one who must look for it. It was all very well for you to chase after me last summer. We were not at war then. Piper, you must go back to your studies at Misthall." He frowned at the boy, who nodded shyly. "Rana—"

"There's no need to give me orders, *my Lord*," she said bitterly. "I know where I am wanted. I will go back to Laurelynn and brew more medicines to heal the wounds made by you warriors."

Julian gaped, torn between relief and astonishment. Angry color burned beneath her pale skin like light through a lantern. Had his gift offended her, or was it something that had happened in the dance?

"Go on," she said more calmly, drawing her cloak around her. "You don't have to worry about me."

Julian wiped his brow with his sleeve. "Silverhair, we both know how cold affects you. You *must* stay in Laurelynn with Lady Rosemary." He waited for some protest, but Silverhair said nothing. The King eyed him warily. As the silence continued, they all began to stare until finally his uncle smiled.

"Why do you all look so suspicious?" said the harper. "Julian is right, this time. If he needed me I would come despite the weather, but I suspect that this quest is going to take him into the mountains again, and I have no desire to flounder about in the snow."

Julian sighed. Did he dare to believe either one of them? Still, he was willing to take what agreement he could get now and put off worrying about how to enforce it. The Hightower folk had all gone back into the hall, the echoes of their singing fading from the air. He took a deep breath. Frederic and Robert were standing side by side, arms folded, watching him.

"What about us?" Robert asked sweetly. "Now that you've disposed of everyone else so neatly. I'm the captain of your guard. What did you have in mind to get *me* out of the way?"

"And I'm your wizard," said Frederic. "I've finished my studies at the College, and I can't try for Awahna until spring. How are you going to get rid of *me*?"

Julian stared, seeing them suddenly grown older; there was gray in Robert's hair and he wore dented armor, but Frederic wore red, like a seneschal. He blinked, and they were in their festival garb again, watching him suspiciously.

"If you two are going to gang up on me, I don't suppose there's any way I can." Julian picked up his cloak and wrapped it around him, grinning at the shock in their faces. He would worry about them, of course, but if that glimpse of vision had been true, they would survive. And they were right—he could think of no way to stop them if they really wanted to come along.

"Piper, wait," said Silverhair as the boy started down the path. Rana had gone already. Julian saw her already halfway to the hall and frowned, more certain than ever that something was wrong. But it would do no good to call to her.

"When do we leave?" asked Robert.

"As soon as I've cleared things with Eric in Laurelynn. Meanwhile, it's getting cold out here," he made himself speak cheerfully. "The only fire I want to see right now is the one that's burning on the hearth inside!"

* * *

In the sacred valley of Awahna, sun-sculptured ice had built a crystal palace around a glade where it was always spring. The sun emerged from behind a cloud and frozen water fractured the light that shone through it into a shimmer of rainbow. When the rainbow disappeared, Coyote was sitting upon the grass.

"Do you think that the King of Men will master the Jewel?" The Lady of Fire stretched on her couch of burning roses, petal flesh at once veiled and revealed by flame-gold hair, and smiled.

Coyote shrugged. "Does it matter? It will be fun to watch him try."

"I have other concerns," said the Lady. The air grew warmer.

"That I believe!" Coyote laughed. "Does it matter?"

"He must be tested," said the Lady, "and so must she!"

Coyote grinned. "That could be interesting. I wonder . . ."

"Wait."

"Oh, I will. Do I have a choice? The Maker made sure of that, giving humans free will. I don't complain," he went on. "If not for that, think how boring our existence would be!"

"You are absurd." The Lady sat up, and two doves that had been bathing in the pool fluttered up to perch, one on her shoulder, the other on her outstretched hand. "You might as well be a man."

"I have been." He eyed her appreciatively. "I will be."

"If the Maker wills," she said as he began to change.

"If the Maker wills?" Coyote blinked eyes that were still amber, even in his new form. "If the Maker did not enjoy a good joke, She would not have created Me!"

FOUR

The scream ripped through Silverhair's dreams. He jerked upright in his bed, heart pounding painfully. A door slammed. He heard the clash of steel, but he was already reaching for his own blade. The corridors of the palace echoed to shouts and running footsteps as he raced down the hall.

Julian! Terror made the thought a silent cry.

"I'm all right, Uncle." The reassurance was instant. *"Someone—in Lord Eric's rooms!"*

Silverhair slackened his pace. Julian was right—the tumult ahead was from the east wing, where the Regent's rooms overlooked the lake of Laurelynn.

"Hold!" Eric's shout ended in a cough.

Metal thunked wood, someone cursed, and Silverhair saw a blur of motion at the end of the hall. His sword sang out unbidden as a dark figure sprang toward him. The man swerved, and Silverhair was turning, thrusting. He braced himself against the sudden weight of his blade and wrenched it free as his attacker fell.

"Silverhair!" Light rippled across the polished boards as someone lifted a lamp.

The harper leaned on his sword, breathing in harsh gasps.

"Have you killed him?" cried Julian. Silverhair bent over the still form, trying to see. Steel sparked in the lamplight; Julian knocked him away as the assassin moved, but the little dagger the man had drawn went into his own breast.

Robert held the lamp high and Julian ripped off the concealing hood. "Who sent you?"

The thin lips opened, but all that came out was a compressed gasp. Then the pale features twisted and the man's whole body spasmed. For a moment he held that impossible contortion; then all of his muscles relaxed and he was still.

"Did I kill him?" Silverhair was finding it hard to breathe.

"Here's where your sword went in—through the shoulder," said Julian. "And here's the mark of the dagger. Neither one of those should have been fatal." He reached for the little knife that lay on the floor.

"Don't touch it!" said Frederic. "I think there's poison on the blade."

"The Regent?" Julian swiveled on one knee, looking up at him.

"Lord Eric woke before the wretch was in knife range," said Robert. "He had to use his sword."

Julian got to his feet. "Take this away." He motioned to two of the guards. "Take the dagger as well, but carefully—you've seen what it can do."

"Julian, come—he wants you!" Lady Rosemary called from the doorway.

The King ran back down the corridor with the others behind him. More slowly, Silverhair followed. When he reached the Regent's room they were all gathered around the great bed, where Eric lay in a welter of bloodstained sheets, grunting as his wife wound his chest with bandages.

The harper stopped, leaning against the doorway. His arm was aching. He wondered if he had strained it somehow in the fight. Then he realized that it was his left arm—his harp arm, not his sword arm—that felt the pain.

"Eric?" Silverhair's voice sounded strange in his own ears, but it must have been loud enough, for his old friend's eyes opened.

"He didn't touch the life," Eric said harshly. "It'll take more than a flesh wound to kill an old war-horse like me!"

"A flesh wound," muttered Rosemary, tucking the last bit of bandage in. "The sword thrust barely missed the lung!"

Silverhair nodded, and felt the invisible hand begin to tighten around his own chest. He recognized the pain now, but it had never been so bad. He fought for control.

"Why, Farin"—Eric ignored his wife—"you're white as my sheets used to be!"

Silverhair glared, for now they were all looking at him. "I'm all ri—" he began, but he could not finish the word.

"Uncle, did that dagger—"

Silverhair shook his head. He saw Julian starting toward him and tried to hang on to the doorpost, but the pain was drawing a red veil between him and the world. The last thing he felt as it mastered him entirely was the warm strength of Julian's arms.

"But I can't run off now, with you down and the Seneschal's Office still trying to replace Tanemun!" Julian glared at the Regent, who lay on a couch in the small council room. The assassin who stabbed Eric had not been alone, and the man who attacked the Seneschal had not failed. Outside a fine rain was falling. It was barely a week past Sunreturn and night still closed in early, but with the curtains drawn, the flames that flickered on the hearth kept the room bright and warm.

"Of course you can!" Eric's voice was still weak, but his gaze did not waver. "Tanemun's deputy can deal with anything likely to come up at this season, and all I have to do is give orders. Unless I die of boredom, that won't do me any harm."

Julian gazed around the table, but he could find no counsel in the serene faces of the Master of the Junipers, who had been summoned from the College of the Wise to treat Eric, or of Frederic, who was sorting through the letters that had arrived that day. Robert's face showed only repressed impatience. Silverhair looked a little haggard, but he met Julian's glance with complete composure. The King sighed. He was worried about his uncle, too, but the older man refused to admit that anything was wrong.

"The Jewel of Fire has been safe for twenty years," he continued. "It can wait a month or two more."

"In two months the ground will be dry enough for cavalry. That's when you'll be needed here," said Frederic quietly.

"Do you think that Westria suddenly can't do without your supervision just because the Council has elected you king?" Eric raised himself on one elbow, grimaced, and let Rosemary help him lie back again.

"Am I worrying too much?" Julian rubbed his eyes. "You ruled Westria well, my lord. The difference now is that the land is my responsibility. Well, let's have a look at the work load." He leaned back in the great chair, pulling from the neck of his tunic the chain on which he had strung his father's signet ring and fingering the jade.

Frederic lifted the sheaf of papers. "The reports from Seagate and Las Costas are good, anyway. Two villages in the south were attacked and none north of the Bay, as opposed to four and three in November. Ardra thinks that the raiders have been driven into winter quarters by the storms.''

''Heavy snow in the passes should have the same effect in the Ramparts and the Corona,'' said Robert hopefully.

''Unless they are already on our side of the border,'' Julian answered him.

''Well, at least they can't get reinforcements.''

''Not unless they come from within,'' Silverhair said grimly. This produced a small silence, in which the sound of the rain against the thick glass of the windows was suddenly audible.

Julian shivered. ''If only I knew what the Blood Lord was planning!'' he exclaimed.

The Master's eyes opened. ''That is something I'm not sure even Caolin knows. What one wants with the heart and with the mind may not always be the same.''

''Does he even *have* a heart?'' Robert lifted one eyebrow.

''Yes, though he may believe he has destroyed it.''

''This letter is from Lion Claw!'' Frederic looked up suddenly from the paper he was reading, and the Master stilled. ''He says that Katiz died at Samaine. His body died, anyway. His spirit was destroyed long ago.''

Julian nodded. ''Katiz was the sorcerer who taught Caolin,'' he told Eric and Rosemary. ''We saw what was left of him when we passed through Awhai.'' He shivered, remembering the darkness that the old sorcerer had shown him. ''Master, what makes you think the Blood Lord is any different?''

''Caolin still hates, and he still desires—''

''Yes, he desires Westria,'' muttered Robert as the Master went on.

''Those are passions, Julian. Where one passions lives, its opposite can grow. We rejoice in creation and fear destruction, but the stillness of complete despair is more terrible. I have been there, and I know.'' His seamed features twisted with an ancient pain. Then the light came back into his eyes.

Julian felt Frederic's shock. The darkness he had glimpsed in Katiz had nearly destroyed him. How had the Master won free?

"What else do you have there, Frederic?" Lord Eric asked finally. Julian looked up. The Regent's voice had been loud, but the King could hear the strain.

Frederic heard it, too. "Nothing that we need to deal with now."

"Nonsense, let's get it all out of the way while you're still here."

"Yes, I am still here, and here I will stay." Frederic managed a smile. "The rest can wait." He held his father's gaze with something of the Master's serenity while the older man colored and then grew pale once more. There was something almost painful in the pride that shone in Lady Rosemary's eyes.

"But you wanted to go with Julian."

"What I want doesn't mean much anymore," his son replied. "I gave up my sword, Father, but I will not abandon you. This task is something that I can do very well."

Yes, you can do this well, thought Julian, remembering his vision at Sunreturn. He had seen Frederic wearing the red robe, not the gray.

"Robert and his guard will be sufficient protection," Frederic continued, "and I think Julian is already enough of an adept to manage the Jewel of Fire."

"That means you're going, Julian," said Silverhair. "And now perhaps we should all go. Eric looks tired."

The Regent protested, but Robert was already at the door, calling for the young guardsmen who would carry his bed back to his room. The Master of the Junipers stood talking with Lady Rosemary.

Julian peered out into the winter dusk where the lights of Laurelynn glimmered bravely through the rain. Somewhere southward, the Red Mountain endured the windy darkness. Though his enemy was invisible, across the miles the King could feel Caolin, hating him.

After a moment he became aware of another presence and turned to find Malin Scar at his elbow. They had all become so used to seeing the man as the Master's shadow, thought Julian—one forgot that he had an existence of his own.

"You seek to master fire?" Malin Scar's voice never rose much above a whisper, and Julian strained to hear.

"I am going to—" Julian stopped himself. There was no need to be too specific. "Yes, I do."

"Ask *him*." He nodded toward the Master of the Junipers. "Ask him how he walked through the fire!"

"What do you mean?" Julian focused abruptly.

Once the Shadower had tried to kill them all. The next time Julian saw him, Scar was nearly mindless and the adept's devoted servant. The King had never dared to ask what caused the change.

"Lord Sangrado told me to kill him," said Malin Scar harshly. "I ringed his house with fire and burnt it to a blackened shell. And in the morning he walked through the embers and touched me with Light."

Julian looked at him in wonder; then his gazed moved to the Master.

"Yes," said Malin Scar softly. "For a long time . . . I knew . . . only him. Now I know myself again, and I do not know him at all."

Julian nodded. *I have always known the Master was like that, haven't I? But did I ever understand?* "Yet you still serve him?" he asked aloud.

Malin Scar's dark eyes brightened with the faintest of smiles. "I serve the Mystery," he said. "When you find out what it is, tell me."

* * *

"So," said the Master of the Junipers, "what have *you* come to ask?"

Silverhair gave the Master a quick glance as the old man finished pouring the tea. A chill wind from the northeast had scoured away the valley's pall of fog and the room was full of sunlight. He wondered if he would have had the courage to come to the Master if the rain had kept on.

"Have you had a lot of visitors?" he asked, taking the mug and cradling its warmth between his hands.

"I suppose I should be flattered," said the priest. "Everyone seems to have been saving up their problems until I come back to Laurelynn."

"Had you no difficulties at the College of the Wise?" Silverhair kept his voice light, like the sheen of sunlight on the surface of his tea.

The Master sighed. "Yes, and I blame myself for some of them—I knew the Mistress better than any. I should have seen—"

"That she was growing old?" asked the harper.

"That the expectations of others had locked her into a prison from which she could not break free. We had forgotten that at their own hearth, to their own land and to each other, every woman and man are priestess and priest. We had forgotten that the differences between layman and lay priest and adept derive from training and breadth of commitment, not from inherent spiritual worth. Too many have sought Awahna only because they wanted to be called Master, and failed. But there are still good people there. I did what I could to set things right again."

The tea was chamomile. Silverhair felt its fragrant warmth uncoiling in his belly and spreading through his limbs. "But you left it," he said then.

"If I had stayed, I would have been caught in the same trap as Madrona. They had too much respect for me. It is better for them to rebuild as equals, and I had to decide how to spend what strength remains to me." The Master's harsh voice rang in the harper's ears like the calling of the wild geese when they summon their stragglers home.

"How . . ." Silverhair whispered harshly. "How did you know that's what I must decide too?"

"I do not *know*, but I can feel your fear."

The harper closed his eyes against the betraying sting of tears. Why should he weep? Nothing had changed. But some of the tightness in his chest began to ease.

"Farin, I have known you since you were younger than Julian is now," the Master went on. "What is wrong?"

Silverhair kept his eyes on the puffy white clouds that were floating across the blue sky. "I have trouble breathing after exertion sometimes. Last time it happened, there was a pain in my arm."

"The left arm?"

Question and answer followed, crisp, without emotion.

"I didn't want Rosemary fussing over me," Silverhair said finally. "And I will not tell Julian. But if it grows worse, I may not be able to hide it anymore. What is wrong?" He went to the window and stood looking out over the rooftops of Laurelynn.

"A weakness in your heart," said the Master. "I have encountered these symptoms before."

His voice was very calm, a smooth sea on which Silverhair maintained a precarious balance while he tried to understand. Why was he so surprised? Despite all the evidence, had some part of him been hoping the Master would tell him an overactive imagination was causing the pain?

At any moment my body could fail me. He tasted that knowledge. "How long?" he asked when he could speak again.

"If you take care of yourself and hang up your sword, you may live to see Julian's children grown."

"You mean, if I play harper-sit-by-the-fire and let them coddle me!" Silverhair said bitterly.

"That is what I have had to do." The priest's voice had sharpened, and Silverhair turned.

"But you came back here."

"Length of life is not the only good. It depends on what that life contains."

The Master of the Junipers smiled, and Silverhair's breath caught, not in pain this time, but in wonder. He stood with his hands open at his sides, feeling joy as sharply as he had felt despair only a moment ago. This time he did not try to stop the tears. He might have expected to find release in sharing his pain, but he had not known that the older man would share his joy.

"Light and music," he whispered, knowing that there were no words for it, as he knew that words were not necessary with this man. "When it happens, I am no longer afraid."

"Try to live in that light," said the Master. "And take care of yourself—Julian still needs you. There are some herbs I can prescribe."

Silverhair laughed a little and sank back into his chair. He felt oddly weightless and happy, which seemed strange for a man who had just had his worst fears justified. But to know that what he had experienced was not just self-delusion, that the joy that drew men to the Master of the Junipers was something that he of all people had somehow discovered as well—this was almost an acceptable trade.

"I will try, but that advice may be difficult to follow." He laughed. "We are in the middle of a war!"

"I have not forgotten. Now you know your life's value. Spend it wisely, Silverhair."

The Street of the Goldsmiths looked prosperous, thought Julian. Even after the disasters that had left much of the city in ruins, the shop fronts here were neatly painted, and gold glittered from signs whenever the sun broke through the clouds. Only Fredegar Sachs's shop remained open to the sky, still cursed by its owner's treachery. One of Eric's elite longbowmen was on guard there. He saluted as the King picked his way across the rose-brick cobbles, avoiding the puddles left by last night's rain.

He could hear his guards splashing after him—Will and Loren this time. They knew better than to ask him where he was going. After the attack on Eric, the King had been forced to agree to an escort, but he felt like a prisoner. He shoved back the folds of the fur-trimmed cloak, which was another thing they had forced upon him, and strode on.

The shop he was looking for was one of the smaller ones, at the end of the row, but the metal of the laurel wreath that marked it had been freshly gilded, and it swung cheerfully in the breeze. He waved his guards toward the seat beside the door and went in. Sunlight poured through thick panes in the front windows, and he blinked at the dazzle of gold and cut stones that glinted from nests of velvet on shelves and tables everywhere in the room.

"I'm looking for Master Johannes," he said as a stocky man with very bright eyes in a round, rosy face came into the room.

The goldsmith's eyes widened and he sketched a bow, then grinned. "Have you come about your ring, then? I wondered if anyone at the palace would remember that the King's signet was made here."

Julian pulled the chain over his head, unclasped it, and dropped the ring onto the goldsmith's palm. "Can you expand it? My hands are bigger than my father's were."

Master Johannes held it up, examining it closely. "I was a child when I saw this last. My grandfather cut it down and resoldered it when your father came to his throne. But it can be changed again."

The King blinked, half-tranced by the shining circle of gold, or perhaps it was the ring itself—an inheritance as mutable and enduring as the blood in his veins. "What must you do?"

"Come with me."

Behind the display room was another realm, with cupboards and marble-topped worktables around an open space with ovens and a large, hooded hearth. Louvered windows were set into one wall, and another was really a pair of large, sliding doors.

A young man with a mop of dark, curly hair was bending over a worktable at one side.

They moved closer. "This is Kieran, my journeyman. He's just finishing the wax model for a brooch. The procedure for your ring will be almost the same."

The design was an openwork interlace of leaping stags. Julian watched the fine point of the graver trace the line of muscle, the texture of horn and hide, each stroke bringing new definition to the design. *Just so have I been formed and molded, and now the hand of the Maker is putting in the detail,* he thought then.

The journeyman sighed with satisfaction and lifted the tool away.

"Now," said Master Johannes, "he must attach these little pipes of wax to allow room for the venting of gases, and provide a passageway through which the melted wax can escape. Then he will make the mold."

With swift, sure strokes of the swab the journeyman painted over the surface of the brooch with liquid clay until every hollow was filled, then added more until it was a solid mass. When it had hardened, he turned it over and carved out the back of the brooch, then filled it in with clay.

"Now this piece must dry, but we've another, my lord, that's ready for the fire."

Julian nodded. This was what he had come to see.

Kieran began to work at the bellows set into the central hearth. The smith took an amorphous lump of clay bound up with iron wire from one of the benches and settled it carefully among the coals. Then he placed a crucible near it, watching carefully as each pulse of the bellows made the flames leap higher and the color of the charcoal began to change.

"This mold has been fired already," he explained. "And the wax that gave it form has melted and burned away, but before it can receive the true metal it must become one with the fire." The goldsmith banked charcoal around the mold.

The heat of the hearth upon Julian's face was like the breath of some great beast of prey. He had likened himself to the finished wax carving, but the wax piece itself was only an intermediate stage, whose single purpose was to leave its impress in the mold. The journeyman worked the bellows enthusiastically. As the coals caught, their red brightened until they glowed with a pale incandescence like the setting sun. Julian was sweating, but Johannes and Kieran seemed unaffected by the waves of heat that came off the fire.

It is beautiful, thought Julian, *but it terrifies me.* Now the mold itself was glowing red, and a little lake of melted gold lay in the crucible. The master skimmed off the film of dross with a piece of flattened iron.

"Sufficient heat will burn out all the impurities," he explained.

Julian stepped back out of their way. With one pair of tongs Kieran held the mold steady while Johannes tipped the crucible carefully toward the hollow at the head of the pouring hole. He was sweating now, the King saw, and the muscles in his arms trembled with strain. Then the gold began to flow from crucible to mold in a thin, shining stream.

In a moment, it seemed, Johannes was setting the crucible aside. Kieran waited a little longer, then began to pull the glowing charcoal away from the mold.

"Now we must let it cool," said the goldsmith, wiping his hands on his apron. "Kieran, why don't you go and draw us some beer!"

By the time they had finished their tankards, Julian was cooling down as well, but visions of molten gold and incandescent coals still blazed in memory. He found his own heart beating with excitement as Kieran unwound the wire and gave a first, swift tap with the hammer. There was a dull clink of superfired clay; first one crack, then another appeared. Kieran was grinning as the shards fell away, and they saw lying among the fragments the glittering figure, perfect to every bristle, of a golden boar.

"You have seen how we work, my lord," said the goldsmith as they moved back toward the front of the house. "What do you think?"

Julian wiped perspiration from his brow. "I begin to see why my ancestors trusted yours," he said aloud. He handed Master Johannes the ring.

The goldsmith weighed it in his hand. Then he went to a locked cabinet and from one of the shelves withdrew a small casket of oakwood, dark with age and carved with the arms of Westria. Its interior was lined with green velvet, empty now except for a fragment of gold.

"Here is the piece we took out when it was cut down for your father's hand." He placed the King's ring in the casket, and Julian saw that ring and fragment were the same.

"How long will the alteration take?"

"This job I must do myself, or my ancestors would haunt me!" Johannes laughed. "There is a power in that gold beyond its common value, and it must be handled carefully. In our craft we have certain rituals for doing such things."

"I understand," said Julian. In some ways, kingcraft and smithcraft were the same. "I will come for the ring when I get back to Laurelynn. Put a virtue of wisdom in the ring for me, goldsmith, and courage as well. I will need them in the coming years!''

Master Johannes closed the casket and looked up at Julian. ''My lord, it will be ready when you return. We kept that casket safe through all the years of the regency, not knowing if anyone would ever claim it. I will not give it less than my best effort now!''

FIVE

Rana heard the door to the stillroom opening, but she had her eye on the decoction of birch and white willow that was beginning to bubble in the covered pot and her mind on the charm that Eva had taught her to empower them.

> *"Birchbark bruised, willow white,*
> *Banish pain by your might!*
> *Herbs of power, in this hour*
> *To blessing I bind ye!"*

She pushed back the hair that had escaped from her braid, and turned to see Silverhair standing in the doorway, drawing in deep breaths of the pungent, herb-scented air.

"If you're looking for me, shut the door behind you. You're letting the cold air in."

The harper lifted one eyebrow. Rana flushed, realizing

how ungracious that had sounded. But there was no grace in her anymore.

"I was looking for Rosemary, actually." He shrugged off his cloak. Beneath it he wore high boots and a loose tunic of gray-green wool. The fleece of a sheepskin vest peeked out from the neckline. It must be colder than she thought outside.

"But you know what's here, don't you?" the harper asked.

Rana nodded. "I can prescribe from a recipe."

He dug into his belt-pouch and pulled out two folded pieces of paper. "The Master of the Junipers gave me these." He began to wander about the room, looking at the labels of the boxes and jars shelved there.

She read aloud: " 'As a tea, one part each hawthorn leaf, sweet cactus flower, and one-quarter part each rosemary, chamomile, valerian.' " The second was shorter: " 'one bottle tincture of foxglove.' "

"Silverhair," Rana said in a shaking voice, "why did the Master send you for these?"

If the prescriptions had been for the Master of the Junipers, Silverhair would have been trying to reassure her. She knew what medicines Rosemary made up for the priest, anyhow—cinquefoil steeped in white vinegar for his aching joints, and *yerba santa buena* tea.

"These are both for heart trouble. That's the one problem the Master doesn't have." She knew she was babbling.

"Just make the stuff up, Rana," he said tiredly. "It doesn't matter who it's for."

"Doesn't it?" She went to the shelf and pulled down the sack of dried cactus flowers. "Would Julian think so?"

"Rana, *please.*"

She bit her lip and got out the rest of the herbs in silence, measured them into the mixing basket, and began to shake them together. Silverhair sat down on the bench, watching her.

"I'm sorry," she said finally.

"So am I." His voice had gentled, and she ventured to look at him again. He seemed thinner, but he didn't look ill, and he was smiling.

"It can't be very bad, or you wouldn't be walking around." She hunted beneath the counter for a bag. "On the other hand, you're sick enough to keep you from going with Julian to look for the Jewel. You were too cooperative when we discussed that. It's got him badly puzzled, you know—he's sure you're going to come sneaking after him."

The harper eyed her quizzically. "And what about you?"

Rana stared at him.

"Why did *you* give in so easily, Rana? Now Julian thinks you're mad at him. Will you trade me your secret for mine?"

She could feel the hot color creeping up her neck, and tried to distract him by scooping the mixed tea into the cloth bag.

"Or shall I guess?" he went on. "You've realized that you love him."

"I've always loved him, Silverhair! He was my hero before anyone else believed in him. Even when I was afraid of any man's touch I loved Julian. If we could live like two spirits of the air, everything would be fine. But I love him as a man now," she said baldly, remembering how her flesh had burned after the Midwinter dance. "And he loves Robert. It serves me right, I suppose, for rejecting him before. But I couldn't bear for him to look at me the way Robert looks at Carmelle!"

"Rana! Nobody's going to confuse you with that little bitch!"

"Silverhair, *please*!" she echoed him. "Here's your tea. If it tastes too awful, you can always add honey."

"Thank you. I won't give you away to Julian." Silverhair touched her shoulder. "Will you keep my secret? What good would it do to have everyone worrying about me?"

Rana looked at him, remembering how hard it had been to reconcile the transcendent spirit she heard in his music with the sharp-tongued human being who produced it. But her own struggles had taught her to sympathize with his, and when they followed Julian to the Ramparts in search of the Wind Crystal, his compassion had helped her to find her own equilibrium.

"Can *I* worry about you?" Rana asked. "And if you need help, will you come to me? Think of it as something that both of us can do for Julian."

He looked at her directly this time and smiled, and she glimpsed what it was in him that had won the love of Mistress Siaran and the Queen of Normontaine.

"Do it for me, Rana," he said softly. "Accepting help is one of the things I have to learn. I'm a sour-tempered, trail-worn old bard, and I have spent too much of my life alone. Loving comes hard to me, but if I had a daughter, I'd wish her like you!"

"A prickly bitch?"

"A cactus flower—to stimulate the heart!"

Through her tears, she found laughter. "If I am your daughter, then I can hug you," she told him. Surprisingly he let her do it.

He was thinner than she had expected, but he was warm. After the scare he had given her, that was sufficient, and when he dropped his head for a moment upon her shoulder she knew that she had done the right thing.

Presently she let him go and handed him the bottle of foxglove. "Now this is for emergencies only—did the

Master tell you that? Take it two or three drops at a time. But I hope you won't need it!''

"So do I, Rana." He kissed her on the forehead. "So do I. . . . "

Rana was still worrying about Silverhair as she struggled to slip the loop over the last of the golden buttons at the front of her garnet wool gown and smoothed it. The neckline was slightly raised into a framing collar that could plunge deeply in front. A little too deeply, perhaps? With evening, the drizzle that had dampened the day had strengthened into a chill rain. She shivered and looped two of the upper buttons closed.

"Rana, are you ready?" Lady Rosemary herself was standing in the doorway.

"I suppose so." Rana turned from the mirror, pulling nervously at her skirts.

"Dear, you look lovely." Rosemary surveyed her, twitched her collar straight, and undid the top-most button of the gown.

With a sigh, Rana followed her down the hallway.

The guards Eran and Marcos stood at attention by the door dressed in black thigh-boots and dark blue capes emblazoned on the shoulder with Julian's star. The rest of the household was gathered around the central fire in the smaller of the halls in the palace. Lord Eric and Frederic were discussing the progress of the outworks that the Regent was building across the river. The fortifications were planned to run in a shallow curve out from the shore. Rana supposed that they would delay an enemy, but it was the spirit of the folk who defended them that would be their real protection.

Robert was in the center of a laughing group, radiant in a tunic of gold and purple brocade. He was rather over-dressed for a family party, she thought sourly, but it was *his* birthday.

Holding her head high, Rana moved on into the room. Near the fire she saw Silverhair, trying to get his harp in tune, and headed toward him. She would be safe with Silverhair.

"Rana—"

He was behind me—I should have looked more carefully. Schooling her features to maintain a friendly smile, she turned to face the King.

"Rana, are you angry with me?"

She stared at him. *How could I be angry, my lord, when you are standing there with the strength of the mountains in your shoulders and the light of heaven in your eyes?* She clutched at the folds of her gown, forbidding her hands to reach out and grip the muscle beneath the rough saffron wool of his sleeve.

Since they had returned from Rivered she had scarcely seen him. She had wondered if that were long enough to dull the physical awareness that had overwhelmed her at Midwinter. She had not expected to want to kiss the tracery of silver at his temple so badly it was like pain.

"Is there some reason I should be?" She licked lips grown suddenly dry.

He shrugged with that nervous gesture he had almost outgrown. "Well, you've been avoiding me, and I don't want to go off on this expedition thinking you're unhappy because I wouldn't let you come along!"

That's not why I'm unhappy, my love. Then she remembered that sometimes Julian could hear words unspoken, and thrust even that thought away.

"Did you think I was going to sit in a corner and sulk because I got left behind? Stop treating me like a child!"

"Rana." He took her hand, and she felt the touch as if she grasped fire. "You know I don't—but with the war—"

"Always the war!" She jerked her hand away and saw

with horror the hurt in his eyes. *Sweet Lady, now he thinks I'm afraid of him again!* But her tongue rattled on.

"Go off with your guard then, and your shiny, sharp-edged swords. I know what war is, too, remember—when the stink of blood makes you gag, and all you can hear are the cries of men in pain!" His face changed, and Rana saw that every word was a sword going into him, and that it was his own horror of the months just past that he was trying to exorcise by keeping her free.

"Julian, I'm sorry!" she cried. "I do understand—that's why I'm trying to become a healer, don't you see?"

His big hands clenched and unclenched at his sides. *Lady of Fire! This cannot go on!* she thought desperately. *When he brings back the Jewel I'll tell him the truth, no matter what he thinks of me!*

"Julian, come!" Robert called to him, pulling out the King's chair at the center of the table. They were bringing the food in. The rich odor of roast beef made Rana's stomach churn.

"Yes, of course." He tried to smile.

Rana watched him walk away, then started toward the seat Silverhair was saving for her, wondering how she was going to get through the meal.

Julian watched as Robert lifted the brooch from its wrappings, eyes widening. The three golden stags chased each other through the forest of their own antlers, tiny amethyst eyes sparkling in the candlelight.

"Do you like it, Buck?" Julian used the name by which he had first known his friend. He had seen Rana leaving the table. She *was* upset, no matter what she said. He sighed in frustration, but he must not worry about her when Robert was turning to him, his fine-boned face shining with joy.

Does it make up for some of the times when I have had

to put other people and things ahead of you? he asked silently.

"This is beautiful!" The others were echoing him, but Robert was the one who mattered now. Apparently the sovereign of Westria had an income, and using some of it to buy the brooch from Master Johannes for his lover was one of the first things Julian had truly enjoyed about being King. For a moment longer, Robert stared at it; then he pinned it to the neck of his tunic, his fingers lingering on the gold.

"I'll have a hard time leaving it behind tomorrow," he said, grinning.

"When are you going?" asked Eric.

"In the morning," the King answered. "It should take us two or three weeks to reach the Mother of Fire."

The rising wind spattered sleet against the window-panes, and Lord Eric frowned. "By tonight, this will be hitting the mountains. How are you going to find the Jewel if everything's covered up with snow?"

Julian shrugged. "I hope I'll be able to sense it."

"Try the crater, where the earth-fire comes to the surface sometimes," said the Master, who was sitting on Frederic's other side. "I searched there long ago, when I was looking for the Jewels, but of course the stone would not reveal itself to me."

"The crater?" asked Robert. "Do you mean it's *in* the crater? How is Julian supposed to get it out again?"

"That sounds like the joke we have at the College about 'an exercise left to the student,' " commented Frederic.

They all laughed, but Robert had come right to the point, thought Julian. At the College of the Wise, the adepts were said to walk on glowing coals. But that was *after* they had mastered the element of Fire. . . . *I can walk upon the earth and breathe the wind of heaven and bathe in the sea,* he thought then. *But where do I find Fire?*

"At the college, they taught us that Fire is not a place, but a process," said Frederic.

"But it has its elementals, its ruler?" asked Robert.

Frederic nodded. "The elementals are called salamanders, for reasons which no one has ever explained to me, since Westrian salamanders, at least, like to live in the damp mold beneath the leaves. Their king is called Djinn."

"Does that mean that Julian can call them and they'll bring him the Jewel?" Robert went on. Frederic looked in appeal at the Master of the Junipers.

"When the fire inside you burns as brightly as the flames outside," said the Master, "the fire of earth will do you no harm."

Julian stared at him. He looked so fragile, and yet the King could see the light that burned in the Master of the Junipers' eyes. *He is like a lantern,* thought Julian. *The outside is only a shade through which the essential spirit shines.* He sought inward for some spark to kindle, but he only felt cold.

"I have enjoyed the party," the Master said then. "But these old bones need to be in bed. Julian, will you escort me back to my rooms?"

However politely put, that was an order that even the King of Westria could not ignore.

"Will you excuse me?"

Robert gave him a compassionate grin as he stood up. Frederic was helping the Master to rise. In his eyes, Julian read a rueful understanding. *Has the Master discussed me with him?* he wondered. But the priest had never needed anyone's help to know things about Julian. *And that's just as well, for if he cannot help me, who can?*

"So what is it you wanted to say to me?" asked Julian. As the door to the hall closed behind them, the sounds of the celebration were cut off abruptly. They moved down a paneled corridor toward the stairs.

"How suspicious you are." The adept's voice held amusement.

"Well, I know you, and you know me!"

"I think it is rather a question of what you wanted to ask me," the Master said when he had got his breath back.

"That's true." Julian gathered his courage. "And I *can* tell you, because I think you are the only one who will tell me to go anyway. The Blood Lord is a familiar evil, but each Jewel leads me into a new and more alien territory. I am afraid."

"They say," said the Master, "that a woman expecting her first child fears the unknown, but a mother of many is apprehensive about labor because she knows how it will be. For a boy at his first battle and a seasoned warrior, it is the same. And for an adept. I would be surprised if by now you had *not* learned to be afraid!"

"I am no adept!" Julian exclaimed.

"Perhaps you are something more. You have been where no Master of the College of the Wise has gone since she who made the Jewels."

"Are you trying to flatter me?" Julian was becoming angry. They stopped before the Master's door.

"Julian, there is nothing wrong with fear. Would you allow a fighter who did not understand it to serve in your guard?" The Master peered up at him.

"No, of course not. He would make mistakes through overconfidence." He knew that much from experience. "But this is different. Fighting I can deal with. Once a battle starts, all the uncertainties are gone. But with magic, the deeper you go, the stranger it gets, until you lose all control." Suddenly it was he who was holding on to the Master of the Junipers as for an instant his world whirled away.

"That is what frightens me, every time it happens," he whispered, "The moment when I have to surrender myself."

"This is too heavy a conversation to support standing," the Master said when a moment had passed. "Let us go in."

Julian opened the door for him, and he lowered himself into the chair beside the hearth. But the King remained standing, arms folded across his broad chest as he waited for the old man to go on. The fire in the Master's grate had gone out, and the only light came from the flicker of a votive candle before an image of the Guardian of Men.

"Julian, what did Katiz tell you about the darkness he showed Caolin?"

Julian shuddered. "The dark nearly trapped us all—only Silverhair's playing got us free."

"To you it was a trap; to Caolin it is a place to hide. But he is wrong about its finality. I myself walked in that darkness many years ago," the priest said softly, "and I know that there is another way to get free."

In the dim light, the Master's face was in shadow, and after a moment Julian was almost glad. He felt as he had when he looked into the sacred valley of Awahna. He rubbed his upper arms nervously.

The adept spoke again, calmly, implacably; so still in his chair that it might have been his spirit speaking now. "You must embrace it, Julian, that is the only way. Fall through your fear, and you will emerge into the Light."

They had opened the door from the hall when Julian returned. Halfway down the corridor he could hear Silverhair singing. The sound was oddly distorted, as if the music were coming from a great distance. He took a deep breath, trying to diffuse the disquiet left by the Master's words.

> "Once in a meadow by the shore,
> The laurel maidens used to dance,
> Till young Ben Bell of Mirador
> Came wandering there one night by chance."

It was a legend of the founding of the city of Laurelynn,
a tale from the times just after the Cataclysm when the
First People were arrogant in their newly recovered sovereignty, the time when men were building up the sand
spit in the river into an island that would protect them
from the wild powers.

> *"The laurel nymphs drew breath a space,*
> *Then, laughing, hid themselves away,*
> *All but the last, who saw his face,*
> *And for a moment, wished to stay."*

He passed through the door and stopped, blinking. The
candles had been put out, and now the canopied hearth
provided the only light in the room. The door was to one
side, and a pillar blocked his view of hearth and harper.
But this was a friendly darkness. It was safe to let it enfold
him here.

He could see Robert and the others, faces lit by an occasional flicker of firelight, and now and again a soft murmur of comment could be heard. But mostly they were
silent as he was, listening to the song. The clear notes
rippled through the shadows like sun on river water, like
light on laurel leaves.

> *"He saw her slender arms outstretched,*
> *The moonlight glistened on her hair.*
> *He reached to clasp her to his breast*
> *And bent his head to kiss her there."*

Julian felt his own pulse throbbing, and remembered
how all through one moonlit night Rana had lain sleeping
in his arms, as near and as unattainable as some spirit of
the sea. It had been months since he had thought of that—
since he had allowed himself to remember it, for fear of

hurting himself or her. But that night on the sea, she had
been so beautiful.

She had been beautiful tonight, too, though in a different way. But he understood her no better than poor Ben
Bell had understood his laurel maid. He thrust the thought
away and moved out from behind the pillar.

> *"A moment then, when neither feared—*
> *The stars were less bright than her eyes—*
> *She shimmered then, and disappeared.*
> *He told himself he must be wise."*

The firelight shone full upon the whitewashed back wall
with its arching ceiling, and upon that backdrop the fantastic shadow of the harper played. Julian looked quickly
back to the hearth, but saw only the curve of his uncle's
back and the jut of the harp leaning against his shoulder,
the gleam of firelight on bronze strings. It was the shadow
harper who was making the music, arms moving in graceful sweeps, fingers dancing swiftly across a shiver of
shadow that was the strings.

> *"And yet when morning came, he sought*
> *Her where the light was green and dim,*
> *And peering through the branches, thought*
> *He saw her peering back at him."*

The chords sounded ever more slowly in sweet melan-
choly and the certainty of loss. Julian moved closer. If he
could only see Silverhair's face, it would be all right. *I'm
the one who's leaving*, he told himself. *Why do I feel as if
he and Rana and everyone I love is slipping away?*

Softer came the harpsong. The voice of the singer rose
above it with piercing clarity.

> *"He searched through every moonlit night,*
> *With grief grew pale, with fasting thin,*
> *And wandered till he passed from sight.*
> *Still calling, calling, 'Laurelin.' "*

Harp strings echoed that plea like calling bells, fading finally into silence. A log popped suddenly and Silverhair's silhouette flared in black relief against the red wall; then it all fell into ash and shadow, the shape of the harper misting away into darkness until it, too, was gone.

SIX

"Fight, wolves, fight! Slash and bite!
Run, wolves, run! Yield to none!"

The torches set around the drill yard of Blood Gard
flared as half a hundred voices took up the cry. Men
stamped around the central bonfire to the beat of the drum.
Caolin climbed to the platform, swaying as the windy
darkness trembled around him. January was drawing to its
end and the night air was frosty, but he felt a surge of heat
as the shout went up again.

"Kill, wolves, kill! Wit and will!
Howl, wolves, howl, wolves, howl!

"The rhymes may be idiotic, but they are effective,"
he murmured to Captain Esteban.

"I am familiar with the practice of raising men's enthusiasm for battle to a fever pitch by chanting," the soldier answered austerely. "But why do it now?"

"To bind them. That stonecutter who calls himself King of Westria has a guard. Tomorrow they leave Laurelynn in search of the Jewel of Fire. The men who pursue them must be a unit as well. Now I will own their souls. They have been carefully selected—the best riders, the best killers. They will be given the best horses and trained as lancers, and they will be the ones whom the others fear."

Captain Esteban nodded. He himself had transmitted the orders that held the rest of the sorcerer's army locked in their barracks. They would hear the shouting and see the glow of the fire, and rumor would build the mystique of the Blood Lord's guard. Caolin glanced at the Captain's fine-drawn profile and smiled a little.

"Would you like to be one of them?"

The Captain shrugged. "I command the rest of your forces. It would not be appropriate."

Appropriate! thought Caolin. *You do not yet understand. Will it still be enough for you to be my general when I am done with this magic?* Half a hundred voices shrieked gleefully from below, and he smiled.

> *"Maim, wolves, maim—slash and shame!*
> *Stun, wolves, stun—hunt and run!"*

He could feel the excitement building. The Wolfmaster moved to the low railing.

> *"Slay, wolves, slay—night and day!*
> *Howl, wolves, howl, wolves, howl!"*

The sound shrilled against the blank black of the heavens. Caolin gazed into upturned faces flushed with torchlight and wine.

"Who are you?" His call drew out the note of their

final howl in a long vibration that they would hear in their bones. This time the response came with full-throated enthusiasm. "Yes-s-s." The hiss stilled them. "You are wolves, *my* wolves! But you must become a wolf *pack*, bound by blood to each other and to me."

The men gazed up at him with here and there a frown as a few, more sober than the rest, began to wonder what he could mean. The swordsman Konradin stood a little apart from the others. Perhaps Esteban was right, thought the Blood Lord, watching him. The captain was too temperate for this, and someone must manage the army. But the sorcerer would need a leader for his guard, and he sensed a suppressed fury in the pale-haired swordsman that might be useful.

Caolin gestured sharply. A gate in the wall swung open. Grunting and clashing, a great red boar sprang through. Men fell back, swearing, then laughed at each other's panic as they realized that twin traces of iron links hobbled the boar's hind legs to a wooden bar. Konradin snapped the biggest chain through the iron loop at its center as the beast surged past.

A roar of harsh laughter momentarily overwhelmed the boar's raging as it fetched up short and fell over. In a moment it was up again, lunging at its tormentors.

Caolin heard the furious snorting and his hands clenched hard on the stone. *He feels the spear in his hands and hears the boar grunt in obscene triumph as its sharp tusks rip upward, splattering the King's blood across the bleached grass. . . .* He staggered and felt the Captain's hand hard beneath his elbow, supporting him, straightened and flung up his hand. The shriek of metal strove with the boar's squealing as Konradin began to turn the wheel.

Caolin had thought he had forgotten the sound of a boar's rage. He blinked away the vision. Soon real blood would wash those memories away.

The animal's charges grew shorter as it was drawn backward. The crowd stilled as the boar's hind feet were jerked out from under it; then the turning wheel brought the frantically scrabbling forefeet scraping across the gravel.

"See how he flies, lads! Feel his fury!" the Blood Lord cried.

Jerking and twisting, the pig was inexorably hoisted into the air. Froth flew from snapping jaws. Now it hung even with the platform. Caolin stared at it, shaken himself by the passion of hatred that pulsed from that writhing form.

Rage on! He glared back into the boar's rolling eyes. *Now you'll pay for Jehan!* Captain Esteban set the cold hilt of a sword into his hand. Konradin was watching him with professional appraisal. *Let him see that I am also master of his mysteries,* Caolin thought with a grim smile, then let the knowledge fade. He took a deep breath and let it out slowly, then another. Consciousness focused to a circle of stone whose center was the red eye of his enemy.

Caolin held that furious gaze, and for one moment the beast was still. It was enough. As when, in the act of love, all awareness centers in the loins, all of the sorcerer's power was channeled into a single swift flick of the honed blade. A red mouth gaped suddenly beneath the boar's tusked jaw. For a moment the victim hung motionless. Then he convulsed, splattering red blood across the stones.

The Blood Lord's stroke had bitten precisely to the depth intended—the beast's struggles pumped the blood out more swiftly, but it would take time for the great body to drain. *Time enough,* thought Caolin as he handed the sword back to the Captain, in whose lean features revulsion and fascination warred.

"Here is your feast, my wolves!" he cried. His robes flared as crimson as the boar's blood as he swept down the stairs. "Here is your sacrifice!" Another man set an iron basin beneath the swinging body. The dark drops of blood rang hollow as they fell.

"Come here!" His gaze caught Konradin's. The man's eyes were almost citrine—wolf eyes. "Look at him, man," whispered Caolin. "Can you feel his fury?" Konradin twitched as the sorcerer's will linked his awareness to that of the animal, and he began to breathe in harsh gasps. Caolin could see the anger, and the hunger, that warred within him. He caught a splash of blood on his own fingertips and smeared the warrior's cheeks and brow, then ever so gently traced crimson across the tight lips.

"Now I have marked you, my cubling," he breathed. "I give you this life. You will never be alone again. What will you offer to seal the bond?"

The man's tongue touched his lips as the dagger gleamed suddenly in Caolin's hand; then, more slowly, he licked them again. He pushed up his sleeve, took the weapon, slashed.

"Say after me," Caolin whispered harshly, "As I give my blood, I give my life to my pack and to my leader!"

Slowly Konradin repeated the words. His feral gaze returned to Caolin as his own blood welled along the shallow edge of the cut and was swallowed up into the red pool of the boar's blood below. Just so, the eyes of the wolf Gerol had followed him when the sorcerer first tamed him, long ago.

Now the men had seen what he intended. The ritual began to build its own momentum, and the space between boar and basin pulsed with power. Some of the men came eagerly, eyes hot with excitement; some reluctantly, revulsion plain in their faces; some uncomprehending until the knife's sting roused them, but by then they too were breathing in the energy raised by the mingling of the offering given freely and that which had been wrested away.

Then the last guardsman had been marked with the bloodsign. One of two looked at the sorcerer expectantly, but they did not understand. The sorcerer fed on the power of others; he did not give it away. The boar, drained now, had ceased to move. But the fierce energy that had kept it fighting to the end shimmered above the cauldron, mingled with the essences of fifty men scarcely less dangerous.

"By the bond of blood, life is shared," said the sorcerer. "Now we are one!"

Caolin leaned over the cauldron. The red pool within seemed to stir with a life of its own. Then he plunged the dipper into it, raised it to his lips, and let the thick liquid slide down his throat. He shuddered, sickened by the salt-sweet, iron-sharp taste; then the power in it jolted every muscle into momentary spasm, and he felt sweat break from his brow as heat flared through him.

I am the Blood Lord. He drank again. *Why did I never think of this before?* He looked around him, and with lips still wet, he smiled and held out the dipper.

"Thus do we drink the blood of death, of life, of brotherhood!"

"Wolfmaster!" Konradin took the dipper.

"Blood Wolves! Now you are fed; now you are mine!" cried Caolin. Somewhere a deep drum beat. The sorcerer's pulse drummed in his ears. Konradin's throat worked as he swallowed. When he held out the dipper again, his eyes blazed. Caolin motioned to another man.

One by one they came forward, drinking in each other's essence with the desperate fury of the dying boar. He saw them look at each other with new eyes, after. He had bound them to each other, and they could feel it now. But the Blood Lord knew them all while himself remaining a mystery. He licked his lips and tasted the soul of each man whose blood had dripped into that red pool.

Your allegiance was mine before . . . but your souls belong to me now!

"What are you?" demanded Caolin when the last man was done. The strength that dreadful drink had given him pulsed hot within. He seized the wills of those whose blood he had tasted and taught them their reply.

"We are the Blood Wolves!"

"Who is your leader?"

"The Blood Lord, who gives us our food!"

"What is your food?"

"Our food is blood and death!"

Blood and death. . . . For a moment Caolin saw the King's blood bright against his white skin, his eyes dark with pain, and fixed on something beyond mortal vision. *If I had drunk your life, my lord,* the sorcerer's new knowledge wondered, *then would I understand?*

Caolin gestured, and Konradin released the ratchet and let the boar's limp body fall.

"Behold your food, oh, wolves!" cried the sorcerer. "Eat well, my children, for tomorrow we hunt a noble prey, and the journey will be hard and long!" And with daggers flashing in the firelight, fifty men who were at that moment no longer entirely human obeyed.

Julian sprang from stone to stone, his feet finding their own way as his eyes searched out the blood trail. The wounded stag might be able to go on forever, but the hunters were beginning to tire. Behind him the land fell away toward the upper reaches of the Great Valley in long slopes that sprouted grass and chunks of volcanic rock in equal profusion, dotted with live-oak trees. From here he could see the Father of Mountains floating luminous on the horizon, and the peaks of the coast range powdered with snow.

Those mountains had been a mirage to lure them onward as Julian and his men toiled north from Laurelynn. For two weeks they had journeyed, but when at last they swam their horses across the upper Dorada and headed eastward into the Ramparts, the clouds still clung cold and gray before them. What lay beyond these barren foothills was a mystery.

"Have we lost him?"

Robert scrambled up beside him, the sound of his breathing harsh above the whisper of wind in bleached grass. A few hardy flowerets were tucked away among them, but the wind that whirled down from the invisible mountains ahead smelled of snow. Julian shook his head and pointed to the slope below, where the wounded deer still ran.

"Well, at least he's slowing!" said Robert. "I was beginning to think we'd die before the deer."

Two more of the guardsmen came up behind him and stood panting. Julian took a deep breath and felt the hot blood singing beneath his skin. Action was a good cure for anxiety.

"Spread out. If we can surround him at the foot of the cliff, we can end it there."

He shifted his grip on the short hunting spear and started down the hill. The stag, betrayed by his shattered shoulder, had veered off on an erratic parallel to the hill. The King angled across the rocky meadow to draw even with Marcos. He sensed the positions of the others as if the hunt had made them one being, sharing each other's wills with no need for words.

"Together now, and slowly, circle round." His spirit spoke to theirs. *"Let him have a moment's respite before the end."*

In a hollow where a great lump of lichened rock jutted like some forgotten altar, they brought the stag to bay. He stood with head a little lowered, as if he were growing too weary to support his great rack of horns. He was old, and perhaps ready for harvest, but all the more wily and dangerous for his years.

Julian kept a wary eye on the sharp front hooves. Once he had seen a man gutted by a slash from a cornered deer.

The blade of the hunting spear was almost the length of a short sword, with a sturdy oaken shaft. He would need that length to match the stag's reach with hoof and horn. He felt Robert's anxiety and an uncertain mixture of apprehension and eagerness from the others.

"Horned brother, I salute you!" Julian lofted his spear. "Thus do I raise the challenge: my weapons against yours in honorable combat, body to body, spirit to spirit, alone!"

"So be it," the others echoed. They drew back as if it had been a sworn challenge between two warriors.

Julian's lips twitched as he eyed those wicked antlers. Was it wisdom to risk his life alone when together they could safely bring the beast down? Then the stag lifted his proud head, and he thought he saw laughter in that lambent gaze. *I will kill you or you will kill me*, said those eyes. *But not without a fight!*

And that was why he was doing it, thought the King as he moved in. What virtue could there be in butcher's meat? Only the flesh of a beast that had fought to the end and accepted its death could give him the strength he would need to master the Jewel of Fire! Consciousness contracted, seeking the point of stillness where all things are one. The deer's head lifted a little, as if in offering. And then, as the stag turned, the King leaped in.

Something stung his side, but all his awareness was on the thrust of the spear, driving, with all the power of back and thighs uncoiling behind it, through the paler fur of the vulnerable throat and up into the brain. Then the spear was wrenched from his hands. He felt the impact of each boulder distinctly as he fell.

By the time he got his breath again, the stag was still. As Julian knelt by the beast's head, he felt a pang in his side, set his hand to the hurt, and brought it away red. He grimaced and stroked the stiff hair above the animal's dulling eyes, leaving a smear as bright as the blood that soaked the ground.

"Forgive me this pain, my brother," he said softly. "Thy life will not be wasted, as I pray that at my own ending my own will not have been!"

"Will, can you run back and bring one of the horses?" called Robert, helping Julian up again. He frowned as he saw the torn tunic and the blood on his side. "And bring the King's pony as well!"

The hunters returned in triumph with the stag slung across one pony and Julian riding on the other. They had set up their camp in a sheltered canyon where the stream had laid a more generous coverlet of soil across Earth's bones. But the river had carved its walls from living stone. The westering sun was sending slanting rays beneath the clouds, brushing the cliffs with a glamour of gold. Last year's pale grasses glistened, and the deep light suffused the new greenery with a golden glow. Opalescent mists made a shimmering ceiling; surely this was a fairer palace than any in Laurelynn!

As the stag roasted over the fire the cliffs rang with deep laughter; Eran and Will and Hal, Loren the Farwalker and the beautiful Marcos, Douglas of Lynxcairne, their best strategist, and Roalt and Kevan, as inseparable now as Julian and Robert had ever been. The King realized suddenly how rare a thing it was for them to sing together this way. Since fall he and his guard had been in the thick of the fighting, too heartsick at the end of each battle for more than a clap on the shoulder and a smile.

"Are you all right?" asked Robert.

"Was I frowning? Believe me, after this much wine, I'm feeling no pain." Julian put his arm around his lover's shoulders and squeezed hard. Fat sizzled as pale flame licked upward from the fire.

"Is the roast ready?" he called.

Eran grinned and carved off a slice from the thigh. The

warm juices ran down Julian's chin as he tore at it. He remembered how the stag had looked at him.

As your body becomes part of my body, brother, may your courageous spirit inflame my own. He swallowed, and felt a warmth go through him.

"Here's to our king, may he always have good hunting!" Hal lifted his mug in salute and the others echoed him, laughing.

"And here's to th' noble stag," cried Eran, "a king of his folk as Julian is of men!"

"But not so lucky," said Robert in an undertone as Julian raised his own drinking horn.

The King shook his head. "That death was no ill-fortune. It was his time. Better a swift ending to some purpose than to be dragged down by wolves, and he knew it. Perhaps it is a royal gift to know when to make the sacrifice."

"Julian . . ." Robert's hand closed on his arm.

"Don't worry, I'm not having any premonitions!" He grinned. "Just a general observation, that's all."

But Robert's gaze was still clouded. "Sometimes it's the privilege of another to die for the King. Remember that, too. That deer died so that we can live. I would as gladly die for you."

"Oh, Guardians, Robert, don't say that! Don't you know that's what I most fear? How can I dare love anyone, or let anyone love me?" He shook his head.

"But you have to, if you are to be any good as a king," his cousin said then. "You have to be able to love all of Westria. I couldn't do it—that's why I didn't want the Crown. I need something more tangible." He squeezed Julian's arm and laughed.

Robert's dark mood seemed to have lifted as abruptly as it had come on him, but Julian could not forget so easily.

"I didn't realize you understood that," he said in a low

voice. "I just hope that the Jewel of Fire can teach me how."

"Here." Robert handed him a flask.

Julian drank, then sputtered. It was brandy, and it went down like fire. The warm glow in his belly burned away his fear. He passed the spirits back again. Somehow, without his noticing it, night had come, and the world contracted to this circle of bright faces, this fire.

"Don' worry," Robert said to him sometime later when the contents of the flask were gone and they had crawled into their blankets. "We're goin' t' live forever." Robert's breath was warm against his neck, the hard muscles of his arms a reassuring defense against the dark.

He must be drunk, thought Julian. *He's using the speech of the mountains.* He opened his mouth to answer, but no words came. *If he's drunk, then so am I.*

But what Robert had said was true. All things that burned with the fire of life were one. He felt the spirit of the stag he had slain as a bright presence within him, and in the others as well. He could sense Robert's spirit as vividly as he felt the intimate pressure of his lover's hands. He knew without looking where to find every man of them, the lovers twined together, comrades curled like puppies or snoring alone. And as Robert strained against him and he poured out his own strength in answer, Julian loved them all.

SEVEN

The mists drew down a glimmering curtain like a veil between the worlds as the travelers passed among the first outrunners of the trees. When they emerged from the cloud, only a few boulders beneath the pines reminded them of the land they had left behind. Julian shivered. From the moment they left the campsite in the canyon, they had been moving into a mysterious land whose ways none of them knew. Even Robert had been this way only once, on a tour with his brother, and that had been in the summertime. Now it was another spring, backsliding rapidly into winter as they glimpsed the first shifting flurries of snow.

Julian wiped wet snow-kisses from his brow and turned to look back down the trail. The powdering of white was thickening rapidly, capping each stone. He reined his rawboned bay to a more careful pace. His men rode hunched into their saddles, their cloaks of tight-woven, oily natural wool already acquiring white capelets of snow. Julian shrugged his shoulders, but the flakes he dislodged were instantly replaced.

The snow was a foot deep on the trail by the time they saw smoke from the holding where the road to the peak branched off from the pack trail. The old couple who lived there were generous with newly baked bread and hot tea, yet even if the troop had been ready to stop, there was no room for so many. But the corral was large enough to hold their horses, and it was clear that they must shift to snowshoes if they wanted to make any speed.

At least it had stopped snowing, thought Julian as they moved out again. The old folks had sent their grandson Tully along as a guide, and the King followed him gratefully. As he settled into the rhythm of the climb, he felt his spirits lifting. The exercise warmed him, and the clouds were parting to show patches of brilliant blue.

In the monochrome world through which they passed now, the sky held the only color. The forest here was white pine and silvertip, but moisture-darkened needles looked black by contrast with the blazing purity of the snow. He trembled at the intensity of that whiteness—frozen light, enraptured radiance, a still perfection that made him feel unclean. It seemed sinful to disturb its serenity.

A snowball spun past his head. Hal was spitting out snow while Marcos bent to grab more. Robert stood in the trail behind them, laughing. Julian's lips twitched suddenly. In a single swift motion he scooped up a handful and sent it flying. It took Robert in the side of the head and he sat down in the snow. For a moment he could only sputter. Then the suppressed grins of the others declared who had downed him. His aim was as good as Julian's own. For the next few minutes, the white snow was no more than a brilliant backdrop for their play.

After that, their feet seemed to move more freely. Extra wrappings were bundled back into packs, and only the mist of their breath reminded them of the cold, as an occasional wisp of steam that curled from beneath the snow reminded them of the heat at the mountain's core. In the white silence they heard the sound of water running as escaping waters from the hot springs carved hidden channels beneath the snow.

"It's like the mountain is breathing," said Roalt as steam gusted suddenly from the bank beside him.

"Then the mountain's been on a three-day drunk in Laurelynn!" Kevan wrinkled his nose at the overpowering odor of rotten eggs that came with it.

"And how'd ye know that, eh? From experience?" Eran's grin became a grimace as he breathed in and the full impact reached him.

"Better get used t' it." The boy, Tully, laughed. "Smells like that lotta places here. 'Tis worse 'n the summer, though."

Julian drew his scarf across his face in a vain attempt to filter out the smell. He sensed the throbbing power deep within the mountain with increasing clarity. Perhaps it was just as well that he had chosen winter for his questing. Now, when the sun was weak and the earth gripped fast by cold, perhaps the magic of the Jewel of Fire would be muted as well.

Then they twisted around another outcropping and saw the white blaze of the trail dropping down through a forest of hemlocks to the gray gleam of a frozen lake. But Julian had no eyes for the road. On his left the Mother of Fire herself loomed up as if a sleeping dragon had roused suddenly, exhaling a lazy puff of steam. Red-black slopes jagged with new stone layered over old defied the snow that clung in scattered dapplings. He gazed upon the mountain and read in her contours the tale of countless rebirths and self-destructions.

The greatest of those had been during the Cataclysm, when the Mother of Fire had blasted what remained of her old crater and built a new summit nobler than the one the

Ancients knew. But two of its slopes had been blown away already, as if she were still unsatisfied by that achievement, so that the peak seemed fluted. From the nearer side, a white curl of vapor uncoiled through the still air.

Tully grinned. "Don' be 'fraid. Th' Mother's mostly quiet in the wintertime, and when she's wakin' we have warning. Th' earth sorta shivers, like a dog turnin' over underneath a blanket."

Julian let his earth-trained senses quest downward. Despite the boy's words, he knew it was not sleep but a balance of forces that held the mountain still. Even now he could feel a faint tremor as superheated steam forced its way through fault and crevass.

"Be still," he said silently, stretching out his hand. *"I mean no harm to you."*

The sun was westering now, rosy light lending an illusory warmth to the snow. Julian peered ahead. "We'll make camp by the lake, and then look for game."

They found a path winding up the draw behind their campsite. Tully came with them, grinning, though he would not say why. A half hour's careful climbing brought them to a tumble of cracked stone that looked as if some giant's fortress had been thrown down. But each chunk bore its own cap of snow, and the going was treacherous. Loren, in the lead, stilled as the slope echoed suddenly with harsh, high-pitched calls of alarm.

"What is it?" called the King.

"Some kind of animal," came the answer. "There's a stack of dried lupine cached underneath this rock." He jerked back as a gray-furred head popped out, round ears twitching.

"What in the Changer's name is *that*?" exclaimed Robert.

Tully laughed. "Pika—rock-singer. They live all 'round here! Thinks yer man in gonna steal its winter food!" The creature disappeared, squeaking angrily.

"The pika is going to be *our* winter food if we don't get moving," said Julian, reaching out to haul Loren upright. "Come on!"

They breasted a height where the hemlocks clung together for protection from the winds and wound downhill again.

"It's getting warmer," said Hal suddenly.

"It's gettin' stinkier," Marcos replied. Julian cast a suspicious glance at Tully's grin, but as the bowl-shaped area they were approaching became clearer, he kept silence. It might almost be worth going hungry to see a wonder.

Clearly the earthfires were close beneath the surface here, for much of the area was clear of snow. Plumy puffs drifted on the wind, and as they approached, one of the fissures belched up a billowing cloud of scalding steam. Roalt yelped in surprise and leaped back, almost knocking over Kevan, and they all laughed.

Julian stayed where he was, looking down at a pool of gray mud that erupted gases like a miniature volcano. Where snow did not cover the banks, the earth was stained red and ochre or speckled with yellow crystals. He could feel the heat in the ground.

"Be careful!" cried Tully. "Stay on rock—ground's not solid, even with snow over. You break through, get scalded to th' bone!"

Roalt and Kevan, who had been about to venture among the mud holes, drew back hastily.

"It is getting late," said Julian. "We can boil dry stuff for a hot meal."

Engrossed by their explorations, they had not noticed how the light was fading. They headed back readily enough; it was Julian himself who delayed, gazing down at the restless surface of the bowl.

"You hide your cruelty, but I know it is there," he said softly to the mountain. And it seemed to him that there was a reply. *"This is only my playground. Tomorrow you will face my power!"*

In the dead hour between night and morning, a line of horses picked their way along the trail that Julian's guard had broken, their riders shrouded in gray fur. But instead of following the fork that led to the lakeside, they dismounted in the shadow of the trees. Leaving two guards, the riders unstrapped snowshoes and began to make their way northward around the base of the Mother of Fire, ignoring the pleas of the old man who was their guide.

By the time the sky lightened, they were ascending the mountain. Their guide was dying, but that did not matter, for now they could see their way. Carefully they crept upward. When the sun pushed its way above the horizon, they were near the top. An icy wind swirled around the peak, probed the folds of wolf-fur cloaks, and chilled the mail beneath, but no one complained. Just below the peak, a command halted them.

"We will wait here. Burrow into the shelter of the stones and cover yourselves well. You'll look like rocks if anyone should chance to see."

"We'll be too cold to move when they come." The protest was very soft, but the leader heard.

"My spells will protect you." the leader said softly. "Be still now, and breathe deeply. That's right." There was a pause as the last man settled into position. "Your breath comes soft and slow, and a drowsy warmth weights your limbs. You will lie still, and flesh and blood will ward you until I call again. . . . Feel warm . . . feel at ease. . . ." The soft voice droned on.

Soon the slope was still once more, and the wind scattered snow across the gray shapes. Only the leader was still visible. And then his blood-red robes seemed to blur. Presently, anyone watching would have seen only a shadow staining the snow.

* * *

Julian sat up in his blankets, blinking away visions of fire and splendor. His skin prickled as if it had been seared by flame. He rubbed the muscle of his forearms, feeling the dark hair unsinged. The campfire was gray ash, but the snow blazed with the first light of day.

"Mmf—*cold*!" Robert tired to pull the covers back around him. Julian closed his eyes again, striving to recover his dream. Rana had been in it, holding fire in her hands and telling him—

" 'S morning already?" Robert reached out to him. "Julian?"

"Robert, take command for me." Julian squeezed his hand. "Get the men fed and packed. We can leave our gear here while we go up the mountain, but keep the others away from me. I have to do this alone."

"You're not going without us!" Robert tightened his grip. He sounded wide-awake now.

"You heard me say *we*," Julian answered gently. "Watch if you want to. Just don't try to talk to me."

Robert's eyes asked, *What use, when you're already miles away from me?* but he nodded. Julian sighed. Just as well that Robert did not know that in his dream, Rana had been the Lady of Fire.

He sat on a rock at the lake's edge while the others got ready. Once Robert approached him with a mug of steaming tea, but Julian motioned him away. One must face such trials alone and fasting. His gaze returned to the mountain. The hushed voices of his men emphasized the world's silence. The sky was cloudless, but the eastern peaks still hid the sun. Like him, the land was waiting for the Lord of Light.

He rose to his feet as the sky grew brighter. *Skyfire, earthfire, fire of life within,* the words repeated in silent litany. He willed himself to *become* fire. Then sudden brilliance outlined the jag-edged mountains and fused into a circle of light that remained imprinted on Julian's vision. *Skyfire*.

He strode forward to seek the earthfire and the treasure it contained.

They climbed slowly, lowland lungs laboring in the thin mountain air. Julian felt his forehead crisping as the sun's rays pierced the fragile shielding of the atmosphere. *I was wrong to think that last element had no kingdom,* he thought. *This radiant silence is the realm of Fire.*

They left the hemlocks behind them, passed grimly clinging white pines. An eagle soared past. The trail twisted through rocky talus slopes and around sheer outcroppings of dark stone. His own pulse drummed in Julian's ears. The world fell away in folded vistas below him: white meadow and black forest; lakes sheened with ice or sparkling as open water caught the sun; the dim expanses of the Valley and the blue line of the coastal hills; and to the northward, the perfect white peak of the Father of Mountains, guarding the land.

The top of the mountain was a tumble of hardened lava, half covered by snow. But it was from the far crater just below the peak on the southern side of the mountain that the lazy trail of vapor came. With scarcely a glance for the splendid scenery surrounding him, Julian began to clamber down.

The others followed him. Julian knew that the men had positioned themselves around the crater's rim, but Robert was keeping them well in hand. The King swayed as he stood, though the curve of the peak sheltered him from the wind. He was used to drawing up earth energies, but here the volcano brought them from the earth's core through tortuous paths of fault and fissure, for its own weight had plugged the original vent long ago. The power pulsed all around him; it shook his bones. No wonder the Master of the Junipers had not been able to locate the

Jewel. Every pebble that crunched beneath his bootsoles vibrated with the name of Fire.

He strove for balance, remembering the Master's words. He was master of Earth, and this was earthfire, solidified into stone. He reached into that hardness, anchoring his will. And he was lord of the Sea Star; this lava had fountained like water, and so he felt his way along the flow. The Wind Crystal was his as well, and the empty spaces in the mountain were filled with air. He let consciousness drift through them.

Earth and Water and Air . . . his identity with them sought their resonance in the Mother of Fire . . . and sought also for the one point in that fiery mountain where there was no identity but Fire. Ever more deeply he explored. His feet carried him toward the crack at the back of the crater. His ears heard Eran's cry of alarm and Robert's anguished order to stand, but neither disturbed him.

Consciousness eased its way between the elemental bondings of the stone, sped through the gaps between them, paused where it sensed stone becoming liquid, all the elements intermingling as they were overwhelmed by the power of Fire . . . *Fire* . . . FIRE!

Julian came to himself kneeling at the lip of the crevasse. Dazed, he stared into darkness like the gullet of a dragon, feeling even with his body's senses the heat that pulsed against his skin. The Jewel was down there. He felt it as a point of incandescence resting on a sea of fire. But if he wanted to hold it in his hands, the Jewel would have to come to him.

"Mountain," he spoke silently, *"you have something that belongs to me."* His inner observer told him that it was ridiculous to challenge a heap of stone, but he had learned how to outargue that voice, these past three years.

A tremor shivered through the rock beneath him. Julian tensed. He had visualized the mountain as a dragon. She was beginning to awaken now. He got himself upright and took a deep breath of sulfur-tainted steam.

"Firemother!" he summoned the power of the Wind Crystal to send his voice vibrating through the stone.

> "—Mother of Fire, hot with desire,
>   hearken to me.
> Graciously giving, light of the living,
>   help me to see—
> Goddess bright-burning, yield to my yearning
>   that deepest part,
> Throbbing with pleasure, grant me the treasure,
>   hid in Thy heart!"

Rock shook beneath his feet; force flared through his fingers. The incantation vibrated through stone and bone. Julian had not planned this. He shivered to a sudden sharp memory of the scent of his first lover's skin. The spirit within him surged toward the Jewel. Fire shocked through him and he felt power pulse in response. Stones showered down the side of the crater, but he could not stop the song.

> "Bloodfire is flowing, the glory is growing,
>   Fire now I summon!
> Loving and moving, giving and proving,
>   Come, love, oh, come in!"

Ecstasy strung taut the sinews of his outstretched arms. His manhood stiffened. The Mother of Fire shuddered as his passion ignited the convulsions that would expel the seed of light from her womb. His hood was blown back by a blast of heated air.

"Now, my beloved, now!" cried the King.

The fire was coming, coming, and his guards were crying out in fear, but Julian did not move. Steam shot upward, men cowered beneath a hail of small stones. Julian coughed as the hot breath of the dragon filled his lungs. The clouds that billowed around him glowed with the heat of the mountain's molten womb, red as Rana's hair. The mountain's tremors knocked him to his knees. Boiling mud gushed past him, but he held on, biting his lip until the blood came.

Lady, Lady! he prayed. The rock leaped beneath him. Superheated steam roared through the vent, ablaze with light.

"Julian!" Robert's call came faintly as the reverberations began to fade.

But Julian scarcely heard. Among the stones that the blast had ejected he saw something that blazed like a tiny sun. He stared at it, afraid at last, for it was melting the rocks around it. Light glowed in the clouds of dissipating steam, glittered on the rocks, danced in his brain.

The mountain had stopped shaking, but he could feel a faint vibration, the tension of some great energy held in check. The stone pulsed with blazing reds and oranges that swirled in dynamic harmony with an almost incandescent green. He stretched out his hand and the heat of it beat against his palm. *If I touch the Jewel,* he thought, *it will sear me to the bone.*

Then he blinked, for suddenly it looked smaller. It was shrinking—no, it was sinking back through the melting stone.

"Well?" said the power of the mountain beneath him.

"Lady of Fire, help me!" Julian cried. His eyes were dazzled by the Jewel's glow. But in that radiance it was Rana that he saw.

"Only fire can touch fire without being consumed," said the Voice from his dream. *"Become Fire, and grasp the flame without fear."*

He closed his eyes. He let the light of her eyes fill his inner sight. He reached out as he had when she offered him the candle, and closed his hand upon the Jewel of Fire.

Agony seared through his skin as he touched it. The shock jerked him upright, and then the power had passed through him, melting the remaining snow for a hundred feet to every side. Now he felt only a gentle glow, but the air around him was shimmering. *"In the Name of Fire I bless you, Child of Light!"* The words flared through his memory.

I burn and am not consumed. He felt the wonder. Then the King of Westria lifted the Jewel, and its radiance burned across the sky. His cry shook the air:

"I am Fire!"

EIGHT

"I am Darkness!"

The radiance deepened to blood red as the sorcerer's shout rolled shadow across the clouds of glowing steam. Caolin stood at the edge of the crater, his crimson robes whipping wildly as the words of Julian's conjuration throbbed in his blood. The King's face contorted as the Blood Lord's negation forced the power that was blazing through him back again. The sorcerer scrambled downward; cold-stiffened limbs carried him clumsily across the rough stone.

Then the King was before him, shuddering as if the mountain's turmoil now raged within. The sorcerer pulled out the square of silk he had brought with him to wrap the Jewel.

"It burns in your breast, doesn't it," he said softly. "You can't control it with my will against you. I can make it easier . . . give it to me!"

The King's head lifted. A spark of defiance kindled in the depths of the dark eyes.

"Julian, watch out!" The sorcerer glimpsed a sword and recognized Lord Robert staggering toward them.

"Konradin." The mental command brought the warrior over the edge behind him. *"Take him. Leave the King to me."* The fighter moved smoothly between the Blood Lord and Robert, but now other shapes were struggling through the clouds.

"Blood Wolves now I summon! Come forth to feed!" he screamed suddenly. "Fire and sword I promised you, and I come with a sword of fire!"

Konradin whirled, and the sweep of his longsword took the legs from the nearest of Julian's guards. Robert leaped in, and steel clashed. But the moment had been sufficient. Released from their trance like dogs from a kennel, the Blood Wolves obeyed their master. Gray shapes appeared at the lip of the crater. A hoarse howl split the sky.

The King's men brought the first wave of wolves down. But soon new gray-cloaked figures were challenging the Westrians. Robert was closest. But Konradin was holding him. Caolin turned once more to Julian, focusing his will.

"Give me the Jewel."

"It would destroy you!"

The answer, like the question, was in the speech of the soul, and it pierced Caolin's darkness like a tongue of fire. Shadow swirled once more as the Wolfmaster clutched its protection around him.

"There is nothing to destroy. I am safe in the dark!" he cried. "Konradin, kill him now!"

Steel flared and Robert leaped back, but blood showed bright through a slash across his thigh.

"He will kill him," said the sorcerer. "He always kills them. I will call him off when you hand me the Jewel!" He saw Julian's hand move, and took a step forward. Konradin struck again. Now Robert was down on one knee. Steel screamed as his blade blocked the next blow.

"I'll throw it back into the fire," came Julian's hoarse

gasp. For a moment the sorcerer hesitated; then he began to laugh.

"You cannot!" Caolin reached out.

"No!" the cry seared through inner and outer hearing.

In the weird light the boy's face was suddenly Jehan's. Caolin's fingers brushed harsh wool, then the mountain leaped beneath him. Hot ash filled the air; with one red-clad sleeve half shielding his eyes Caolin saw Julian lurching away.

"It's exploding! Run!"

Konradin struggled back to his feet as a dark young man with beautiful eyes helped Robert toward the edge of the crater. Men screamed as burning rock showered down. Another tremor threw the King forward and the sorcerer staggered after him.

Let the world explode! Rage, mountain—consume my enemy! Caolin's shout had no human words. He felt the fury below and laughed wildly. *I am the volcano, Julian, see how I burn!*

Julian fought for balance as the world erupted in fire and thunder. The Jewel of Fire was a flame in his fist. The mountain shuddered beneath him; the air seared his lungs; he scrambled out of the way of the flood as heat turned snow to mud and steam. He tried to call on the other elements, but the clash of Caolin's rage against his own had turned everything to Fire.

Rock cracked beneath him and he slid down the slope. Roalt launched himself after him, was struck by a flying boulder, and went down. Julian tried to reach him, felt the volcano's violence sear through him, and was lost in his own struggle to survive.

Shield the Jewel. Distant memory yammered in his awareness. *It can't be controlled so close to its source. Put it away or it will destroy you!*

When he could think once more, he was at the end of

a slope where the ground leveled briefly. They had rested here on the way up, sheltering in the lee of a knot of twisted pines. For a moment the mountain was not moving, though smoke and steam rolled from its summit in angry billows of gray and brown and red-shot dirty cream. Julian fumbled for the silk pouch that hung from a thong around his neck, and groaning, thrust the Jewel of Fire inside.

Fire faded within. Suddenly he could feel the throb of seared tissue in his lungs. He took a step and cried out as wrenched muscles stabbed him with pain. Gasping, he fought to control the agony. Two of his men were crumpled on the mountainside above him. The gray-cloaked shapes of several of Caolin's wolves lay still nearby. But more were gathering around the pale-haired man who had been fighting Robert.

"My lord—my lord, are you all right?"

Julian winced as a hand touched his shoulder, saw Loren's lanky frame, and tried to smile. He let the man lead him toward the trees where his own men waited, awareness questing inward as he sought an answer. Nothing seemed to be broken, and his breathing was growing easier now. Perhaps it was not so bad.

"Why should men kill each other when the mountain waits to devour you? Save yourselves, Westrians. My business is with your king."

At the first words, Julian looked up and saw beyond the Blood Wolves the crimson robes of the sorcerer. He reached for his sword, and fire blazed through his arm. He must have cried out then, for Loren stopped. Julian stared down at the seared flesh in the palm of his right hand.

"Tell *me*!" Robert limped forward. Someone had tied a cloth around the wound in his thigh.

"I can't fight," Julian whispered, looking from Robert to his hand and back again. "I can't hold a sword."

"You may go free," repeated Caolin. "If you give me the Jewel or the King."

Robert laughed. "My King has business elsewhere, but I'll keep you company." The other guards spread out between Julian and his enemies, and Loren began to pull him away.

"Konradin." The sorcerer's command seemed to shadow the sun. No, it was the cloud of ash that the wind was drawing across the heavens. The light grew bloody. The robes of the sorcerer burned like a dark flame. But the warrior Caolin had summoned glided across the rough ground. The side of his face had been grazed and his cloak was torn, but a feral light glowed in his eyes.

Robert's face grew intent. He brought up his sword. "Finish him."

"No!" Julian jerked free and started toward them.

"Julian, run!" Robert cried. "If you weren't here, they wouldn't care about me!" His opponent struck and Robert saved himself with an awkward parry. Blood Wolves spread out to either side.

The King stopped short, shaking. *True . . . it's true . . . run now.* The groan that wrenched him did not come from his body's pain. As if in response, the mountain belched up a new cloud of superheated steam. Julian saw Robert's blade connect as his opponent was thrown off balance. He began to move.

"Leave him! Follow the King!" Caolin shouted.

Again, Julian chanced a glance backward. The man called Konradin blurred suddenly into motion. A flare of red seared the shadow as his sword slashed across Robert's body and the warrior ran past him. For a moment Robert wavered, eyes widening as the blood began to flow. Then Marcos caught him in his arms. Kevan leaped into Konradin's path, sword raised, and with scarcely a pause the warrior struck him down. Once more Julian slowed.

Flee, cried the voice within him. *How many more must die for you?*

"Mother of Fire, avenge them!" Julian cried aloud, clutching the pouch with the Jewel in his burned hand.

The mountain roared. Its next heave knocked the warrior's feet from under him, but with the pain, power flared from Julian's hand through his body, and each new tremor sped him on his way. Even the air was burning. A last time the King looked backward, saw the clouds lit red from below, and then, at the lip of the crater, the first incandescent edging of liquid flame.

Julian lay in a snowbank, breathing in harsh gasps. He had come down the mountain with the Blood Lord's men behind him baying like wolves. He buried his face in cold whiteness, letting his heartbeat slow. Above him the mountain was still peppering the snow with ash, but the lava was darkening as it cooled. After a time Julian found his face wet. The heat coming off his body was melting the snow, but the burning within had begun to ease. Carefully he opened his hand. The Jewel had seared a crimson circle into his palm. The tissue beneath it was puffed out with fluid, but the skin was unbroken. It would heal.

He heard a wolf's howl from above and tensed. First, he had to survive. On the trail, they could surround him. He moved back into the forest, reaching out to the spirits of the trees. Somnolent with cold, they were hard to rouse, and he had so little time! But as he pushed onward, branches rustled. Anyone who came through after him would find it hard going—until the trees sank into their winter sleep once more.

But the King made no effort to conceal his trail. The Blood Wolves had to follow him until Robert and his other men were far behind, or else this retreat they had forced upon him would be a coward's flight. Smoke from the volcano spread a pall across the sky. He smothered the fear that these evasions had done nothing but deny him the privilege of dying with his friends.

Once more he heard howling, and pushed himself harder.

It was going to be close. He would betray Robert if he let Caolin's wolves catch him now, and all he knew of this land was what he had seen in the past three days. Julian stopped abruptly, thinking, and a swinging branch showered him with snow. Perhaps there was a way to change those odds.

He hurried toward the trail up the mountain behind the lake. Making a swift detour to their camp, he grabbed his pack. The pika shrieked warning and popped back among their rocks as he clambered over the scree behind it. He heard a shout from below and paused at the summit to let his pursuers see him. Then he trotted down the far slope of the hill.

Julian strode through the snow straight toward the steaming fumaroles, making sure his tracks were deep and clear. Smoke-stained light tinted it almost the same dirty pink as the open rock beyond. He drew on Jewel-enhanced senses to probe beneath the surface, to understand what kept the stone too warm for snow.

Fire . . . molten rock that for eons has been ever so slowly cooling, hardening, releasing water as mineral-laden steam. His nostrils flared as the wind brought him the rotten-egg smell. *Earth cracked by stress or dissolved by acrid streams, thick and solid or thin as eggshell—a deceptive crust across a boiling cauldron of mud and steam. . . . There . . .*

The King opened his eyes. *There!* He scooped up snow, made his way lightly around the hidden mud pots, dropped handfuls at the edges where they might have fallen from the boots of a fleeing man. Then he reached ground that was as solid as its seeming and flogged himself into a run. Halfway up the slope he heard his pursuers give tongue again and stopped, though every instinct counseled against it, clinging as if exhausted to a tree.

He saw three men, then a dozen, cloaks flaring red as speed blew them back to show the linings, moving down the hill. Another came smooth and deadly as the lava's flow behind them. At the top he glimpsed crimson. . . . Someone pointed at the smoking stone, he heard voices. *Don't stop to think about it, you bastards! Just come!* Julian began to stagger upward, looking back to see if they were following.

The howling broke out again, cruel and triumphant. They had seen him. They thought him already in their hands. Men dashed forward. The first made it in safety, but the next group saw the snow that Julian had dropped and followed it. Crusted mud gave way beneath them. Suddenly wolf calls became screams of agony.

Boil in hell, wolves! And your master with you! Julian thought viciously. But the first man was already on the slope below him. The King scrambled around a tangle of trees, backtracked, and waited. His left hand was skilled enough for stabbing—he struck from shadow and felt the point go in.

By the time night's shadows began to reinforce the volcano's darkness, Julian was nearing the crossroads. But there was no need to tell the old couple what had happened to their grandson, for when he reached it, the buildings were smouldering with a stink worse than that of the volcano, and the only reproach he heard was the lonely whinnying of wandering horses.

His own big bay seemed relieved to see him. Julian found an undamaged saddle that would fit. A new storm system was drawing in to challenge the volcano's clouds, and by the time the King was ready to go on, gray snow was already giving the ruins a rough burial. He welcomed it, knowing that between the storm and the darkness, even the Blood Wolves would find it hard to follow his trail.

They would expect him to take the shortest way back to the valley, and they might be able to overtake him on the pack trail. But the track that twisted southward through the mountains should bring him to the valley above the fortress of Elder in two days' time.

And then I will raise the land against them. . . .

Julian gazed back at the serrated silhouette of the mountains, shading his eyes with his hand. If he hadn't been checking the straps that held his bedroll he would have missed it, if there was really anything to see. The day was bright, spent clouds scudding eastward while the wind herded a new storm system over the coastal hills. But after two days of flight it was hard to focus. As the trail descended, forest slopes were giving way to banded stone tortured by wind and weather into sagging fortress walls. Exhausted and heartsore, he rode through a fantastic dream.

A moment longer he looked behind him, and something flashed like a star trapped in the trees. The King brought the bay to a sudden halt, staring. That had been sun on metal! His own men, or Caolin's? His skin went cold. The road he followed had been too hard for wounded, and he knew his guards would never leave their own. The Blood Wolves probably killed their injured, or left them for the real wolves. They could have followed if Caolin had guessed which way he would go. After the first day of storm he had not taken the time to conceal his trail.

There was one way to be sure. He slackened the reins and the bay horse, gaunted from two days of fast travel, began to tear at the new grass that edged the trail. Julian closed his eyes.

"Who are you?" Awareness arrowed northward, seeking the spark he had seen. Like a rebounding thunderbolt, his sending returned. Julian held his head, shaking. *Red darkness . . . a wordless rage . . . Caolin . . .*

He slashed at the pony's neck with the reins. It would be a race, then, and the bay was already tired. He bent over the tangled mane, trying to gauge the extent of the oak-studded foothills before him. Rising with astonishing abruptness from the dim sweep of the valley beyond them, he saw a jagged bulk of stone.

The Dorada Buttes. In the hours that followed Julian came to know that contorted silhouette too well. He had seen them from the other side of the river on his way to the Mother of Fire. Now they loomed like a mirage on the horizon, dominating vision. With each hoofbeat he willed those twisted turrets to grow more clear.

But as miles and hours went by, each step the bay horse took came slower. Julian pushed on till light failed, slowing then only because the ground was strewn with volcanic stone. For a time he walked, pulling the stumbling pony along behind him; for a little while they rested. But when dawn came they were moving once more. The sun was nearing mid-heaven when the bay stumbled. Julian pulled him up; a nudge with his heel produced a few more limping steps and then no more. Regular tremors shook the gaunt frame.

To the south, smoke from the cookfires of Elder twined lazily toward a cloud-layered sky. But between him and those red-tiled roofs horsemen were moving. He thought he glimpsed a flare of crimson. He felt the horse sway beneath him, and slid from the saddle.

Julian's own weariness overtook him and he clutched at the sweaty neck. But it seemed to him that the earth trembled beneath the hooves of his enemy. He pulled himself upright. With hanging head and angled flanks, the horse was a caricature of the beast on which he had left Laurelynn.

"I'm sorry, old fellow." A swift yank loosened the cinch. The horse never moved as Julian hauled off the saddle and then unfastened the bridle, too. "Rest now," he whispered, stroking the sweat-stiff hair. "If you die, at least you'll be free!"

The Blood Wolves were between him and Elder, but the Dorada Buttes shimmered before him no more than five miles distant now.

It is a fortress. If men can't defend me, I'll trust myself to the land.

At times the trail grew so steep that Julian had to pause and think what the next step must be. There would be moments then, when the pounding of his blood slowed and he saw his enemies picking their way among the rock-strewn lower slopes of the Buttes, that he knew he was very near the end. Then he would catch his breath and reach for the next handhold—the trunk of a stunted live oak or a skin-shredding outcrop of amber-brown volcanic stone—and the compulsion to escape would drive him on.

The three great buttes rose above a multitude of lesser towers. The south butte lifted now above him. Julian crawled along a spine of stone crested with formations like frozen flames. His hands left crimson smears where he gripped the stone, and Caolin's wolves howled behind him.

A blood trail . . . but he knew that was not what they were following. Caolin must be able to feel his presence by now, a molten throbbing in the gut, as he felt that of the sorcerer. A thin wisping of green grass clung to the slope, ending in a sharp curve against the sky. He dragged himself upward, and then there was nowhere left to run. More raw stone thrust back the soil at the summit. Here, too, earth's fires had breached the surface, but long ago. The volcano's fury was only a memory.

Julian lifted his head and felt the damp breath of the storm system whose clouds rolled low above him, weighted with snow, but he did not feel the cold. The skin on his brow was tight and dry. He could hold a sword now, if he ignored the pain, but the seared flesh in his hand was hot and angry as well.

A figure came into view on the slope below, gray fur ruffling in the wind. In ten minutes they would reach the top. Julian rested his aching head on his arms. It would be so much easier to lie here and let them take him.

But not the Jewel . . .

Perhaps it was the stone itself, speaking to his spirit. Julian's lips curled back in a grim smile. There was a crevice in the rocks before him just the right size to take the stone. Grunting, the King pulled the pouch over his head, feeling it burn even through the silk. Then he thrust it into the hole. With another piece of rock stuck into the opening, the place was unremarkable.

But there was a way to hide it even more surely. Julian scraped a handful of soil, summoned energy he had not known he still had, and spoke to the grasses whose seeds waited within. Soon the gaps around the opening were filling with green.

One thing more remained to ensure its safety. Painfully the King clambered back the way he had come, willing crushed grasses to straighten behind him. Down the ridge he made his way to the saddle below it, where piled chunks of stone could support him when he made his stand.

Caolin felt his enemy burning before him.

"Sir, here's blood," said one of the men. The sorcerer reached out and touched the darkening stain. He had seen this, he knew, in some dream.

Someone gave a bark of triumph. "He's up here!"

Of the fifty men who had set out from Blood Gard, a dozen remained. They should be quite sufficient to deal with one man. Caolin continued his steady climb. This time the boy could not escape the Blood Lord's hand. He heard the scrape of steel and an exclamation of pain.

"Hold!" the sorcerer cried in a great voice. "He belongs to me!"

The sorcerer stepped out into a miniature amphitheater, scattered with twisted piles of stone. For a moment he saw a pillar of fire burning in the shadows; then he caught his breath and focused on this world.

His wolves had spread out around the man who stood with his back to the highest heap of stone. One of them lay crumpled in a pool of blood, but the blades of the rest were ready. The tip of Julian's sword rested on the rock before him, still red. As the sorcerer came forward, he saluted with a surprisingly steady hand.

Caolin found himself bowing as he would have bowed to the King. *He* is *the King.* The realization came with appalling clarity. Bloodstained, with skin and clothing shredded, Julian had armored himself with a dignity that made Caolin recognize his resemblance to Jehan.

It does not matter. It cannot. I killed Jehan, too.

"Where is the Jewel of Fire?"

Julian laughed. "You will never take it from me!"

There was a little growl from the men, and some of them moved closer, glancing at the Blood Lord hopefully.

"Let me kill him for you," said Konradin.

"Stone him if you won't give him to the sword," said one of the others. "Plenty of ammunition here!"

He turned back to Julian. "You have no chance, boy. Surrender to me."

"So that you can kill me without losing any more of your dogs?" He glared at the sorcerer with fever-bright eyes.

Caolin raised one eyebrow. "I have no need to kill you." In the distance, thunder muttered, and some of the men looked over their shoulders. This height would be a bad place to be caught in a storm. The Blood Lord focused his will.

"You are burning with fever," he said softly, compellingly. As he drew closer, he could feel the waves of heat coming off the King's body, as if the Jewel of Fire were consuming him from within. "You're dizzy, aren't you, and that sword is far too heavy for your arm."

Julian's blade began to waver, and the sorcerer smiled. Then a sudden gust sent his cloak flaring out behind him; he winced at the first splash of rain.

"Here's Air and Water, Caolin!" Julian dropped his weapon and lifted his hands. "And a land full of green things is waiting to devour you!"

The wind roared down on them. Caolin clutched at his robes. Had the earth really quivered beneath his feet? He reached to the nearest rock, felt slick wetness, and snatched his hand away. He focused his panic into a blow to crush Julian; it was deflected by a will as strong as his own. Light blinked across the valley, then the thunder came.

"Stone him!" he shrieked suddenly.

Above the roar of the rain he heard Julian's cry as he tried to shield his head and dodge the stones. The wind swirled as if he were willing it to blow them away.

Light flared down between them, negating vision as hearing was destroyed by the next second's crash of pure sound. Caolin felt himself falling, his throat scraped by a scream that no one heard. But when his senses at last began to recover, he saw Julian lying close beside him. Dark blood trickled sluggishly across the tracery of silver at his temple, and his eyes were closed.

The sorcerer pushed himself up onto his knees, nostrils flaring at the scent of burnt air. He grasped Julian's wrist and felt the pulse throb thready and slow.

Konradin pushed forward, sword glinting coldly. "He destroyed the mountain," said Konradin. "His blood is power. Let us drink it now, before he wakes."

"No. He is my meat," said the Blood Lord. "Bind him." Someone brought thongs to lash feet and ankles while the sorcerer yanked at the ties of the King's tunic and pulled it open. There was nothing—no medicine bag, not even a crystal on a chain. Swiftly he patted down the sides of his jerkin, dumped the contents of the King's belt pouch on the ground. His boots yielded nothing. What had he done with the Jewel?

"He may have hidden something before we got here," he told the men. "A small pouch or packet. Search the rocks."

The rain was coming down harder, with occasional stinging pieces of hail. The sorcerer stared into the unconscious face of his enemy.

"You defied me, yet there you lie," he said softly. "As your body is broken, I will break your will. Did you think death was the worst fate I could give you? You will beg for my mercy, boy. You will lick my feet and beg." He shuddered suddenly at the vision of that dark head bending before him.

"My lord, we cannot find it!" The Blood Wolves were standing in a ragged circle around him. "In this light, with the rain . . . are you sure the talisman is here?"

Caolin stilled, twitching as he sought the fiery touch he had sensed so strongly at the Mother of Fire. He still felt its essence in Julian—had the fool swallowed the thing? He would squeeze the knowledge out of him! But not here, not now—hail stung his skin and water weighted his robes. The clouds were covering the world in a darkness through which distant lightning laced white fire.

"Carry him down the hill and sling him over one of the ponies." Caolin gestured toward the body. "He will sing a different song in Blood Gard."

NINE

In the light of the setting sun the great split dome above the Sacred Valley of Awahna glowed red as a coal. Tatters of cloud smoked off to the eastward in swirls of mingled gray and flame. Like a spark cast off from the conflagration in the heavens, a fire challenged the shadows of the valley floor.

With a roar it blazed upward, though there was no wood to feed it and no wind to fan the flames. Then the form of a woman appeared within them, Her body incandescent, hair whipping toward the sky. For a moment longer the fire flared around Her, then She absorbed it back into Her glowing flesh and turned to face the two other flickers of light in the clearing, which brightened until they seemed as solid as She.

"Well, th' first test has been interesting," said Coyote, hunkering down. "What do ye have in mind for th' King o' Men now?"

"My plan went well. He courted the Mountain, and She

gave him the Jewel!'' The Lady of Fire shook bright hair back over Her shoulders. ''What happened after cannot be blamed on Me!''

Coyote shrugged. ''But it did happen. An' now the Jewel's lost again, and so is the King!''

''A man captured him, men must rescue him,'' said the Lady slowly. ''How can we interfere?''

Both turned toward the third figure in the clearing, whose skirts were the pale gray of shadowed snow, but whose cloak glowed now with the radiance of the winter sky. She looked back at them, and the air grew brighter with the movement of Her golden hair.

''We must do something about the Jewel of Fire,'' said the Lady of Westria. ''If it stays where it is, when the weather warms it will set the valley ablaze.''

''And the King?'' said Coyote. ''As I recall, he served ye well.''

The Lady's light intensified. ''I have already given him what help was allowed,'' She said unhappily.

''What about his woman, then?'' Coyote answered Her. ''It's all very well for Julian t' disport himself with You, but what about that girl he wants t' make his queen? I think *she* deserves a little fun!''

''You would—'' the Lady of Westria began, but the Lady of Fire started to laugh.

''I like that! They must come together as equals, and the poor child needs someone to teach her how!''

''Are you volunteering, Fire-bringer?'' the Lady of Westria asked then.

''Sure.'' He grinned widely. ''If we're all agreed.''

The Lady of Westria frowned. ''We forbid men to upset the balance, but we must give them free will. Still, the Blood Lord perverts all powers. This much I will allow. The girl also most prove herself worthy by finding the Jewel. And if she wants your help, first she has to ask.''

Coyote stretched, and the radiant human form he had

worn settled into the ginger-gray four-legged body he preferred. He shook Himself, lifted His muzzle, and sniffed the air.

"She'll ask. She likes rescuin' people, and she thinks she knows Me!" In a blink He was gone.

Only a memory of light remained above. The bright figure of the Lady of Westria faded; then the Lady of Fire disappeared as well. But where they had stood the snow glistened until the earth slept and the only fires still visible burned in the star-strewn sky.

"Julian!"

The call deepened to a hoarse scream as Rana stumbled to Robert's bedside.

"It's all right! Lie still now, you're safe here!"

She turned up the lamp, knowing already that she would see a new red stain spreading on his bandaging. Lady Rosemary's skillful surgery had pulled the edges of the sword slash neatly together. But Robert had endured over a week in a horse litter before the survivors of the King's guard got him to Laurelynn. It was the part where the blade had bitten most deeply that bothered her. Bloody serum oozed through the bandage every time he moved. Perhaps in the morning they could try poulticing it with comfrey and mugwort again.

"I'm safe, but is *he*?" Robert winced as Rana pulled the pad above the great slash across his chest gently away and patted another into position. "Why am I still living?" He turned his head restlessly. "Why?"

"If you don't lie still, you won't be, and then Julian will come back and blame *me*!" Rana said tartly, smoothing the damp hair gently back from his brow. Robert sighed, and his eyes closed. Rana left the lamp burning. He might feel more secure that way. It was just past midnight. The only sounds were the occasional creak of a beam in the walls of the palace and the harsh breathing of the wounded man. Her own eyes began to close.

"Where is he, Rana?"

The question came so quietly that for a moment she thought it was her own soul speaking. It was what all Westria was wondering: *Where is the King?*

"He's not dead, anyway. The Master of the Junipers has gone out on the Spirit road, and he says that Julian is not in the Otherworld."

"But he should have been here before me." Robert held her in his blue gaze.

"Remember, he's always disoriented until he gets used to the Jewels. The Jewel of Fire must have been hard to handle. And then the Blood Lord came. Perhaps the shock . . ." Rana stopped speaking. She had meant to reassure Robert, and now she was scaring herself again.

"Fire," muttered Robert. "He called fire out of the Mountain, and something so bright you couldn't look at it. And then he picked it up, Rana, and he *shone*."

Rana nodded. She had seen the King in the glow of Midwinter morning, brushing away the earth of his grave, and she had seen him in the silver light of the sea, commanding the storm. She had seen him glittering like crystal as he called the winds. He had mastered all of those. He was the Jewel Lord. But Fire was the most dangerous of all. Did Julian wander in the mountains, blasted by the powers he had summoned, or had his return been prevented not by magic, but by men?

"He couldn't die," she said stoutly. Or if he did, what grave could hold him?

"He shone," Robert repeated. "Give me something to drink, please?"

The knot in Rana's stomach tightened as she felt his forehead. It was hot again. Swiftly she poured out some of the tea Lady Rosemary had left for him—yarrow and willowbark with a little honey to take away the bitter taste.

Robert drank thirstily, but it did not seem to ease him. He lay back on his pillow and closed his eyes, but his breathing was too careful; he lay too still.

Rana looked at him and bit her lip. The stubble of beard only emphasized the gauntness of his cheeks. The skin around his eyes looked bruised. Now that the sheer physical beauty that had always daunted her was gone, she realized that it was not only for Julian's sake that she cared for him.

"Julian *is* back, isn't he?" Robert whispered finally. "I wanted to stop the Blood Lord all by myself so that he would be grateful, and I made them pull him away. He blames me, and no one will tell me. That's why he hasn't come to see me. I understand."

"Robert, what are you saying? Julian loves you!" She bent over him.

"He always wanted *you*, Rana. Maybe it will be easier when I'm out of the way!"

"Robert, don't you dare die!" Her hands closed on his shoulders.

"Why should you care?" His eyes were open, but she wasn't sure what he was seeing. "I took him away from you so you couldn't hurt him anymore. But now you want him, don't you? *Don't you?*"

Frantically Rana sponged his brow with cold water. "Robert of Rivered, I'll smack you silly if you don't listen to me!" Perhaps the absurdity of that threat got through to him, for suddenly his gaze was focused on her face once more.

"Last summer you saved Julian. You were right to love him. And in all those weeks of tromping around the mountains I learned to value you. Can't you believe that a woman can love you without wanting to eat you alive like Carmelle?"

"It's hard," he whispered. "They say she married some

poor fellow from Las Costas right after the Autumn Sessions, and the cow is pregnant already!''

''Don't change the subject,'' said Rana, taking the hand that had been twitching at the sheet and clasping it in her own.

She could feel the life in him, but it seemed strange to touch it directly, without Julian to mediate between them. There was nothing in Robert that responded to her as a woman. But when she had danced with Julian at Midwinter, there had been. Did Robert know? He relaxed suddenly, and for a moment she felt a stab of fear.

''Love him, Rana . . . when you find him.'' Robert's breathing grew calmer and she realized that he was falling asleep again.

I seem to be learning how to love quite a lot of people these days, she thought wryly. *You . . . Silverhair . . . Even if he never loves me, Julian has already taught me that love is like a fire—the more you feed it, the more warmth it gives.* She settled Robert's hand beneath the blanket and tucked the covers snugly around him again.

Silverhair brushed his fingers across the harpstrings, and sound shimmered softly through the room. They had opened the windows to let in the morning light, but the smell of sickness was still heavy. The harper shivered a little as cold touched him, but each chord modulated sweetly into the next unhindered, sound fading and building and ebbing without conclusion, an endless flow of music to bring the spirit peaceful dreams.

But the spell did not seem to be working. Robert had kicked off his covers again despite the chill. Rana and Rosemary bent over him, sponging his hot skin. The murmur of their voices rose and fell along with the harping. Silverhair let the music flow through him. In his current incarnation as harper-sit-by-the-fire, playing for the wounded was one of the few things he could do, and in the past weeks he had played endlessly. He focused once more on his harping, trying not to remember those weeks long ago when he had played for a dying king.

"Run, Julian! The mountain's going—holy Guardians, look at the *fire!*" Robert's cry made a sudden shrill descant. "Burning—the air is burning! Marcos, get back, boy. Crouch down and shield your heads, everyone!" He twisted, huddling with his arm across his face.

The two boys from the King's guard who had come to visit their commander stood with fists clenched, staring. "That's the way it happened," said one of them. "I thought the world was goin' to explode." In the three days since Robert had been brought in, his ravings had given them all a vivid picture of what had happened at the Mother of Fire.

"Dark—why's it gone so dark suddenly? It's the Blood Lord! Julian, get *away!*"

The harper looked at the gaunt frame that a month ago had belonged to a vital young man and thought of that other young man whose strong body might even now lie stiff in the snow. What gave him, with a damaged body and a life already half gone, the right to save his own life when these boys were risking theirs? *Would this have happened if I had been there?*

Robert's ravings faded into muttering, but he was twitching as if his muscles were still trying to fight his enemy. "The darkness—so dark—oh, Guardians, there are *faces* in those clouds!"

"What's wrong with him?" said the younger of the two guardsmen. "Is he going to die?"

"If he would stay quiet, he could heal, but his fever makes him live through it all again," Rana answered him.

"Come away, Marcos," said his companion. "There's nothing we can do."

"Julian, where are you?" wailed the wounded man. "I've failed . . . why should I live when I've lost you?"

"No!" The guard called Marcos stepped to the bedside. "My lord—Roberto—I love you! Don' leave me alone!" He held Robert's face between his hands until he stilled. "Listen t' me, lord. Ye've got t' get well for me, huh? Please, Roberto, please—" His slim brown hands smoothed the sweated hair back from Robert's brow, stroked down cheek and neck, sending their own messages through the skin.

Lady Rosemary put her finger to her lips and drew Rana away. "Look," she said in a low voice, "He's growing quieter!" The women pulled the bedclothes back over Robert's long body.

Marcos settled down beside the bed, gripping his lord's hands. "Roberto, I won't leave ye alone!"

Silence fell in the room. Carefully Silverhair set the harp aside and followed Rana out to the balcony.

"Love . . . who would have thought it!" he said as the door closed behind them. "Perhaps this will make him want to live." Banners of flame flew across the western horizon as the sun went down behind the coastal hills.

"Sometimes love is not enough." Rana rubbed her eyes with shaking hands. "We all love Julian!" She turned to Silverhair. "I've been mewed up here since they brought Robert in. It's been over a week now. Has there been any word?"

"Frederic sent men to backtrack the guards as soon as they got here," said the harper. "They went all the way to the Mother of Fire, but between snow and ash fall, there wasn't much of a trail. They're coming back slowly, checking every holding along the way, but the messenger said that they'd found no sign of him so far."

She leaned against the railing with a sigh, and the sunset light aureoled her hair with its own flame. "Silverhair, at Midwinter we gave Julian a promise. Do you think it holds us now?"

The harper met her clear gaze with his own slow smile.

"We promised not to seek the Jewel of Fire. We said nothing about looking for *Julian*."

"That's how it seems to me." Rana gazed northward, shading her eyes with her hand as if she could see through the gathering mists to wherever the King had gone.

"But where do we look?" he added reluctantly. "My trailcraft is nothing out of the ordinary, and if the experts Frederic sent found no trace, I doubt there's a tracker in Westria who could pick up the King's trail now."

"No human tracker," she agreed. "But I think we know Someone who could find him if we can figure out how to attract his attention."

"Now if you were Coyote," said Rana, "what would make you come?"

The harper stared at her; then one eyebrow went up and he grinned. "From what I've heard, almost anything."

Abruptly she realized what she had said, and she felt the hot blood rise in her face. With great deliberation she continued to arrange kindling on the hearth before the altar, waiting for the betraying color to fade away. Perhaps they would have gotten better results out-of-doors, but the night was cold, and if they went very far from Laurelynn they could be snapped up by Caolin's men. At least the shrine in the palace was quiet and secure.

"Rana, are you sure you want to do this?" Silverhair said then. "Coyote is not a dog to come at your command—" He stopped. "Sorry," but now she was laughing too.

"Caolin thought he had tamed Mañero—I know better than to even try. But he might find this quest amusing." She tapped experimentally on the drum.

The fire was blazing strongly now; the juniper twigs interwoven among the oak sticks fell away in glowing curves. She let those lines trap her vision, stilling until her only movement was the slap of her fingertips on the taut skin of the drum. She heard the first harp note come in on the beat. Silverhair's music rode the rhythm, flickering up and down the scale as the fire leaped and fell. Rana bowed to the fire and tried to remember the words of the traditional summoning.

> *"Grandfather Coyote, great spirit of creation,*
> *Dance from your southern plains.*
> *Your grandchildren call you!*
> *Fill us with your passion for living,*
> *Enliven us with the flame of your spirit,*
> *Give us the skills we need to grow.*
> *Welcome, Grandfather!"*

It did seem to her that when she had finished, the fire burned brighter. She felt a warmth in the room, but she needed more than the benevolent attention that one expected from the Guardians during a ceremony. She glanced at Silverhair in appeal. Still playing one-handed, he cast a handful of sage leaves where they would smoulder at the edge of the fire. She took a sharp breath and her vision was filled suddenly with the sweep of bright hillsides where the pungent aroma of sagebrush was released by the sun.

"Coyote, Changer," Silverhair half chanted, *"can you hear our calling?"*

> *"Fancy dancer, far-farer, undefeated, ever falling—*
> *Fast talker, feast-stealer, insatiable lover*
> *Fire-bringer, imitator, swift to recover . . ."*

Rana swayed, staring into the fire. The harper's chant was only part of the rhythm, like her drumming, like the beat of her heart. The fire was pulsing, too—dark/light, dark/light. Two round coals at its center glowed.

"A cold trail and a hot kill, Death-faker,
A new love, a good laugh, Life-maker!
That's what we offer you—
Take what we proffer you."

Rana heard no more. At the fire's heart two bright eyes were burning. She met the lambent gaze unblinking, her consciousness kindled in the pulse of the light.

The fire was dancing—no, *she* was leaping and whirling to the music of harp and drum. She tried to see who was dancing with her. Folk said that once Coyote had danced all night with a patch of wind-blown reeds. At least one pair of eyes was glowing through the smoke that swirled off the fire.

She circled the flames, and suddenly the figure whirled before her. She tried to stop, for he had a stag's horned head atop a man's strong body, but the deer-dancer seized her and began to spin her around and around.

"Let me go!" she cried. "You're not the one I'm looking for!"

The dancer released her suddenly. She stood, still swaying to the rhythm, and saw him grasp his head with both hands and twist it. As the deer's head came off she saw another one beneath it—a brown bear's head that surveyed her with a broad grin.

"How about me, then?" The voice was furry, too. He grabbed her in a great hug, but before she could scream he had let her go.

"No." She shook her head emphatically. "Just let me dance!"

But this head, too, was coming off. She held her ground, wondering what lay beneath it. It was a hawk this time, who swung her over the fire in a trail of sparks like scattered stars. And beneath that one was the head of a hare, of a raven, of a stallion. She danced with all of them until she had almost forgotten why they kept changing or what she was looking for.

Then she found herself staring at a pointed fox face and realized she was getting close now.

"You look like Coyote."

"I'm his brother," said the dancer. "Won't I do?" The flames blazed up with a roar behind him as someone threw more wood on the fire. She saw white teeth and glinting red fur.

"Take off your mask, Coyote," she said. "I know you now!"

And he grinned and peeled the fox away, and it was Coyote, as she had seen him when he revealed himself on the roof of the Council Hall.

"Doubt it," said he, "but this'll do for now. Why d'ye want me?"

"I need your help to locate the King. You can follow his trail even if it's been hidden by magic. Help me find him, please!"

"What ye gonna give me?" asked Coyote. The fire was dying down again, leaving his face in shadow.

"What do you want?" She peered at him, trying to read the gleam in his eyes.

"That's a question. If ye got th' answer, ye don' need me t' help you, eh?"

No, that was another riddle, thought Rana, but she had not time for games. "Well, that's what I'll give you," she said in exasperation.

"*Whatever* price I ask?" He cocked his head to one side, grinning at her.

"Anything!" Her answer came, and Coyote began to laugh.

"Meet me, dawn tomorrow, north bank o' the river just past th' ferry. An' bring plenty supplies."

"Then you'll do it?" It was growing darker. He was only a shape now, furry ruff and pointed ears and two glowing eyes. But the body beneath that coyote head was still human. She wondered suddenly what she would have seen if she had asked him to remove the final mask.

"Of course. I got your promise. But you gotta come alone."

Silverhair stared at Rana across the embers of the dying fire.

Fires glowing in a land of darkness populated with towns and holdings whose folk are invisible in the light of day. He blinked and forced himself to focus on the real world again. Was it a dream or a vision that he'd had? *In that land of shadow, Jehan and Faris are reigning. But Julian is not there.*

"Are you all right?" Rana seemed dazed. He wondered if her dreams had been as strange as his. The coals were fading, and with them, the images of his dream.

"I'm dizzy. I think it was the smoke." She set down the drum and began to massage her hand without meeting his eyes. The harper's arms and shoulders were tired, too.

We failed, he thought, watching her. *If she had made contact with Coyote, she'd be bubbling over with triumph now. But I did—* The rest of his dream came to him suddenly. *Coyote was with me in that Otherworld, explaining what happened the time he went there. But why did I dream that? Did I hear that story about how Coyote tried to bring his wife back from the dead somewhere long ago?*

He shook himself, willing the memory away. He believed that he wanted to go on living. And if there was something unsuspected within him that considered death a blessing, it could not be allowed to matter. He had to live long enough to save Julian.

"I'm sorry it didn't work, but neither of us is really trained for this kind of thing," he said firmly, as much for his own sake as for hers. The girl looked exhausted. "It was worth a try." He reached for the harp case, surprised at the effort it took.

Rana nodded. She tied the drum to her belt and got stiffly to her feet.

"In the morning we'll go to the Master of the Junipers," Silverhair said reassuringly. "We'll have to bring him in on it—he'll know how to make Coyote listen, I'm sure."

"Oh, yes." Rana looked a little alarmed. She began to pinch out the candles.

"You haven't gotten cold feet about this, have you?" He shouldered his harp case and followed her to the door, stiff as if he had in truth been to the Land of Death and back again.

"I haven't changed my mind." She smiled at last, and he relaxed. It had been a crazy thing for them to try without telling anyone.

"It must be very late, and I'm cold," Rana went on. "Come down to the kitchen and I'll make us some spiced tea."

It was blessedly warm in the kitchen. Silverhair leaned back on one of the benches set against the wall, watching with half-closed eyes as she puttered about with the teapot and her packets of herbs. It was a big, comfortable room, with whitewashed walls and dark beams strung with braided bulbs of garlic and red peppers dangling in rows. Burnished copper gleamed in lamplight, and the air was rich with the scent of soup stock simmering overnight on the hearth.

"Do you want to talk about what happened?" he said softly as she put the kettle on.

"Not now. I'm still too confused." Her back was to him, but he thought she was measuring out spices.

"Just like a daughter," he said, still trying to put her at ease, "making tea for her old dad. Rana, I'm beginning to be very glad that you adopted me!"

For a moment she stood very still. Her bright head and the copper pots had the same gleam. *Did I embarrass her?*

he wondered. But it had been her idea, after all. He grinned.

Presently he heard the kettle whistling, and she brought him a mug almost too hot to hold. Silverhair warmed his hands on the rough surface, blowing away steam and smelling cinnamon and honey and other things he could not identify. It was heavily sweet to the taste—she had put in too much honey, but he would not hurt her by saying so.

"This will relax you and make you sleep," she said abruptly as he finished it.

"Yes." He gave the mug back to her and let his hand fall to his side.

Sleep . . . yes . . . He felt sleep stealing along his limbs. A first tremor of alarm tickled awareness. He couldn't fall asleep in the kitchen! Silverhair shook his head and tried to sit up, but his limbs would not obey him. Mist swirled slowly upward, like the steam from the tea. All he had to do was close his eyes, and it would carry him away.

Rana was speaking. He concentrated his remaining awareness on trying to hear.

"You'll be all right, Silverhair. I'll get you to your room, and tomorrow you'll wake just fine. Forgive me."

He forced his eyes open and looked up at her, understanding finally that she had drugged him. He saw tears on her cheeks, then the cool cloud drew a veil between them.

In that gray peace he hears a bark of very familiar laughter.

"Don' blame her," says Coyote, *"I made her promise not t' tell. This quest is for th' girl. But you need me again, just call. I'll come t' you."*

TEN

Rana shivered beside the willows and watched the chill mists of dawn smoking off the river. The world had gone gray—no life or light anywhere. Her feet were getting cold already, and the splash of the ferry had hardly faded from the air.

But mostly she felt foolish. There was no chance the ferrymen would forget a lone woman with a riding horse and a cranky pony laden with awkwardly bulging bags, and even if Silverhair slept until noon, someone in the palace kitchens was bound to discover her hasty scavenging. It hardly mattered what they did to her. She would die of embarrassment, trying to explain what she was doing out here with all this salt beef and smoked ham.

Rosemary was going to know she was crazy anyhow when she read the note: *"I've run away with Coyote to search for the King."*

In the tree above her a bird tried out its morning song. Silver ripples lapped the shore as an otter surfaced in midstream. Was the sky brightening? She did not know whether to desire or fear the day. The ponies ceased browsing on the coarse grass and lifted their heads, ears pricking in curiosity.

She soothed them, grateful that she had not lost her touch with horses during these past months indoors. *I'm just a dumb human*, she thought, straining to listen. *Tell me, what did you hear?*

The fog began to shimmer with gold. *It's only the sun rising*, she told herself. *It happens every day.* But the pounding of her heart shook her bones. *"Why are you worrying?"* A deeper knowledge spoke within: *"Behold the wonder."*

And then the mists kindled suddenly into splendor, and all her yammering fears were stilled. Beyond the screen of the willows the blush of rose deepened swiftly into flame. Above the molten flicker of light on the river, the next group of trees was a burning shadow; veils of light shaded one into another from the soft flutter of the willows to the most distant delicate tracery uplifted against the sourceless golden radiance of the sky.

"So where's my breakfast?"

Her senses still ablaze with wonder, Rana turned. A glowing shape that had not been there before wrapped mist around itself, and as if memory were altering her perceptions, the dancing motes of light became pointed ears and a ruff of fur, and they in turn shifted until she saw a skinny, grizzled tribesman in buckskins with a blanket wrapped around his shoulders for a cloak and an old hat drawn down over bright eyes.

"Mañero!"

"Oh, no, I was him, but he's dead now."

"What do I call you, then?" Nerves made her shrill. She had been so sure that he was not going to come.

"Huh, I got lots o' names." He grinned and got to his feet. "Some folk call me Sinkalip or Manabozho, I been

Vegtam the Wanderer, and I been Iktomi. Other places, people call me Esacawahta, I'wi or Oleli, baby Hermes, or Tsistu, Loki or Ellegua—you pick one.''

She had thought she knew him, but that was when he was only Mañero. His reality frightened her.

''Old Man! That's what my people call you!'' Rana crossed her arms defiantly, but he only laughed, and she realized that this was the right way to deal with him. His amber gaze fixed on the packs the pony bore.

''Then you're my Old Woman, huh, and you better fix me somethin' hot if you want me t' take ye anywhere!''

''Old Man, you want me to cook food for you, you better build me a fire.'' She turned away to hide her grin.

She stopped worrying about discovery. Anyone who came after her would see whatever Coyote chose to show them, if they saw anything at all.

Rana straightened in her saddle, rubbing at back muscles that had begun to complain after a day on the road. Coyote was a gray shape meandering among the grasses. Four-legged, his pace was better than any speed she could get out of the laden ponies, but he was easily distracted by fleeing field mice and rabbits who always seemed to get away.

She had never in her life seen so many animals. Deer looked up from their grazing, tiny jaws continuing to move as velvet ears flicked forward. It seemed to her that rodents poked their sleek heads out of every hole. Along the river, beavers smacked the water with their tails in greeting, and twice, brown bears shouldered aside the tangled brush to watch them pass.

It lent interest to a dismal journey. Low clouds lay heavy above the valley, covering the tops of the coastal mountains and merging into the first ridges of the foothills that hid the Ramparts. Beyond the lumpy hills north of the river, the flat expanses of the valley stretched dim and featureless to either side. Only when the wind set the pale wisps of last year's grass rippling above the new green like the guard hairs on Coyote's fur did Rana believe that spring might return to the world.

Their road was clear enough, at least for now. They were taking the swiftest way up the valley to the Mother of Fire—the way that Julian and his guards had gone. Coming and going, their traces were plain on the trail, but Coyote had found no sign of the returning hoofprints of Julian's big bay.

From somewhere ahead she heard a regular creaking. When the road dipped again she saw a farm cart jolting along ahead of them, piled high with bundled cornstalks. Coyote was laughing. Rana saw that he had resumed his human shape and frowned.

"What are you up to?"

"So suspicious! Like an old wife already, you are." He untied the pack pony's leading rein and began to tug the beast along, shoulders slumping wearily.

Rana sighed. The day before, Coyote had stolen a pie set out to cool on a windowsill. She had ridden for two hours with her head crooked over her shoulder, waiting for someone to come galloping after them. Traveling with Coyote involved hazards she hadn't considered when she invoked him.

As they drew even with the wagon, his pace slowed. A woman was driving, her features weathered to agelessness by long hours out in all weathers, her stocky body strong. Her face brightened as she saw them, and they exchanged the courtesies of the road.

"Don't often meet folk traveling, this time o' year," said the woman. "I've got a holding over by the river. Promised my daughter I'd bring her some extra fodder for her beasts. You folks going far?"

"Toward the northern end o' th' Ramparts," answered Coyote.

"You better cross the Dorada by the Meridian Bridge, then, and go north through Elder—we've had a lot of rain this winter, and the water's running high."

"Guardians bless ye for the news, mother. 'Tis a weary way even on a good road!" His shoulders bowed a little more and he sighed.

"Hmm, that your daughter?" asked the holder.

"Oh, that's my old woman." Coyote's whisper was clearly audible. "Pretty thing, huh? Got t' keep 'er sweet, though, so I let her ride the mare."

The woman turned and favored Rana with a disapproving stare, whether because she believed Coyote or because she disapproved of the difference in their apparent ages, the girl could not tell, but she could feel the blush burning from neck to brow.

I should offer to get off right now and let him ride! she thought furiously, well aware of her guide's aversion to traveling on any four feet but his own.

"Well, there's certainly room for two up here," said the holder. "You can sit by me till I turn off the road, and rest your legs a little while."

Rana caught Coyote's grin as he pulled himself into the wagon, and realized that this was what he had been angling for all along. She could hear the slow rise and fall of their voices, and presently, the woman's hearty laughter.

"You ever hear the story about the time Coyote dressed up like an old woman an' put his penis into a basket so he could pretend it was a baby?" His voice was quite loud suddenly. Rana pulled her shawl over her face and rode on, pretending not to hear.

"Wolfmaster, you honor us." Konradin stepped aside so that the Blood Lord could precede him down the narrow passageway. In a rock-cut storeroom in the foundations of Blood Gard, Caolin's Wolves had made themselves a shrine. He found a curious fascination in the idea that the ritual he had devised had taken such root among them.

He pushed open the iron-bound door and saw them waiting, their wolfskin cloaks reversed so that the crimson linings flowed into the bloody swathe of the hangings that covered the walls. He heard the shuffle of boots on stone as someone moved, a stifled cough. Their eyes followed him.

From above the altar, the skull of the sacrificed boar leered down with empty eyes. There were dark stains on the gray stones. From a spike in the wall hung the mummified head of one of Julian's men. The Blood Lord had not ordered that, but he could think of few things more calculated to spread terror among his foes.

So, fierce spirit, are you pleased? He grinned up at the boar, and it seemed to him that something glimmered from those shadowed sockets in reply.

"Is it well?" Konradin's pale eyes fixed his master, hungry for something more than food. The sorcerer projected some of the illusion that veiled him to lend a momentary glamour to the other man.

"Yes, my wolves, it is very well. The boar blesses you and will give you the power to devour all your foes."

"*You* give us the power, Wolfmaster!" corrected Konradin. "You led us through the fires of hell and captured him who raised them. We sacrifice in your name."

Caolin looked at the stained altar again. He could feel their belief in him giving him power, as their blood had empowered him when he killed the boar.

"There are men in your armies, lord, who wish to join us," said Konradin.

Caolin nodded. Ordrey said that the other men muttered about the rituals, but the Blood Lord had given his wolves a barracks of their own. They had the finest horses, and daily training was developing their skills as lancers into something uncanny. Let the common soldiers whisper, and let those who proved worthy fill the places left vacant by those who rotted now beneath the Ramparts' snows.

"Test them, and for those you accept, we will hold the blood rite. When they are trained, I will send you forth once more to savage my foes." Caolin smiled. Who could stand against him when he had the service of such as these?

They bowed before him, and the sorcerer deepened his illusion until they saw him gray pelted and yellow-eyed, and the thin lips beneath his long nose twisted in a lupine grin.

Julian struggled upward from caverns of fire-shot darkness. He was lying on something hard, and all around him he could sense stone. Was he underground? He opened his eyes and saw only blackness, but there was a smell of old incense in the air. He tried to sit up then, and pain seared through every limb. There had been fire in his dream, too, he remembered, but his fever had left him. He fell back, licking parched lips.

"Are you thirsty?" said a voice that he ought to know.

Julian nodded, wondering whether the other could see his movement. But in a moment he felt a hand beneath his head, something hard against his lip. He opened his mouth and drank greedily. The stuff was cold, with an odd sweetish flavor that repelled him even as his body demanded the moisture. He had tasted it before.

He tried to guide the cup and found that his arm was tethered. Cold iron bound both wrists; he heard the clink of chains. For a moment then he lay very still, reaching out with other senses, but all his probings rebounded upon his own awareness; his head swam. Silk hangings shielded the stone, but that was not what had stopped him. Everything in the chamber pulsed with the imprint of a powerful will.

"You can't escape, you know. The chains hold your body and the drug keeps your mind from flying free. But don't complain—even your nightmares will seem sweet by comparison when my master allows you to wake up again!''

Julian took a swift breath, seeking the twist in consciousness that would release his spirit, but instead he felt himself falling deeper into his body, his momentary clarity submerged in a chaos of sensation. As the darkness took him, he realized that the voice that had mocked him was that of Ordrey, and the identity that permeated his prison was Caolin.

For a time beyond measuring Julian wandered in darkness. When he came to consciousness once more, he was still in the black room. There was a blanket over him, and he lay on clean straw. He still could not free his spirit, but at least his skin was cool. His right hand seemed sore; he tried to make a fist and felt bandaging. They wanted to keep him alive then—that was not necessarily a good sign. His other muscles were working, but weak. He touched his ribs and found that he had lost flesh, too. How long had he been lying here?

Perhaps they were trying to make him afraid. He supposed that most men would wake screaming if they had been left this long alone in the dark. He smiled grimly. Caolin himself had forced him past that fear when he struck him down on Spear Island. Dark as it was, this prison was not so lightless as the grave.

Something squeaked—metal, not the mice that he dimly remembered hearing before. He felt footsteps vibrate through the stone. There were more sounds, and then an agonizing point of light. Julian shut his eyes tightly and turned his head away.

He felt them coming closer; someone yanked away the blanket. Bare skin pebbled at the touch of cool air.

''Well, well, is this the hero King of Westria, blind as a beggar and naked in the straw?'' There was an indecent triumph in the voice. Julian got himself upright and forced open his eyes.

It was only a candle. Light-starved pupils adjusted painfully. But he made himself bear it until the knowledge that the Jewel of Fire had given him kindled, and his spirit fed upon the flame.

Holding the candle was the pudgy ginger-haired man with whom he had traded blows near Registhorpe. The man who had drugged him a little while ago—Ordrey.

"Well, well, and is this the Blood Lord's tame cur?" Julian's voice was harsh with disuse, but he had managed to echo Ordrey's tone. He saw the man's pale eyes open in momentary surprise. Then he smiled.

"A cur with teeth, boy. You're my meat now, don't you know?"

The smile became a grin which Julian did not much care for. He tugged experimentally at his chains.

"Oh, are they too loose?" asked Ordrey. "We can do something about that. Come, boys, let's make him more comfortable!"

Julian tried to fight, but any two of them could probably have taken him, weak as he was now. Swiftly he was unchained and hoisted onto a sturdy wooden framework beside a square stone like an altar, limbs splayed so that his only choices were to stretch on tiptoe or to put his whole weight on his arms.

"That's better. One would think you didn't appreciate the Blood Lord's hospitality." Ordrey moved around the frame, checking Julian's bonds.

"What do you want with me?" He had to at least try for answers. "I won't—"

"Well now, *my* wants are very simple," Ordrey interrupted him. "Just stay right where you are. Later, when you've become more cooperative, the Blood Lord may have some questions." He gave his captive a friendly slap on the buttocks as he went by.

Julian jerked in his bonds. They were grinning at him, damn them, laughing at his nakedness. But they had forgotten that the King of Westria was also Master of the Jewels! He took a careful breath, reaching inward for the tone that would command them.

"Oh, no, I know that trick!" cried Ordrey. One of the guards slammed Julian suddenly in the gut and the breath exploded out of him in a soft grunt. As he opened his mouth to gulp more, Ordrey jammed a gag into it. Julian struggled to spit it out, eyes bulging, but one of the men had him by the hair, and suddenly it was only by taking slow, careful breaths through his nose that Julian could get air at all.

"The first lesson," hissed Ordrey, "is to learn that you are vulnerable to pain." He held up a whipstock with a knotted bullhide thong. "It's a simple tool, but you'd be surprised what it can do to the human skin."

He is trying to frighten me, thought Julian. *And he's succeeding, too.* There had been a man in the Border Patrol who had been a slave in Arena and whose back still bore the marks of the thong. When he had drunk enough he used to talk about it sometimes.

The first stroke touched him, and Julian leaped in his bonds. The men laughed. The King bit down on the gag, waiting. *This is just the body, not really me!* The remains of the drug held his spirit half tethered, but as a second line of fire crossed the first that repeated affirmation made it easier to endure.

Another blow bit, and another. Was it better to concentrate on counting them or to push one's consciousness away? He felt warmth trickling over buttocks and thighs and knew that he was bleeding. The goal was not to move, not to let the dog know that he felt the pain as the whip sang and his back became a net of fire.

Presently all the blows merged into one another. And the pain, too, began to spread until Julian's shocked system overrode his will. Now he recoiled with each touch of the thong. He fought for breath, the panic of suffocation adding to his extremity, and rough hands took the gag away. It did not matter. They knew that all he could manage now was the shaken gulp of air before Ordrey's next blow.

He retched and sagged in his bonds as consciousness started to whirl away. But a pail of cold water brought him gasping to awareness again. He had not expected this dreadful sickness. The pain could not be escaped, could not be resisted, could at the last only be embraced. . . .

Julian remembered the glowing heart of the Mother of Fire and gave himself to those flames.

The candle flame was flickering as if unwilling to dwell on the ruined flesh it revealed. Caolin lifted it higher, surveying the damage, but the man who lay sprawled on the floor never moved. Only the dark hair and broad shoulders assured him that it was Julian. The back itself was raw meat, glistening now with the ointment with which they had treated it. Sometimes men died after a flogging like this, but Julian's harsh breathing went on.

"I gave him syrup of poppy as you ordered," Ordrey spoke behind him. "He didn't fight me this time. It seems a pity. If he is drugged, he cannot feel the pain."

"He feels it," said Caolin. "You know so much about the men's bodies, do you think the spirit is only nerve endings? What do you understand about the downward spiral into darkness that destroys the spirit? See how he twitches—the body's shock and the drug together have trapped him in nightmare. He still feels pain, Ordrey. More terrible than any torments you can devise for his body are the self-wrought sufferings of the soul."

He moved closer to his captive and stared down. The pure curve of the boy's cheek and brow contradicted the maturity of the dark beard. One manacled hand lay open and outstretched in mute appeal.

There was a curious stillness to the air. Here at the foundations of Blood Gard, the living rock blocked sound, and the heavy black silk with which the sorcerer had hung the walls added a psychic insulation that completed its isolation. When it had been the Blood Lord's temple, that had helped him to concentrate on the symbols of the elements that it contained. Now, instead of altars, it held instruments of torture, but the principle was the same.

The sound of Julian's labored breathing only deepened the silence. Had he ever seen Jehan lie so very still?

"I wish you would let me take him to my workshop," Ordrey complained. "It's not fair to ask me to do a job and then deny me the proper tools."

Julian's hand clenched suddenly and then opened once more. Caolin brought the candle closer and saw in his palm the mark of the Jewel of Fire.

"Be still!" The sudden harshness drove Ordrey toward the door. "Your tricks work on the vermin who man my armies, but you do not begin to understand how to deal with a man of power! What you do to his body matters only if it weakens his spirit!

"This man has wielded the Jewels of Westria—do you think that metal and stone could hold him without the wardings that I have built into these walls? This is the fortress of my spirit! The manacles are only to convince the body that it is bound. A man might break his chains, but what holds Julian captive is my will!"

The body twitched. Caolin bent over his prisoner. "Sleep," he whispered. "And may your dreams be evil!" The dark head moved a little, as if in denial. "Does your spirit listen?" the sorcerer said more softly still. "Good— I am going to devour you, do you hear? I will absorb you into my own darkness, and that is a prison from which there is no escape for body or for soul!"

* * *

"No . . . no more . . . Let him down."

The voice came to Julian through roaring waves of red pain. Presently he realized that he was lying down once more, and the agony in his hand where his fingernail had been torn away became a localized pain. They had not flogged him again; each day brought a new assault on his senses and his endurance. But no one had ever stopped it before.

Slowly he opened his eyes. Ordrey and his helpers had gone.

A pale glimmer of skin above a dull red glow filled Julian's vision; then his focus sifted and he saw a face worn as weather-stripped bone and mottled with old scars, pale, lank hair that had once been gold, a thin frame swathed in heavy crimson robes. He blinked. At the Council Hall, the Blood Lord had been a man in his prime, with golden hair.

No, that is the face he made me see. The gag was gone, too, but Julian kept silent, content for the moment simply to savor the decrease in pain.

"I am sorry things went so far," said Caolin, shifting on his bench so that his prisoner could meet his eyes. "We don't want to damage you."

He sounds like a company commander after a tavern brawl. A flame of resentment kindled and Julian got himself upright. Naked he might be, but he would not lie beaten before his enemy.

"What *do* you want?" he asked aloud.

"Not to kill you—you are already too familiar with the Otherworld." Caolin smiled, and Julian realized that the sorcerer was trying to charm him. *Does he know that now I can see him as he is?*

"I want you to tell me where you left the Jewel of Fire."

"You know my answer," said Julian. "What would you do with it? You could not use the Jewels even when you held all four of them in balance. Fire alone would destroy you.''

"Perhaps all I require is to keep you from using it," said the sorcerer. "Or perhaps I will destroy it. That might be interesting."

"You might destroy Westria." Julian rose to the threat and saw Caolin's eyes gleam. "I don't believe you. You have spent too much of your life trying to conquer this land."

"Perhaps there comes a time when there is no difference between hatred and desire." Caolin's gaze had shifted to the lamp.

Julian looked at him curiously, perceiving beneath the sagging flesh the fine bones of the face whose beauty had once been no illusion.

"Did you hate Westria when you were her seneschal? There was truth in one thing you said in the Council Hall— the country was never ruled so well as when you carried the key. Why did you put on the red robe?"

He waited for an answer, forcing himself to ignore the ache in his maimed hand. *I can be charming too, you bastard. Remember? You forced me to learn how to use words.* The flattery might work, he thought, just because it was true. And so long as they were talking, no one was torturing him.

"Because I could not put on the gray."

Julian held his breath. Had Caolin realized that he had spoken aloud?

"Prince Jehan . . . came for his training at the College of the Wise the last year that I was there." The Blood Lord's voice strengthened, and Julian knew that this was what the sorcerer wanted him to hear.

"They were a crowd of holy fools, more concerned with the minutiae of tradition than with the meaning of magic! The Prince had been brought up to wear silk, not sacking.

I excelled in my studies, though it won me few friends. But I understood him. I protected him.''

The Blood Lord's voice had sounded almost tender. Julian turned his disbelieving grin to a grimace as the sorcerer looked at him.

"Does your finger pain you?''

The question brought awareness throbbing hideously back again, but the King managed a shrug. How did the man expect it to feel?''

"I will bind it for you," Caolin said kindly. "I grew quite adept at treating Jehan's wounds when he came home from his wars.''

Not wounds that your own servants had given him! thought Julian with mixed amusement and outrage.

"After I left the College, Jehan begged me to come to Laurelynn.'' The Blood Lord grasped his captive's hand and poured an ointment over the raw flesh of the nailbed. Julian gasped in spite of himself. "He got me a place in the Office of the Seneschal. They laughed at the Prince's favorite. But not for long.''

He slid a kind of wooden cage over the finger and began to bind it in place to keep anything from touching the wound. *He had it all ready!* thought Julian. *He intended this all along!*

"In a month I knew all their secrets. In a year they had realized that they could not do without me. By the time the old King died, no order left that office that was not approved by me.''

Caolin tucked the last bit of bandage in place and released Julian's hand.

"No king ever had a better servant. And Jehan knew it. He left the governing of the country in my hands. For fifteen years I poured out my life for Westria. I knew the destination of every sack of salt and load of iron; I knew where every stalk of grain grew!''

The chains were just long enough to let Julian cradle

his arm against his chest. He stared at the sorcerer, thinking that if Tanemun had possessed half Caolin's ability, the Blood Lord would not threaten them now.

"He who makes a thing owns it, boy! I built Westria. The land is mine!"

"Nobody can own Westria," said Julian steadily. "Not the Seneschal, not the King. We only serve her."

The sorcerer leaned forward, pale eyes blazing from the fortress of his skull.

"Westria will be mine, whether as a wasteland or a garden pruned by my hand. Those are the only choices I will allow."

"Then kill me now," cried the King. "Because while I am living she shall do neither!"

"No?" The Blood Lord drew one thin finger along his prisoner's cheek, and Julian jerked away as if he had been burned. "You don't understand. You are part of Westria, Julian. You too must belong to me!"

ELEVEN

"A time will come," Caolin had said to him, *"when you will envy the dead."*

Julian gasped at the outrage of overstressed joints and tendons as they strung him up again. He was beginning to understand. They did not want to kill him, but to break his mind. Each time he thought he would die, but after each descent into darkness he woke, and it was all to do again.

I will scream this time, he told himself. But when, by way of introduction, the clamps began to pinch his skin, something more fundamental than the gag held his throat closed.

"My expertise," said Ordrey briskly, "is in the human body's response to pain. I have worked on animals, of course. But animals die so easily." He leaned close and Julian flinched from his foul breath as he grinned.

"I've never understood it," said the torturer. "A dumb beast with no understanding will give up and escape the pain, but a man . . .'' He jerked his captive's head back suddenly. Julian tried to twist away, then stilled, feeling at the base of his throat a sharp point of pain.

"That's right," cooed Ordrey. "You don't want to move. You see, a man knows what is being done to him." Something scratched downward, then dug into the muscle above the left nipple and twisted viciously. "And can anticipate what more his enemies might do." Julian flinched as the thing pricked his solar plexus. "If I push just a little harder, this blade will go in. Through skin and muscle, and then, oh so easily, through the pleura, and into the hot, throbbing muscle of the heart." Julian's heartbeat shook his whole body beneath Ordrey's hand.

"You know that, but your heart keeps beating, and you want to live!" The grip on Julian's hair was released abruptly. His head fell forward, and Ordrey laughed. He held up a gray goose feather with a sharpened quill. "Of course, sometimes I lie."

Julian hung in his bonds, willing the gallop of his pulse to slow. *I want to live . . . but why? They may let me go alive, but never whole.* One of the other men removed the clamps, and returning circulation brought its own agony.

"But that didn't matter, did it?" said Ordrey. "Your imagination was doing all the work for me. After this you'll never know. If you can't see it, something that feels dangerous might be nothing." He snapped the quill between his fingers and tossed it away. "And something that touches you softly might be deadly."

Julian took a deep breath. *I am not this body . . .* he told himself, trying to believe it. He closed his eyes, seeking the stillness at his center, since he was cut off from earth and sky and sea. There was something there, like a bright spark. He had almost touched it when Ordrey grabbed his hair again.

"You're not taking me seriously!" the torturer screamed. He gestured to one of his men. "Unlock his left hand!"

As the manacle opened, Julian tried to fight. Agony flared through him as he moved. When it faded, his arm was locked securely, and they had already clamped the pincers on the nail of the first finger of his hand.

"I'll let you watch this," said Ordrey. "You know what's coming—you've already lost two fingernails this way."

Julian flinched and the pain increased; he leaned forward, and the sinews of his other shoulder throbbed at the strain.

"Now, my lads!"

The pincers ripped. And then, muffled horribly by the gag, came Julian's scream.

Caolin jerked at the sting as the strap smacked Julian's naked skin.

"Enough!" He stopped massaging his arm as Ordrey looked around. Odd how he had seemed to feel it, almost as if a memory.

"That's got his attention!" said Ordrey. "Shall I release the tension now?" The Blood Lord peered into Julian's face as Ordrey loosened the ropes that had racked him. The pulse fluttered in his throat like a dying flame. A touch could extinguish it. But then the boy would be free, and Caolin would become *his* prisoner. As the ghost of Jehan held him still. . . .

I cannot reach you, my lord, he told that specter, *but through your son, you are mine once more.* His hands closed on either side of Julian's face. "Come now, lad, you're rested. Wake up, I'm waiting for you . . ." He clothed his face with kindness, but when the dark eyes of his prisoner opened at last, they were like dead coals.

"What . . . do you want of me?"

The Blood Lord stared at him in frustration. "I want

you to serve me," he said finally. He felt the faintest twitch of denial through his hands. "You have no hope, Julian." He signaled Ordrey, and the ropes began to tighten again. The sorcerer saw fear in the boy's eyes then, and smiled.

"An army is coming from Elaya, lad, and this time every blow it strikes will be mortal, for it will be under my command!"

"Can't . . ." A sheen of sweat glistened of Julian's chest and beaded on his brow. "They kicked you out . . . long ago."

"Is that what the lords of Westria believe?" He stopped Ordrey, saw Julian's apprehension become endurance as he set himself to deal with a constant level of pain.

"When your uncle betrayed me in Santibar, Prince Palomon was forced to deny me the city, but I was rewarded well. By the time Prince Ali ascended the Lion Throne, the economy of Elaya was in my hands. Palomon's nephew is not well loved. Whether I dwell here or in the south, he must obey me, for he knows that I have only to open my coffers and his lords will rise against him."

Julian's eyes had closed again.

"Look at me!" hissed the sorcerer. "Shall I prop your eyelids open with splinters? You cannot escape me that way!"

"You . . . tried to take over . . . in Westria." The King drew breath harshly. "But even if you kill me . . . they won't serve you."

"I am not going to kill you!" Caolin felt his illusions waver and reconstructed a compassionate smile. "You are going to serve me! What gives a hill-bred brat like you the right to sit on Westria's throne?"

"I love . . ."

"Love! You fool! I have governed two great kingdoms, and there is nothing I do not know about ruling men. You will be served best if they are afraid. I know what men fear and what they need and what they desire."

"And what they love?" The King seemed to gulp in strength with the air. "Do you know what they will die for? I never thought I had the right—but I was chosen. The Guardians—"

"—deluded you! They are evil—evil! They would rob us of all that makes us men!" He gestured and the ratchet began turning again. Julian whimpered as some new muscle took the strain.

"Where were the Guardians when I captured you? Where are they now? They have betrayed you! The only power left for you to love or fear is *me*!"

The tendons stood out on the boy's neck. Caolin signaled to Ordrey and then, lightly, almost tenderly, ran his hand across the tight, slick skin of Julian's chest and arm. The muscles were set in spasm. He bent close, breathed in the sharp-salt scent of Julian's sweat.

"It will dislocate your shoulder soon," he whispered. "Say you will serve me! Say it and save your arm!"

Julian's throat worked helplessly, but his gaze transfixed his tormentor. *"What do you love . . . Caolin?"*

The words had not been spoken aloud. The sorcerer jerked back, and Ordrey, taking it for a signal, released the ropes. Then Julian fainted at last.

"You lie over there alone all night and yer gonna freeze!" said Coyote.

Rana clutched her cloak around her and stared into the fire. This was the first time they had camped in the open. She should have anticipated the problem, but she had not realized how cold the northern valley in mid-February could be. Coyote was very likely right, but she did not trust him.

"Would ye feel better if I was a woman?"

"I'll be fine," she said through clenched teeth. "I can sit here and feed the fire."

"And fall off your horse tomorrow 'cause yer too tired? Look at me!"

The voice had changed. A cold wind coming down the valley whipped up the flames, and for a moment Rana saw clearly. It was Coyote Old Woman who sat on the other side of the fire.

"Nothin' t' hurt ye here—see?" Coyote hoisted her skirts to show grizzled hair covering the slit between her plump things.

"Nothing at all, Grandmother!" Rana burst into laughter. "But how do I know you'll stay that way?"

"Swear by th' Lady? By th' Lady o' Fire?" The old woman picked up a coal that glowed like a fiery eye against the night. Coyote might quarrel with any of the other Guardians, but would he/she dare deceive the Lady of Love?

Lady, if your bright eyes see, watch over me! Rana prayed silently.

"Oh, very well." She gathered up her things. Their cloaks, with the blankets they had brought with them, would do well enough for two people curled spoon-fashion before a banked fire. Rana eyed her companion appraisingly. Coyote Old Woman was still grizzled, with a face brown and creased by many suns, but comfortable breasts filled the loose tunic, and she had a well-padded rear. Only the amber eyes that laughed back at Rana never changed. The girl thought suddenly of her own grandmother's ample lap, and wondered if that had been intended.

Silently she crawled beneath the blankets and was enfolded by the warmth of Grandmother Coyote's embrace. Her companion radiated heat like a stove, but no fire ever accommodated itself so conveniently. The tension that had held Rana wakeful vanished suddenly, and she slid unresisting into the friendly dark.

In the hour just before the dawning she thought she dreamed. She lay cradled in someone's lap as if she were a child. Was this some memory of being taken to rituals by her mother when she was small? She stared up into firelit faces, made fearless by the strength of the arms that held her.

The murmur of grown-up conversation checked. Suddenly they were all looking back at her, and their faces were masks, like the age-sculptured faces of mountains. Not all of them were even female. And they kept changing. She clutched at the One who held her.

"Mother!" The cry came from Rana's heart, but it was not for her own mother, at home in Registhorpe, that she called.

"Hush . . . hush, child. My arms will always enfold you, didn't you know?"

"Mother, I walk in darkness. I am afraid."

"Seek for the Eye of Fire and you will find your way." The eyes that looked down at her shone with a light that overwhelmed the world.

When Rana opened her eyes again, the sun was shining full upon her face. She smelled wood smoke and saw that Coyote, brown and grinning and more masculine than ever, was building up the fire.

Rana strained to hear the hollow ring of hooves on the wooden bridge above the rush of the waters. Swollen with winter rain, the Dorada tugged at the posts and swirled around the trunks of the cottonwoods. Rana looked at the river suspiciously. Coyote had gone first with the pack pony. Unless they wanted to spend a night in the marshes, they too must cross. Her pony tossed its head uneasily at the vibration in the boards, and she touched its neck, sending reassurance. She sensed the moment when the horse began to trust her again, and a soft command moved her forward.

As Rana pulled up beside Coyote, she felt a breath of wind on her cheek. Golden light deepened; they stood in a mist of cold fire, and every hair on his head was jeweled with flame. The wind grew stronger, unveiling the tree-tops. In the west the clouds were withdrawing from the purple-gray peaks of the coastal mountains. The arch of the bridge was gilded by the long rays of light.

Coyote chirped to the pack pony, and both horses began to pick their way along the raised dike. Rana saw the red gleam of light on standing water ruffled by the wind. And then the mists rolled away, and she saw to the east a great shape fashioned of frozen flame.

"Dorada Buttes," said Coyote, seeing her still staring. "Pretty, huh?"

Rana shook her head. What was this fantastic bastion of stone doing in the middle of the valley? She looked at Coyote as if he had put it there to confuse her, urged her horse forward, and found herself stopped at the edge of the bank.

"No, no—ye want t' see, ye gotta follow th' road!" Coyote was laughing at her.

"Yes, I do want to see it!" Rana pulled herself together, wondering why. It was only an upthrust of volcanic stone. "Can we stop there? It wouldn't take long to climb, and think how far we could see!"

"There's a road." Coyote's eyes burned as if the fire of the sun had kindled something within. "I think you'll find th' way."

That evening they sheltered in an abandoned barn at the foot of the Buttes, whose lure had grown stronger as they neared them. Still wondering why they fascinated her, Rana was already cuddled up with Coyote before she re-alized that he was still male. She stiffened, but already his warmth was relaxing her. And what was the difference, really? She had been silly to fuss so.

In the deepest part of the night, she found her eyes open and realized that Coyote's hand was cradling her breast. Rana lay very still in the darkness, wondering what would happen now. But he did not stir, and after a time she decided that to try and move his hand might bring on the very attention she was trying to avoid. And there was something friendly in that pressure, a warmth that spread slowly through her body and made the other breast tingle faintly in sympathy. She sighed, felt his body curve more closely around hers, and slept again.

Rana woke laughing in a golden haze of light. The haze, returning awareness informed her, was a swirl of dust motes catching the sunlight that shifted between gaping boards in the old barn. She was giggling because Coyote was tickling her.

"What are you doing?" She sat up, stiffening in outrage.

"Makin' you laugh." His hand slid between her legs, and as she struck it away, his other hand flicked her breast.

"No, you aren't!" But the clever hands were everywhere, and where they passed, her flesh tingled. She slapped him, laughing in spite of herself as she tried to dodge away.

"What're you afraid of?" He sat up in the welter of blankets. His skin was like polished wood; his hair all gingery with little sparks of red in the sunlight, and hardly a hint of gray.

"You know what I'm afraid of!" She crouched on her knees, panting. "And what happened to old Man Coyote?"

"Ye mean this?" He patted his crotch. His tunic made a little tent above it that grew taller as she looked at it. Old or young, Coyote was definitely male today. "It's just my little friend . . . Maybe I should take him off and let you play with him!"

"Oh, blessed sweet Lady!" Rana jumped to her feet and began to look around for her boots and breeches. Her face was burning. She must be as rosy as the rising sun.

He was teasing her, wasn't he? She remembered some of
the stories she had heard and began to blush again.

"No?" he said plaintively, looking down at himself with
interest. "Well, there's no pleasin' some people."

"Get your clothes on, you dirty old—" There were no
words in which she could swear at someone who was neither man nor beast and more than either. She told herself
that he was just being Coyote. Rana picked up his pants
and threw them at him, and suddenly she was laughing
again. "We have a mountain to climb."

He continued to be Coyote throughout the morning.
Rana learned to keep her distance as they rode to the base
of the Buttes, and after the second time he goosed her, she
made sure he led the climb. Then they found the body.

Rana had never before had to look at what a few weeks
in the open could do to the body of a man. What was left
was only a man-shaped tangle of bone and meat half
wrapped in some kind of fur. After a quick glance, she
looked away, wishing she had not eaten breakfast.

"About a month old, I think," Coyote sounded mildly
interested. "Might be a sword thrust did for him, though
'tis hard t' tell. Look at this, though."

Controlling her stomach, she turned, and saw on a scrap
of leather jerkin a wolf's head badge.

"A month ago," she said slowly "was when Julian disappeared, and the guards said Caolin's men wore wolfskin
cloaks. Do you think they chased him here?"

She gazed around her, seeing the soaring stone with
new eyes. They had reached the saddle beneath the southern butte, oddly populated by weather-cracked chunks of
golden rock and treacherous with scattered stones. Could
that white scratch on the rock have been made by a sword?
Rana turned and saw Coyote watching her.

"You're the tracker," she yelled suddenly. "Why don't
you sniff the ground? Was Julian here?"

"This is all rock, an' there's been a lotta rain," he said

quietly. But something unhuman burned in his eyes. "Look around—see what you find."

Rana felt his gaze still upon her as she stared around. Her insistence on climbing the Buttes had found them a clue, but what had compelled her to climb? The sun had broken through the clouds again and the clear air was ablaze with light. She closed her eyes, but the radiance grew greater.

Julian was fleeing from the Blood Wolves. Why didn't he keep going across the valley? He must have known they would catch him. Why did he come here?

And then, because she had also for a time borne one of the Jewels, and because she understood Julian, she knew. But if the Jewel of Fire was here, then surely the Guardians must realize. . . .

"Old Man!" She turned, but what she saw was a coyote who laughed at her with amber eyes.

"So—" She sighed. "You're going to make me do it all by myself, are you?"

"Why complain?" came the reply. *"I can't goose ye with paws!"*

She knelt and set her hands upon bare stone. Once more she closed her eyes, striving to open another kind of awareness. She was not Mistress of the Earthstone, and the rock did not speak to her, but she had found the Sea Star. What had she felt then?

I was desperate, that day, she remembered. *I wanted to get away.* And perhaps her own love for the sea had attracted her. *What in me is akin to the Jewel of Fire?*

Love. It was always love, wasn't it? Rana stilled, suddenly seeing patterns in things that she had thought pure chance. Even Coyote . . . Suddenly she wanted to flee down the mountainside.

How much do I love Julian?

It was now, she realized, that she must decide—not when she found the King, not even when she faced Coyote again. She held out her hand to the light. She had begged the Lady of Fire to protect her. Now she asked that all her protections might be taken away.

"Lady . . . Lord . . . You!" she prayed to the white radiance around her. *"Fill me so full of love there is no room for fear!"*

Light burned through her closed eyelids. A tremor rippled through her solar plexus; she gasped as if pierced by a fiery arrow that exploded in her belly, burst through her breast and womb, out through her limbs. She felt Fire, Heat, Light . . . and with them a surge of love that could embrace the world.

And for a moment then, Rana *was* the world. She was the rock beneath her and the turning earth and the great arching sky above. She was the sunlight and the sea. She was all creatures, even Coyote, and all things were One Thing, and just for an instant then, Love was the only thing there was.

And then the radiance became no more and no less than the living light of day. She found herself weeping, but she could not have said why. Now the fire was only sunlight and her body's heat and one burning point that radiated from the butte above. Without wondering how she knew that, Rana began to climb.

The butte was raw stone and gravelly soil, and a thin scattering of grass. She could see no sign of disturbance, but Rana sought the pulse of power as if there were eyes in the palms of her hands. Heat pulsed through the earth as if she held her hands up to one of the great ovens in the palace at Laurelynn. Gently she scratched the turf aside. There was a crevice in the rock . . . her fingers found the way.

Rana folded back the silk and blinked at a blaze of green and crimson fire.

"As once unknowing I took up a Jewel, knowing, I claim you now," she whispered, and in the same instant of vision, she knew that she would also bear the other Jewels of Power one day.

Holding the Jewel, she felt the kiss of sunlight on her skin and the green fire burning in every blade of grass. She ached with need beyond desire, for the matrix of the Jewel held a spark of Julian's life fire, and as she touched it she was overwhelmed by awareness of his radiant spirit, and of the living body through which it shone.

Rana got to her feet and gazed southward, knowing now where he had to be.

I see the fire of life in everything! Julian, burn bright until I come to you!

TWELVE

"*Far away, far away, wild echoes are flying,*
Softly, now softly, the fall wind blows,
Sadly, so sadly, the pine trees are sighing,
Slowly, so slowly, the cold stream flows."

Above the pure music of the harp Silverhair's singing soared like an echo of pain. Outside, wind sighed in the rainy darkness, blending with the whir of Rosemary's spinning wheel. Eric had put down the report he was studying and lay back in his chair, watching her.

"*The warriors are gone, and my soul goes with them—*
The beat of their hooves is the beat of my heart.
Neither tears nor embraces can I longer give them,
Silence and longing remain my part."

The harper drew out the minor chords with bitter clarity.

"The rich fields abandoned, their harvest awaiting,
The beasts without herdsmen wander still.
No news comes to comfort, my heart's fear abating—
I look at the places no one may fill."

"There's many a woman in Westria who could sing that song tonight," said Lady Rosemary as Silverhair let the harp continue the lament alone.

"Not only women." Silverhair's frustration erupted finally into words. "We've been a month with no word of the King! If Julian is alive, even injured, why hasn't he sent us word?"

"Perhaps he is a prisoner."

"What prison could hold the Master of the Jewels?" exclaimed Silverhair.

Eric lifted his head. "Caolin's."

"Caolin must know that we would pay almost anything to get the boy back," Silverhair began.

"Does he?" asked Eric. "I refused to ransom my own son when the cost was too great, and the Blood Lord knows that Julian wouldn't consider it."

"Julian would have no say!" the harper said grimly. "And Caolin knows that as well."

"That's true," said Rosemary reflectively. "You'd think he would at least try."

Silverhair started to agree, and then another thought struck him. His face must have shown it, because after a moment he realized that they were both looking at him.

"I keep forgetting that we're talking about *Caolin*, not some bandit from the Barren lands," he said unhappily. "I keep forgetting how Caolin can carry a grudge. I should know, considering how persistently he's hated me all these years. I think that since last fall Julian has become his personal enemy. And without the King we can't defeat the Blood Lord. We found that out at the Council. Caolin was there. Oh, yes—he knows!"

"If he harms Julian . . ." Eric's big hands clenched as he fought for words.

"He may not *have* him, love," said Rosemary soothingly.

No, thought Silverhair, *but it's horribly possible.* He thought of some of the threats that Caolin had made to *him* and shivered.

"There is no point in getting angry until we know for sure." Rosemary let the wheel draw out the last of the handful of wool she had been spinning and tucked it in. "We must find someone who is *not* a personal enemy of Caolin's and send him to Blood Gard to see."

The harper met her warning gaze without expression; only his fingers moved more strongly upon the strings as he gave them the final verse of the song.

> "Gone, they are gone, to the trumpets' harsh crying,
> On a hard battlefield, far away.
> Where they lie now, as the daylight is dying,
> Alone, I may wonder, but cannot say."

Julian burned in the furnace of the Blood Lord's hatred as the days of his captivity dragged on. Outside the hours of light were lengthening, but the only light in Blood Gard was the flicker of the torturer's fire. Flesh abused beyond endurance whimpered even when they were only lifting him into the frame. The manacles were becoming formalities. The soles of his feet had been beaten and most of his toenails were gone, every joint throbbed; he could not have walked out of his prison unaided if Caolin himself had opened the door.

When Julian wakened, he knew it was because the potency of the herbs with which they had drugged him must be wearing off, and each time he had a moment's hope that his spirit could break its bonds before his tormentors came. But he had never achieved more than the first faint flutterings toward freedom before he heard the scrape of the key. Julian wondered sometimes about those who were said to have achieved enlightenment through pain. His own agony was just another shackle, a distraction that kept him from concentrating long enough to get away.

Perhaps even then he could have achieved it if there had been no other barrier. But the King lay in Caolin's shadow, and if that was not yet so secure a prison as the well of darkness from which he had tried to free Katiz, still, the Blood Lord's personality permeated the stones. When Julian tried to speak to them, he heard only Caolin's hatred and despair. Only the mouse that ate the crumbs of his meals answered his calling, and its tiny teeth could do nothing against steel.

Julian tried to remember love and laughter, but as time went on they became more unreal than the chaotic dreams that haunted his drugged sleep. The sorcerer had not yet taught his captive to serve him, but though Caolin might not know it, the King was learning hatred, and that was a dark flame that grew stronger with every day.

If Caolin remakes me in his image, he will have conquered as surely as if he broke my will, thought Julian. *I cannot reach the Light outside me, but is there no light within?* He drew a careful breath, striving to focus his awareness. . . .

The door slammed open. Flaring torchlight shattered into a flicker of light and shadow as something wrapped in the remains of a green cloak was flung into the room. The shock left Julian shaking. He had been succeeding— he had not heard them coming or the turn of the key! His groan of frustration was echoed by a moan of pain.

"There 'e is, parrot! Ye want news o' th' King, ask away." Both light and laughter were cut off as the door slammed shut once more.

Julian heard someone else gasping for breath beside him.

"Who . . . are you?"

The harsh breaths stilled. "My lord?" came a whisper out of the dark.

"Yes . . . I am . . . Julian."

"Oh blessed Guardians, we feared it when—oh, my lord, what have they done to you?" A babble of words burst over him in a voice that sounded too young to be here.

Do you really want to know? thought Julian. "That . . . doesn't matter," he said aloud. Speech was coming more easily now. "Who are you?"

"Oh, forgive me. I'm Tarran Fairchild, from the Heralds." There was a rustle in the straw as if even bound, the boy had tried to bow. Julian grunted with something that was supposed to be laughter, felt Tarran flinch, and laughed again. "They thought a herald's cloak would be honored, even at Blood Gard," the boy went on.

Honor, from Caolin? Julian winced. "Did Caolin send for ransom, or was this just a wild guess by Frederic or Silverhair?" he asked disgustedly.

"It was Silverhair, I think. But, my lord, tell me how you are. I don't know how long they'll let me—"

"No, you tell me!" Julian interrupted him. Did this child really believe the Blood Lord was going to let him go? "What's happened since I was captured?"

Tarran took a deep breath. Julian could almost hear his training taking hold.

"It was near the end of February when your guards brought Lord Robert home and told us—"

"Alive, or his body—is Robert still alive?" Julian tried to reach out and cursed at the chain.

"He's getting better," Tarran said hastily. "He was terribly cut up, but now they think that he'll fight again. Everyone took turns to nurse him, especially Lady Rana, but 'til that lad Marcos from the guards came to sit with him nobody could quiet him."

Marcos . . . The King remembered a slight young man with lovely dark eyes. Robert had liked him—perhaps more than liked him, he thought, remembering some things he had been too busy to notice at the time. *Should I feel jealous?* he wondered. His most powerful emotion was a profound relief that he did not have his cousin's death upon his soul. Tarran was still babbling.

"Just as well there's someone to manage him, now that Lady Rana's dis—"

"What?" There was a sharp silence.

"She disappeared."

"Before or after they figured out that Caolin had captured me?" Julian knew that his voice had grown terrible, but that did not matter.

"No, my lord!" Tarran protested. "It was before that, a week or so before!"

Julian relaxed with a painful sigh. There was one more thing to be thankful for. If Rana did not know where to find him, at least he did not have to fear that she would try to sneak into Blood Gard.

"And what about the fighting?" he said then.

"Lord Eric's outworks are finished, and the ditch between the two walls ready to be filled," Tarran said brightly. "So Laurelynn is safe, but there has been fighting in the valley." Tarran gathered himself and began the sad tally of battles lost or all too occasionally won. "And then there's the Blood Wolves," the herald said finally. "They're the most vicious of them all. Terrible fighters, of course, but it's not that—they take prisoners—"

"Torture?" asked Julian.

"No, lord. Folk say they *eat* them and take their heads to decorate their temple here."

Julian was still trying to comprehend when he heard the opening of the door. Torchlight and lamplight dazzled him. This time the guards had come to stay.

"So," said Ordrey, smiling, "have you had a nice chat?

But you wanted to see him, didn't you?'' Guards hauled Tarran upright and he gasped as he got his first good look at the King. ''There now. Isn't that a pretty picture to take with you into the dark?'' The men dragged their prisoner toward the rack.

''Halt!'' Julian put all the strength left to him into the command, and the guards stood still. ''He is a herald, sacred in his office. Let him go.'' He drew on the Wind Crystal's power to find more words. ''Let him return to those who sent him. That is the Law,'' he crooned. Then Ordrey giggled, and Julian saw the gag in his hand.

''No!'' cried the King, but despair robbed the force from his tone. The herald had finally realized what was happening, but the guards only laughed at his struggle. Ordrey jammed the gag into the King's mouth as they finished tying Tarran down.

''Stop fighting, lad,'' jeered one of the men. '' 'Tis a King's bed yer lying on!''

''You see, my master won't let me kill *you*,'' said Ordrey pleasantly to Julian. ''It made me sad to think you'd never see all my skills. But now I can show you—yes, stretch him a bit farther, lads, until he sings!''

It was almost worse to watch, thought Julian, as every painfully educated nerve twitched in sympathy. But Tarran began to scream quite quickly as agonies that had been carefully spaced to spare Julian were inflicted in swift succession. Soon what had been a nice-looking youth became a piece of meat which only imagination would call a man.

But he was still alive. Julian had never felt such fury for his own sufferings. If he had had the use of his voice, there was a Word that could have ended it.

''Tarran!'' He put all his power into the mental call. It was the first time since his capture that Julian had been awake, undrugged, and neither suffering nor fighting for his sanity. He focused his forces, tried to let awareness slide out gently.

"Tarran, listen, I'm with you, hold on to me." This time he thought he felt an answer. What Tarran sent was pure uncomprehending terror, but Julian endured it as he had learned to live through his own pain. *"Hold on to me, lad, and I will help you. He can only torment your body— your spirit is safe with me."*

"My lord." There was relief beyond words in that greeting, and a trust that would have appalled Julian if he had been in any normal state by now.

"Tarran, I will show you how to escape him. Leave your body behind you, it is useless now." Julian reached out for the struggling spirit and felt his own soul at last slip free. He was gazing down at his own slumped body from somewhere near the ceiling. The body on the rack looked like a shredded rag doll. One of the torturers pulled up its eyelids, swearing.

Julian held out his hand and the transparent form of the soul who had been called Tarran came to him.

"Don't look behind you," said Julian. *"Here lies your way."* The entire fortress was a latticework of energy, no more solid than spiderweb to the form he wore now. From this center he saw the refractions of myriad realities. He drew Tarran toward the brightest passageway, and the silver cord that connected him to his own body began to thin.

"You see, King of Westria, the consummation of my art!" crowed Ordrey. He turned and saw Julian's abandoned body, and his face went white as ash. "Call the Blood Lord!" he screamed hoarsely to the guards, and started shaking the slumped shoulders frantically.

Julian felt as if he were being buffeted by a strong wind. The cord was tightening again as his body called. He nudged Tarran forward. Radiance took shape within the bright passage and held out welcoming arms. Then the door of the chamber swung open behind him and shadow flowed in.

"No!" came the cry of Julian's spirit. In a moment he

would have been free! *"Go now, go swiftly!"* With his last strength he propelled the other spirit into the light.

And even as he did so, he felt himself rebounding. Shadow swirled widdershins around the room, flowed between him and the Light, clung and contracted and forced him, struggling furiously, back into his body as Caolin came in.

Rana realized that she was singing when Coyote looked back at her and grinned. Before they had gone half a mile she was humming again. Her pony shook its head and danced along more swiftly.

Why shouldn't I sing, she asked herself, *in such a world?* Since they had come down from the Buttes the sun had shone brightly, and the flower-starred meadows glowed with the vibrant green and gold of the Westrian spring. No one but Coyote could hear her, and surely she was past being embarrassed by him!

She grinned up at the sunshine, and the Power hidden at her breast responded with a pulse of joy. *Did Julian feel this way when he bore the Jewel?* she wondered then. *Was the scent of green stuff on the wind an intoxication? Did the touch of the sun send a shiver of delight through his skin?* But the King had been fleeing with the Blood Wolves on his trail.

Suddenly there were tears in Rana's eyes, but she blinked them away. *When I give him the Jewel, he will know joy!*

Coyote led the pack pony, and Rana's mare followed without need for guidance. Rana wondered if she *could* speak, or only sing. Once she had seen water elementals aglimmer in the mist above the waves. Now it was the spirits of flowers who shimmered in the haze of light above the fields.

When she heard voices, she thought at first that they

were part of her ecstasy. But surely flowersong would not be accompanied by men's deep laughter.

> *"Light and Dark divide the days,*
> *Balanced voices sweetly sing.*
> *Man and maid unite to praise*
> *The focal flowering of Spring!"*

Was it the equinox already? During the dark days when she was nursing Robert, Rana had lost track of time. They would be celebrating the return of the Maiden now in Laurelynn. Then they breasted the rise and saw a cluster of horses ahead of them. She nudged the mare forward.

"The Maiden! The Maiden! Spring is here!"

As they reached the square at the center of the town, people began to pelt them with flowers. Someone threw a garland over Rana's head. It was only then that she realized that the shouted greetings were for her.

"Will ye be our Maiden, lass?" A tall woman wearing the broad ribbon of a guildmistress took Rana's rein. "The girl chosen got a stomachache, and a stranger is better. The best of everything and a soft bed after. What d'ye say?"

"I don't have anything to wear," Rana protested. And how could they spare the time to indulge themselves at a festival?

"Please, pretty lady?" Someone held up a small child, who pressed a limp bouquet of brodeia into her hand. The Jewel of Fire burned at her breast, and suddenly a love that she could not contain blazed out to encompass them all.

Lady of Fire, this is for You! she told that radiance within as they drew her from her horse and carried her into one of the houses to be washed and dressed and decorated like the Goddess of Spring.

Elk Crossing had put its heart into making a good thing

of this festival. There were races, and prizes were put into Rana's hands to be awarded those who won. There were competitions in baking and brewing, and Coyote was only too happy to help her with the judging. And lambs and puppies and calves were brought to her for a blessing, and that was the best of all, for when Rana held those new lives to her breast she touched the power that had filled her on the Buttes once more.

When night fell, the folk converged on the center once more, and Rana found herself enthroned on cushions between two bonfires with a kitten in her lap, feasting on spring greens and roast lamb. As the darkness deepened, drum and fiddle struck up a quick rhythm and the people began to dance.

Everyone seemed to move a little more swiftly where Coyote passed. After a time one of the drummers did a solo, and one by one everyone but Coyote drew back to the sidelines, clapping and laughing as their strange guest leaped and waggled his rear end at the fire.

"They say that Old Man Coyote is a fine dancer," said Rana maliciously when the drummer gave up at last and her companion sat down again. "But it would be hard to equal that performance!" One bright eye glinted at her as he reached for a meaty bone, but he did not deign to reply.

"Tell us a Coyote story!' said one of the children.

"It's not quite summer yet," said the Guildmistress, smiling. "I guess it's still allowed. And since it is the beginning o' the warm time, I guess I'll tell ye the story of how Coyote stole fire t' keep th' people warm!"

Oh, no! Rana put her hand over her mouth to hide her laughter. Coyote was cheerfully cracking lamb bones beside her, but she knew that he was listening.

"It started at a dance, ye see," the storyteller began.

"Like this one?" asked the children.

"Not quite," said the Guildmistress. "This village was on top of a mountain made o' black stone, and they guarded the fire very carefully, 'cause in those days they were the only ones in the whole world who had flame.''

"Selfish, y' know," said Coyote, leaning over to twitch a candied fig from Rana's plate. "Can't keep all th' goodies t' yerself, huh?" The children began giggling.

"Indeed. Folks had no way to heat their food or warm their homes, and so Coyote decided to steal the fire."

"An' he took his friends with him, didn't he? I remember!" cried one little boy.

"Oh, he was just bein' nice," said Coyote. "He coulda done it by himself if he'd wanted to." He cracked a walnut and began to pick the meat from its shell.

The Guildmistress frowned. "Eagle and Hummingbird went with him, and Puma and Fox and Frog, and he told them just what he wanted them t' do. And he made himself a long wig of reeds, and when they got t' the village o' the Fire People he challenged them to a dance."

He's gotten better at disguises since then, thought Rana, glancing at her companion. The walnuts were disappearing fast.

"And they did dance," said the storyteller. "All through that night until the bonfire was burning low. The Fire People were getting sleepy, but Coyote was still going strong. And then suddenly he howled! The people thought a coal had burned him. But his friends got ready. Then he howled a second time . . ."

She paused for effect, and Coyote tipped back his head and a shrill yip startled the dancers.

"That was very realistic!" said the Guildmistress tightly, and the children laughed.

Rana dug him in the ribs. "Will you stop that?"

"Why?" whispered Coyote. "I'm havin' fun!"

"And the other animals started to run." The storyteller hurried to finish her story before she was interrupted again. "But Coyote shoved his reed wig into the fire an' set it ablaze. Then he ran too—down the mountain and across the valley, as fast as he could go. The Fire People chased him, howling. He passed the fire to Eagle. One after another the other animals took over, and the chase went on.''

''Like our relay races!'' said one of the girls.

''Just like,'' the Guildmistress agreed. ''And they kept running 'til everyone was exhausted, and still the Fire People came after them. So Coyote grabbed the reeds and tied them to his tail to carry, and that's why his tail tip is black today. Then the Fire People made it rain and snow, so Coyote hid in a cave and covered the entrance and kept feeding the fire with dry wood 'til dawn.''

''Did the Fire People give up?'' asked the children.

''Eyah—they thought they'd frozen him. But come morning, Coyote opened the door, and a warm wind began t' blow, and all the snow melted away. Then he came out of the cave and gave the fire to everybody.''

Rana's companion hunkered forward. ''So you all thank Coyote when that fire keeps you warm,'' he said gravely. ''That was a hard race he won.''

The Guildmistress favored him with a crooked smile. ''Maybe I'll let you tell it next time.''

''Oh, no.'' He cocked his head at her. ''I can't eat an' talk at the same time!'' During the story most of the leftovers had disappeared.

''Is that how it happened?'' Rana whispered to Coyote when the conversation had turned to other things.

''That's what folks say.''

''But is it true?'' She gripped his arm to make him look at her.

''Oh, everything's true, some way.'' He grinned at her, and suddenly his arm was free. ''Think I'll go see if they got any more beer.''

Rana sat back with a sigh. Some girls were coming up to sing for her, and after that she supposed there would be dancing again as the Festival went on.

And then, somehow, it was midnight. Sleeping children

lay curled in knots like kittens, covered by their parents' cloaks. The drumming had slowed; the men circled one fire and the women the other with a smooth rhythmic stepping that Rana could feel in her bones.

"Come on," said Coyote. "Let's join them!"

She looked at him in alarm. His own performance had been bad enough, but she could feel the Jewel of Fire pulsing in time to the drumming. What would happen if that Power got loose at this festival?

"Come." His hand closed on hers, and suddenly she was standing.

"Yes, go on!" The Guildmistress was encouraging her. "The Maiden has t' join in the dancing."

A slow, sedate dance, thought Rana as she let the rhythm take her. *I'll dance one round and then sit down again.* Step-together-step, her body swayed as she adjusted her movements to those of the other women.

It was good to move after sitting so long. She felt her muscles begin to slide more easily as they warmed, and stood straighter, enjoying the swing of hip and thigh from a limber back as the dance went on.

Then the circle began to wind outward. The drumming quickened. More muscles came into play as Rana was drawn into the central space. The lines of men and women passed each other; she saw Coyote, but he had shed his clownishness. Was he really glowing, or was his hair backlit by the fire?

Faster and faster the drumming drove them. The blood raced through Rana's veins. Now the women faced outward and the men danced around them with their backs to the fires. She took small steps, feeling the energy build within her, and Coyote's longer steps kept pace across from her.

I can't go on this way! she knew suddenly. *I'll fall! I'll explode!*

But it was the drumming that crescendoed. Dancers

spun outward like showering sparks and the Jewel of Fire amplified their ecstasy. Rana spun in place, trying to spend that energy in motion, but it built—built—

Coyote set his hands upon her shoulders, and the world spun on around them, but they were the still core at its heart. She looked into his eyes, and they were flame.

And then he kissed her, and his lips burned, and the fire fountained through her into the world.

This is what a priestess does, she thought as she felt the power pulse from her outstretched hands. *This is how the Jewels are used to revitalize the land! But why me?* Thought itself kindled and fed the flame as the energy blazing through her continued to grow.

As if the fire itself had taken the shape of a woman, Rana danced, and light flickered from the tossing of her bright hair and the swirling skirts of her yellow gown. Entranced by the dance and the firelight's bright beauty, Rana danced. Lifted by love above sense of herself, the self incandesced in that flame and even the name then of Rana was gone and the One who had filled her before now flared high.

The fire leaped for joy and the stars sparkled with laughter. All over Westria, man and woman lay down in love. Even in the shadows of Blood Gard, torches blazed more brightly, and for a moment Julian found ease from his tormented dreams.

The Lady danced.

THIRTEEN

"You see, he has become a sovereign, too!" The King moves his pawn into the King's Eighth square and smiles at Caolin. His blue eyes glow. Outside, a dark wind rattles the windows, but the sitting room is warm. The King's golden chessmen gleam in the dancing light of the fire. But the Seneschal only shakes his head and returns his bishop to its own square to protect his king. His own pieces are cast in lead, heavy in the hand.

"I have you surrounded and outnumbered. Jehan, did you really think that you could stand against me?"

"That depends on the game." The King bends over the board.

A sudden thunder of knocking brings them both to their feet, sending the chess pieces flying into the fire. Caolin leaps for the hearth and tries to snatch them out of the flames, but the King holds him.

"Jehan! They'll be ruined—the heat—"

"No."

Caolin looks up and sees the King grown broader, his eyes dark brown now, and blazing. The knocking comes again.

"This is the crucible in which lead is transformed into gold."

"My lord Caolin!" comes a call from outside. "Are you awake? My lord!"

As the door bursts open, Caolin looks through the flames and sees pawn and bishop, melting together in the same fire.

"Lord Sangrado, pardon! I heard your voice and thought you were awake." Captain Esteban was standing by the bed, a lamp in his hand.

Caolin fought his way back to awareness. There were no chess pieces, no fire . . . no King. The curtained windows of his chamber already glowed with the first light of dawn.

"There's word from Konradin, sir. His attack on Elder has been successful, and the city is in flames. He says"— the soldier's voice thinned—"that he has made a pyramid of skulls at the town gates to be its monument."

"That disturbs you." It was not quite a question.

"I do not see the military necessity," Esteban said stiffly.

"You are true metal," the Blood Lord said softly. "But I tell you that terror can be as potent a weapon as the sword."

He considered his officer curiously. Esteban had only once in his life betrayed his own strict code, but that lapse had been sufficient to make him Caolin's man. Could he have endured the slow destruction to which the sorcerer was subjecting Julian?

The Captain shrugged. "We shall see. Konradin wishes permission to attack the fortress at Rivered."

"Permission! He has lost surprise already. Why is he

wasting time sending word to me?'' Caolin thrust back the covers.

"He hopes you will direct the attack in person, my lord,'' said Esteban.

"No! I have no time." *Julian is waiting for me to continue our game. Let the Blood Wolves play. It is here that the war will be won.* "Reply. Tell him to remember that our purpose is not to gain military advantage, but to spread fear.''

"But, my lord, I do not understand—''

"Never mind!'' Caolin pulled a wool cloak around him. It was chilly here in his chamber, but in the temple at the roots of his fortress it would be warm. In the temple, where Julian was waiting to be tried in the sorcerer's fire.

"Do what you will,'' he snapped, "but don't disturb me again!''

Smoke spread across the valley in a brown pall. Coyote waved Rana to a halt and bent to the earth, listening.

"Horsemen comin'!'' He trotted back to take the pack pony's rein. "Don't think we want t' meet 'em. This way.'' He started toward the winding tangle of trees that marked a watercourse, and Rana kicked her mare into motion after him. As they reached the edge she looked back, and saw that the flowers had closed up behind them with never a hoofprint to show the way they'd gone.

The mare slid down the bank into a tangle of blackberry and wild rose and then stood trembling until Coyote cleared a way for her to join the other pony where the willows screened them from view. Rana found herself sitting eye level with the prairie. She sucked at a scratch on her hand, then stared as riders who wore cloaks of gray fur appeared on the horizon. The foot soldiers who followed carried shields and spears, but the riders bore seven-foot lances, each of which seemed to be topped by a small dark ball.

"What are they carrying?" she whispered.

Coyote slipped back down from the edge of the bank and came to her. "Children's heads," he growled.

"They must be the Blood Wolves!" Rana swallowed bile.

Coyote's form began to shrink and shimmer as he changed. *"Gotta find out where they're headin' before we go on."* Four-legged now, he scrambled up the bank.

"Don't let them shoot you!"

He paused at the rim, and cocked his head at her, grinning. *"Ye won't get rid o' me that easy—remember, I always come back t' life when I'm killed!"*

Rana waited for him, shivering despite the brilliance of a suddenly comfortless sun, and clutched the Jewel that hung at her breast as if it held the only warmth left in the world.

"Are you trying to frighten me by crying wolf?" Julian straightened, trading the torment of putting weight on his feet for a momentary relief for his shoulders. "When I'm at your mercy, why should I care what your dogs do?"

"So!" jeered Caolin. "Does the suffering of Westria seem secondary now?"

Julian tried to shut away visions of murdered children and burning towns. He no longer tried to hide his own agony, but he had hoped to conceal his anguish for the victims of the Blood Wolves. *I failed them . . . I have failed everyone. I am no longer King.*

The Blood Lord limped forward as if his own joints had stiffened, though he never displayed any awareness of pain.

He is not human, thought Julian, as the sorcerer peered into his face. *He was born evil. There is no way this demon could have ever been a child!* Long teeth jutted yellow from receding gums as Caolin smiled.

Since the death of the herald, the Blood Lord had taken personal charge of the King's interrogation. There were times when Julian felt as if only they were left alive in the world. He tried desperately to think of some question. When Caolin talked, he sometimes forgot to inflict pain.

"There is a nerve . . . here," said Caolin, "that governs the whole leg and thigh." A thin finger jabbed Julian's buttock and suddenly his entire leg was in spasm, sending spurts of agony through the rest of his body as other muscles took the strain.

"And my touch is not only pressure, but power. The nerves transmit energy, and when I disrupt it, so . . . the spirit body begins to disintegrate as well."

Julian writhed in a net of flames. *Is this how gold feels when it is tried in the fire?* he wondered as the sorcerer lifted his hands and the agony ebbed away. *Does it shriek as its form is destroyed so that it can be reshaped to the goldsmith's will?*

But the goldsmith's goal was beauty. Did the sorcerer have a purpose, or was his captor also trapped in this relentless cycle whose only product was pain? He let out his breath in a long sigh. He could not goad Caolin into killing him. But if escape into death was denied him, perhaps he also could learn to destroy.

You are casting the metal into the weapon that will end you, Caolin.

"As Ordrey would say, the human body is a fascinating machine." The Blood Lord's long finger scratched a tingling trail across Julian's chest, and he tensed, waiting for the agony. Then the sorcerer's voice came from behind him. "Jehan taught me that, when I took the tension out of his shoulders at the end of a day."

Caolin's hands dug suddenly into the King's shoulders and he gasped, only realizing a second later that what he felt was not pain. Those hands moved down his back now, kneading, smoothing, easing, and then, when he had ceased to tense against them, attacking with a sudden intimate, appalling penetration that set him screaming once more.

He was still twitching when he felt the sorcerer's manipulation of his body continue. The instinctive shriveling of his flesh was countered by an expert pressure; tension grew, but before it could be released it was transmuted into agony again.

"Pleasure and pain . . . one and the same . . . pleasure and pain . . . what's in a name?" chanted Caolin. He laughed, and Julian saw the skull beneath the skin.

"What are you doing?" He was beyond speech now. Pain he understood, but now his own body had betrayed him in a way he could not comprehend. His violated spirit shrank from the sorcerer's invasion, but there was no escape for either body or soul.

"Did Robert touch you this way?" asked Caolin. "When I am done with you, you will no longer be able to tell the difference between his caresses and mine. This is the truth; both pain and pleasure are illusions; and love and hatred are the same."

"But why? What do you want from me?" All Julian's strength was in the call. The sorcerer took a quick step back, eyes blazing.

"I want you, soul and body." The answer chilled Julian's soul. *"I want you."*

By the time Rana and Coyote reached the Red Mountain it was April. The road that followed the eastern bank of the Dorada had become hazardous. Several times they hid while Caolin's armies rolled past them, trampling the flowers. Then they fell in with the refugees from Elder, and until Rana had used up all her salves and bandages she would not go on. From Elder to Laurelynn hardly a village had been left standing. In dreams Rana saw the heads of the children of Elk Crossing nodding from the

Blood Wolves' lances and woke screaming in Coyote's arms.

But at last they came to the crossroads where Julian had taken leave of Rana when he sought the Earthstone.

"We'll come in from th' south," said Coyote. "Find us a hollow on one o' th' hills facin' the fortress an' watch till we figure out th' routine."

Rana nodded. She knew this would be more complicated than swimming out to the *Lioness* to rescue Frederic had been. Caolin's wolves had been terrible in their devastation of the valley. What an abode of dread must their own lair be?

But Coyote never asked her if she had changed her mind. Even when they had worked their way through the flanking hills and found a vantage point where they could see clear to the great gate of Blood Gard, he never questioned her determination to go in.

Rana lay on her belly, peering through the screen of laurel leaves at the stark walls of the fortress, and knew that she must be insane. In the light of the setting sun its dark stones were the color of old blood. A slaughterhouse reek tainted the spicy scent of sun-warmed bay laurel whenever the wind shifted their way. There were heads on spikes above the gate. A red banner flared from the tower.

Crazy as Coyote! she thought as she wriggled back into the laurel copse, *without His powers.* On the brow of the hill a ring of young trees arched inward to form a green dome that seemed solid from outside. But the space in the center was open earth with only a few blades of grass where shifting leaves admitted a dappling of sun.

Rana and her sister used to play hidey-hole in such copses. She had never thought her life might depend on the protection of a laurel tree. She remembered Silverhair's song and reached out to touch the nearest silverbrown trunk, wishing she had Julian's ability to speak to the trees.

"*Sister, protect us,*" she prayed. "*It is the Master of the Earthstone I want to save!*"

She began to lay a fire, for if they wanted a hot meal, the time to cook it was now, when any chance-seen sparkle of flame would seem a reflection of the setting sun, and any smoke that filtered through the leaves would merge with the darkening sky. Coyote had gone on four feet to take a closer look at the fortress. She wanted to have something ready when he returned.

But when she reached for her flint and steel, the bag in which she carried it was gone. Had she left it at their last campsite, where they set the ponies free, or had it come loose somehow as they wriggled through the brush? She sat back, wiping away angry tears. In theory, she could have used the Jewel to start her cookfire, but the gates of Blood Gard did not seem the place to experiment with a power that could set the mountain ablaze.

"Trouble?" Coyote's voice roused her.

"I feel so *stupid*! I've lost my flints, and now I can't light the damn fire!"

He looked at her as if he understood that she was really weeping from a fear for which she had no words. "Stupid female, you only know one way t' light a fire?"

Rana stopped crying. "All right, show me!"

"Fire's in th' wood already. Just gotta set it free." He searched around until he found a weather-softened branch and gave it to her to split while he gathered tinder and chose a smooth, straight stick. "Put a point on it—that's right. Now watch me!"

Sitting on his haunches bent over the wood, Coyote made it look easy. But Rana had tried using a fire stick once or twice, and knew how difficult it was to keep everything at just the right angle. He rocked a little, humming softly as the stick began to twirl.

"Got t' set it just right so it goes in. Then it's the friction that does it, back 'n' forth, an' back again, the hard goin' into th' soft, till the wood starts t' get warm.'' Amber eyes gleamed as he grinned up at her, and abruptly she understood the double meaning and laughed. In the days since they encountered the Blood Wolves there had been no time for his teasing. It was oddly comforting to hear him trying to embarrass her again.

"Fire in th' wood all the time. Just needs the right tool an' a little energy!" Coyote blew, and a spark of light flickered into life, growing swiftly as he thrust in more kindling.

By the time the star fires were kindling in the heavens, their little blaze was nearly spent. As Coyote went off scouting, Rana lay staring at coals that still retained the form of the twigs from which she had built the fire, a bright sigil that held the answer to all her questions, if only she could understand.

I will break him, thought Caolin, looking down at Julian. *I have found the way around his defenses now.* A week of irregular alternation between physical and mental stress had visibly advanced his disorientation. The boy's eyelids were twitching. He would regain consciousness soon. He set down the tray and lifted the cover from one of the bowls. The enticing scent of lamb stew filled the air. Julian lay too still for sleep, and his nostrils were flaring. For a moment Caolin himself found the odor pleasant, but he repressed the awareness.

"Breakfast, my king," the sorcerer said sardonically. "I used to bring your father his breakfast when he lay late abed. Sit up and eat it now."

"Would you eat, if you were my prisoner?" Julian levered himself upright.

Caolin flinched. For an instant he had felt walls close around him and been sick with despair. Was he identifying with his prisoner? Staring at Julian, who was using the piece of bread and his fingers to gobble down the food, he began to recover his composure. The body wanted life, oh, yes. The body was a donkey, easy to trick into defying its owner's will.

"There, isn't that better? You see how I care for you."

Julian glared at him, but now his eyes held a deeper fear. He did not yet realize that Caolin had invaded his body only in order to break down the last defenses of his soul. The sorcerer laughed.

"You cared for my father, and yet you killed him."

"Your father did not understand!" Caolin paced across the floor as a sudden rush of memory overlaid the darkness of the chamber with other scenes.

"He understood you well enough to make you serve him," Julian began, but the Blood Lord turned.

"He knew nothing! Not even what he had done to win my loyalty!" His voice was shaking. He waited a moment to let the shadows flow back in. *Nothing . . . Jehan is nothing . . . nothing can disturb me now.*

"Tell me about him." The other voice was very quiet, a word spoken by the dark.

"He was very beautiful. And like me, he was very much alone." Caolin fell silent. *As I am still.*

"How can I understand unless you tell me?" said the voice. "Remember."

Carefully he opened the door to the illusions of the past. "It was just before the old King died. Jehan and I got lost hunting and we had to share our blankets to keep from freezing." Once more he felt the warmth of Jehan's body not quite touching his own and glimpsed the clear line of his brow against the afterglow of the fire.

"Caolin, tell me." The words were without sound, but he heard the command in the voice of memory. *"Caolin, tell me how you knew this place was here!"* Jehan says softly. *"You seem to know everything—you make me afraid sometimes."*

Caolin shakes his head. *"No."* Somehow it's important

to deny that praise. Everything? He does not have the knowledge that all other men were born with. He cannot speak with his heart.

Jehan raises himself on one elbow and looks down at his companion. "Did you find this place when you made your pilgrimage after leaving the College of the Wise?"

Caolin turns his face away, heedless of the cold. The memory of that journey is a horror beyond bearing. He remembers only that the road to Awahna is closed to him, and desolation has replaced his dreams.

"Never mind," comes Jehan's voice close beside him. "I was glad when you came back to Laurelynn. I needed you!"

Caolin is finding it oddly hard to breathe. "Prince, why are you saying this to me?" He feels himself being watched. Then the Prince delicately, tenderly brushes back the lock of hair that always falls across his eyes, and kisses him.

"Did you ever do this with others boys at the College?"

Caolin remembers unrewarding couplings with women in the rituals—a momentary contact and exchange of energies in polarity, a brief release. Perhaps the girls were satisfied—he does not know. Even at the moment of union he has always been alone. Nor have there been any comradely contacts on the playing field or in the bathing pool. He would not know how to offer such an invitation or how to reply.

He shakes his head in the darkness, but Jehan's hands are continuing their questions, sliding beneath his shirt and across the skin. If Caolin refuses him, the Prince will be offended. He must not make the heir of Westria his enemy.

"What must I do?"

"Do?" Jehan's breath tickles his neck in the darkness. "Just . . . let me love you."

It is not so bad—and then it is not bad at all, but so

good that Caolin is suddenly afraid. And as he yields to Jehan's possession of his body, he feels that other mind opening like a flower within his own, and he is not alone anymore.

Afterwards, he weeps into the tunic they have folded for a pillow. When the Prince tries to comfort him he turns, and wordless, grips him in an embrace that makes him wince. Jehan laughs softly, a little shaken himself at the intensity he has awakened, and then falls asleep in Caolin's arms.

"And that was the illusion," he told the Other, "*that bought my love. And that was what he betrayed.*" He turned, and saw Julian's eyes wide with a terrible knowledge that Caolin had never meant to share. And yet perhaps this was the inevitable sequel to what he had done to Jehan's son the day before.

"*But I am not alone now, am I?*" Those dark eyes narrowed and he knew the boy had heard. "*I can hear you, and you hear me. There is only one thing remaining. I will bring you into the darkness that Katiz showed me. You will be safe there, in the heart of my power. And then I will never be alone again.*"

"You gonna just march up t' the gate an' ask them t' let you in?" Coyote shook his head. "Give 'em a free gift o' womanflesh, and if yer lucky, rape is all they'd do. Th' Blood Lord knows ye, remember. He'd enjoy t' let them poke you in front o' Julian."

"I know, I know!" Rana hid her face in her hands. "But we've been here four days! How long can Julian endure?" The noonday sun shone through the leaves and the laurel copse glowed around her like a living flame, but the fire that burned in her breast was pain.

"Th' walls can't be climbed, an' if they could be, they're guarded anyhow. Ye gonna get in t' Blood Gard, you need an army, or a disguise."

"That's all very well for you, Shape-changer!" She

wiped the perspiration from her face with her sleeve. "You could put on the face of the Blood Lord himself if you wanted to!"

"Can't—told you. We're not supposed t' get involved in human wars." Crickets chirred in the silence as he stretched out on the blanket, paused, and then struck up their song again. He had stripped down to breechclout because of the heat. Rana felt sweat trickling down her back beneath the light tunic that was all she wore.

"But you led me this far. If I could get in, would you come with me?"

"Might be interesting." His eyes glinted oddly.

"Well then, Changer, why don't you just put a different shape on me?"

"Oh, that's harder. You gotta be really close t' me for that t' work." He waggled crossed fingers at her.

"We've been traveling together for weeks. How much closer can we be!" Rana exclaimed. Coyote grinned, and her eyes widened. "You mean I have to sleep with you?" For the first time in days she really looked at him. His lean body was younger than she had once thought him, but he was still Coyote, with his long nose and brush of ginger-gray hair.

"We've been *sleepin'* together for weeks. I had somethin' more active in mind." He pushed himself up on one elbow, eyeing her appreciatively. "You still owe me, ye know . . . *whatever* price I ask!"

Rana swallowed panic, hearing her own words used against her. She had forgotten . . . no, when he had asked nothing, she had believed that *he* had forgotten. . . . No. In the glaring light of this moment of reckoning, Rana knew that she would have said anything to persuade him to help her find Julian. As she would *do* anything to get his cooperation now. She began to pull at the laces that held her tunic closed.

"What a face!" He shook his head at her. "Who'd ye

think you were dealin' with, woman? Eagle, or maybe Sea
Mother? This is Me, Coyote, an' I got a reputation to
uphold!''

''Is this supposed to be a seduction? You could at least
say you think I'm beautiful.'' She tugged her tunic over
her head and glared at him defiantly.

''You need to be told?'' His yellow eyes rounded. ''You
are beautiful—no, don' take off the Jewel.'' He looked her
up and down. ''It belongs between those two lovely
breasts. An' you got a nice smooth tummy . . . nice round
thighs.''

His gaze had focused on the spot between them. Rana
felt a sudden heat. She lay down on her own blanket.

''All right. Go ahead.'' She shut her eyes.

''Oh . . . I see.'' He chuckled softly. ''A virgin sacrifice!'' She could hear him moving around the circle, humming softly. And presently, though it was still warm, the
heaviness seemed to leave the air. There was a new, shimmering scent in it, too. She felt a tingling in her skin.

''Did ye think that would—ah—unman me?'' He was
dragging his blanket over beside hers now. Rana felt him
ease down beside her and her heartbeat drummed in her
ears. ''Ye promise somethin' t' th' First People, woman-
child, ye gotta pay!''

A hand closed on her shoulder and she jumped as if she
had been burned. But he only lifted her a little and curved
himself around her, spoon-fashion, as they had lain so
many times before. She relaxed a little, grateful that he
had not pinned her beneath him. That had been the worst
of it when the reivers attacked her—the feeling of being
suffocated and unable to get away.

She felt his breath warm on her neck, and then his lips.
Everywhere he had touched her she was tingling, and then
his fingers brushed her breast, and for a moment she forgot how to breathe.

''There now, love—is this so terrible?'' His hands

moved over her body as if he were gentling a frightened mare. Rana was still trembling, but she was no longer certain that it was from fear. She stared straight ahead of her, but the air was glowing, and the leaves of the laurel trees were all ashimmer, though she could feel no breeze.

His knowing fingers danced lower, and a slow fire began to build between her thighs. Rana felt the wonder of it sweeping through her, and forgot to be afraid.

"Was this really necessary for you to give me a disguise or for you to help me?" she whispered. Once more she heard his low laughter.

"Wondered if you'd ask. I could disguise your outside, anyway. But it's the inside that wants changin', isn't it, or what good are ye gonna be t' Julian?"

Yes . . . change me. Changer! she thought, and knew how the wood felt just before it burst into flame.

"Anyway, he had his fun with th' Lady o' Westria. Seems only fair."

But Julian had not known that the old woman he was comforting would change into a goddess in his arms. He had not known with whom he lay that Midsummer Eve, before he had even known his own true name.

And do I? she wondered suddenly. *Do I?* She shut her eyes again, suddenly afraid to see Who held her in His arms. His hands and His lips moved like fire upon her body. She fought to retain awareness.

"But Julian is the King. Who am I?"

"After you danced at the Springfest, lady, don't you know? *Don't ye know?*"

And then He curved closer and Rana opened herself to receive Him, and she understood why He was called the Bringer of Fire.

While Caolin heard the reports of his captains and Rana burned in Coyote's arms, Julian struggled to emerge from his drugged sleep, and dreamed.

He is lying before a glowing fire with his beloved in his arms. He turns, a sleepy arm is thrown across his chest, he moves closer, and the other embraces him. It must be Robert, but when he opens his eyes, he sees that his lover's hair is bright. It is a man, though. Who? It doesn't matter—his body is responding; he begins to climb the slow sweet spiral of passion again.

His lover clings to him, whispering, "Jehan, I love you—forgive me, Jehan."

And then Julian recognizes him and tries to break free, but it is too late.

Julian shuddered to release and woke, weeping, in the dark.

FOURTEEN

"There is safety in the darkness." Caolin set a cushion behind Julian's back, then wrapped the fleecy cloak around him once more. "This is the truth that Katiz taught me. No one can hurt you when you have attained the emptiness at the heart of all things." Julian felt the tension going out of him, knew it for the same trick he himself had used to soothe wounded men, and still felt himself succumbing to its power.

The sorcerer moved around the chamber with a lighted taper, and the ring of candles set into the walls flickered into life behind him. *Why light?* wondered Julian. He coughed and then relaxed further as the scent of smoking grass mixed with incense swirled through the room. There had been something in the tea he had drunk, too, that detached him from his body just enough so that what was happening here already seemed unreal. The silk-hung walls wavered like smoke in the uneven light.

"Whatever it is you're trying to do to me, I won't agree

to it, Caolin.'' He flexed abused muscles, hoping that pain would counter the spell. But there was no strength left in mind or body to resist what was happening.

''I will take you into my darkness, Julian,'' the sorcerer said softly. ''Once I feared it, but now I know that the only safety is here.'' He fanned the sickly-sweet smoke over his prisoner's body. ''Be you purified,'' he chanted. ''Breathe in emptiness, and let all the distractions of the flesh be borne away.'' Caolin stroked the lank hair away from his prisoner's forehead and smiled. Then he began to trace a hypnotic spiral around the room, softly humming in distorted harmonies.

This was the chant that had captured Katiz's soul; had once, in Awhal, almost caught Julian. Already his limbs were growing too heavy to move. He floated in a space just outside his body where pain was only a memory. *Why fight him?* whispered a treacherous voice within. *Isn't this better than suffering?*

Julian watched Caolin return the censer to his altar and knew despair. He had thought he had drained that cup when Ordrey killed Tarran or when his captor invaded his body. But then he had hated, and hatred made him strong. Despair was now, when the man he hated touched him with gentle hands and evil whispered to him like a lover in the dark. His lips were still saying no, but Caolin assumed his consent, and something within him *was* consenting, and there was no harpsong here to break the spell.

''Nothing . . . nada . . . nothing to feel; nothing, nada, nothing to heal . . .'' the voice of the sorcerer slid from tone to tone.

> *''There is no body here, no soul,*
> *Neither separate nor whole;*
> *Nada empties all of meaning now . . .''*

Widdershins the sorcerer circled the room, and each

time he passed one of the candles died and another veil of darkness separated Julian from the world.

> *"Nothing good and nothing ill,*
> *Nothing's done, do what you will;*
> *Nada empties all of meaning now . . ."*

I am dying, thought Julian as his sight dimmed. Caolin lifted a mirror of polished obsidian from the altar; the King gazed at features distorted by shadow.

> *"Life's delusion. Death's illusion—*
> *Embrace despair . . . nothing's there . . ."*

The voice was whispering in his ear. He could see nothing but the slack-lipped face in the mirror, and that was growing darker with each moment that passed. With sight, all other awareness drained away.

> *"Nada empties all of meaning now."*

The last light went out.

Caolin knelt in the darkness and fought to extinguish the flare of triumph as he had put out the last candle flame. *Nada empties all of meaning now.* The Other was a dim shape in darkness, sensed, rather than seen. He would be losing all awareness of his body now, and the sorcerer settled himself to do the same. They were very close to their goal. He smothered another flicker of pride at the ease with which he had conquered the King of Westria.

That did not matter now—nothing mattered but the endless, empty dark.

"Listen . . . you are nothing, you are floating, you are able to hear me, nothing more. . . . Come with me now and I will carry you to comfort . . . you are not real—you are only a dream, *my* dream! You are safe now . . . you belong to me.''

There was a faint whimper, as some deep denial reached across the gulf between the wandering spirit and a body that like a mute beast, could only moan.

"Julian, don't fight!" He felt the spark of contact from his captive.

"Where are you—where is this? I don't want—"

"Follow me deeper, deeper." The sorcerer's will overwhelmed the protest. *"Follow me where you and I will be safe from all suffering in the dark."*

"No." But that denial was growing fainter now.

Caolin pressed harder. *"Give me your knowledge, Julian. Give me your memories . . . they only torment you. Give me your power—you will not need it, for I will take care of you. I love you . . . give yourself to me."* This was the triumph, to utter words of love without being trapped by emotion. This was what he should have done with Jehan long ago. The sorcerer felt a flicker of vision— mariposa lilies nodding above a lonely grave. He penetrated that other awareness and began to draw into his own darkness the succession of bright images that were Julian's memories.

Julian felt the words to a bawdy trail song flowing out of him. He remembered the trust in the liquid eyes of a fawn he had raised, then the image misted away. He grieved for the first man he killed, groaned with delight in the arms of the first woman who had let him love her. He felt the memories being sucked out of him, but how could he fight darkness?

"I love you more than she did. Let me take the burden away."

Julian knew how it felt to wander bodiless. But here there were no lines of light to show him his way. He had been cast out of his body and received a new one in the realm of the dead. But this was not the Otherworld. Here he had no body at all. Here he had no will. As the things that had made him who he was dissolved away, he knew that this was the second death that kills the spirit, the true death that destroys the soul even if the body lives on.

"I love you. I love you . . . give yourself to me."

Once more he plucked the Earthstone from the roots of the Red Mountain. He held Rana in his arms and knew that he loved her. He felt the hard clasp of Robert's hand. That was love, not this bodiless invasion that was tearing his identity away. The Wind Crystal shimmered in his awareness, but it was gone before he could say the Word that would set him free. He saw the blaze of sunlight on snow, and then the rainbow incandescence that was the Jewel of Fire. . . .

An explosion of Light blazed through Julian's awareness. None of the older memories had been so vivid— Julian felt heat sear—his hand! He had a body again, and it was made of light! His glowing arm grasped the raw Power of Fire.

And in that brilliance he saw the sorcerer, striving to shield himself like a spider swept suddenly into the full light of day.

"Caolin, I see you!" Julian's voice resonated through all the worlds. *"I see every livid, curdled scar that distorts your body."* As the sorcerer had raped his memories, he drove into the mind of his tormentor and read and rejected all that Caolin himself had locked away.

"I see every evil that scars your soul! Diseased, corrupt, and wretched—you have failed, Caolin. You cannot love, and no one loves you. No one would ever have loved you if they had known what you are. But I know you, and I will show your ugliness to the world!"

Julian snapped back into his body, power pulsing around him. He pointed, and candles spontaneously reignited all around the room.

"One thing you have taught me, sorcerer, and that is hatred!" he screamed. "And now you will see what the rage of the Master of the Jewels can do!"

"Look as if ye know where yer going," Coyote mind-spoke, pushing Rana ahead of him into an archway. He gave her an encouraging squeeze.

Rana hit him, but she could not suppress a reminiscent throb of pleasure, and reminded herself that soldiers of the Blood Lord did not blush. Then she grinned. After Julian's night with the Lady of Westria, he had awakened to a glorious sunrise. *She* had been roused by a dig in the ribs and told that it was time for her to turn into a man.

Inside, the fortress was more complex than it had appeared. The mule train to which they had attached themselves had entered at the lowest level, where stables and storerooms had been carved out of the side of the hill. Wooden barracks were built out above them, curving around the mountain. A broad, stone-paved road led past them to the peak. Stone walls surrounded an arena near the summit. Above it reared a square building surmounted by a sturdy tower. The men wore odd assortments of looted gear, but they all carried serviceable swords.

"Can ye sense the King's direction?" asked Coyote. "Too many people here for tracking, and anyhow, 'tis likely he was carried in."

Rana set her hands about the Jewel and concentrated. It seemed to warm when she faced the peak, but not when she tipped it toward the tower. "Could they have dug down into the mountain?" she asked softly. "I feel something straight ahead of me."

"Could be," replied her companion. "Gotta go up before we go down, though. Need a reason t' be goin' in there." He peered around him. Suddenly he grinned. "Take that bucket!"

"Those are slop buckets." She frowned at him suspiciously. "And"—she recognized the sweet stink—"this one is full!"

Coyote nodded. "Ye meet someone, tell 'em yer on yer way t'empty it 'n got lost. Or maybe ye'll find another use for't, who knows?"

"What about you?"

"Got another idea." A water barrel rested on brackets across from the buckets with a wooden mug hanging from a nail. Coyote stared at it for a few moments, then took the mug and turned the tap.

"Beer!" He took a swig and yelped happily. Rana stared as he brushed past her. The whiff she caught from the mug was unmistakably alcohol. "Hey, lads, this goddam barrel is full o' beer!"

"Go on, girl, they'll all be here in a minute, but nobody's gonna follow you!" Coyote's voice spoke in her head, but a hubbub of excited voices followed her as she hauled the reeking bucket up the stairs.

As she reached the landing it occurred to her that there was something unfair about an arrangement that left her carrying slops while her ally got drunk—even if he was the one who had changed the water into beer. Then two officers came hurrying down the passageway toward the tumult and passed her without a glance. Coyote had been right about that, anyway.

She found a door, and a wooden staircase winding downward into the mountain. As she stepped from the last stair onto stone, a lance of fire stabbed her breast. The Jewel was burning her—she yanked it free. Even through the leather bag its radiance lit the passageway. She started forward again and the light grew greater, drawing her down a branching passageway. It was not until she was turning the corner toward the next that anyone challenged her.

"Passage restricted? But th' lieut'nant said—" She tried to look as stupid as she sounded. The guard's hand moved toward the hilt of his sword. Suddenly she remembered the bucket. She doused the man with its contents and dashed past him while he was still sputtering, slammed the next door shut behind her, and drew the bar.

Light pulsed frantically between her fingers. She heard a man's hoarse screaming and ran forward. At the end of the passage there was a black door. Another corridor led off at right angles, and as Rana neared, she heard booted feet approaching. These passages had been carved down into the living stone of the mountain, with projecting pillars to take the weight of the crossbeams for the floors above. As Ordrey and four of the Blood Wolves emerged from the other corridor, Rana shrank behind one of the pillars, the Jewel pressed between her and the stone as if her body could absorb its gathering light.

Light, and *pain*! Julian's words were the lightning glare that etches every stark detail upon the awareness and leaves its afterimage burned into the brain. Caolin curled away from the vision that illuminated all his self-deceptions and came to his feet, screaming.

Reflex spun an illusion of radiant youth around him, and he saw the dissolution of all that he had been reflected in Julian's eyes.

He sees—he sees me! His denial of the truth that the King saw was absolute.

But I am still the Blood Lord, and he is in my power! Caolin felt his enemy's fury and slammed it back at him. Master of the Jewels the King might be, but Caolin had a lifetime of practice in directing rage. He blasted Julian backwards and snatched a candle from the wall.

"You desired light, and light you shall have! Here is the fire you have summoned, Jewel Master—now burn!" He threw the candle into the straw where Julian had been lying, tossed another, and laughed as his captive began to jerk uselessly at his bonds.

"I would have given you existence unending, but you

rejected me!" he shrieked. "You wanted death—you have it now!"

"Ugly, unloved," Julian chanted, "your hands are webbed with scars, your face is slipping from its bones!"

"Kill him, *kill him*!" Caolin raved. He yanked open the door, and as the draft swept in, the fire in the straw roared up in a wall of flame. "Guards, Ordrey! Bring doom, bring destruction!" He darted toward his enemy, screaming, and was driven back by the heat of the fire.

"You will be alone forever, and I will be free!" shrieked Julian.

Where were the guards? A spear would go through the flames! He wanted to see Julian's guts sizzling before him, make him roast meat for his wolves. He coughed as smoke caught in his lungs, couldn't stop, and knew that he had lost control. It didn't matter. What use was reason now!

"Bring water!"

"No, it's got too great a hold!" A babble of speech rose behind him.

"There's the Blood Lord, grab him!"

"My lord, my lord!" Ordrey's voice shrilled through the din. Frantic hands clutched Caolin's sleeve and yanked him toward the door as the fire caught the silk hangings and a new wave of heat seared his skin. "My lord, you'll be killed. Come away, oh, please come away!"

Julian stood shaking as rage flamed through him, watching Ordrey drag the Blood Lord away.

As if fed by his fury, the fire roared higher. He felt sweat start on his skin and dry instantly as the furnace around him sucked moisture from the air. Already it was growing hard to breathe. *Better this way than the darkness*, he told the terrified animal that whimpered within him. *My spirit will fly free on wings of flame.*

Vision pulsed dizzily, and Julian did not know if it were weakness or heat shimmering in the air. He could not stand much longer. But the wall behind him was too hot to touch already; it would not take long. Through the wavering veils of light before him he saw the walls of the chamber hung with silken flame.

Each breath was agony, and the metal of his manacles seared his skin. His life was running out of him like melting wax from a mold, he was almost ready to be filled by the true gold.

Rage! Rage on! His silent shout soared with the flames. *Consume me and my enemy in a single pyre!*

"Burn, let it all burn, as long as *he* dies!" Caolin's shriek echoed down the stone passageway. He was moving, but whether he ran or was carried he could not tell. Bitter smoke flowed down the passage after them. On his back he felt the hot breath of the fire.

He heard Ordrey telling someone to get Captain Esteban, to start men passing buckets, but he could not get his breath to tell them how useless that would be. The foundations of Blood Gard were stone, but the upper levels and the bracing within were built of stout timbers from the coast. If once the fire got a good hold, there would be no controlling it. In that moment the Blood Lord counted the loss of his fortress a fair exchange for the destruction of his enemy.

As they came out onto the parapet above the arena, a plume of black smoke was already billowing into the sky. Caolin sank down upon his stone high seat, heart racing, and gulped in great breaths of clean air.

"They're all drunk." Fragments of sentences filtered through his awareness.

"Impossible."

"Yes, sir, I know, sir, but all the water casks are full of beer!"

The sky shimmered as waves of heated air billowed from the burning fortress. *Drunk!* thought Caolin, *And so am*

I—or why is the world spinning around me? Why do I want to weep when my enemy is roasting? He shook his head, trying to clear it, and saw men scurrying across the arena, heard the shrill whinnying of terrified horses as they smelled the fire.

"Captain, I don't think we can control it."

"Get the men out, in whatever order you can!"

"My lord, can you walk now?"

Caolin felt someone shaking him, forced himself to focus, and saw Ordrey with a smear of black across his brow.

"Of course." Someone else seemed to be using his lips to reply—he sounded so calm when what he wanted was to shout or to scream. Ordrey helped him up, and the same automatic response moved his limbs. "We'll evacuate the fortress and withdraw into the Domain," his voice said calmly. "And when we have regrouped, we will march on Laurelynn."

"Yes, my lord." Now it was Captain Esteban, searching his face with worried eyes. "I'll send the Blood Wolves to you and see what I can do with the rest of them. Good thing most of the army is in the field already. Rendezvous at Wilhamsted? There's room to lodge most of the officers there."

"Send Konradin to me," said Caolin. He felt the stone quiver beneath his feet as something below gave way.

"Yes, sir." Captain Esteban gestured, and they were moving again. Two of the Blood Wolves took Caolin's arms, but he shook them off again. He could walk. It was the ground that was shaking. Men were screaming, some of them still drunk; screaming and running until the lances of the Blood Wolves herded them toward the gates of Blood Gard.

All but one.

Nobody but Caolin seemed to have noticed the one man who was leaning against a shed, cradling a beer mug in his hand. The sorcerer halted, signaling his escort to be still.

"Hola, Señor Sangrado, there's a bit o'beer left, won't ye have some?" asked the stranger. "Ye must be gettin' thirsty by now!" He wore the remnants of a uniform, but no soldier of Blood Gard ever had such insolent yellow eyes.

The men began to murmur behind him, but Caolin stepped forward. "*You!* You brought the beer."

"My very self!" The yellow eyes seemed to grow more slanted. Caolin had seen those eyes before. "Did ye think ye were done with me? But 'tis yourself lit th' fire that's burnin' yer fortress down!"

"I lit a fire to burn my enemy," said Caolin harshly.

"An' me an' th' lady came t' save him." Coyote grinned. "Now d'ye see the joke, master? Now ye gonna laugh with Me?"

Caolin stared. Flames licked from the windows above him; he could hear them roaring, no, they were laughing— Julian was laughing at him from the fire.

Pain tore through his gut and he screamed, but what came out was a harsh scrape like a raven's call. It happened again. It was laughter; shattering peals of laughter that set men shivering as they pierced the din of the fire. Caolin laughed as he had once when he burned the work of another lifetime in Laurelynn. And now a second life was burning, and again he had kindled the flame.

He fell back into Ordrey's arms, still laughing. The Blood Wolves' lances stabbed at the stranger, struck a sparkle of light, and stuck fast in the wood beyond.

Coyote was gone.

Julian was trying to say good-bye to those who had loved him. But instead of their faces, he saw fire. Still, he must be succeeding, for he saw Rana coming to him through the flames. Rays of green and crimson light blazed from between her fingers. He had seen this before, in some dream of life when he was a man. Was he remembering how she had come to him from the ocean to offer him the Sea Star? In his delirium it seemed to him quite reasonable that her spirit should offer him the Jewel of Fire. . . .

"Julian, come through the fire! Julian, break your chains and come out to me!"

He smiled. *"My beloved, I am coming. In a moment this body will release me, and I will slip through these bonds and be free!"*

Rana looked angry. Didn't she understand him? Why was her spirit dressed in a stained and dirty tunic? Why was her face shining with tears?

"Julian, damn you, come out of there!" The radiance in her hand swirled as she shook it at him.

Abruptly the king realized that he was hearing her with his mortal ears, that somehow she was really here, and that in a moment she was going to be crushed when the ceiling fell.

"Rana, get out! I'm trapped here! Take the Jewels and save Westria—Rana, I always loved you—get away!" He stretched out his arms to her and the hot iron of his manacles seared his skin.

"Use the power of the Jewel! You can't die this way!" She lifted it, and a blast of cool radiance gave him a moment's freedom in which to breathe.

I am dead already, protested reason. *Then what matter a little more pain?* a deeper knowledge replied. The King lifted his hands, felt the power of the Jewel shock into his palms. Gasping, he pulled it into him; his manacles cracked and fell away. But his body was still in ruins, and between him and the door rose a barrier of flame.

To walk through the fire, you must become fire. That inner awareness spoke once more.

He had begun to learn on the Mountain, when he first took up the Jewel. He had learned the same lesson in the earth and the sea and the sky. *Now I die the death of fire*, thought Julian. He lifted his arms to embrace the flames, felt a greater agony than any he had known as he breathed, and then the tingling exhilaration of pure power as the mold was opened and the true gold poured in.

In one incandescent instant each cell of his body reaffirmed its identity. Then the Master of the Jewels walked out of the Blood Lord's furnace, and the divine fire that filled him flared out in two horns of light from his brow.

The smoke of Blood Gard's burning hung in the heavens. The light was like sunset by midafternoon. It burned from the inside out, an incandescent heart of fire that glowed through a skeleton of stone that collapsed as rock cracked and timbers were consumed. Blood Gard burned as Elder had burned, and the College of Bards; it flamed like any of a hundred villages in the mountains or up and down the coasts of Westria, but longer and more fiercely. The College of Bards had fallen with a sound of dying violins. Blood Gard's stones screamed with pain.

The men who had garrisoned it fled, some into Westria to be killed by the folk who found them; some farther, to carry to Elaya and the Barren Lands the tale of the burning of Blood Gard. But most, lazier or less cursed with imagination, went only so far as the valley below the Red Mountain, where their officers herded them into encampments again. Soon raiding parties were riding out to scavenge among the holdings there.

From those valleys they watched and listened to the Blood Lord's laughter as the day darkened into true sunset and the smoke of the burning kindled the heavens into a greater conflagration still.

Rana winced as the last of the light showed her the livid bracelets that the Blood Lord's manacles had burned into Julian's arms. Never, even after Spear Island, had she seen him so thin. He had walked through the fire like a god, but what lay on the ground before her seemed scarcely a man. How had she gotten him this far?

Blood Gard was still burning behind them, challenging the sky. On the slopes beyond she saw dark shapes moving and knew them for the last of Caolin's men. She hoped Coyote would come back soon.

"Alive." She turned. Julian's eyes fixed on the green leaves as if he had never seen them before. *"They're alive!"*

"Yes, and so are you, though only the Guardians know why!" Her own words sounded strange in her ears, and the stinging in her eyes did not come from the fire.

His gaze shifted. Rana saw awareness of who she was come slowly. "Once more . . . you followed me. . . ." There was no emotion in his eyes.

"Forever, Julian! Do you want the Jewel?" She touched the pouch that held it, cool at last, as if the presence of its master had quenched its fire.

"You carry it. The fire . . . is here." His lips thinned as he gestured toward his own breast. His hand fell back, and Rana saw sudden beads of sweat on his brow.

"Just wait until I get you back to Laurelynn!" she exclaimed. "You're hurt, I know, but there's nothing that can't heal!" Nothing unless shock killed him before she could get him to shelter. *Where* was Coyote? With the tag ends of the Blood Lord's garrison still roaming the mountain, she dared not even build a fire.

"Nothing physical." His eyes had closed once more.

Reaction, she told herself. *He's been pushed past human limits.*

"Thank you . . . for coming after me."

Rana stared at him. "I love you," she said flatly. "And Coyote tells me that I'm going to be your Queen."

"Yes. You will bear the Jewels." Julian did not seem to be surprised.

She raised an eyebrow. Wasn't he even going to ask her?

He gathered his strength to speak again. "But I cannot love you."

"Because of Robert?" Rana bent over him, forgetting pride, physical awareness of his body stirring in her even now.

"Because of Caolin." And then the King did look at her, and she recoiled.

"Caolin is dead!" she protested.

"Do you think so? They will tell him that *I* am dead, but he will know better, as do I. Better than any, Rana, you should understand!"

Julian's voice shook as he tried to lift himself, and she got her arm beneath him. She felt the strength going out of him, but she held him tight.

"The reivers raped your body, Rana. The Blood Lord possessed my body and my soul!"

"I understand!" She bent over him, not caring that her tears burned his seared skin. "But that's no reason for you to be an idiot like me! I'm not a gentleman, Julian, and I've had a good teacher. I'm not going to let you run away the way I did two years ago!"

"A teacher." His brow furrowed a little as she kissed him, then he sighed.

"Never mind . . . never mind," she murmured. "Just let me hold on to you!" He relaxed against her breast, and she rejoiced that at least he did not fear her. The trees made a black barrier against the dimming glow of the sky.

"Wouldn't want t'interrupt anything, but there's Blood Wolves rangin' this way, and a horse an' wagon's hard t'hide."

Rana sat up suddenly, and Julian's gasp of pain turned to surprise. Coyote was holding the branches aside, and beyond him she saw a wagon silhouetted against fading clouds.

"You!" The King's whisper held a hint of laughter. "I should have known!"

"Blood Lord's holed up in the valley," said Coyote as they wrapped more blankets around Julian. "Got most of his men out, but no supplies—an' when they get hungry, where they gonna go?"

"Laurelynn!" The King tried to sit up.

"But not yet—they're still runnin' about like ants from a smashed hill. Lie still, King o' Men, we'll get ye there in time!"

Then they lifted him into the wagon, and he fainted again. As Rana took up the reins, Coyote turned four-footed and trotted ahead to scout the road.

The horse was a poor beast and went slowly. It was full dark before they reached the main road into Laurelynn, but the bells of the city were sending a wild clangor across the waters. Then Rana saw fire flickering along the road ahead of her. She pulled up, her heart thudding out its own alarm. Why hadn't Coyote warned her?

But it was Silverhair. His purple cloak glowed like wine in the light of the torches.

Rana stood up, waving wildly. "The Blood Lord is coming—warn the city!"

"Yes, we guessed it!" He spurred toward her. "But how—" He realized there was someone in the back of the wagon, and stilled. Rana understood what the harper dared not say. Riders swirled around them and light danced across the huddled shape inside.

"Julian's hurt, but he'll heal!" She saw hope come back to Silverhair's eyes. Then he turned to her. She managed a grin. "He has to. I'm going to marry him!"

FIFTEEN

The survivors of Blood Gard howled like hungry wolves at the walls that Eric had raised to protect Laurelynn. From the King's chamber, Silverhair heard them when the wind changed. Rana raised her head, listening, and set down the military text from which she had been reading to Julian.

"What's happening?" The King raised himself on one elbow, wincing as the movement jarred his hand. They had built little cages over the dressings on his raw toes and fingers to protect them, but any movement gave him pain. The air was pungent with the scent of salves and ointments.

Silverhair shook his head. "They'll send word if there's news."

"I should be out there! Every day Caolin's forces grow greater while ours are weakening. Our outworks have been taking the brunt of the attack, haven't they? Does Eric have the strength to rally the men? How many men does he have left to lead?"

"The Regent is quite recovered, and he knows what he's doing," said Rana calmly, returning the book to the pile of works on tactics and strategy on the floor.

"He can't be everywhere." Julian let her help him lie back. "It's been three days since the burning! What's Frederic doing? Have our supplies been counted? Caolin's got the grain from those supply barges and perfect weather for camping. He can sit there and worry at us until he gets in! Our food will give out before his does. We were better off when they were sitting in Blood Gard!"

"It's not your fault that they are not, Julian," said Silverhair. "At least you're not still there, too!"

Warm air drifting through the open window brought the scent of early roses, and the King quieted, turning his signet back and forth on his hand. It was too big now, but he would not be parted from it. Then the wind shifted once more, and they heard the sound of horns. Julian jerked upright again.

"That's the retreat! They're falling while I lie here like a log."

"In the name of the Guardian of Men, Julian, you can't even hold a sword! You need to rest now!" exclaimed Rana. "Shall I give you something?"

"No!" Julian's face set. "No drugs. At least I know I am alive when I feel the pain!"

"Have some mercy on yourself, boy!" said Silverhair.

"Mercy?" Julian stared at him, and Silverhair was the one who had to look away. "There will be no mercy in the world while Caolin lives!"

Silverhair bowed his head. There had been a time when he had said the same, after his sister disappeared. But in Elaya, Caolin had saved his life and set him free.

"Shall I play for you, then?" he said at last. He took the King's silence for assent and unlatched the straps of his harp case.

"Play a spell of safety, Uncle," said Julian softly, "that will drive the nightmares away."

Silverhair struck a series of ringing chords, hearing suddenly in memory a snatch of music that had survived from the times of the Ancients as an example in one of the books in the College of Bards.

> *"Harper David, won't you play,*
> *Drive the demons of the dark away,*
> *With your music ring us round,*
> *Fill the air with sacred sound!"*

"I've never heard that before," said Julian.

"It's from an old tale about a harper who played for a mad king."

Julian gave a short laugh. "I am not mad, not yet, but Caolin is. He drew me into his darkness, and now I share his dreams."

Silverhair drew a ripple of harmony from the strings. "Here is another song for you, then." Reconciliation flowed through his fingers, shimmered in the strings, and spread through the warm air.

"Play me to sleep." The King closed his eyes. "In Blood Gard I tried to remember your music, but the screams of all the men who died in those dungeons still throb in the air. Play me a song of healing, Silverhair, and drive the dreams away."

Agile fingers danced up the scale in a series of ascending chords. *Listen,* said that music, *this is the Divine Harmony. . . .*

When Eternity had ended and time resumed once more, Silverhair realized that he was still sitting in Julian's chamber. The King's breast rose and fell in peaceful rhythm. The harper could feel the fading vibrations of his music through Swangold's soundboard. How long had he been gone?

"Farin, I have never heard such playing from you." The quiet voice came from the doorway. Silverhair turned, and the Master of the Junipers limped into the room.

"If you are here, then I can leave him." Rana stood up abruptly. "I need to brew up more tea." As she passed, the harper saw her cheeks wet with tears.

Poor child—no, it was a woman who had brought her beloved out of the wreck of Blood Gard and nursed him so patiently. A few words spoken before witnesses were a sorry betrothal, but there had been no time for rejoicing. It was as if they all had laid upon Rana the responsibilities before she ever tasted the joys of being Queen.

The closing of the door brought Silverhair's awareness back to the Master again. "That was not me! I was— somewhere—and I didn't want to return!"

"Don't you think I know?" The Master bent over the sleeping King, felt his forehead appraisingly, then took Rana's place in the chair.

"Do you? While Julian was captive, I stayed earthbound. Even Swangold could not set me free. But now— I hear music or see the glitter of sunlight on the river, and then comes the Calling. It gets easier to answer each time. Someday will I go too far to return?"

The Master sighed. "Your loyalty may hold you to life more strongly than you know. I envy you. I have my own bliss, but no way to share it with others—I saw Awahna while you played."

Silverhair remembered the soaring granite walls of a valley that he had seen once in vision, and a radiant hawk bearing his spirit into the skies. *Was that the goal of all my wanderings?* The tangled tale of his life unraveled in memory.

"What is it?" asked the Master.

The harper tried to control his features. "Shame. My

life has been such a sorry story! I have husbanded no woman, fathered no child, spent my life running away. Why should I taste Joy when so many better men live in pain?''

''Perhaps because through all your bitterness you still believed in Beauty? Perhaps because the Love that made all things is not constrained by Justice, and will break through any gap in our defenses to manifest that Beauty in the world?'' asked the Master. ''Farin, I don't know the answer, but the Gift must not be denied! Let the Music make you its instrument, and play so compellingly that everyone can hear the Call!''

As the siege settled into a routine, Julian gained sufficient strength to direct the defense of the city, and the people of Laurelynn had leisure to consider what manner of master had returned to them out of the crucible of Blood Gard. When the soldiers cheered him as he limped out to inspect the walls in the mornings, he did not smile. When the Blood Wolves catapulted the heads of the slain into the city, he did not weep.

Julian knew how the whispers followed him as he went by. Months in darkness had sharpened his hearing; he knew that they wondered whether his spirit was Caolin's captive still. Sometimes he wondered, too. He squinted at the jagged ruins that crowned the Red Mountain and rubbed his eyes as if he could wipe his visions away.

''They're still there,'' said Robert as they made their way along the battlement. ''You can smell their garbage when the wind blows this way.''

Julian nodded. The growing light showed him the Blood Lord's encampment with pitiless clarity, black clots of men who had already trampled the ripening grass to dust while the smoke of their cookfires smudged the blue sky. In the center of the camp a crimson banner drooped from its pole. Around it clustered a circle of rough shelters, separated from the rest of the camp by a ring of poles. Some of those branches bore evil fruit—the severed heads of men. But the rest of the camp was laid out with a military regularity, one fire for every twenty warriors.

"Someone there understands defense," said the King. Using a spear shaft for a staff, he limped along the walkway to the next embrasure. Two men in the brick-colored uniforms of the City Guard bowed and edged back, eyeing him curiously.

"Captain Esteban, they call him," said Frederic. "The only sane man in Caolin's army, from all I've heard. He seems to have come from Las Costas originally."

"You have been busy." Julian looked at his friend.

"Sometimes information can be as valuable as a sword." Frederic brightened at the praise. "While my father was recovering and you were lost, learning about the enemy seemed to be the only useful thing I could so. That's when I found out that this Captain Esteban was wounded and deserted Brian's standard at the Battle of the Dragon Waste. The Elayans took him, and he ended up in the mines."

"That must be where Caolin picked him up," said Silverhair. "He was collecting an elite force of fighters when he was the Protector of the Campos del Mar. He would have made it his business to know what Westrians were prisoners.

"Westrian renegades and Elayan rebels form the core of his forces," said Lord Eric. "Don't despise them— some of them were well taught before they became outlaws. They are all the more effective because they have nothing to lose.

"You, there," he called to a man who was passing below the walkway. "That piece they're fitting to the coping is not straight—go down there and tell them so!"

A lucky cast of the enemy catapult had broken the rim. Otherwise the inner wall was still holding, protected by rubble from the first outwork, which had fallen a few days before, and the ditch, flooded with water from the river now.

The King leaned on the wall to take some of the weight off his feet. His joints still ached sometimes, but he could ignore that, and his burns were nearly healed. Now only the raw nail beds where toe- and fingernails were slowly growing in still gave him real pain. A drum began to beat in the enemy encampment. Men were forming up beneath the red banner. They would be attacking soon. He reached for the edge of the wall and winced as his fingers jarred against the stone.

"Have you had more dreams?" asked Silverhair. Julian stared at him, remembering the other torment that had not gone away. Then he nodded, looking from the harper to Robert, and from him to Frederic and his father until they flinched from what his face revealed. What he learned from those dreams was military intelligence, though he cringed from remembering. They had a right to know.

"You have seen the severed heads the enemy cast into the city after the first outwork across the river fell. In my dreams . . . I see what has become of the bodies to which they belonged."

He swallowed as vision overwhelmed him again—the crimson banner from which a wolf's head snarled; men in wolfskin cloaks who watched, grinning, as the sorcerer lifted a sword above a naked man bound to a rough altar of stone. The blade gleamed as it fell. Blood gushed into a bucket, and as one man stuck the head on a pole and added it to the grisly palisade that surrounded them, the Blood Wolves attacked the body with knives and their own fangs and began to feed. But the blood was for their leader, and as he drank it, Julian felt the red flame of power that kindled new life in every cell.

"They *eat* them?" Frederic's voice shook.

"I wish I could believe these were nightmares, but I

recognized some of the victims even before I saw the lists of those of those who did not make it back.'' Julian saw the faces of the others twisting with revulsion. They must not learn that when he shared the Blood Lord's unholy feasting, he experienced Caolin's exultation as well.

''We knew they were evil,'' Eric said harshly. ''It changes nothing to know the manner of it. Our real problem is this siege. We make them pay for every advantage, but in time we will be forced to destroy the bridge and retreat to the island.''

Julian turned to gaze back at the rose-brick walls of the city, glowing in the morning light like a city in a dream. But those walls had been built to stand against the incessant pressure of the river, not the harsh impact of flung stones. Did they have men enough to defend the entire shoreline once those walls came down?

''Does Caolin want to take Laurelynn for military advantage or just because it's handy?'' asked Robert. A horn blew again and the enemy began to move.

''Laurelynn is a commercial center, not a military stronghold,'' answered Lord Eric, eyes still on the enemy. ''We can repel attackers, but we do not control the surrounding countryside. If we did, Caolin would never have gotten so far. The only effective fortresses in Westria are the provincial capitals. In the long term, the loss of Laurelynn would weaken the economy of the nation. But its most immediate effect would be on our morale.'' He lifted his hand, and a trumpet call sent Westrians moving into positions on the walls.

''Perhaps he is attacking us for revenge,'' added Frederic. ''He must be very sorry he did not kill you, Julian!'' They moved out of the way of the squad posted to this sector and followed Eric along the wall to the command platform.

''You don't understand. If I were dead, I would be beyond the Blood Lord's power. It was my soul he wanted—that's why he kept me captive." He shivered, remembering. "The city is only another prison as long as the siege goes on." He hurried to keep up with the others, though each step was a stab of pain.

"Do you want to leave? Could you?" asked Eric. "If we attacked their outposts on the north bank of the river we could cover an evacuation of noncombatants. Our food will run low soon, and it's hard to get supplies past their catapults. Better to get those who cannot fight out of here if we can. You could go with them, Julian, and rally support in the countryside."

For a moment the King considered it, wanting a good horse beneath him and an open road before him as he had rarely wanted anything before. Then he shook his head.

"Frederic is partially right. Wherever I am, there will be danger. The Blood Lord holds us in check, but our resistance immobilizes him as well. Better make him spend his strength against our fighters here than let the Blood Wolves loose upon the people of Westria."

"For the present, that's true," said Eric, "but we can only grow weaker, waiting here. We must get rid of that army, by whatever means we can!"

"Are you asking me to break the Covenant by using the Jewels to destroy?" Julian's voice grew terrible. Eric flushed uncomfortably.

"My lord, I can't give you orders, but you must understand. As long as we are on the defensive, we are losing. This war has to end!"

There was a whirring in the air and the platform shook as a rock struck the wall. Shrieking, the Blood Lord's men poured across the wasteland before the outworks, and the Westrian arrows began to fly.

"Come on, Julian," said Frederic, gesturing toward the bridge.

The King's hands clenched impotently, but already it

was becoming hard to stand. Raging silently, he let his friends help him away from the fray.

The Beltane fire blazed defiantly from the tower of the palace, sending showers of sparks up to challenge the early stars. The opening at the top of the stairwell framed it; from the platform above came the irregular ring of boot heels on stone.

"He's still limping, isn't he?" said Robert, waiting on the last landing for Rana to catch up with him.

"A little, when he thinks no one can see." She took a deep breath, willing the pounding of her pulse to ease.

"Perhaps we should wait. He did say he wanted to be alone."

He reached out, and Rana gave his arm a comforting squeeze. Her heart was still racing. She heard the pacing overhead pause, and realized that she too was afraid.

"If Julian was refusing food, you would make him eat, wouldn't you?" she murmured. "What he needs now is love!"

"But I deserted him! He belongs to you now," Robert whispered back.

"Nonsense! He left *you*—and betrothed or not, he doesn't seem to want *me*! But it's Beltane." Rana started up the last flight of stairs. She could hear Robert's soft laugh as he followed her.

Julian was waiting for them. Had he heard them, or had other senses told him they were there? The patience in his face was more daunting than anger.

"Hullo, Julian." Robert held out a flask of wine, and when the King did not move, took a swallow himself. "We thought we would come help you to celebrate."

"Just like everyone else in Westria. In the Sacred Wood, the tree spirits will come out to join the dancing," said Rana brightly, "and the fisherfolk of Seahold will be doing their ceremonies on the bay."

"With Ardra's warships to guard them," answered Julian repressively.

"Frederic took a boat downriver to join her. By now they will be together, honoring the Lord and the Lady." Rana pressed on. Robert was leaning against the parapet, watching warily.

Julian's dark glance moved from Rana to Robert. Did Rana see in their depths a spark of amusement, or was it only the reflection of the fire?

"Aren't you going to even kiss me?" She moved between him and the fire, knowing that its glow would shine through the yellow silk of her gown and backlight her hair.

"I can't."

She grasped his shoulders, trembling as she felt the warm life in him beneath her hands. She had suppressed her own responses while she was nursing him, but tonight the land itself cried out for love. But Julian did not move.

"Oh, Julian, I'm touching your body, but there's a wall of ice around your soul!"

"Rana, I *dare* not kiss you. I would be as mad as the Blood Lord if once I let go." He stepped away from her. "Robert, my answer to you is the same."

Face flaming, Rana looked at Robert in appeal. *You see?*

"I understand," he said painfully. "When I didn't help nurse you, you must have thought—"

Julian shook his head. "You were wounded too. I was not neglected."

Oh, Robert, move! She glared at him. *If he won't take me, seduce him as you did before!* But Robert was lost in his own pain.

"No, you don't understand. I was afraid to face you!"

"Because of Marcos?" Julian asked gently.

"You know!" Robert's blue eyes lifted for the first time.

"They let that poor herald, Tarran, talk to me in Blood Gard before he . . . died. I suppose they thought it would weaken my resolve. He told me that Marcos was taking care of you, and I guessed how it would be. Lady of Fire! Did you think I would rather have you dead and faithful than alive and in love with another man?''

Rana turned away, tears prickling beneath her eyelids. *Julian, don't you understand that I would rather have you Robert's lover than able to love no one at all?*

"Julian! Oh, Julian!" Robert sat down suddenly. "He loves me, you see. No complications, just someone who is always there for me. But I still love you, too." His gaze slid sideways to Rana, then returned to the King. "Julian, what did the Blood Lord do to you?" Robert cried.

The King closed his eyes, and Rana remembered what he had said to her on the Red Mountain. Of course he would not want to tell Robert. A man had violated him, and Robert was a man.

From the streets below she heard laughter, and the spark that Coyote had kindled within her began once more to glow.

"You want more time to heal—don't you think *I* know! But can't you feel the Land's need throbbing in the air? The Land must be served, Julian, and you are the King!''

"And you've agreed to be Queen!" Julian cried. "If you think it's so important, why don't *you* make love to the Land!''

Rana stared at him, a heat pulsing through her that owed nothing to the fire. Sweet Lady, Julian was so beautiful! Robert's eyes were glowing, and she realized that he was feeling the same rush of desire that was overwhelming her.

"I will," she said harshly. "I will do the rite for you, as you should be doing it for Westria. Robert, you are his lover and his heir, will you stand in the King's stead, and lie down with me?''

Robert's eyes widened, but the power of the Lady of Fire knew neither preference nor personality. When Rana stretched out her hand, he laughed and came to her.

* * *

Robert and Rana had been gone a half hour before Julian stopped trembling. Had they known how they were tormenting him?

In the streets of Laurelynn those soldiers who were not on guard were drinking and singing. Those who had found lovers in the army must be embracing already, and tonight the public women who had remained in Laurelynn would do good service to the Lady of Fire. Julian thought of bodies moving together in the darkness and twitched, remembering how Caolin had touched him. His gaze sought the fires that were burning across the river.

What are you doing tonight, oh my enemy? Does the blood lust sunder your soul from your senses, or do you seek the embrace of the darkness, hoping to find me there? The flames were whispering their own secrets; faint from below came the sounds of Beltane revelry. But those noises only emphasized the stillness by the fire.

Julian took a deep breath and let it out carefully, staring into the flicker of light. *Let me open up just a little, Lady. I would not deny you your due.* The fire blazed brighter, gold and crimson and blue.

A log broke, and in the sudden flare he saw the bright form of a woman with hair of flame. *"Use the Jewel. Use the Jewel, Julian!"*

"But Rana has it," he began to answer Her.

"Does she? See, the Jewel of Fire is here."

Julian stared into the flames and saw a coruscation of green and crimson, reached out and plucked it free. It was like being in the heart of the fire. In that blaze shimmered Rana with Robert in her arms, but what they saw was not each other but a god whose eyes burned like flame. Julian's awareness moved outward to participate in the passion of all who lay together on this Beltane Eve. The heat of the fire seared away all inhibitions. His body shuddered to release as he shared their joy.

After a time he became aware of himself once more and realized that he was holding a dead coal. He dropped it back into the fire and looked at his palm, but the only mark upon it was the one that had been seared into it the first time he picked up the Jewel of Fire.

Shortly before morning, the enemy fires began to fade. It seemed to Julian that on the other side of the river masses of shadow were moving, but he did not dare to speculate on what that might mean. Nor did he dare to send his spirit winging where it would be easy prey for the sorcerer. He waited, wearing out his eyes in a vain attempt to scan the darkness, until the first light of morning showed him what he had not allowed himself to hope for.

The army of the Blood Lord was gone.

SIXTEEN

Darkness . . . The prisoner starts to turn over, and cold iron jerks him down. He lies back, but his pulse races again as something brushes past his foot through the straw. He gasps beneath the invisible weight of tons of stone. . . . As his body weakens, the close darkness makes him more afraid. If only someone would come— even the torturers!

"No! This is not my dream! Get out of my head, demon! You were my prisoner!" Caolin clutched the soft fur of his bedding. He tried to open his eyes, but fatigue sucked him back into the dream.

"Why should I release you?" A harsh voice answers him. "You tried to seduce me into this darkness. Why are you afraid?"

Awareness of the other presence recedes. Caolin reaches out. The wall he is touching is wood, not stone, and very near. He lies coffined in a lightless, airless box. His small hands beat against rough walls until they sting. His whim-

pers dwindle into sobs. No one will come. What did he do wrong?

The dark presses in and he cries soundlessly. Alone . . . alone . . . alone . . .

Caolin woke weeping as the terror faded. The uneven light from the oil lamp chased shadows across the stretched fabric of his pavilion. It was an Elayan field tent of tightly woven canvas with gilded poles. *They honor me,* he thought, feeling the softness of silk and fur around him. *I am still in control.*

It was almost dawn, but the great army encamped around him was not sleeping. He heard the measured step of a sentry and the soft challenge as two Elayan officers came by; the whickering of tethered horses; singing from the Tambaran campfires, the soft beating of a drum; and more faintly still, the sound of screaming as soldiers ravaged some yet unplundered quarter of the town.

Sanjos had been easy prey for the combined forces of the Blood Lord and his Elayan allies, a much better target than Laurelynn. By now someone must have told Julian where his enemy had gone, but he would not dare move for fear they might just as swiftly return.

Prince Ali had sent him a full impi of eight hundred trained foot soldiers with assegais and cowhide shields under the command of Lord Rafat Elawi, a powerful man whose tribal tattoos were overlaid by the slashes of a lion's claws. With the troop of fully armored heavy lancers came another Elayan of great pride and impeccable pedigree, Don Niero Alfonso de Vega y Costanza. Allied with the Blood Wolves and his own irregulars, they had found the city easy prey. Only the fortress itself still resisted. The screams grew louder, and Caolin shivered, remembering the emotions of his dream. His hands smelled of carrion; his fingernails were edged with brown. How had they gotten that way?

Today there will be more screaming, and the sick reek of blood. They will all want orders, and I am so very tired.

He lay back on the cushions, breathing harshly. He wanted to go back to sleep, but he was afraid what he might dream.

"The Drylands engineers must tackle the gates to the fortress, but I'll hold the Caballeros in reserve." Were those his thoughts? Caolin felt as if he were being crowded out of his own skull. *"The Elayan foot can make the first assault, Esteban the second. By then my spy should have opened the secret gate."* Whoever was thinking those thoughts knew his business. Let *him* deal with the complexities.

The pressure grew greater. With a little sigh, Caolin gave up the struggle and let go.

When Ordrey entered the pavilion, his lord was scrubbing his hands in the basin, calling for more water, demanding a clean robe.

"Summon Captain Esteban, and Don Niero and Lord Rafat."

"Yes, Caolin, I'll tell them," Ordrey began. But his master fixed him with a cold glare.

"Sangrado . . . I am Lord Sangrado. . . . Who is Caolin?"

"Wolfmaster, Wolfmaster, come here!" cried Konradin. "There's more of them, skulking like rats in a hole!" He waved toward a carven archway emblazoned with the Las Costas arms. Four of the Blood Wolves followed him down the stairs.

"Alexander—where is he? I want the man who betrayed me!" The Blood Lord stumbled over a body, then lurched across the stone-paved courtyard after them.

He was tiring again. Alien thoughts whispered at the edges of awareness but he could sense the heat of many bodies ahead of him—bodies full of hot, pulsing blood. Alexander's fortress rang with the cries of the dying as the impi rolled forward, assegais stabbing like the blades of some swift, efficient machine. The Blood Lord sank down on a stone bench at the head of the stairs. Smoke from the burning gatehouse billowed toward them as the wind changed, and he coughed. There was someone who was afraid of fire . . . someone he knew well. He tried to remember.

"No! We've no weapons, we surrender!" The protest was cut off abruptly. Konradin appeared in the doorway, his arms newly crimsoned, holding a vessel of dark glass. The Blood Lord sensed its energy and held out his hand.

"My Lord is served!" Kneeling, the Wolf offered him the chalice. His pale eyes glittered. Blood burned in the sunlight; the Wolfmaster gulped it eagerly. New strength coursed through his veins and the whispers faded. The blood had come from a young man, a musician. As the life force dissipated, the impressions grew less clear.

Booted feet rang on stone behind them. At the first clash of metal, Konradin was between the Blood Lord and the passageway, sword drawn. A man in a bloodstained black-and-gold surcoat burst into the courtyard, looking behind him. He glimpsed the Wolf; his sword was still swinging around when the warrior's blade took him in the neck. The head rolled to the Blood Lord's feet as another leaped past. Konradin's movement continued; the man was flung aside, lifeblood pouring across the stones.

There was a pause, then three came through at once, spreading out with swords ready. Konradin smiled. For a moment no one moved. Then they heard more men coming behind them. The Westrian on the left panicked and Konradin's sword took him; the blade scythed round across the second man's body; for a moment the last held him, then there was a clang and a slither of steel as the sword slid over the defending guard and into the other swordsman's breast.

"You might have left something for us to do." Captain

Esteban's calm voice echoed from the passageway. Slowly
he moved out into the courtyard, followed by half a dozen
of his men. Konradin grinned and wiped his blade.

"My lord, except for a few holdouts, the fortress is
ours," the Captain went on. "But Alexander . . ." He
paused as the Blood Wolves came back up the stairs, dragging a woman who struggled and cursed them with an
astonishing vocabulary.

"Wolfmaster, this one's noble meat!" sang out one of
the Wolves. "We gonna eat her or ransom her?" He licked
his lips, and his captive stilled, her eyes going from the
bloodstained chalice to the man who had drunk from it.

"Oh, she's an old hen, good only for stewing or for
sale!" One of his companions pinched the woman's arm
and laughed.

The Blood Lord rose to his feet. Despite her gray hair and
her torn gown, he recognized her. Memory flickered: the
sighing palm trees of Santibar, and her face, exultant, as
Prince Palomon's nod denied him the city he had won; afternoon light slanting through the windows of the Council
Hall in Laurelynn, and her voice accusing him. Brian's
widow, Alexander's mother—*Alessia of Las Costas.*

"An old lioness, rather!" he said aloud. "Where's your
cub, old cat?" Alessia was an ancient enemy, but Alexander's treachery was still green.

"Monster, my son is safe from you!"

"She speaks truth. The Lord of Las Costas is nowhere
in the fortress," put in Captain Esteban.

"Alexander lives, and while he lives, so does Las Costas, no matter what you do to me or to the city here!"
hissed Alessia.

"Kill her," suggested Konradin. "The cub ran off and
left her—he won't care!"

"Maybe not." The Blood Lord stalked forward, and
Alessia's eyes widened as she saw the bloodstains on his
robe. He dipped a finger into the chalice and drew a red

stripe across her face, then opened his hand. She quivered as the glass smashed upon the stones.

"Now my mark is on you, Alessia. If Alexander will not surrender to save you, we'll try Julian. Or perhaps we can think of some other way to use you." He stroked her drooping breast and cackled as she flinched from his hand.

"No? Well, my men don't like old meat. But perhaps Ordrey could use a servingmaid!" he laughed. "Oh, Alessia! The ghost of Brian is wailing in hell today!"

"Alexander will avenge me," Alessia snarled. "He'll see your blood, Caolin!"

The Blood Lord frowned. Caolin—he knew that name. Caolin was the one who was afraid.

"We waited by the old well, and I watched my city burn, but she never came!" Alexander's voice was scraped raw by fatigue.

Julian watched as light from the river, reflecting through the long windows of the little council chamber, showed him the ravaged features of the Lord of Las Costas, and wondered why it gave him no satisfaction to see that proud head bowed. Perhaps the marks of the Blood Lord's manacles were too enduring a reminder of his own humiliation. He touched Alexander's shoulder, and the other man looked up in surprise.

"We will rescue Lady Alessia, or we will avenge her!" he said harshly, hoping it was true.

"If she needs it," put in Silverhair. "Your mother is a remarkable woman. Give her a week, and Caolin may be begging us to take her back again!"

Alexander's lips twitched in a wan smile, and Rana pushed a steaming mug of chamomile tea into his hand.

"And you say they're coming north now?" Eric asked finally.

"The advance guard was moving out when I left, and the rest were breaking camp. My people . . . are dead or scattered into the hills. But an Elayan garrison still holds the fortress,'' Alexander replied.

"How many?'' Robert seemed still shaken by the news.

"The Blood Lord had a thousand already, and the Elayan force numbers as many again,'' said Frederic, "plus whatever tag ends of raiding parties may come in.''

"Not from the east or north,'' said Julian. "We have men waiting at Altamont and on the Laurelynn road.'' He shifted position on the hard seat as his tender joints began to ache once more.

"What force do you have to bring against him?'' asked Alexander. "Besides the two companies from Laurelynn that I met returning here?'' As Julian started to speak, he put up a restraining hand.

"No, my lord, I don't blame you—by the time you got my message it was already too late for them to help. It would have served no purpose for them to throw their lives away. The fault is mine. If I had come to your aid in your extremity, you might have been able to help me in mine!''

The anguish in Alexander's voice pierced Julian's heart, and he reached out to him. "It has been too little and too late for all of us ever since this war began!''

"My king, will you forgive me? The word will go out to my people, however slowly, that I live and fight on. Whatever strength and loyalty I can command are yours from this day forward, Julian!''

He reached out across the table, and Julian gripped his clasped hands. A glimmer of light from the river filled the room, dazzling him.

"Alexander of Las Costas, will you bear me faith in all things according to the Covenant and the laws of Westria? Your truth for mine, your sword and mine raised in common cause?'' He felt another voice speak through him, heard his words echoed up and down the years as if all his ancestors and Alexander's were renewing their bond through their clasped hands. Yet still he trembled, for how could he offer a king's protection to anyone as things were now?

"In the name of the Guardian of Men, I swear it."

Julian trembled at the rush of emotion that came to him through the other man's hands—a release of tension like that of a weary child entrusting itself to a parent's arms.

"Alexander, my faith I give to you, as I am pledged to the Maker of All Things for Westria. Beyond love or liking, there is loyalty. Let us not forget it again." Julian forced out the words.

Then he stiffened, feeling his own hands held in a grip of such force that his senses swam. *"Julian of Westria, I am here. I have always been here! In your time of trial, hold out your hands to Me!"* For a long moment he sat rigid; then the Power that had spoken released him, and he let go of Alexander's hands.

"Oh, Alexander, now you are worthy of your father's signet ring that I gave you when you were a child," said Eric hoarsely. His eyes were wet with unshed tears.

But the shadow that had weighted Julian's spirit since he heard of the fall of Sanjos was gone. He did not have to bear the burden all alone! He opened his eyes, and the light that he saw in the faces of the others dazzled him. Or perhaps it was the fire that burned within them that he was seeing, for the illumination that came through the long windows was as evanescent as their present danger in the long tale of years.

Alexander looked dazed, and Julian smiled at him. "This is the beginning of the restoration of Westria."

He smiled at them all, though returning awareness showed him how the stress of the siege had loosened the flesh on Eric's bones, the new lines of pain around Robert's eyes, and Frederic's perpetual frown of responsibility. Only Rana shone like a newly lit flame, and his uncle had a radiance about him that was more than the shimmer of sunlight on his silver hair.

"We have already asked every province to muster its men," he said briskly, and the others sat straighter as if kindled by his sudden energy. "The situation in Las Costas and Laurelynn we know. I'm hoping for axemen from the Ramparts. The Corona"—he nodded toward the painted arms on the tiles set into the mantel over the hearth—"has been summoned, but it will take time for their horsemen to reach us here.'

"And I have written to Queen Mara of Normontaine," said Silverhair, "asking for troops and a commander. She may send them. She may even come herself, though I told her not to."

"But that will take time. Seagate is the only healthy province close enough to offer effective resistance to the enemy," said Lord Eric. "We breed good heavy cavalry, and though they're unblooded, we have kept up the competitions in the yearly Games. My younger son, Theodor, is in Bongarde, supervising the weapontake, but with a good horse I can be there in two days' time. The question is, 'Where is Caolin going now?' "

All eyes returned to the map in the middle of the table. The light was dimming as dusk came on, and Frederic lighted a lamp so they could see.

"It seems to me that he has two choices," said Robert finally. "He can come back upriver to finish off Laurelynn and then tackle Rivered. That would be easiest. We're both weak, and he doesn't have to cross any rivers to get to us."

"But he would have to divide his own forces to garrison them, while giving Seagate and the north time to gather their strength against him," said Eric grimly. "He might be wiser to try to take Bongarde before we can all combine!"

"My own preference is for a pitched battle before any more cities burn!" said Julian. "We must draw this viper's teeth even if we risk everything—better that than the constant skirmishing that has been bleeding the country dry!"

"Well, that's agreed, then!" said Robert brightly.

"Where shall we fight him, Julian?" They all looked back at the map.

"Not *we*, Robert," said Julian slowly. "I want you to stay in Laurelynn."

Robert's face paled and he started to turn away. "Is it because I failed you at the Mother of Fire?" he began, but the King gripped his shoulder.

"You almost died on that mountain, defending me! Think, Robert—I must leave someone I trust to defend the city. If I fail, that will be vital, and there's none else among our kin who is both free and of age to bear the crown! For Westria's sake, one of us has got to survive!"

"Oh Julian, Julian." Robert's head bent until it rested against the King's hand. Julian waited until his cousin nodded acceptance, gave him a swift hug, then let him go.

Lord Eric sighed. "All this is irrelevant until we figure out how to delay the enemy until we're ready to give battle, and then tempt him to some spot where we'll have a reasonable chance."

"I'd like to draw him north, across the river," said Julian thoughtfully. "There are hills enough for concealment, and broad valleys where we can use our cavalry."

"And very few holdings for the Blood Wolves to destroy," added Frederic, tapping the shaded hills between the north bank of the river and the top of the Great Bay. "Do you think we could catch him between the hills and these marshes?"

"I was going to order the ferries at Julian's Isle destroyed," said Lord Eric, "but perhaps we should make it easy for him to cross the river there."

"If it's too easy, won't he suspect something?" asked Rana.

"Perhaps if we leave a token force to defend the crossing . . ." Suggestions were coming quickly now.

"Let that be my job," said Robert. "Don't worry, I

won't risk myself,'' he added bitterly. "Damn it, Julian, you've got to give me something to do!''

"We have to make the Blood Lord want to go north,'' said Frederic into the silence. "What do you think will draw him?''

"Me,'' the King said suddenly. "He might go if he thought I was still too weak to fight and had fled to Bongarde.''

"Are you?'' asked Alexander. "Are you fit for battle?''

Everyone looked from him to Julian, and the King realized that the Lord of Las Costas had asked what they all wanted to know. Julian got to his feet. Despite the special boots, they hurt, but he could ignore that. Unsmiling, he lifted the heavy oak chair and held it at arm's length over Alexander's head.

"Do you want me to give you an accolade?''

Robert grinned, and then all of them, even Alexander, were laughing.

"That leaves us with only two problems,'' Frederic said wryly. "The first is how to thin their ranks enough before we come to battle so that we can handle them.''

"Archers could hide in the hills around Misthall and worry their flanks,'' said Silverhair. "We've got refugees from the Royal Domain here who know the country. I remember it pretty well myself from the year I lived at Misthall!''

"Oh, no,'' said Julian. "I want you to sing me into battle, Silverhair!''

"You'll have your battle music, I swear it to you, Julian.'' The harper smiled at him. "What was the other problem?'' he asked Frederic.

"How to tell the Blood Lord a lie he will believe.''

"Here they come.'' Aurel held the branch of eucalyptus aside and pointed southward, and Silverhair squinted to see. A pall of smoke still hid the sky above Sanjos, but the road glittered with spear points of light.

Aurel swung his sling experimentally. "I used to scare the crows away from my father's corn! My eye should still be good enough to wing these." He had made the weapon from a bit of old burnishing leather and some spare strings he kept for his viol.

Silverhair surveyed him sourly. He had intended simply to leave the horses at Misthall, but Aurel and some of the livelier students had insisted on joining him. By now they did know the area, and at least this way he could keep an eye on them.

"You stay here, remember! You're a hundred yards from the road, good range, if that thing works. And for Wind Lord's sake, stay among the trees."

"I could say the same to you," said Aurel, smiling. "You'll be closer."

Silverhair nodded. A quick glance up and down the road showed him the others settling into cover where the trees came down nearly to the road—five who had once lived in the shadow of the Red Mountain and another ten from the shore of the bay who swore they were good with sling or bow . . . and the six from the College of Bards.

"At least leave the harp here," added Aurel.

"And let it be lost or trampled if we have to run? I won't even notice it. The harp case is a part of me by now." There was a sound behind him. "No," Silverhair added without looking around. "I want you to stay with Aurel."

"You need talk t' others, gonna whistle?" Piper moved between him and the other bard. "I hide easy, move fast . . . know all the paths." The harper was still shaking his head, but Piper only grinned. "Only fair—you followed me!"

Silverhair sighed. Short of tying the boy up, he knew no way to make him stay away.

"Stick close, then! And don't make a sound!" It was only when Aurel suppressed a snort of laughter that Silverhair remembered to be grateful that Piper could speak at all. Crouching, he began to work his way down the hill.

He had chosen a clump of coyote brush a quick dash away from the trees as his hiding place. He glanced back at the dappled light and shadow of the eucalyptus grove. It looked farther now.

"Learned all th' songs in your book," Piper said softly.

"Already?" Silverhair felt an unexpected flush of pleasure. Music was such an evanescent art, yet a song could survive its maker if it was passed on. During the past year Aurel had been transcribing the harper's music to replace the first collection, lost when the College in Las Costas was burned by Caolin's men.

"When we get back, will you sing them for me?" He reached out to ruffle the boy's brown hair and saw Piper's eyes glow. Then the jingle of harness set them both staring at the road, and Silverhair thrust the boy down.

"Crossbows!" Beyond the first troop of mounted officers marched foot soldiers in the kilts of the Drylands; they carried the same formidable weapons that twenty years earlier had nearly been Eric's bane.

"Tell the others to hold their fire," he whispered, pushing Piper away. "Wait for the bowmen; they're the danger. Take out those crossbows and we'll save lives!"

As the boy slithered off through the grass, Silverhair plucked an arrow from his quiver. Sweat trickled down his back, but he did not stir. He had learned his shooting in a rough school, but now he chose his target as carefully as any hunter. There . . . that patch of unarmored neck, reddened now from marching in the sun. *For Eric and Brian,* he thought, and let fly.

A dozen arrows hummed through the air, and the lead pellets of the slingers whistled after them. Men fell, screaming. Packhorses plunged as spent arrows rattled among their feet. Eucalyptus branches rustled as archers shifted position and shot again.

Silverhair aimed once more. *A dozen down—good! Get off another volley and then away!* The advance guard was already wheeling. The ground trembled as men in wolf-skin cloaks cantered forward. Foot soldiers with long cow-hide shields were coming after the bowmen. Before they realized they were in range, several fell. The surviving crossbows fired fruitlessly into the grove.

A shouted order brought a line of foot from the impi marching up between the bowmen and the hill, lifting their long shields to cover both lines. A well-slung lead pellet might penetrate the hardened hide, but Silverhair's bow was useless now.

The harper reached for his silver whistle and blew the retreat with one piercing call. Self-sacrifice had never seemed less attractive. He crawled awkwardly toward the trees, wishing he had taken Aurel's advice and left the harp with Siaran at the College of Bards.

As the harper pulled himself upright, panting, he saw one group of riders swing away from the rest and start up the road toward Misthall. Several of them bore torches, and beneath the sweat, Silverhair's skin went chill. All the bards who might have been able to defend the hall were with him here! He lifted the bow, desperately seeking a target, and saw one man in a plain tunic among the wolf-skins, a little round man with a bald patch surrounded by graying ginger hair.

"Ordrey!" he fought for breath. *"Or . . . drey."* He put all the compulsion a lifetime of training had taught him into that call. "Does Caolin still want the harper? Here he is, Ordrey—he is here."

There was a confusion of sliding hooves and jingling harness as the Blood Wolves reined in. Ordrey stared into the trees.

"Where are you? Is that Silverhair?"

"Your old friend." The harper pitched his voice to bounce off a eucalyptus trunk a few paces away, and he had barely spoken when an evilly barbed dart thudded into the tree and hung quivering as the pull of its wooden stock and lead weight bent the soft iron shaft.

"No, don't!" screeched the little man. "The Blood Lord wants him!"

"Alive—that's right, Ordrey." Silverhair thinned his voice; let it float mockingly through the trees. "Why don't you take me to him now? Let Misthall alone for a while— you can always come back again."

"Your life for an old house?" Ordrey laughed.

There were faint rustlings on the hill behind him. The others would be carrying the warning now. Once when frustration had driven Silverhair to fantasies of sacrificing himself for Julian, the Master of the Junipers had made him promise to risk himself only for the sake of his own truth. His heart hammered painfully. *My life for Siaran and the others so that the music can go on.*

"That's my price," he called. "You'll never find me in here!"

"Burn the grove, and the harper in it," suggested one of the Blood Wolves.

Ordrey shook his head. "Lord Sangrado would burn *you!*"

Silverhair watched him, hoping that the memory of his defeat on the road to Registhorpe three years ago still rankled. The little man gave an order, and the harper felt a moment's unwilling admiration as the Blood Wolves turned their horses with knees alone and loped back down the hill.

"Come out, harper!" Ordrey's voice cracked with excitement. "Come out, Farin Silverhair, and play!"

Silverhair reached for the radiance that had ravished his spirit, but all he found within was necessity. He let the bow slip from suddenly strengthless hands, and walked out into the pitiless sunlight on the hill.

SEVENTEEN

Smoke filled the sky above the city. Rana coughed as the reek caught in her throat, remembering Blood Gard. But these were forge fires, and it was the King himself who had ordered them to burn. She watched him sidelong as he walked beside her. His shoulders were hunched with anxiety, but his limp was almost gone. Rana knew his joints still ached, but he would not allow that to matter. If only he would let her try to soothe the pain away!

Then he held out his hand to her, and if the warmth in his face did not quite reach his eyes, at least he was trying to smile.

"Listen—there's a warrior's music!"

Rana shivered. "I prefer Silverhair's!"

Julian frowned, for the archers the harper was guiding were late getting back to Laurelynn. Then they turned the corner to the broad alley behind the Street of the Smiths, where the air itself was at war with the clamor of hammers on steel.

"Look—there's the King and his lady!"

Rana glanced back. Two women with bundles of kindling balanced on their heads grinned and curtsied without losing a stick. She waved, then glanced at Julian, who had not heard. Slowly her smile faded. What use was it to be called Queen if Julian could not love her? What use all her care to heal him if he was killed in the battle they were making these weapons for?

New hearths had been built along the center of the alley, shielded from the winds by movable screens, with quenching vats close by. Charcoal lay stacked ready to feed the fires. At one end of the alley, crucibles of ore glowed in the hottest furnaces, and cranes of cast iron swung them over the molds of carven stone. At the other end stood the anvils, where the smiths were beating the rough blanks into weapons of war.

"Is every smith in Westria here?" exclaimed Rana, staring.

"All those in Laurelynn, and some from the Free Cities," answered the King. "A pack train is coming from the Ramparts with poles for axe handles and spears. It has been twenty years since Westria went to war, and rust and dust have eaten most of what was in the armory. Men can fight with pitchforks and pruning hooks, but they will do it more effectively with spears."

Rana nodded. Roughly cast heads and sword blades lay on a hide. One-handed, a smith used tongs to lift a glowing triangle of metal from the coals to the anvil. Stripped to breechclout and padded gloves, glistening with sweat and grime, he looked more like some elemental than a man. Sparks flew as the hammer crashed down, making its own metallic music as it danced across the steel.

"You'd think it would break." She winced at a particularly violent clang.

"No, the hammering makes the steel stronger," said Julian.

There was something odd in his voice, and she looked at him quickly, but his eyes were as opaque as charcoal before it goes into the fire.

"And what about us? Will this trial make Westria stronger as well? Or will it destroy us? This used to be a pleasant little lane."

"What do you mean?" His hand closed on her shoulder. "Rana! You saw Blood Gard—at least these folk labor like free men!" Julian's voice had risen.

A man who had been busy with the bellows turned, grinning, and Rana forgot her disquiet as she recognized the Artificer who had built the catapults for their battle on the sea. His white hair stood out around a balding pate red now with sun, and there was a large smear of soot across his brow.

"My lord! You're looking well indeed, and your lady, too! 'Tis been a time since that sea fight, but I've not forgotten!"

"Nor have we!" said Rana. "But what are you doing here?"

"New bellows!" He pointed proudly. "Gets the air just where it's needed—"

"And with less labor," said the smith, clapping the old man on the shoulder. The others let the work go for a moment to cluster round.

"What word of the enemy?" they asked. "Who's going to use these blades? D'ye think the Blood Lord will come this way?"

"Not if I can stop him!" The King answered the last and loudest question. "We'll give you what warning we can. You have wrought wonders, my friends. But as you labor, set your prayers upon those blades."

There was an odd silence. Then Master Johannes the goldsmith stepped out from the crowd.

"You are a Master in your own way, Jewel Lord; surely

you know that each craft has its mysteries. Did you think we would work without using *all* our skills?''

The King bowed his head. ''I should have known that. The valor you forge into these blades will strengthen our arms.''

''I see that you are wearing your signet on its proper finger again,' said the goldsmith, looking at Julian's scarred hand. The king turned the ring in a gesture that had become a habit with him since he returned.

''My hand is still a little thin, but it grows stronger. I will not ask you to alter it again!''

''Then you will accept another gift from me?'' Master Johannes beckoned Julian and Rana to follow him down the alleyway to an open door.

''This is the back way to your shop,'' said the King.

''Yes. My first love is goldwork, but my forges will melt harder metal.'' He led them to the hearth where Kieran plied the bellows, and pointed to the glowing coals.

Lying among them was a sword made of Light.

''It is almost ready for its first quenching. Will you accept it as a gift from me?''

Rana stifled a gasp, looked closer, and realized that it was only steel—it must be steel heated to incandescence. Hot air seared her skin and she flinched away. But Julian never stirred.

''Did you know that the Blood Wolves broke my blade when they captured me?'' he asked very quietly. ''This blade shall be born of blood and fire! When you finish it, make a setting in the pommel to receive the Jewel!''

''You would set it in a *weapon*?'' Rana exclaimed.

''I will never use the Jewels for destruction''—he gave her a quick glance—''but their protection I may claim. The Earthstone gleams already from the boss of my shield, and the Sea Star from my battle horn. I will set the Wind Crystal in my helm. But until now I did not know where to use the Jewel of Fire.''

He turned to the smith. "Johannes, you called me Master. Will you trust me to meddle in your mysteries now?"

"My lord, it is *your* blade!"

"And my blood will feed it!" A swift slash of Julian's dagger opened a red gash across his scarred palm, and he let the blood drip into the quenching vat. "Fire in the blood cools fire in the steel! Fire in the heart no pain will feel!" He took a deep breath, then reached into the fire and gripped the glowing bar of steel.

For a moment the King held it high, and the air shimmered in a visible aura of power. With a cry, he plunged it hissing into the red-stained water. When he withdrew his hand, Rana saw that the steel had seared the dagger slash closed. Beyond that livid line and the old scarring where he had first grasped the Jewel of Fire, Julian's hand bore no burn.

"Jewel Lord!" Master Johannes bowed more deeply than before. Rana's heart was pounding in her breast. Why was she so surprised? She had seen Julian walk through the fire. She herself had been a vehicle for Power. But Julian had not looked entirely human as he brandished that blade.

As they emerged from the goldsmith's front door, they saw Frederic pelting down the street toward them. Rana gripped Julian's arm.

"What is it?" she cried. "Is the Blood Lord coming here? Is he coming through the Misthall pass?"

"Not Misthall!" Frederic gasped. "The Blood Wolves were going to burn it in revenge for Blood Gard, but he stopped them!"

"*Who* stopped them?" Julian found his voice at last.

"Silverhair." Frederic gulped for air and reached out to them. "Silverhair is in Caolin's hands."

"No," whispered Julian. His fingers curled defensively as if to protect the half-grown nails. "Oh, Guardians, *no!*"

He closed his eyes. Rana put her arms around him, trying to still the fine tremors that shook him, but he burst free.

"Johannes!" he cried. "I want that sword by tomorrow dawn! Frederic, summon Eric and the commanders. If Caolin has hurt him—" He could not finish. He began to run down the lane, and Rana and Frederic followed him.

"Kill him!" shrieked the Blood Lord. "I told you to kill him three years ago!"

As brutal fingers dug into the harper's arm, a memory surfaced—a sullen crowd watching soldiers march along a street in Saticoy.

"Desterrado! Desterrado!" he cried. "Do you remember me?"

The red-cloaked figure stilled, and Silverhair stopped struggling. He took a calming breath of the cool air that was blowing across the road from the bay.

"*Desterrado* . . . but that was long ago," said the sorcerer.

Silverhair stared. He had never in all these years seen Caolin anything but immaculate, but now his tunic was soiled and stained. The flesh hung too loosely from its bones; the sorcerer was making no attempt to disguise the old scars that curdled the skin on one side from neck to brow. But it was the eyes that appalled him—oddly unfocused as if blinded from too much light.

"Landless no longer, Silverhair! Did they send you to plead with me?" The Blood Lord laughed, and Silverhair felt the fine hairs tingle along his spine.

"Julian did not send me," he answered quietly. "I came of my own will, Caolin."

"Many things might have been different if you had done that ten years ago." The sorcerer's voice cooled suddenly, and for a moment Silverhair saw the man he had met in Santibar. The sorcerer beckoned, and the guard let go. The canvas field tent was already up. An old woman brought a folding stool. As she set it down, she pulled back her ragged shawl, and with a shock he realized it was Alessia. A warning shake of her head redirected his attention to his enemy.

"And you brought your harp!" said Lord Sangrado silkily. "Will you die, I wonder, with it in your hands?"

"I would rather live," said the harper truthfully, "and play for you!"

The sorcerer laughed. "Do you think you can escape by charming your guards again? These men of mine are protected. Play if you like. You will make a different kind of music soon."

"Once you, too, were a musician, Caolin," whispered the harper. The Blood Wolves were laughing, and Silverhair did not know if his captor had heard. With trembling hands he eased Swangold out of the harp case.

Now he must play as he never had before. He watched Caolin covertly as he continued to test the strings. Julian had feared madness, but here was its source. He had already seen two different men look out of Caolin's eyes. He remembered so clearly the Seneschal's cold splendor when they both were young. Caolin had possessed such gifts—his potential for good was the measure of the evil he had done. *And what have I done with my own gifts?* the harper thought then. *But perhaps that doesn't matter. Only the music matters now.*

Unwilled, his fingers began to caress the strings. The melody that emerged was the chorale from the play the College of Bards had performed when they came to Laurelynn to tour that last summer before Jehan had died.

The camp was quieting as the confusion of putting up the tents ended and the cookfires began to burn. Golden light lent a richer glow to the dun hills and glittered on the sighing wavelets of the bay. Silverhair let the slow, sweet chords blend with the hush of waves sliding up the sand. Music trickled from beneath the harper's fingers like a rush of cool water. *Receive this gift of beauty from me,* thought Silverhair, *and remember that summer evening when we were all at peace. Listen, and remember the days when you were Caolin.*

The tide was coming in. Silverhair felt the music lifting him as a grounded boat is freed when the waters return. *This,* said the music, *is the meaning of everything—not conflict among men or between man and nature. But peace . . . peace . . . peace. . . .* The harmonies resolved and then continued as the incoming waters spread their shining veils across the sands.

From outside the Blood Lord's perimeter came faint echoes of laughter or cursing as the army settled in for the evening. But within earshot of Silverhair's music all was still.

"I remember." Caolin's voice was a whisper. "We sat by the lake in Laurelynn, and the water was like a mirror of gold."

"It was a mirror of light," Silverhair's voice echoed. "I looked into the lake and saw the bright spirit within me. . . . Look into the light, Caolin. What do you see?"

"Nothing!" The shout ripped mind from memory in a single searing blast. *"There is no Light!"*

Silverhair screamed as Swangold was ripped from his arms. The peace of the evening was shattered as rough hands hauled him upright.

"Traitor, were you trying to trick me again?" The hideous face that snarled into his own belonged to no one that he knew.

"Every crime that has been committed against me, every slight, every treason, burns in my memory! I never forget, harper, *never,* and you have owed me a life for twenty years!"

They let him fall, and booted feet thudded into ribs and spine, rolling him over and over. Already his heart was

leaping like a trapped hare. In a moment it must give out
and set him free.

"Roast meat, lord?" cried someone with hoarse glee.
"Tough meat, but fresh! May we eat him now?"

"No. He's the yokel-king's uncle, remember? He's deep
in their councils." The Blood Lord's laughter screeched
up the scale. "And now he is going to tell me everything
he knows."

Silverhair willed his heart to keep beating as he was
dragged upright again. *We wanted . . . to misinform
Caolin. Give me strength . . . to do it now.* A point of
light captured his vision, and he felt the sorcerer's mind
begin to bore into his own, *for Julian!*

*"Listen to me. . . . You hear no other voice, no other
will. Do you hear me, harper?"*

What a stupid question, thought Silverhair. He let his
head fall in a nod, and someone jerked it up again so that
he had to meet the Blood Lord's mad eyes.

"Speak to me!" The sorcerer mouthed soundlessly, but
the words reverberated inside the harper's skull.

"Yes, I hear you." The Voice drove out all other awareness. Silverhair's captive mind fluttered painfully, trying
to remember what he had to do.

"What is Julian doing?"

"Getting ready." That was an easy one. His head lolled
forward. The prick of cold steel at his throat brought
awareness jolting through him, and for a moment he was
freed from the sorcerer's will. *Music!* his spirit wailed.
Wind Lord, help me before I betray them all!

"Where is he now?"

"Bongarde," whispered the harper. There had been
something about Bongarde that he was supposed to say.

"Is Julian in Bongarde?" the Voice probed once more.

Silverhair shook his head. "Hurt—"

"You will hurt a great deal more if you do not answer
me!"

The blade pricked deeper and the harper focused again. His eyes rolled upward, and fixed on a red-tailed hawk that circled serenely above the bay.

"Tell me, harper—tell me about the King."

Silverhair's mind seemed to have divided. Part trembled at the sorcerer's unclean touch, but his spirit was with the hawk, and it seemed to him that the hawk was telling him what to say.

"Lord Eric . . . has sent Julian to Bongarde . . . to protect him. Gathering men . . . resist siege."

"Will we go to Seagate then?" Ordrey's voice seemed to come from very far away.

"Yes, I will take Bongarde and the King," replied the Blood Lord. "After that, the capital and Rivered will be easy."

Silverhair felt his senses leaving him, but it did not matter. He had done what he intended. The hawk spiraled into the sun.

When he became conscious once more it was dark, and the camp was quiet around him. Pain shot through his bound arms as someone turned him, and he moaned. He felt something warm wrapped around him; water touched his lips and he swallowed automatically; a dry hand smoothed back his hair. He was still alive. He wondered why.

"Alessia?" Silverhair recognized her profile against the sky.

"Forgive me," she whispered. "If I had known how Caolin hated you, I would not have made you tell me who he was at Santibar! They're taking us north with them tomorrow; I'll help you if I can."

"Don't risk yourself," Silverhair began, but she had straightened, listening. Alessia was a survivor. He wanted to give her a message for Julian, but she was already flitting away.

* * *

The sparrow hawk soared in the bright blaze of the afternoon sky. To the men who marched below, she was only a speck, of no interest to eyes that scanned the folded straw-colored hills through which they were marching, and squinted against the dance of sunlight on the great river as it rushed through the narrows into the bay. Even the Blood Lord, riding at the head of his Wolves, sensed no menace in that distant gaze.

But the bird's keen eye saw everything, and what the bird saw was understood by the man whose body lay motionless in the shadow of a ruined tower north of the river with a clear crystal winking upon his brow.

The mind of the Jewel Lord sent the bird soaring above the line, counting weapons and warriors and searching for Silverhair. Through the eyes of the bird, the King knew the moment when Caolin's scouts saw the men who were waiting for them where linked barges bridged three low islands and joined them to the causeway through the marshes on the other side. His control faltered as they closed. But Robert's frustration at being left to delay the enemy was now avenged, for the agony of watching someone he loved ride into danger without him drove Julian back into his own body again.

"What is it? Are they coming?" came Lord Eric's frantic questioning as the King groaned.

"I didn't see," whispered Julian. "They are at the barge bridge now!" He writhed with the need to know if Robert had escaped, and if the Blood Lord was going to cross the river. But the link with the bird had been broken. To try again with another would take time and energy that he did not have to spare. Fighters were still coming in to add to his army, and there were a thousand things yet to do. He struggled to his feet, leaning on a broken wall, and gazed across the flat marshes. But human eyes saw only the distant glitter of the river, with the jagged bulk of the Red Mountain rising beyond.

I was mad to pin all on one hope! he thought as he drank the barley water Rana handed him. He shivered despite the hot air. Not knowing was the agony. He forced himself not to think about Silverhair. Both he and the Master of the Junipers had searched for the harper's spirit, but if he still lived, the Blood Lord's wardings had hidden him.

"Our watchers in the marshes will signal if they cross the river," said Frederic. "If they press straight on, they should be here tomorrow afternoon."

Julian stared at the pale ribbon of road that led between the southern spur of the mountains and the hill with the tower. Once that fortress had guarded the road; in the time of the Jewel Wars brigands had swept down from it to prey upon the caravans. Now it was a king's stronghold. But still it watched the road.

Tomorrow . . . What would the tower see then?

Silverhair deceived me!

Caolin's gaze fixed on the green banner that had suddenly unfurled from the broken tower on the hill to the left of the road. Below it snapped a blue pennon with a single argent star. The clamor of the Elayan horns was transforming the column of marching men into a line that spread out to face the bristling barrier that had sprouted across the road. Behind it, the sun glittered on helmets. But the sorcerer scarcely saw them. He yanked his gelding's head around.

"My lord." Captain Esteban spurred toward him. "Don Niero and Lord Rafat are coming to confer."

Yes, of course, they would want orders. Was Julian behind that barrier, or was the King watching from the tower and laughing at his enemy?

"Bring the harper to me." At the Blood Lord's look, the officer's protest stilled. The gelding half reared as he pulled back, and one of the Blood Wolves took the rein.

"Lord Sangrado, we must make decisions!" Don Niero reached him first. The sorcerer stared at him, forcing back his rage.

"What decision?" Lord Rafat booted his pony forward, plumes waving. "The enemy is there; we fight! You think we should run away?"

"No son of the House of Alfuera has *ever* flee from a battlefield," Don Niero said silkily. Sun glared blindingly from his cuirass and his helmet's silvered steel. "Or refuse a challenge!"

"We *will* fight them—" Lord Sangrado's voice rasped across the Elayan's. "Soon. Our men must have a chance to arm, and to catch their breaths." He looked back at the barrier and the gap it guarded, trying to remember the lay of the land.

"Konradin! Take the Wolves and scout to either side. How soft is the ground in the marsh to the south of that hill? Make a count of the enemy." His glanced moved to the tangle of hills that marched away northward, covered with live oak and pine. No way through there, but he would have to keep a watch on the road eastward to the Great Valley.

The Wolf brought his hand to his chest in salute, then, without perceptible signal from its rider, the horse wheeled on its haunches and away.

"Wait." The Blood Lord's gaze returned to the two Elayans.

"Can your men overrun those defenses?" he asked, and the darkness of Lord Rafat's face was broken by a tight grin. "Of course you can," he went on. "The barrier is only woven brush, and the men behind it are only half-trained farm boys, after all."

"And the caballeros?" asked Don Niero.

"I realize that horses will not charge that barrier. But be ready, as the smith's hammer is ready to strike the anvil, to smash the foot soldiers when they flee.'' He tensed as he saw Ordrey approaching.

''Here he is—what's left of him!'' Ordrey smacked the mule's rump and the animal gave a little buck and trotted into the circle of Wolves.

''A prisoner? Now?'' The Elayan looked at the slumped figure on the mule's back curiously.

The sorcerer shook his head. He could feel Lord Sangrado's calm being overwhelmed by the Blood Lord's red rage, but for a moment longer he resisted it.

''We have lost the advantage of surprise,'' he hissed, ''but we can still shake them. . . . Cut him loose!'' he said to Ordrey.

Silverhair swayed as Ordrey slashed the bonds that held his ankles, then slid bonelessly to the dry grass. But his eyelids were quivering.

''No, you are not yet dead! Not even unconscious, though you may wish you were. Open your eyes, Farin Silverhair! Friends are waiting up on that hill!''

The harper's dark eyes opened, unfocused with pain. That would never do.

''Ordrey, give him the stimulant. I want him able to understand!'' The Wolves had not been kind. Blood and dust had grimed the captive's white hair; bruises mottled the skin that showed through the torn tunic and trews.

''Your slut at Misthall would not take you to her bed as you are now, harper!''

''There is . . . an army waiting for you, Caolin. Why waste time taunting me?'' Silverhair's words came distorted through swollen lips. The Blood Lord felt a hot pulse begin to beat in his temples.

''We don't have her here to play with, but perhaps there is something else you'd not see broken? That harp, for instance.''

Somehow Silverhair struggled upright, gaze flickering frantically until he saw the harp case tied to the saddle of the mule. The Blood Lord clambered out of the saddle, moved stiffly to stand above his captive.

"Caolin, you used to love music! The harp didn't harm you—punish me!"

"Very well! If you wish the harp to survive you, surrender your soul! Now that I know where to look, I will have the tally of Julian's forces." As Silverhair shook his head, the Blood Lord gestured, and Ordrey reached for the harp. The harper's dark gaze came back to his captor, and the sorcerer took his head between his hands so that he could not turn away.

"That's better," he whispered. "Farin Silverhair, answer me! How many foot soldiers does Julian have?"

"I don't know . . . when I left they were still gathering."

"How many did he expect? And the north? How long ago did he ask them for aid?" He saw the torment in the harper's eyes and laughed.

"Maker of Music! Wind Lord! Winged One! Deliver me!" cried Silverhair.

The sorcerer's grip tightened. "He cannot hear you. He cannot help you! You will speak to no one but me!"

The harper whimpered, but Caolin shuddered suddenly as his inner hearing was assaulted by a shimmer of sound that grew into a vibration that shook his soul. He glared around him. They could not hear it—it was all illusion, like beauty, like love! He reached within for his own perverted power song, but the other melody already possessed him. The music grew softer . . . pure sound resolved into a song that Caolin had once played for Jehan.

"Stop him!" The sorcerer jerked back. Silverhair's fingers were moving as if he plucked invisible strings. "Ordrey, stop the music. Break his hands!"

"Are you so afraid that you send a servant to take your revenge?" Silverhair's voice was faint, but in Caolin's inner hearing, the music surged and sighed, fingering the strings of memory. Ordrey weighed the pommel of his sword and wrapped cloth about the blade. All around them, men were whispering.

"Caolin, look at me! *I* am your enemy!" In the harper's voice he heard pity, and that was the most terrible thing of all. "You cannot do it, Caolin. If you let your minion destroy me, I have defeated you, and the music will never end!"

Harp notes rippled across his memory. *"The Lord we loved is gone."*

One voice emerged from the murmur. "He is mad."

"It shall not master me!" The sorcerer shrieked suddenly. *They shall not see me fail!* He ripped the sword from Ordrey's hands. "Bring me a stone!" The Wolves who had stayed with him bayed, scenting blood. "Hold his hands," he growled as they set the rock before him.

Silverhair stared at him, and Caolin saw the fear in his eyes, but the music soared triumphantly. "I will kill the music—so!" He gripped the cloth around the sword blade and brought the weighted pommel down upon the harper's hand.

Silverhair screamed. The heavy hilt cracked down upon the thumb—*there is no rhythm!* Upon the forefinger—*there is no harmony!* The pommel of the sword smashed into the clever fingers that had made Swangold sing.

There is no music; there is no love; there is no light! Caolin continued to hammer at the harper's hands long after the bones had shattered; he felt neither the tears upon his cheeks nor the smart as the edges of the sword cut through the cloth into his palms; he struck again and again, beating out upon the anvil of his hatred all of his own pain and fear.

And then, finally, the terrible music was still.

Caolin rose to his feet, and the sword slid unheeded from his bloody hands. All the world seemed silent—the men around him, the hawk that circled the sun. But that sun had scarcely moved in the sky, and his scouts were still galloping across the plain. So short a time to kill the music. Really, it had taken no time at all.

"He's still alive," Ordrey said presently.

"Yes." Caolin's voice sounded leaden in his own ears. If the harper ever woke, it would be to the knowledge of what he had lost, as once Caolin had awakened to— He shivered, and walled the memory away. "Sling him over the mule, and find a white flag, Ordrey. Once more you shall be my herald to Julian!"

EIGHTEEN

The King gave a last whack to the stake he was hammering into the ground and straightened, staring at the mass of men that had appeared like a mirage on the road. Why should he be surprised? The earth herself had told him they were coming—as the Blood Lord's forces drew closer, the message had passed from root to root through the grasses they trod.

He set his hands around the wood. *"Root fast, hold well."* He sent the mental command into the soil and felt a response vibrate along the tangled barrier of vines and coyote brush and manzanita from the hills. Awareness shifted to the humans who manned it—young faces flushed or pale, or grimly frowning veterans who had seen those fluttering Elayan plumes at the Battle of the Dragon Waste.

Behind the Westrian barrier stood four hundred unmounted fighters with swords and pole arms, interspersed with blocks of bowmen and slingers armed with pouches full of the lead pellets they had cast in Laurelynn. They were brave, but so few were trained! What could they do against these warriors who moved together like the limbs of a single monstrous beast?

"Time to get back to the hill, my lord." Loren Far-walker touched his arm.

Julian nodded. He knew that the total numbers of the two forces were almost equal, but the hollow boom of assegais on cowhide shields set his own pulse leaping. Then the swaying line opened to let a horseman through. The King saw the flicker of a white flag.

"They're sending someone out to parley!" Loren exclaimed.

"I wonder if our little hedge has frightened them!" said Julian loudly, and someone giggled. "The heralds will never forgive me if I don't let them go see. Warriors, don't expose yourselves unnecessarily—remember, your spears are two feet longer than their assegais. Archers, remember to shoot together at the first wave, then choose your targets carefully. And when you retreat, don't turn your backs to the enemy! You are taking the first shock, but the rest of us are waiting behind you, and the earth herself will give strength to your blows!"

"Hurrah for Julian!" came a call from down the line. "Julian and Westria!"

The King glimpsed the green blaze of Mistress Anne's cloak emerging from among the trees.

"Go out and see what they want," he said as she drew rein beside him. And then he could only wait as green and red cloaks moved toward each other across the straw-gold field. His guard was waiting beneath the trees at the base of the hill. Loren brought out his big bay mare and held her while he mounted. His shield already hung from the saddlebow. Still watching the field, he put on the helm the guard handed him. Sweat curled down his back beneath his mail and padding, gluing the shirt Rana had made him for his knighting to his skin.

In moment, it seemed, the herald was returning with another horse trailing behind her. Julian had no awareness of having set his mount in motion; no memory of the moment when he knew that the bundle slung across the beast's back was a man. His questing spirit touched a flicker like a guttering candle flame.

"Master! Rana! Frederic!" His mental call winged toward the healers' camp on the oak-covered knoll on the other side of the road. *"It's Silverhair!"* Julian flung himself from the mare's back as Mistress Anne reached the Westrian lines. The harper's dark eyes opened as the King lowered him carefully to the ground.

"I brought Caolin where you wanted him." The harper's eyes began to lose focus, and Julian held him tighter.

"You promised to play me into battle! You can't desert me now!"

The King felt the tide of sorrow as Silverhair's gaze moved to his hands. His own glance followed, and for the first time Julian saw what Caolin had done. The Jewel in the hilt of his sword blazed. Word whispered through the host like a sudden wind, fanning their own hatred of the Blood Lord to flame.

"Julian . . ." For a moment the touch of his uncle's mind held him. *"Better to lose me than the war."* Then Frederic and Rana were lifting the harper onto a litter. The King fought the compulsion to charge, shrieking, into the foe. *The Jewels—* He staggered as they amplified his own emotions back at him. *I have the power to destroy them all!*

"Julian! Stop! Caolin wants you to lose control, that's why he did this!" Rana was stroking his hair.

"He miscalculated," the King said tightly. "We all have reason to hate him now. Take care of Silverhair!" He squeezed Rana's hand. "Save him for me if you can!"

The booming of the enemy shields grew louder. The Westrian horns squalled their challenge, and suddenly the dark line with its fringe of white feathers began to move. The enemy came swiftly, almost dancing. Guttural cries throbbed through the air as they shook their short spears.

"Get back up the hill!" cried Julian, shoving Frederic away. He felt Rana's lips brush his, then she was following. As he hauled himself into the saddle he heard the enemy's chanting deepen; the Westrians' defiance shrill in reply. Archers and slingers were already busy. Some of the white plumes fell.

Then the first wave of Elayan warriors struck the Westrian line.

Julian stood in his stirrups as the fourth Elayan attack hit the Westrian line. His raw recruits had held longer than he would have thought possible. As each line of foes danced forward, the withdrawing warriors crouched so that their fellows could leap over them, then formed a new battle line. The enemy struck the barrier in a confusion of flashing spears. Behind them he glimpsed the sorcerer's red shape like a clot of blood upon the gold grass.

Now some of the spikes spitted bodies; men were scrambling over them until the enemy charged across the bodies of his own slain. So far the longbows positioned on the side of the hill had been able to guard the Westrians' southern flank, and scouts hidden among the reeds were bringing down any of Caolin's riders who got through.

The King stiffened as the tossing plumes speared forward. Was the line giving way? The neat diagrams in the texts he had studied had been deceptive. Battle was dust and the stink of blood and the confused cries of struggling men. More Elayans surged through where the weight of piled bodies had crushed a part of the barrier. The enemy column was cutting the Westrian line in two.

He grabbed for his horn, and the notes of the retreat fell through the air. Another horn call echoed from the top of the healer's hill. Julian smiled grimly, knowing who waited to hear that song.

The Westrians began to give way. Many were killed when they forgot their orders and tried to run from the enemy. But the more experienced fighters steadied the others. Spears bristling in a protective hedge, the foot soldiers moved backward, providing cover for the archers as they paused and shot, ran and knelt and shot again.

"Brave spirits!" whispered the King, "Steady now, steady as you draw them in." His foot soldiers were doing better than he had dared to hope, but now he could see how many fell beneath the impi's dreadful stabbing spears. His guards tightened shield straps and fidgeted with their lances. He glanced back and saw them watching him: tall Loren and Hal without his laughter, Alix and Davina, Roalt, burning to avenge the death of his lover Kevan, and the rest. Their eyes spoke for them: *"Our people are dying! When will you loose us upon the foe?"*

Then he felt a vibration in the earth more regular than the frantic scrambling of fighting men, and sensed before he heard it a rumble deeper than the clatter of steel on wood and mail. The Elayan column stretched out as the Westrians moved faster. He saw a blur of motion beyond them and laughed.

Once more his war horn blared; the Westrian foot strove to stop and lock their shields, and in that moment, Eric's heavy cavalry swept out from the fold in the hills where they had been hiding to strike the right rear flank of the foe.

"Now, friends, let's hit them!" He dropped the knotted reins on his mare's neck and booted her in the sides, getting a good grip on the lance in his right hand as she leaped forward and grasping the others with his left, behind his shield.

As the Westrians turned at bay the front rank of attackers was thrown back upon those who followed. A ripple of confusion spread through the Elayan ranks as the men in the rear tried to turn their assegais toward the cavalry who were thundering toward them, and those in front saw Julian's more lightly armed horsemen galloping in from the other side.

But Guardians, they were good! Even as the King's guards neared, the men of the impi were reforming, shields locking and assegais bristling into a barrier that no horse would charge. Julian shifted the mare onto her right lead and began to turn.

"Ready your lances! We've got to break that line!" He hefted his own weapon, gauging his moment, wondering if this would work after all. They were almost within range now. He spied a spot where the mass seemed thinner. "There, lads—there!"

And then his arm was swinging. He felt the wrench as the lance left his hand, grabbed for the next as he saw a plumed warrior go down. He kneed the mare around, headed her back toward the line at an angle and flung his other two lances into the press of men. From the other end of the column he heard shouting, but he could not stop to see. He urged the mare toward the gap in the line.

"Swordwork now, my comrades—into them and through!" Fire shot through him as he gripped the hilt of Master Johannes' sword. The blade sang sweetly from its sheath and the air blazed. Against that radiance, the enemy were shadows. The sword struck and struck again, and those who faced it fell.

Dust rose in choking swirls from the battlefield. But the Blood Lord knew it was not the dust that reddened the sunlight, but energy from the blood that was soaking into the hard-baked soil. There was so much! He felt it like the heat of some great fire. He drew it into himself with each breath, gorged but not glutted, until the air around him crackled with power. Never had he suspected the harvest of life energy that the sacrifice of so many lives would yield!

As the fighting surged back across the field the Blood Wolves tried to make him retreat, but they could not touch him. When some of Eric's heavy cavalry swept toward his command post, the sorcerer blasted them senseless. The throats of the survivors were cut by his Wolves. As Eric's tired men and horses withdrew to ready another charge, the Blood Lord mounted his rangy gray gelding. At his right hand rode Konradin, with the blood mark on his brow. With the pack trotting behind them, they advanced onto the battlefield.

> *"Blood Gard is blazing, now falls the dark fortress,*
> *But the Wolves of War live and they harry the land—*
> *What radiance shall scatter the shadow that rises?*
> *When blood feeds the battle, then how shall men stand?"*

Silverhair opened his eyes. "I didn't write those words." He could only manage a whisper, but Piper turned.

"It's your song. I've learned all your songs. I said I would sing them for you."

"I thought it was mine, long ago." The harper's grimace was meant to be a smile. "But I was only an instrument to set it free."

Rana was laying out more rolls of lint and muslin. He could hear the murmur of the Master's voice, keeping a patient in light trance as he finished sewing up a wound. But from below came the desperate shrilling of a horn.

"The battle—how goes the battle now?"

Piper shielded his eyes against the sunlight that slanted through the leaves. "It's all a confusion. Eric's knights and men in shiny armor are fighting. Ardra an' her sailors came up in boats a little while ago—can't see where they got to."

"Where is the King?"

"In the middle. Not much o' his guard left now."

Silverhair groaned. His fingers contracted as if to grasp a sword, and the pain swept him into the darkness again. But he was still conscious. He had visited this shadowland before. He looked around and saw a figure that shone through its veil of flesh as the red-hot rocks that warm the sweat lodge glow through their skin of stone.

"Coyote!" he spoke to the shadows.

"I am here . . . . Have you finished your work in the land of men?"

What did that mean? Was there a reason that his heart had continued to beat so long? Memory shook his serenity. *"I promised Julian a battle song!"*

Agony flared down his left arm. He was going to be sick—sight returned as he finished retching into a basin. His heart was hammering against its cage of bone. He whimpered as gentle hands eased him back against the blankets. Through a haze of pain he saw the Master of the Junipers and Malin Scar looking down at him.

"Am I dying?"

For a moment the adept did not reply. "If not, only the Guardians know why! If you cling to life strongly enough, you could live."

"And my hands?"

The Master's face told Silverhair all he needed to know. *"Your enemy will break your harp and the hands that made her sing."* A girl called Thea had prophesied it long ago. Siaran had repaired the harp, but even the Master could not restore smashed bone.

"No sword . . . no song," he whispered. "No use to anyone without hands. Now I know how Piper felt without words."

"But . . . you still loved me," said the boy.

The Master set his hand on Piper's shoulder. "And you still have the music within!"

"Caolin's bringing up his crossbows!" Rana hurried toward them. "Julian is surrounded—" She realized that Silverhair was conscious and broke off abruptly.

The harper shook his head. "Now I understand why my sister chose as she did, so long ago," he whispered, and saw the Master flinch, remembering how Faris had fought her last battle and why. *Coyote, wait for me,* he thought then. *I still have something left to do.* He forced more breath into his lungs.

"Set Swangold in my arms," he said aloud. Frederic looked quickly away and Rana was blinking back tears. But as Silverhair rested his cheek against the polished wood and felt the familiar weight against his breast a great content filled him. The pain seemed to belong to someone else. His spirit was free.

He wanted to say more, but Coyote was beckoning. With the harp clasped closely in his arms, Silverhair followed him.

Julian grabbed the rein of a riderless palomino Elayan battle charger and swung himself into the silver-mounted saddle. As he turned the beast, he suppressed a sense of disloyalty to his bay mare, who had taken one of the Blood Wolves' evil darts in the chest and died even as his own stroke sent the man's head flying. But the palomino was scarcely sweated. He felt the strength in its springy stride as he headed it back toward the fighting. He wished he had a fraction of that energy. He sucked air into his lungs and tried to draw up earth-power, but even that effort was almost beyond him.

It was all falling apart. He had not allowed for the impact of the highly disciplined Elayan forces on his untrained fighters. They were equal in numbers no longer. Even a late-arriving contingent of heavy cavalry from Las Costas had been unable to help them. Charging into the battle without plan or warning they had galloped straight into the path of Caolin's crossbows.

Oh, Robert, how I wish you were here beside me! he thought despairingly. *And how glad I am you're safe in Laurelynn!*

Julian glimpsed blue surcoats surrounded by the red cloaks of the Blood Lord's riders. He gave the palomino its head, feeling the elemental energies he had called on renewing him at last. The drumroll of hoofbeats was the enemy's only warning. The King saw them turning, white faces and dark stamped with a single shocked identity.

Then he was among them. One man fell beneath the palomino's feet, another was still lifting his sword when Julian's blade sliced down. A lance glanced off his shield and jabbed through the mail that covered his thigh. Then the palomino's hindquarters heaved beneath him as iron-shod hooves lashed backward, and he blessed the horse trainers of the Campos del Mar. When he reined the beast around, the other attackers were running away.

Hal and Alix were standing back to back above Davina's motionless body. He suppressed his sorrow, searched the field for other survivors. These two looked nearly done for—the Jewel Lord could draw power from his magic, but where was he going to find new strength for his army?

"Warriors of Westria, to me, to me!" he cried, and the Wind Crystal's power carried his voice across the bloody grass.

"For Julian and Westria!" came the answer. Like spirits coming out of the earth on Samaine Eve, his battered soldiers were rising from the battlefield. They staggered with exhaustion, but still they came, and an enemy that had thought them defeated was paralyzed by astonishment long enough to let them by.

We will make a last stand here, thought the king as he saw red cloaks and white plumes beginning to mass a few hundred yards away. A quick glance backward showed him the Seagate road open and empty. His reserves had already thrown themselves into the battle. Archers and slingers, their missiles exhausted, were picking up maces and swords. The axemen Philip had sent him from the Ramparts seemed to be the largest surviving unit. They should make up his center. He saw Eric's banner at the foot of the healer's hill—the Regent was trying to reorganize the remains of the cavalry. As Caolin's forces formed up, Julian began to shout orders. He swung off the palomino, told a man with one arm already in a sling to lead it to the rear. Then he checked his shield strap and took his place in the center of the Westrian line.

The earth was already trembling beneath the tread of his foe when a whisper of music reached Julian's ears. *It's the strain,* he thought, setting his feet more firmly. Again it came, at first faint as memory, then rising in ascending harmonies that banished weariness from the body and gave the spirit wings.

Harp music . . . Swangold's music . . . but that was impossible.

Even if Piper had tried to play, no harp that size could be loud enough to carry this far, and it was no fumbling touch that struck those strings. A sigh of wonder rose from the men around him. They heard it, too—a singing, swinging music that strengthened the heart and set the feet to stamping out a battle dance.

"Oh my comrades!" he cried as his sword flared high. "This is Silverhair's last miracle! Let his music bear us to victory!"

In the hidden land, a shadow harper played a shadow harp. At first the sound was only a whisper, but it grew stronger, and as the music soared, light sparked gold from the strings. Now brightness was flickering across leaf and stone. But the shadow land burned without being consumed, for the fire the music had ignited blazed within.

The harp glowed and the swan upon its pillar raised her head and spread her shining wings. Silverhair had thought the bright figure who had led him here was Coyote, but now he saw a hawk with eyes like the sun.

His fingers flashed across the harpstrings with the flexibility of his youth and the mastery of his maturity. And the light grew brighter still.

The Blood Lord heard that music and screamed in disbelief and rage. The rags of the Westrian army were charging like men in the first melee at the Summer Games, feet stamping in time. The sorcerer's fury forced his own men out to meet them, but they stumbled like village boys at a court dance. He let the remains of the impi and his own infantry stream out ahead of him.

"Esteban!" The mind touch reached the captain, whose troop now supported the formation's right wing. *"Take a dozen men to attack their healers' camp, on the hill."*

He sensed resistance. The enemy was in front of them. Why attack noncombatants? How could he leave his post now?

"The harper is there—his music is their weapon!" the sorcerer's thought pressed in once more. *"I should have killed him. Kill him now! Destroy them all!"*

The captain's pennoned lance came up in acknowledgment. The Blood Lord's center slowed a little, letting the sides curve out like a bull's horns to enclose the foe. But one group of men continued running. The sorcerer saw Captain Esteban outflank the Westrian left and pass it, heading for the hill. Then he focused upon his fighters, letting his own power flow out to feed them, struggling to keep his concentration against the terrible music that tormented his ears.

On the hill, the music overwhelmed all other understanding. It was like standing beneath a falling wave or in the midst of a forest fire or in the eye of a storm. Rana's heartbeat shook her whole body. Her hair lifted and sparked in an electric wind.

The wounded who could walk were reaching for their weapons; even those whom Rosemary had dosed with poppy twitched and murmured in their drugged sleep. Only the harper did not stir. But Swangold was a blur of brightness, vibrating as if invisible fingers were plucking that music from her strings.

Rana started toward Silverhair, and the music made her steps a dance. She felt the flutter of the harper's pulse, and fear fled before the glory of his song.

Her ecstasy was shattered by a scream.

Still half-tranced by the music, she seemed to turn in slow motion, saw bloody swords and wolf's-head badges and cloaks whose red stains mocked their crimson dye. Piper grabbed a broken spear that had been part of someone's stretcher.

"Here!" she yelled. "They're here!" Suddenly she understood the music. As the warriors ran toward her she felt no fear. She heard the spear shaft break and glimpsed Piper being flung aside. Red-clad men yelled as the wounded swarmed over them. Then harder wood clanged against metal and Piper's attacker staggered as Frederic's staff whipped down upon his helm.

Now Frederic was between her and the enemy. She saw a man who still looked like a soldier running toward them. A dark figure struck down the next two attackers and then came on like a shadow behind them. There was one left now—

"Esteban!" The voice of the man who had once been Caolin's most feared servant scraped across the music. The soldier whirled, staring.

"I know you," he began, but the other man was coming in.

They moved too fast for Rana's comprehension; steel rang a descant to the music, then the combatants sprang

apart again. Captain Esteban's brigandine was slashed, but
the padding had protected him. Wind shivered through the
oak leaves, and shifting sunlight struck red sparks from
the bright blades.

A ripple of harpsong filled the waiting silence. The distant clamor of the battle below was part of it, as was the
harsh breathing of the two warriors and Silverhair.

"You're Malin Scar," cried Caolin's captain suddenly.
"But you died three years ago!"

The music surged, steel flared and fell, and one sword
flew across the clearing in a wheel of fire. Captain Esteban's face paled as he realized that he was weaponless,
but Malin Scar only smiled and lowered his sword.

"The Shadower you knew is only my shadow now."

Captain Esteban shook his head uncomprehendingly, but
he made no resistance as Rosemary began to bind his arms
with a roll of bandages.

The enemy formation was disintegrating. The harpsong
soared, and then it was lost in the sweet calling of many
horns. Rana gazed toward the gap in the hills that led
toward the Great Valley and saw a host of spear points
catch the westering sun in a river of light as they flowed
across the plain.

She gripped Silverhair's shoulder. "Do you hear that?
Can't you hear it—we've done it! We've won!" She closed
her eyes; her awareness rushed outward in a flare of exultation, seeking his.

She heard the music of the horns and distant shouting.
She heard the hard-fought rasp of his breath drawn once,
again, and then no more. Silently she began to call his
name.

Silverhair's glowing hands played a harp fashioned from
flame. He felt Rana's joy, but he could not stop playing.
His harp was the sunlight, his harp was the wind. Light

danced with light in unending vibration of particles as he touched the strings.

"Silverhair, can you hear me? Silverhair . . . we love you!"

Astonished, he understood that what Rana said was true, and believing that, believed at last that Julian and the others loved him, too. He felt her love lifting him.

He was the light, he was the music. The last fear that had constrained him was consumed. His awareness expanded, and in a surge of Light and Music beyond the comprehension of human senses was swept away.

NINETEEN

"Renegades of Westria, you are surrounded. Send the traitor Caolin out to me!" The King pitched his voice to carry across the battlefield. The gray ranks of the Blood Wolves hid the sorcerer, but Julian could feel him behind them burning like a dark fire. Triumph made Julian's pulse leap wildly. *Now you will be* my *prisoner!*

The swords and the assegais that the Blood Lord's Elayan allies had cast down when they saw they were surrounded lay piled before him. Their owners were being guarded by Westrian archers until someone had time to arrange terms for ransom. The field was Julian's. Someone had even rescued Lady Alessia, battered but undaunted, from Caolin's baggage train.

Others were quartering the battlefield, searching for signs of life in the bodies that covered it—so many bodies! Already the coyotes were summoning their brethren to feast on the slain. Only the remains of the army of Blood Gard still stood in arms, locked shields facing Julian's tattered infantry and the scarcely blooded knights of the Corona and Normontaine. Behind them, a swollen sun sank through the dust-stained sky and its deepening light touched the dry grass with flame.

"Do you think you have won, little king? This day has been no more than a winnowing!"

Julian stiffened as every cell in his body recognized that voice, and yet it seemed disembodied, as if the wind had spoken, or the stones. What if the sorcerer took another form in order to flee? The King touched the Jewel set into his shield and let his consciousness sink into the earth, asking the people of root and blade to tell him if his enemy moved.

"You cannot escape, Caolin," he said tiredly. "Why sacrifice more men?"

"Why, indeed?" came a new voice. A man stepped out from the ranks of the Blood Wolves. "I am Konradin, and I challenge you. Why should tired men fight when the issue can be decided by a combat of champions?"

The King glimpsed fair hair beneath the gray wolf's mask that covered the man's helm and for an instant he thought it was Caolin. He opened his awareness a little, sensed an almost feral excitement and a mind fixated on a face that shone with a terrible beauty—Konradin's vision of his master. With a visceral shudder, Julian realized what he might have become if the Blood Lord had conquered him. The other warrior was his distorted mirror, and behind him the shadows of Caolin's torture chamber swirled.

"No! There's no need!" Eric shouldered his way through the ranks and gripped the King's arm. "We have the force to mow them down!"

All day he had controlled his rage. He had killed without hatred, from necessity. But now he understood what wrath was for. Julian blinked, searching for logic that would not betray his compulsion to destroy what he saw in Konradin's eyes.

"The horses won't charge that shield wall, and our infantry are exhausted. It's going to get dark soon. Shall we give Caolin all night to think up new deviltry?"

Eric's face showed that he was obeying the King's tone, not his words, but after a moment he let go, and the King strode out to face the Blood Lord's champion.

The man moved like the wolf whose pelt he wore, efficient, flexible. Konradin grinned, and for a moment the King was horribly reminded of Coyote. But Julian's own resolve was fueled by the passion of the Westrian army. The King could feel Caolin's power blazing through the man before him. His greaves creaked as he settled into a defensive crouch, peering at his enemy from beneath the brow band of his helm. More than two warriors faced each other here. His enemy was Blood Gard; and Julian *was* Westria.

Konradin padded to the right, gripping his long blade two-handed, and Julian turned to face him, their shadows shifted across the burnished ground. Now the world was no more than this widdershins circle; its only inhabitants, Julian and his enemy.

Don't think! the King told himself. *Be!* There had been no time to worry during the battle, only the moment between action and reaction when even as the brain was registering danger, trained reflexes responded. He strove to recapture that mindless balance. *I am the Sword . . . I am his Sword . . . I am . . .*

Shadow flickered between them, merged and parted as the blades belled. Julian staggered as Konradin's counterstroke carved across his shield; then his turn drew it free, the momentum brought his own blade flaming through the space where his enemy had been, and he whirled away once more.

Konradin leaped after him. Off balance, the King swerved; steel scraped, then he felt a sting as his foe's blade struck past the skirts of his mail and sliced into his thigh. His return stroke brushed grizzled fur; his enemy's laughter thinned, descanted into an exultant howl.

Julian's heart drummed in his breast. The Wolf stalked at the end of his shadow and Death danced between them. *I accept you,* said the Warrior within him. *I accept all.* His thigh was throbbing, not to be trusted; he rooted himself in the earth, licked dry lips, and steadied his breathing as his foe came in. His lifting sword flared in the sunlight. For a moment the Wolf's lope faltered.

The King's sword seared the air. The twist of his hips shifted weight: the blood-tempered blade bit through the leather sark that protected his enemy, through shirt and skin and the protecting cage of bone. Konradin lurched and his sword arced skyward in a wheel of flame.

"Wolfmaster!" The wounded man staggered backwards, holding his guts in with clasped arms. The Wolves stepped aside. Was that cry an accusation or an appeal? Panting, Julian glimpsed the sorcerer, red robes redstained, pale eyes burning in his skull.

"Drink—" In the silence even that whisper seemed loud. Konradin slipped to his knees before his master, clawing the leather armor away. "Drink . . . life!"

Blood gushed from the wound. As Konradin collapsed, the Wolfmaster stooped. There was a swift jerk, and the sorcerer held up something red and pulsing. In his dreams Julian had seen this—he had thought himself beyond horror—but Konradin's blood filled the world.

Bile burned his throat, but he could not look away.

Sweet, cloying . . . salt sour tang . . . For a moment, the sorcerer felt regret, then exultation as the hot sweet blood set new life leaping through every vein.

"Konradin lives!" the Blood Lord cried. "He will live forever!" The air shivered to the Blood Wolves' ecstatic howls. The sorcerer tore into Konradin's gift again, gulping, swallowing. The drifting life energies that had intoxicated him during the day were like the scent of a feast, but the Wolf-warrior's heart blood was the reality; he quivered with power.

"Caolin, surrender!" came a cry. "Or you betray the word of the man who gave his life for you!" Horns blared. Through a red haze, the Blood Lord saw men approaching; a sweep of one arm sent them reeling, leaving Julian standing alone.

"I am the Blood Lord! Puny mortals, do you think I play by your rules?" He laughed and changed his semblance. Now they would see him robed in living flame, towering above the battlefield. He masked his face with his own most perfect beauty, then replaced that calm smile with the contorted grimace of a Nippani demon and laughed again when men's bowels betrayed them in their fear.

How they cowered! How they ran! And this was an old magic. The power of illusion had been his first mastery, long ago, when he had been . . . Caolin. Memory struggled to assimilate that purity of control with the savor of his most recent dreadful meal. *It was necessary . . .* came the cold conclusion. *It is a means to power.*

"Caolin, Caolin, I see you!" The voice of the King slashed through his concentration. "You are scarred! You are ugly! You are old!"

Reflex wrapped shadow around him—but Julian's eyes were still fixed upon his face. *"I know you,"* said that gaze. Bound by the awful intimacy of the torture chamber to his enemy, the sorcerer felt his control wavering. He needed more power—

—and suddenly energy blazed once more before him. He focused outward, saw one of his Wolves sway as a red dagger fell from his hand. He reached out, and the man collapsed into his arms, blood spurting from a slashed throat. The sorcerer bent, drank blood, drank life, then let the limp body fall.

"Oath-breaker! Blood-drinker!" screamed Julian. "Do you think you can destroy *me*? I slew your champion. I challenge you now!"

Caolin felt the King's rage resonate against the fury that fueled his own soul and snarled. Did the boy think to defeat him with his own weapons?

The sorcerer reached inward, and a low vibration tormented the air. Katiz had taught him this song, but the old shaman of Awhai had never sung it with such power.

*"Darkness flows, darkness grows, darkness knows
How to blind, how to find, how to bind!"*

He pitched the evil song to carry outward in wave upon wave of distorting vibration that disoriented thought and warped memory, and the shadow that shielded him thickened and began to roll outward. No harper's melody would ever heal this music!

"I summon light of dawn—now shades of night be gone!"

Another voice soared above Caolin's dissonance, so strongly that for a moment he could hear nothing else, and radiance flickered painfully through the shadows that protected him. He drew breath, began anew:

"Shadows fall, as I call, smother all!"
"I summon light of noon—all shadow's banished soon!"

Again came the alien singing, trapping each note of the sorcerer's song in a terrible harmony. New chords quivered in the heavy air. Caolin felt the sound as a physical pain. He glimpsed white light blazing from the King's brow.

"No!" he cried suddenly. "I killed that song!" Silence, abrupt and deafening as the stillness after thunder, surrounded them. And then Caolin tasted the red pulse of life again as another of the Blood Wolves gave him his soul. Power flowed from his fingertips and the darkness surged outward again.

> *"Circle round, sight and sound now are bound,*
> *Circle back, all goes black, reason, crack!"*

Darkness spun around him in a widdershins whirl that widened suddenly to encompass the sorcerer's enemy. The Blood Lord heard wailing from the Westrians as it swallowed their king, and the hurtful radiance that had played about him dimmed.

> *"I summon sunset light to challenge shades of night!"*
Julian cried.

> *"Gather night, darken sight, extinguish light,"*
the Blood Lord answered, then laughed. "What will you summon at midnight, little king? Admit yourself beaten! Now you belong to me!" For a heartbeat he waited, but Julian had no reply.

Caolin gestured, and another of the Wolves came to him eagerly. Once more the sorcerer drank power, and this time when he lifted his hands a shadow passed across the sun. The sphere of darkness was expanding. Soon it would overwhelm the world!

> *"Summer day pass away! Night will stay,*
> *Night is here, death is near, see and fear!"*

No eclipse had ever been so complete, no darkness so terrible. The fear of the Westrian armies fueled the Blood Lord's spell and the land trembled at the early nightfall, like a pendulum checked before it had completed its swing.

"Once I offered you the Void as a haven," cried Caolin.

"Now it will be your prison, Julian. *Nada empties all of meaning now.*"

A dim glow pulsed feebly ahead of him. The King was trying to conjure up the fire that had freed him in Blood Gard, but this darkness was not simply that of the spirit. Using the physical energy of human lifeblood, the sorcerer had warped the laws that allowed light to reach the world.

The sorcerer swept toward Julian with the remaining Blood Wolves behind him. The darkness pulsed with pallid flickers as the life energies of the men around him gave them an eerie visibility. He licked his lips, anticipating how they would feed his hunger. And then there would be no one to hurt and no one to suffer. There would be nothing at all. . . .

The King lifted sword and shield to guard as the sorcerer approached him. The radiance of the Jewels he bore had paled to a ghostly glow.

"Now it is midnight," said the Blood Lord. "Now I will drink your soul!"

Julian stood in a realm of ghosts and shadows in which only the crimson glow of the sorcerer was real. But that red shimmer emitted not light, but its opposite. In this realm all laws were reversed—death was life, and darkness visible. The Blood Lord lifted his hands, and the shadows around him curdled toward his foe.

"I summon hidden light," whispered Julian desperately. But what did that mean? He tried to remember what the world had looked like in the sunshine, but all his memories were shadowed. Julian tried to lift his sword, but there was no strength in his arm.

Now the sorcerer was before him; his mouth red with other men's blood, their life force glowing in his eyes. Bony hands reached out, skin stretched skull-tight as Caolin grinned, and for a moment, Julian wanted to go to him.

I can't just stand here and let him take me: I am the Jewel-Lord! Julian told himself. His awareness tried to tap their familiar powers, but they belonged to the world of sunlight and rain. He could sense only the faintest glimmer of their forces here.

"Ah . . . the Jewels . . ." said the sorcerer. "Once I desired them. Now I will destroy them."

"If you do, you will destroy Westria, and there will be nothing for you to rule!"

Caolin nodded. "Just so. Life is a delusion that I have done with, Julian. Our battles have taught me that the world of the elements is untidy, imperfect, obscene. When I have conquered, there will be nothing left at all."

He blinked and beckoned. One of the Blood Wolves came forward, smiling ecstatically.

"My body for your food, my blood for your drink, my spirit for your life, my lord!" The dagger in the man's hand flashed and fell. As he staggered, the Blood Lord grabbed him in a parody of an embrace.

Julian stared. Was he becoming used to this horror? No, this time it was not revulsion but pity that tightened his throat, and suddenly he understood.

"You reject the physical, Caolin—but that is what gives you your power!"

The sorcerer let the body of his sacrifice fall, and Julian took an involuntary step backward.

"Death is sweet when freely offered! But for you it will be pain!" raged the sorcerer.

Julian lifted sword and shield defensively as a tendril of darkness snapped toward him. He braced himself, but his shield seemed suddenly lighter, and as if from a great distance he sensed a shudder of pain. *The Earthstone!*

Darkness lanced toward the crystal on his brow, and the stones in the band of his horn and the pommel of his sword. The King's spirit curled away from the pain, toward that deep place where he did not need to touch the

Jewels to use them—into that sanctum where his soul-light blazed. . . . Words roared through his awareness.

"I summon hidden light, and see with spirit sight!"

Julian opened his eyes.

All around him he saw the spirit shapes of leaves and grasses and men. He saw the soul-fires burning in Caolin's soldiers, saw the confused flicker of stolen lives in the body of the sorcerer. And the light of the Jewels blazed all around him, glowing through clouds and green leaves, flickering in fire, sparkling on the sea. How could he not have known it? The Jewels were only a focus, not the source of the Power.

Suddenly Julian laughed, and the darkness rippled around him.

"Do you want the Jewels? The sacrifice is sweet when given freely!" Still laughing, he detached the Jewel of Fire from the hilt of his sword and held it out to the sorcerer. "You asked for it!" he cried. "Take it now!"

The Jewel touched Caolin's hand, and the Blood Lord screamed.

Agony blazed through every nerve in Caolin's body as the Jewel of Fire touched his skin. The Lady of Darkness rose before him and burst into flames. Suddenly he saw Blood Gard burning and heard the screams of trapped horses and hurt men. No, it was a cabin they had torched when he rode with the northern woods rats; there had been children inside. He heard their cries, and they were his own; he felt their pain. A hundred other memories seared his awareness, burning away the illusion of separation that had armored him.

Caolin tried to cast the Jewel from him, felt the sharp jab of the Wind Crystal replacing it, and screamed again as a great wind whirled the shadows away. Light exploded through his darkness. Words exploded through his consciousness—a babble of dialogue that he had thought banished from memory.

"Caolin, what do you love?" It was Julian's question, but the sorcerer had not answered it then.

"Caolin, remember that I have loved you." That was Jehan's voice, and now he could not escape the knowledge that what the King had said was true.

"My little one, Mama loves you—see, I'll kiss the pain away." Those words came from a place beyond memory; even now Caolin dared not wonder if she had lied.

"Please," he whispered. He dropped the crystal, but his groping hands closed on the Sea Star, and a great tide of emotion rose and carried him away.

He was weeping; he knew only the sighing of the waves and the surge of their music and the pure pain of loss as the receding tide drew all his dreams down into the depths of the sea.

Dizzied, he fell, arms flailing. Then Julian pressed the Earthstone into Caolin's palm, and everything grew solid once more. The dry grass beneath him was real, and the soft light of sunset. He stared at a stalk of wheat beside his outstretched hand—an old man's hand. *I am old.* Awareness grew within him. *Like the earth, I am dust.* The Jewel rolled from nerveless fingers.

The wheat trembled as men rushed past him. Caolin heard cries and the clash of steel. He would not have moved, but suddenly someone was lifting him. Shadow shapes of soldiers slipped between him and the brilliance of Julian's eyes.

"My lord! Caolin, we've got to get you away!"

It was Ordrey, with Blood Wolves behind him. Caolin smelled fresh blood and gagged. Julian's sword flashed and one of them fell, then the others swept in between.

"Oh, Guardians! Look at the barrier!" came a scream. "The vines are moving, they're dragging our men down!"

The voice was cut off and he glimpsed Julian turning to see. Then Ordrey hustled him away.

What was he doing here? This was not Spear Island—he hurt too much. Was it the Red Mountain? The scars where the Jewels had burned him ached furiously. His mind was still reeling from the explosion that had torn them away. *Jehan . . . wait for me!* his spirit cried, but the King was gone.

"My lord, can you walk? I can't carry you any farther." Ordrey was panting. Caolin tried to focus. The plain behind him pulsed with struggling men as the Westrian army fell upon the last of the Blood Lord's irregulars.

Not the Red Mountain—that was twenty years ago. But Ordrey was still helping him. He forced his feet into motion, then stumbled again as a sharp howl split the air.

"Blood Wolves, stop runnin'." The call trailed off into a yip and the Wolves who followed their master stopped in their tracks. Caolin whimpered as he saw a coyote trotting across the field. *"Beasts yer named, an' acted worse than men! But yer not my business—let Wolf judge ye!"* Coyote sat down, tipped back his pointed muzzle, and howled.

A glimmer of silver light flared suddenly beside him, outlined a wolf shape that lengthened into the figure of a man. But this man was crowned with a mane of silver-gray hair, and he observed them from glowing yellow eyes.

"You have perverted the name of Wolf," he growled. "You have broken the Covenant. Blood Wolves you called yourselves, and fed on others—you shall feed the blood of wolves now!" His laugh became a deep howl; light blazed around him, and then he was gone.

"Wolfmaster!" One of Caolin's men turned with dagger half drawn. "Help . . ." The next words were a terrified squeak. Before the knife hit the ground the human form was dwindling. In moments, a brown field rat was scurrying through the grass.

"Oh, demons and devas!" muttered Ordrey. "He's changed them all!"

The trodden wheat was all aquiver as the rats sought safety. One of the coyotes that had come to scavenge pounced suddenly and came up with a twitching brown body in its jaws.

Caolin felt the world rush away from him, as if he were falling down a well. All he could see was the look in the Blood Wolf's eyes. *Even then, he was trying to offer his life to me.* He was walking again, but he could see nothing at all.

But his sacrifice would have been willing, he told himself. *"Who gave you the right,"* came a second voice within him, *"to eat the lives of men?"*

I had the will and the intelligence . . . should I have let myself be ruled by fools?

"And where," came the voice implacably, *"has your intelligence brought you? Master of fools, where is your magic now?"*

Caolin reached for his power, and there was nothing there. A void, an emptiness . . . a refuge? He could feel it sucking him in and twitched away in fear.

"That is where you trapped Katiz—that is where you would have trapped Julian," said the Judge within him.

I don't want to remember that! He thrust the memory of Katiz's terror into the darkness and saw it disappear. Was this the way to evade his accuser? His giggle of triumph died as he heard once more how Silverhair had screamed as he broke his hands, remembered the pity in the harper's eyes and then, across the years, the terrible beauty of Wind Lord's song. *But I killed the music.*

And then the Void took that memory, too. But there was no time for peace. He remembered Ardra's revulsion when she learned that he had fathered her, remembered how he had blackmailed Prince Ali; the faces of all the men and women he had used and betrayed swam before him. *I don't know you!* he cried, and all those parts of his life disappeared.

"Master, we can rest here—the sun is going down. Maybe we can get through their lines when night falls."

They stopped moving. Caolin let his legs give way beneath him. He could see again, but only dimly—perhaps that was the fault of the failing light. Ordrey was still taking, but Caolin paid no attention. The images that filled his inner vision were so much more real.

Now it was Jehan whose face filled his awareness. He remembered all the love that had been between them and the final betrayal, and, trembling, thrust the memories away. But that only led him to Faris, and then to Julian. Ordrey pulled him down in the grass as knights from the Corona rode past them through the gathering dusk, but Caolin was remembering how Julian had screamed beneath the torturers' hands, and how, for a moment, he had not hated the boy at all. *No, don't remember Julian or he will hurt you again.* Shuddering, he extinguished the memory.

At the College of the Wise they had taught this kind of self-examination. Briefly he relived the terror of his failure to reach the Sacred Valley and then gave up the memory. But before he attempted to reach Awahna, he had sat for three days on a mountainside, trying to purge his soul. What had he remembered then? What, even then, had he refused to recognize?

He was striding up the road from the steading at Round Hills on his way to the college. Behind him his mother was weeping, but he did not turn. Why hadn't he looked back at her? He tried to remember her face, saw a woman old before her time with a bruise on her brow. *She betrayed me.* But even the Judge within could not find a way past that knowledge. Caolin whimpered and felt Ordrey patting his shoulder.

"Don't worry, my lord. Even Julian's not going to find us once it's full dark here!"

"Who is Julian?" asked Caolin.

"Oh, dear," said Ordrey. "The sooner I get you to shelter the better it will be! Let me just have a look." Ordrey pushed himself to his feet and turned to gaze back at the hill where the ruined tower poked jagged teeth against the darkening sky.

There was a sound. Caolin knew he should recognize it, but he could not remember. Ordrey grunted, and his master looked up at him. In the middle of Ordrey's pale tunic, a gray-feathered arrow was still quivering. Ordrey shook his head, then sat down suddenly, coughed and fell backward into the grass.

"Master, be careful." He frowned and coughed again, and then the meaning faded from his eyes. Caolin reached out to touch him, but he did not stir. A fragment of knowledge brought his hand to the fat throat, but no pulse beat there.

"Ordrey." His vision blurred suddenly, but could not blot away memories of the laughing young man who had become his first agent when he was still a deputy, of the hours Ordrey had spent nursing him after he lost the Jewels, of a service that had lasted over thirty years. "You never betrayed me!"

"You killed your friend!" Suddenly that pain was too great. The darkness was gathering. Let Ordrey go—let it all go, everything!

He allowed the darkness to flow over him, erasing all the knowledge that remained until there was nothing in his memory, not even his name. He had sworn to obliterate the realm of Westria, but it was the citadel of his reason that had been destroyed.

Nada empties all of meaning now.

The Void gaped wide before him. But it was no longer

empty. Faces glimmered there, watching him with snarling lips and glowing eyes.

"He burned me!" One of them darted toward him. *"He drank my blood!"* hissed another. *"He tortured me!"* The man in the bloodstained red robes flinched. Perhaps he could have named and repelled these spirits, but he had given up the memories that might have defended him. Now all light was gone from the sky. The Void surrounded him, and gibbering ghosts thronged the shadows.

And then suddenly, other spirits were darting between him and his tormentors—warriors in wolfskin cloaks who used ghostly swords to keep the attacking ghosts away. He wondered who they were.

"Run, my lord!" cried the ghost of a fat man in a bloodstained white tunic. *"We'll cover you!"*

The man tried to understand. Perhaps if he moved they would not want to hurt him anymore.

Could he walk? He staggered upright. In the darkness, his red robes were only a darker blot against the reeds. While the Westrians searched the battlefield for their slain, the man in red stumbled through the marshes toward the river.

No living soul saw him go.

TWENTY

Slowly Julian climbed the knoll beyond the healers' hill-top where they had built Silverhair's funeral pyre. Behind him, cleft peaks lifted starkly against a golden sky, but the marshes and all that lay beyond them were lost in a shimmer of haze. Two crows flew silently across the valley and settled upon the top branch of an oak tree, watching him.

The body wrapped in the purple cloak seemed smaller than Julian remembered, but the harp was still cradled in Silverhair's arms. When at last the King had found time to go to him the night before, it had been possible to imagine that the harper was only sleeping. What the King saw now looked like an image lying there.

It was the end of the day after the battle, and only now had they finished scouring the hills for stragglers and made a final tally of the slain. The bodies of the Blood Lord's men had already been burned in a pit at the edge of the marshes and covered with stones. Ordrey's was among them, but no one could say what had become of his master. For Julian, it was enough that Caolin's name was gone from the land.

This was not how the King had expected to feel after the battle. He ought to be elated. They had won, and though he ached in every bone, he had scarcely been touched in the fighting. But there were so many dead, so many still suffering. What he felt, it occurred to him suddenly, was shame.

Silverhair would have had some sardonic comment to comfort him. Silverhair could have made music to charm his grief away.

A pure thread of flutesong soared above the silence, as if the winged spirit of Music was singing Julian's sorrow to the world. He blinked and realized that the slopes of the knoll were filling with people. Was it time already? The wings of the golden swan on the harp gleamed softly in the fading light.

"They shouldn't burn th' harp that saved us," whispered someone. " 'Tis magic!"

"Only in the hands of the harper," a woman answered, and Julian recognized Mistress Siaran. He was glad that the message he had sent by one of Bird's hawks to the College of Bards had enabled her and Aurel to get here in time. "And the pillar is cracked through the grain. Neither Swangold nor Silverhair will ever sing again."

She had been weeping. Everyone had been weeping. *Only I,* thought the King, *am like a barren tree in a burnt land.* Tears would bring healing, they had told him. But if he wept, the shell that had upheld him since he walked out of the Blood Lord's furnace would shatter, and there was only emptiness inside. Still turning, he met Rana's clear gaze. *Don't you understand?* his own look replied. *I have nothing to give you or anyone!*

The Master of the Junipers was sitting in a huddle of gray robes on the other side of the pyre. *He looks half dead himself,* thought the King. *Has he slept since the battle began?* By now the worst hurt were dead or mending. Rosemary and the other healers were here. Robert had ridden straight from Laurelynn.

Silence gathered as the light faded. Julian touched his torch to the lamp that was burning beside the pyre and watched it flare.

"The wanderer's path is at an end," he spoke the words. Even if he could have trusted his voice, to sing Silverhair's song would have seemed a blasphemy.

> *"The quest complete, the task all done,*
> *And we who gladly called him friend*
> *release him with the setting sun,*
> *for he has ceased from wandering."*

There was a little murmur as folk who knew the harper's road song realized how Julian had altered the ending. The King moved around the pyre, and the torchlight, already brighter than the radiance of the fading sky, warmed the faces around him, and touched the still features of the dead with illusory mobility.

"The first time I ever saw Farin Silverhair he played for me. He played for us all at the end." He looked at faces rapt with remembered wonder. Had the others heard words within that music? The harper's voice had spoken to his soul: *"Music never dies; love never dies; my love for you will never die, Julian!"*

"Now"—he swallowed"—it is time to say good-bye." He bent to kiss the cold brow, and knew finally that Silverhair was gone.

Frederic helped the Master of the Junipers to get up, but the old man seemed to put on power like a priestly garment as he moved around the piled logs, sprinkling them with sweet herbs. The flames were blowing backward from the torch as if reluctant to touch the pyre. The Master began to sing.

> *"Ashes fall to dust,*
> *Blood become a mist,*
> *Breath smoke from the pyre.*
> *Spirits spark the fire!"*

The King thrust the torch between the logs and stepped back. The sudden heat seared his skin, yet he found himself shivering. He wanted to weep as the others were weeping, but his eyes burned.

"Oh, Rosemary, Julian's eyes are like holes in a blanket!" exclaimed Rana as she watched him follow the Master around the pyre. "Silverhair looked healthier!"

The oil-soaked logs caught quickly, veiling the still shape of the harper in bright flame. As the wind freshened, showers of sparks went whirling up to challenge the stars. Lord Eric and Rana's father cast sweet herbs on the fire and spoke of Silverhair's deeds as a warrior; then Aurel Goldenthroat stepped forward to praise his music.

"A singer of tales, his life was a greater legend than any story he sang." The bard's head bowed, firelight gleamed from his bright hair. "My masters at the college taught me *how* to play—Silverhair showed me *why*!"

Rana fingered the garland of flowers she had made to throw on the fire. What would she say when her own turn came? Better than most here, she understood the reasons for the choices the harper had made. She had been holding on to him when he died; she still felt the exaltation of his victory. It was the living man who stood beside his pyre who concerned her now.

"He was like my father." Piper marched up to the flames, clutching his flute. "He—" His faced twisted. "I'll sing his songs, best I can!" he burst out after a brief struggle. "An' carry his name."

"Farin Piper I name you!" exclaimed the King, and

something in his face relaxed a little at last. "When your training is done, come to me and be my bard!"

At least he's beginning to think about the future, thought Rana. Frederic and Ardra gave their tribute together, and Rana watched them with envy. Ardra's arm was in a sling, but they had finished with fearing for each other, and their faces shone.

As the flames devoured the stacked logs, others were coming forward, casting their offerings on the fire and sharing their memories. Silverhair had always seemed so alone, and yet in his death all Westria was his family.

Two figures moved toward the pyre at the same time, and Rana stiffened, recognizing Mistress Siaran's purple cloak and realizing that the other woman was the Queen of Normontaine. Rumor whispered that Silverhair had been more than a student to the harp mistress, and more than court harper when he was in Normontaine.

"He was a lover of music and music made him a lover!" said Siaran, not caring that all could see her tears. For a moment Mara of Normontaine paused; then she threw back her veil and gave the other woman a little complicit smile.

"He touched a woman's body as gently as he touched his harp, a giver of delight who let Love make him its instrument—"

"—as Music spoke through him when he sang," added Mistress Siaran. The rumors, apparently, had been true. As Silverhair's two ladies spoke of him, their faces shone with the memory of joy.

That's what love is supposed to be! thought Rana, listening. *A service and an offering! Did Silverhair ever understand why women loved him?*

Once more her gaze moved to Julian. The sheer physical presence that was sometimes so overwhelming was muted now, but even grief could not extinguish the strength in him, the grace—all those qualities that he had begun to manifest as he mastered the Jewels. Yet what made her want to hold him was none of these but simply the patience with which he stood there, enduring his pain.

The framework of logs fell inward and flames bloomed above the coals with sudden splendor, as if the Lady of Fire Herself had been drawn by the praises of the two women who mourned him to carry his spirit away.

"Lady, listen to me—I have a living man to awaken, and I don't know how!" Her prayer whirled upward with the flames.

"Elements reclaim," said the Master of the Junipers, raising his arms in blessing and farewell.

> *"All except the name.*
> *Our ritual is done;*
> *Let spirit seek the One."*

They watched while the fire burned, and one by one the torches of the night were lit in the heavens to show Silverhair his way home. And when the great pyre began to sink in upon itself in a heap of glowing coals, as silently as they had come, the people disappeared. Only the King stood without moving. For a long time Robert waited silently behind him, but Julian never stirred, and when Marcos came, even Robert turned away. Finally, when they were almost alone, Rana went to him.

The King looked around, blinking, as she touched his arm.

"Rana." He spoke as if saying her name made her more real. The last faint glow of the firelight glinted on his hair, but his face was in darkness.

"I'm tired, Rana. I feel like a shadow, and you are a shadow too. Nothing has substance now." He gestured at the dim shapes of the trees. "Did Caolin win after all?"

"You need to rest, Julian. I have a bed—come with me."

Rana steered him through the darkness to her tent. His

tunic was soaked though with perspiration from the warmth of the night and the heat of the fire. Briskly she stripped it off of him and handed him a mug of wine.

"I should make the rounds," he muttered as he finished it. Rana refilled the mug and handed it back to him.

"The last of the Elayans are on their way home by now. Robert and Lord Eric are perfectly capable of watching over your army. Drink this."

"Have you put herbs in to make me rest?" he asked. "Silverhair told me how you drugged his tea. We laughed about it." His fingers clenched as he remembered; wine spilled and he set the mug down. "I should know that death is not the end! I have walked in the Otherworld! But I will never hear him play the harp again!"

"No." She moved both mugs aside and began to knead his neck and shoulders.

After a time his muscles started to feel like human flesh instead of stone. Rana pressed him down upon the blanket then and began to work up and down his spine until the rigidity went out of him and his arms lay relaxed, hands open and nerveless as if they had never grasped the hilt of a sword. Gently she rubbed the cool skin as if he had been a horse that had been worked too long, letting her love flow out to him through her fingers. And presently, when his breathing deepened, she blew out the lamp and lay down beside him, still holding him. . . .

"Rana! Where are you?"

Heart pounding, Rana struggled to one elbow, fighting her way back to wakefulness once more.

"Caolin's face floats in the darkness like a skull!" muttered Julian. "There were skulls in Blood Gard, and dry bones, do you remember?"

His hands closed hard on her shoulders and she bit her lip to keep him from knowing that he was giving her pain. There would be bruises later, but that didn't matter, for the armor that had imprisoned him was cracking. She had prayed for this, she dared not stop it now. Even after her own torment, she had not understood the depth of his pain.

"Hush! It doesn't matter," she whispered. "I'm here, love, I'm here!"

His head dropped against her shoulder. "Rana, don't leave me. We'll celebrate the marriage as soon as we get back to Laurelynn."

She turned her head and kissed him on the brow, and as if that had released him from some final constraint, Julian groaned and grabbed her, skin sliding against sweat-slick skin. At Beltane his will had enabled him to resist her seduction, but his body was asserting its own need now.

She had forgotten his strength, too. His grip tightened, bending her backward painfully, and she stiffened in instinctive resistance. She felt his muscles spasm; his breath came out in an agonized gasp that she realized was her name.

"*Julian.*" Perhaps the speech of the spirit would reach him. "*It is all right. I love you.*"

"*I don't want . . . to rape you,*" came the answer, "*like Caolin—not like I wanted it to be.*"

And for that, even mind to mind, words were no answer. He was almost beyond reason, trembling like a strung bow; a moment more would break him. Rana realized suddenly that the unbalanced energies raging within him must be earthed whatever the cost.

He groaned again and tried to pull himself away, and his movement released her enough to shift position beneath him. She could have escaped then, but instead, she forced herself to open her thighs and let him in.

Rana held on desperately as Julian battered against her, his body striving to touch the life in hers and claim its immortality. When it was over he wept, and she accepted his grief and his shame as she had accepted the fury of his need.

She held him until the racking sobs ceased and sleep left him emptied and unconscious in her arms. No more than he had she believed that their first night together would be this way. But as his tears dried upon her skin she understood that even this violence could bring healing. Aching in heart and body, Rana cradled that knowledge to her as she cradled the King safe in her arms, waiting for the dawn.

The sun blazed from a brilliant sky as the royal procession marched toward the central square of the city of Laurelynn. Every window was hung with bunting; bright banners sported with the wind. Julian and Rana moved through the streets beneath a rain of flowers.

"Hail to the Peacebringer! Hail to the victor of the Suisun field!" they cried. "Hoorah for the King of Westria and his Queen!"

Where is the triumph? Julian wondered, hearing them. *Would they wave their flags so exultantly if they knew they were getting such a poor excuse for a king?* At least he knew now that he was still potent, and the marriage to which the people were cheering them would not be a total sham. Caolin had only crippled, not destroyed, him. Rana's embrace had released the worst of his anguish, but it had been pity, not passion, that had opened her arms.

There was a fine, dry heat in the air already, but the sun's fires caused him no discomfort. Light shimmered from the heavy green silk of the royal mantles he and Rana were wearing, and kindled her flowing hair. On the white skin beneath her dark gown there were bruises, but he saw only serenity in her eyes. Looking at her, he was blinded.

"I am with you," Rana's thought came instantly. Through her he sensed the solid support of the cobblestones and regained contact with his body. Perhaps it would be all right. He was not the first man to walk to his wedding with a dry mouth and twisting gut.

The noise intensified as they came out into the open square. On a shaded dais before the Council Hall the Master of the Junipers was waiting for them. Trumpets blared imperiously.

"Hail to the Lady! Hail to the Master of the Jewels!" the people cried.

"People of Westria!" Mistress Anne's voice rolled out across the crowd. "Julian of Misthall and Rana of Registhorpe stand here ready to be pledged before you. Do you accept them as your king and queen?"

As the crowd exploded once more into acclamation, the heralds set the shepherd's crook into his hand and gave to Rana the cleansing broom. Robert took his place at the King's right hand, and as their arms brushed, Julian realized that his union with Rana had restored his ability to respond to the man who had been his lover as well, and that, too, made him afraid.

How will I get through this? Panic slowed his steps. *I have given everything already. I should refuse it—give Robert the Crown. I have nothing left for Rana, or for the land.*

But still they were cheering him. Robert's ceremonial gravity slipped as they reached the center of the square and he grinned like a boy. Julian tried to return the smile, and Robert punched him playfully.

No, thought the King. *He has already poured out his blood for Westria. I will not weight him with the burden that is destroying me.*

Rana had not denied him in his need, and he would not deny that of Westria. Despite his fear, Julian had never drawn back from his duty since the day the Master first told him his father's name. The raw emotions of the crowd were an elemental power whose energy carried him toward his destiny.

The ruined framework of the Council Hall had been hung with the Cloth Guild's finest weavings; as the wind off the river stirred them, the hangings shimmered like a rainbow. The Master of the Junipers stood on the broad porch, waiting, and on the altar beside him the crowns of Westria glittered in the light of the sun.

In the front ranks of the crowd Julian saw men and women who had fought beside him, who had sheltered him; the purple cloaks of the College of Bards and the red and green and black of the officers who had pledged to serve him. Frederic stood with the seneschals, the crimson cloak of his new office covering his white priest's gown. Robert had marshaled the guards behind him; Megan and his foster brothers had come from Stanesvale. He saw Rana's parents with Eric and Rosemary; Cub and Piper stood next to old Eva. Of the living, all those he loved were here. These were the people who had chosen him for their king. Why did he feel that there were others, not human, who should have been in the circle, too?

And then they were standing upon the first step, and the voice of the Master of the Junipers rang out above them.

"People of Westria, we are gathered here together to witness the pledging in marriage of a man and a woman, and in their union, the consecration of a king and a queen."

Julian bowed his head beneath the promises and bindings.

"As you shall see each other as Lord and as Lady, as such I salute you," the Master said at last. "As priest and priestess shall you be to one another, celebrating the Great Marriage that renews the world."

Julian shivered; remembering how he had taken Rana in need and violence three nights ago. Could the ritual renew his spirit, or was he desecrating the ritual? But the face of his bride was focused and calm as she offered a piece of the loaf on the altar to the earth, then held it out to him.

"As I break this bread, I offer my life to nourish you."

"As I receive it, my flesh becomes one with yours!" Julian ate, and was suddenly overwhelmingly aware of her physical presence. As he gave the bread back to her they moved closer; he felt their life lights merging as she repeated his words and ate the bread he offered her.

"As this wine is poured onto the earth, so I will pour out my spirit for you." He tipped the chalice, and the red wine flowed. Then he held it out it to Rana.

"As I drink it, my spirit mingles with yours."

Once more the exchange was completed. Julian felt his awareness twinned, so that he saw the world at once through her eyes and his own. Hope stirred within him—perhaps this marriage of the spirit would be enough for them, after all.

Julian and Rana turned to face their people, and a roar of acclamation shook the air. The sun blazed on jewels and hangings. The faces around them seemed lit from within.

"Julian, what gifts will you offer this woman to seal your union?" said the Master. "Rana, what gifts will you give to this man?"

In any other marriage, they would have given each other the fruits of the field and flowers. But what the King and Queen of Westria must exchange were the Jewels of Power. Julian had not touched them since an ecstatic certainty that now seemed to him madness had inspired him to give them to Caolin, and they had found the Jewels abandoned in the grass when they were searching for the sorcerer. The King bore his enemy's mark upon his soul already. Had the Blood Lord's touch tainted the Jewels?

The crowd had grown very still, waiting to see if the power Julian felt wakening as he reached out to the Jewels would blast his Queen.

Earthstone. He lifted the Jewel and remembered the weight of stone, the moist embrace of the earth that had been his grave. Then he clasped the belt that bore it around

Rana's hips, and suddenly he could not move. Her flesh was solid beneath his hands. The power of Earth rose through her legs and thighs as it did through his own, then uncoiled suddenly up their spines. They stood like two trees, rooted in the strength of Westria.

Rana's gaze had gone inward in wonder. Then she smiled as she had smiled at him in the Sacred Wood on Midwinter Day.

"Initiate of the Mystery of Earth," said the King, "I invest you with its power."

When the world steadied around him, Julian reached for the Sea Star. Rana understood its nature already, and as he wound the silver belt in which they had set the Jewel around her waist, he felt once more the ebb and the flow of the waves and remembered how she had come out of the sea with the Sea Star blazing on her breast and all the mystery of Deep Ocean glimmering in her eyes. Now her eyes were brimming with memories. An answering tide of emotion surged within him, but this time, it was not tears of grief but of healing that welled from his eyes.

But a cool wind off the river dried Julian's cheeks as he lifted the Wind Crystal and fastened its chain around Rana's neck. Her breath came in swift gasps, and brilliance flashed from the stone. He thought of summer storms and lightning, and memory resonated with the Crystal's mighty music. Then, very clearly, he heard a ripple of harpsong.

"Remember, the music never dies."

The voice was Silverhair's, and when he could breathe again, Julian saw Rana's eyes shining, and knew that she had heard it, too.

"I love you!" Her words were his own.

Radiance blazed between his fingers as he set the Jewel of Fire upon her brow.

"As you have given the Elements of Life to me, so I return them." Rana's voice carried clearly. Julian blinked as vision returned to normal, and his heart leaped at the joy in her smile.

She embraced him, and as the Jewels were pressed between them the people gasped at the visible outpouring of power. Then she belted the Sea Star around him and crowned him with the Jewel of Fire, but even when Rana wore Earth and Air, Julian still carried their essence within him, and he felt in her the balancing energies of Water and Fire.

"Behold," said the Master, "the Jewel Lord shares his power with his Queen."

Julian shook his head. Did not the adept understand that it was Rana who had blessed *him* today?

"Hail to the Master and the Mistress of the Jewels!" came the cry.

A trumpet blared, and the officers of the kingdom moved forward to surround them. The crimson cloaks of the seneschals glowed in the sunlight, the square blazed with purple and blue and green. A rising wind drew out the banners of the provinces in rippling waves of color against the sky.

"In the name of the Estates of Westria, will you consent to bear the crowns?" Lord Eric cried.

Borne up by the Jewels' incandescent energies, even this was possible for him now.

Frederic opened the casket, and the royal crowns flashed silver and gold as if the sun and moon were nestling there. Medallions with the arms of the Estates glowed from the interlace of metal—golden laurel leaves for the King, silver roses for the Queen.

Julian lifted the Queen's crown from its bed of silk.

"As my Queen I crown thee, as Sovereign Lady I salute thee! Lady of the Land, I offer thee my service—Lady of Life, awaken me!" he cried, and his soul was in that prayer.

He set the crown upon Rana's head, and the light of the morning sun was refracted back from it, radiant, dazzling.

Julian blinked. Was it the crown that had turned to gold or her hair? Her gown grew bright, and she was becoming taller. . . . He stepped back, the fine hairs on back and arms lifting as he realized Who stood before him.

And the Lady of Westria smiled, and took up the crown of gold.

"As King I crown thee, as Sovereign Lord I salute thee! Lord of this Land, well hast thou served Me—long life shalt thou have, and grace and glory!"

He felt the weight of the gold and bowed his head, accepting Her blessing without understanding it as he had accepted the comfort of Rana's arms. The light blazed around him, and in that moment he was complete once more.

Then the glory began to diminish. He looked at the woman beside him, and it was Rana, but she still wore the Lady's smile.

"Lord and Lady of Westria, behold your kingdom!" Eric's voice rang out across the square. "Come now, and let us keep the festival!" He drew breath to continue, then turned, frowning, as a knot of confusion erupted at the edge of the crowd.

Through the afterglow of the Lady's blessing Julian felt the first foreshadowing of fear.

"My lords, my lords!" Shouting erupted beyond him. The crowd eddied in confusion and separated to make a path for the boy who was struggling toward them. "You must come to the Red Mountain!"

Julian stiffened. It was not over then, and somehow he had known it. That was why he could not rejoice in this day. The messenger fell to his knees on the first step of the porch, fighting to get out the words the King already knew he would say.

"The Blood Lord is still alive!"

TWENTY-ONE

Rana followed the King through the charred gate of Blood Gard, trying to forget the last time she had walked that way. As she looked around her, she understood suddenly why Caolin had chosen this place for his citadel. The wind had swept away the pall of dust that usually veiled the valley, and one could see from the white-tipped cone of the Mother of Fire far to the north to the dim expanse of the Dragon Waste at the southern end of the valley; from the floating peaks of the Ramparts to the Far Alone Isles in the glittering western sea.

But the noon sunlight blazed straight down upon the summit of the Red Mountain, casting stark shadows as Julian clambered over the blackened timbers where the stairs into the barracks had been. Even from here she could feel his tension. She flinched from the reek of spilled blood and the echoes of pain imprisoned in the scattered stones. Then Julian stopped short, looking into the wreckage, and Rana felt his shock.

She felt a sick twist in her gut—or was that Julian's reaction? What she saw in the ruined dungeon seemed scarcely human. A skinny leg showed beneath the rags of a red robe as the creature tried to burrow beneath a fallen timber. "Is that really Caolin?"

"He's afraid of the light," said Julian softly. "See how he tries to cover his eyes. Just like Katiz." His voice shook with revulsion. "He tried to prison me in that darkness, and now he is trapped there."

He climbed further down, his white festal robe a glimmer in the shadows, and at the sound of his footsteps, the wretch who had once been the greatest sorcerer in Westria cowered.

"Kill him, Julian!" Robert had followed them, with Frederic and Ardra helping the Master of the Junipers down behind him. "This is too horrible!"

Julian stood gazing at his enemy, fingering the hilt of the sword he had girded over his festal robe.

"What will happen to him if he dies this way?" Rana asked the Master.

"He will be lost in that darkness forever. He is very close to it now."

The Master looked as if the ride had exhausted him, but there was a suppressed tension in the way he watched Julian.

"Give him the mercy stroke, lad! I would grant even a rabid dog that much kindness," said Lord Eric. But the King did not move.

One thrust of the sword . . . it would be no murder, but an execution.

Yesterday I could have killed him without hesitation, but if I strike him down now his shadow will never leave my soul.

Slowly Rana realized they were still linked by the Jewels. These were Julian's thoughts, not her own.

"Is there no other way?" she said aloud, and knew that

this was his thought, too. The King had turned and was looking up at them.

"You know the way," said the Master painfully. "If you have the courage. But you cannot walk it in hatred, Julian." He was trembling visibly now.

Julian bent. "Caolin, can you hear me?" The creature before him flung up its hand as if expecting a blow. Once more the King's hand clenched on his sword. Then he let it go.

"Rana—help me!" came Julian's mental call, and suddenly she understood what the Master was really asking him to do. Shivering in the sunlight, she hitched up her skirts and made her way down to him.

When he touched the sorcerer's mind, he met darkness. The flesh beneath Julian's regrown finger and toenails ached painfully. Panic was very close to the surface as he allowed those walls of darkness to close around him once more.

"You don't have to do this." Rana's arms anchored him and his fear became more bearable.

"Darkness can't be destroyed by a sword! If I kill him unhealed, the shadow will pass to me." He waited for Rana's assent, then summoned up the song of Katiz that opened the dark doorway. The bright sky and the friends who waited for him faded. He set himself to follow the road by which Caolin had invaded his memories.

"There is no body here, no soul."

He floated in the endless, empty dark.

"Caolin, where are you? I command you to answer me, Caolin."

There was no response. The name he called was only a collection of meaningless syllables. But as he probed, another presence fled him. As he pursued it, he had a sense of passing through a series of empty rooms that held the lingering scent of memories whose substance had disappeared. This was what the sorcerer had tried to do to Julian. The last of the King's hatred turned to horror as he realized the extent of the sorcerer's self-destruction.

I could find him if I knew his true Name. . . .

Julian pressed onward. Could Caolin have extinguished everything? Only his connection to Rana kept him from panicking anew at the thought of seeking this lost soul forever through the dark. But if the nameless awareness that had been the sorcerer kept running, he must have somewhere to go. Unrelenting, the King pursued him.

At the center of the darkness there was, finally, a locked room.

It was small—only a cupboard, really. But from inside Julian heard the uncomprehending sobbing of a little child.

It's dark here, and cold. He bumps his head if he sits, but his back smarts too much for him to lie down. A mind that will not cease functioning even when he is terrified is trying to understand what he did wrong. His small fists beat against the door, he hears soft footsteps and the scrape of the bolt, then a door slams against a wall.

"Lettin' him out, bitch? Not 'til he stops tellin' stories! Not until I say!"

A chair crashes over. There's the sound of a fist hitting flesh, and then his mother's despairing sobs.

"Soft, both of ye! I'll teach ye not to fill th' boy's head with lies!"

The cupboard door rattles. The child gasps, eyes tight shut as he waits for the great bright monster to drag him into the light and hurt him again. Then the bolt snicks tight once more. Heavy footsteps leave silence behind them.

"Luz, it will be all right."

His mother is still weeping, but through the spaces between the boards he can smell the sweet scent of her hair.

"Luz—my own sweet shining brightness, bright in mind and body and spirit, my radiant one!"

The child does not reply. What she says is a lie. He is not good—he has been punished too many times. The lovely spirits he thought he saw were a lie, and his mother has no power. But someday he will be big and strong, and nobody will ever hurt him again.

"Luz, I love you."

The child turns his face to the darkness and refuses to hear.

"Luz." Julian spoke the name into the darkness, then stilled in wonder, realizing that its meaning was the same as that of his own. He knew that the other had heard him this time. He drew the bolt on the cupboard door.

"Child of Light, it is the Child of Light that calls you. There's no need to be afraid."

But all that Julian could feel in that cupboard was fear. Shadow flowed from the open door. Even when he was a child Caolin's mind had been powerful, and his belief controlled his reality.

"You are a man." Rana's thought touched Julian's. *"He is afraid that you will beat him."* Her spirit took shape beside him. Her cheeks were wet with tears.

"Luz!" she knelt before the cupboard. *"Come out of the darkness and be free!"*

"You are lying," came the answer. *"You can't help me!"*

"Do you think so?" said Rana. She got to her feet again. Her black robe became a shadow as her body brightened. Now he saw her as he had this morning, clothed in the radiance of the Jewels.

"I am the strength of the Mother, and I free you!" Her brilliance increased, and the outlines of the cupboard wavered and disappeared.

Before them crouched a golden-haired child with the

sorcerer's crystal eyes. His terrified glance moved to Julian, and pity left no room for any other emotion in the King's heart. It was for this that they had crowned him. He knelt and held out his arms.

"I am the tenderness of the Father, and I love you!"

For a moment the child stared at him, and then, wailing, he flung himself into Julian's embrace.

The light around them became blinding as the King held him. He could feel Rana's arms around them both, but the light was too bright for vision. The light was singing, he heard harpsong, suddenly there seemed to be a great crowd near.

Then he was blinking in the living light of day.

"Forgive me." The murmur of supplication came from the man he held in his arms. Julian realized that he was in his own form again, and that the wasted body he cradled belonged to Caolin.

"We do." Gently Rana smoothed back the old man's matted hair.

"I forgive what you did to me," Julian added, "and what you did to my parents as well, and to Silverhair." Abruptly the King understood what else was required. "Can you pardon those who harmed you?" he asked.

The gray eyes met his, vulnerable as Julian had never seen them. "They *hurt* me."

Julian nodded. "That is why you must forgive them."

The old man's breathing was harsh in the silence. The others waited in a circle around them, but Caolin did not seem to see. Once more Julian had the sense that unseen Presences were near.

"Do you love me?" It was the voice of the child. Julian nodded, and in that moment, if only because the other man's need called it out of him, it was true.

"Then I give up . . . that . . . too." Caolin coughed, and Julian felt the life in him waver like a blown candle flame. "I am nothing now."

"You are the Child of Light!" said the Master of the Junipers, his voice harsh with triumph and sweet with pain. "And the way to the Light is opening."

Caolin focused on his ancient enemy and his eyes widened. He tried to speak, but no sound came. His lips formed the words *"I am afraid."*

Julian shivered, for as the Master named the Light he felt it flare through him. With doubled vision he saw the faces of his friends and the radiant shapes of those Others who waited around him. Behind them glowed the bright doorway through which he had guided the spirit of the herald Tarran.

"Let go," he said in the speech of the spirit, *"and I will show you the way."*

Caolin's eyes fixed on Julian's, trusting as a child's. And then suddenly they were empty. The flesh grew heavier in the King's arms.

But Julian was rising from his own body and reaching out for the drifting spirit, turning it toward the Shining Ones who stood by the Door. For a moment he saw his own father's face clearly as he had seen it once in the Otherworld. He thought he glimpsed his mother as well, and Silverhair. Then the radiance of that gateway expanded, and Caolin was gone.

"Now you are the child of earth and heaven—the stone and the star. Now you are King!" The voice of the Master of the Junipers rang like a gong.

"He forced me to become those things," said Julian somberly. "He made me learn, and so did you. Long ago at Registhorpe you said something about a promise. Have I fulfilled it?"

The Master nodded. "He could not accept forgiveness from your parents, but now at last he is healed."

Behind him, the escort were bringing up the horses to take them back to Laurelynn and the interrupted festival.

"Let the body stay here, then," said the king. "These

seared stones will be his monument. But more than Caolin needs healing now.''

"You will do it—you and Rana will do it, Julian. This place shall be cleansed and holy,'' said the Master. "Here will you establish your high seat. From this place will the healing of Westria flow.''

As the sun of the longest day sank toward the western hills, the waters of the Dorada flowed downstream from Laurelynn like a river of gold. Rana rested oars and squinted back across the glittering water. The city's walls were still crusted with scaffolding, but Midsummer bunting fluttered from every tower and rooftop as if the town had burst into belated bloom. The sounds of the festival echoed across the water as the people of Laurelynn exulted in the death of their enemy and welcomed the Jewel Lord and his Lady to their thrones.

It was only the King and Queen themselves who could not share the rejoicing, Rana thought as she angled the boat toward the island before her. That morning she and Julian had blazed with the power of the Jewels. Beneath the light of noon, they had gone into the kingdom of darkness to rescue Caolin. But as people of Westria celebrated beneath the setting sun, their king and queen had put off their power and found themselves imprisoned once more in their separate humanity.

Rosemary said their trouble was at least half exhaustion. She must give Julian time to recover, but if Rana had been patient, she would never have followed him on that first quest for the Earthstone! For a moment, understanding of just why Julian needed her teased at Rana's awareness; then the prow grazed shoaling shoreline, and she grabbed for a trailing branch to pull the boat in.

Julian has achieved so much, she told herself as she drew the rowboat up on the bank, *but we cannot wear the*

Jewels all the time. Can we somehow heal ourselves as we healed Caolin?

The isle was just downriver from the city, but it belonged to the elder kindreds. Rana called it Green Island. She had discovered it the previous winter when she needed a place to get away from Laurelynn. Willow and cottonwood grew in a tangle around the island's edges, thickly laced with vines, but the center was open, luxuriant with grasses that even at Midsummer were lush and green. In the center of the glade lay a large, water-worn rock—a natural altar stone.

Rana tied the boat and hauled out the canvas bag in which she had packed her candles and sweet herbs, a comb and a mirror for the Lady, cakes and sweet wine. In Laurelynn they would be wondering if the bride had run away from her wedding, but Rosemary knew where she was and what she was doing, and the Master of the Junipers had given her his ambiguous blessing.

Already she was humming. *Mistress of Mistresses—*

"Are you listening?" she asked the green silence. "Are you there?" She stripped off her clothes, perspiring in the close silence, and began to arrange the kindling for her fire.

By the time the sun slipped behind the western hills, all Rana's tools were laid ready. Dusk laid a hush across the river, and the red-winged blackbirds, still at last, perched like jewels among the reeds. She had bathed and rubbed her skin with scented oils, and her hair spread like a copper mantle across her shoulders. She stood before the altar stone and lifted her arms.

> *"Mistress of Mistresses—Lady of loveliness,*
> *and World's Desire—*
> *The heart She binds, the eyes She blinds,*
> *for She is Love's fire."*

Rana knelt and kindled a flame with the fire drill as Coyote had taught her. Soon a sweet-scented smoke was curling through the leaves.

> *"She is the force of men's striving; its source,*
> *just as She is the goal.*
> *Women She blesses, for we are Her dresses*
> *as She is our soul."*

As she moved, Rana glimpsed her own reflection flowing across the silver mirror on the altar. She had always thought her neck too short, wished her waist more slender, but against this backdrop there was a balance to her body that pleased her. Once more she sang.

> *"Fairest of goddesses, when we pray, heed us,*
> *and show us Thy face.*
> *Bearer of Beauty, bestow on us ecstasy*
> *in Thy embrace."*

She picked up the hand drum from the altar. Around her wrists and ankles there were bracelets of chiming bells. Herself the source of her own music, Rana began to dance.

"Lady, where are you?" her heart called then. *"How shall I find You? How shall I call You here?"* She tried to remember how the heat of the Jewel of Fire had filled her when she danced at the village festival.

A fire at her breast, a flame in her heart. She heard an echo of teasing laughter. And then the tender skin between her breasts was burning! She looked down, glimpsed a radiance, and her step faltered. After the fall of Blood Gard Julian had said that she could bear the Jewels because he no longer needed them—were they now a part of her too?

"If the Power of Fire is mine, then, Lady, I conjure you, come to me!" she cried.

Rana began to move once more, dancing as that beat demanded, and letting that compulsion carry her call. The sky was still blushing with memories of the departing day. The leaves glowed with their own green fire; the flame before the altar burned pale and bright. She felt a silken prickle of power sliding beneath her skin.

"Lady, come to me! Lady, be with me! Lady, come to me now!"

Light flowered before her.

She jerked as energy rushed up her spine and lifted her hair. The drum dropped from her hand, but it didn't matter. The world was pulsing to the drumbeat in her veins. Light edged every leaf and flickered through every tree; each grass blade glowed.

But the source of the radiance hovered above the altar—tumultuous as a flurry of failing blossoms or a whirl of doves, brilliant as the evening star. Rana saw a white hand beckoning, and heard a voice that called her name.

"People of the Wood, behold the Queen—let us array her for her bridal night!"

The flickering lights trailed green fire from the trees, and though Rana never knew whether it was they or her own perception that had changed, she saw them as olive-skinned maidens, slender and laughing as they joined the dance. This was what had been missing that morning. Only the human people of Westria had been at the wedding. Senses awakened by the Jewels of Power expanded the Queen's awareness. As they circled around her, Rana raised her arms in greeting and delight.

Garlands decked the altar now, and beside it the tree maidens were laying down a bed of sweet grasses strewn with flowers. She stilled as she recognized the smooth red-brown skin and curled bark hair of the Lady of the Madrones.

"From the People of the Wood I bear blessings. Heal the King and the land, Daughter of Men." As the Lady spoke, Rana felt the earth grow solid beneath her feet once more and remembered why she had come.

"You love him, too," she said softly. "Give us your blessing. How can I help him now?"

"Sing!" cooed the doves that swirled above the altar. "The midsummer moon is rising. Go down to the water and sing your lover to your side!"

They gave her the comb of cedarwood from the altar. And then as the mirror of the moon lifted above the valley, Rana went down to the river's edge, where she could gaze toward Laurelynn, and sat upon the bank and began to comb her hair, and sang. . . .

The newly crowned king of Westria stood on the porch of the Palace in Laurelynn, gazing downriver where the last memory of light still glowed in the sky. In the hall behind him, Robert and the guards were singing. Robert's notions of what to sing at a wedding feast were crude, and the rest were already drunk enough to join in with a will. Julian would not deny them their pleasure—he found it hard to refuse anything to those who had survived that battle. But he did not feel like singing now. Tonight he was probably the only man in Westria who grieved for Caolin.

Robert and the others had laughed when he and Rana excused themselves from the festival, and ribald remarks about the way in which the King and Queen would finish their celebration had followed them from the hall. But when Julian had changed from his robes and come back into their chamber, Rana was gone. Why was he surprised? Threatened with a repeat of their first lovemaking, why shouldn't she run from him as she had once before?

There had been no chance to tell her that he would not trouble her. The ceremony that morning had given him the strength he needed, and Westria required only that she be Mistress of the Jewels and his Queen.

The city below him glimmered with lanterns, and a bonfire burned beside the lake of Laurelynn. They were singing in the taverns, too, or perhaps they were drumming. Somebody was drumming—he could feel it like a pulse beat in his belly. Instinctively he swayed.

I learned to sing when I sought the Wind Crystal, he thought wistfully. *I should have learned to dance when I mastered the Jewel of Fire. But there was never time.* His feet were trying to dance now, though. Where was that drumming coming from?

The beat was hypnotic. Julian felt a prickle of energy along his spine and suddenly he began to wonder if what he was hearing came from the city at all. Across the river, a coyote howled. From somewhere surprisingly close to hand came an answer. Julian's fingers clenched on the railing.

"Firebringer." He cast his awareness outward. *"What is going on? Is that you?"*

"Wondered if ye'd notice, Jewel Lord!" came the answer. *"Magic's afoot t'night—go for a swim, an' maybe ye'll see!"*

In the river, at this hour? Julian stared around him, and heard coyote laughter again. Suddenly he didn't care. If Rana had left him, what did it matter where he went or with whom?

And the night *was* warm. Sweat trickled beneath his tunic even as he thought about it. Behind him the moon was rising. He saw it glimmer on the river and could almost feel the cool water soothing body and soul. Grinning, he ran up the stairs to his room. He had already stripped down when it occurred to him that the citizens of Laurelynn might be startled, even on Midsummer, to see their king completely skyclad.

Draped in a light cloak, he could have been anybody. As he slipped through the streets toward the river no one questioned him. He had a moment of uncertainty as he reached it; then a V-shaped ripple broke the silver sheet of the water.

"Will you come with us, King of Men?"

As Julian let his cloak fall, a second otter popped from beneath the surface. Moonlight glistened on stiff whiskers and sleek fur. Julian grinned. It had been too long since he had been in the water. With the grace the Sea People had taught him, he dove in.

He let the current take him and felt the tensions that had plagued him beginning to dissolve. The otters were playing around him, but when he veered toward shore they popped up before him, guiding him back to midstream. Testing his powerful muscles against the current or letting it carry him, Julian was content to let the otters guide him downstream.

Then once more he heard the drumbeat. He felt a stirring in his loins, and at last he began to understand.

Now he cooperated consciously with the river's cleansing. Beavers as well as otters were escorting him, trout and salmon flickered through the water nearby. Deer lifted their heads on the shoreline; a grizzly paused in her fishing to see him pass; he sensed raccoons and possums, a skunk and a family of water rats, owls hovering softly in the moonlit air. Each creature touched him with its power as he passed.

The otters slowed. Treading water, the King saw an isle that glimmered with green fire.

He came up out of the river with the water streaming off him like silver and was met by a blast of air as dry and fragrant as a meadow on a summer day. He stared into a sphere where air flowed like water, and tried to understand the bright shapes that swam within.

"The Lady invites you to Her feast," came a voice like silver bells. *"But you must be arrayed for the festival."*

"I left my clothes behind in Laurelynn!" stammered Julian.

"Quite right, too," came the reply. *"But have you no friends to lend you their semblances?"*

The Guardians wore the appearance of human beings when they wished to communicate with men. But it was as the Elder Kindreds that they had summoned him. Whose shape would suit him now? He thought of the strength that had so often served and sometimes embarrassed him, and suddenly he felt his limbs covered by the grizzled fur of the great bear. He lifted his head, remembering himself a king, and felt upon his brow the weight of an antler crown. Fire coursed through him, and his phallus filled with power.

Fur and feathers, scales and skin, all of these clothed him, and when man and beast were one, the Lord of Westria arose, and the barrier of light opened and he entered into the sanctuary.

Rana felt the presence of the Lady behind her, as if she stood before a raging fire, and heard Coyote's howl. All the Guardians of Westria had come to the wedding now. On her right hand, the heated air was rippling with invisible currents. She sensed the mighty wings of the great Eagle fanning the blaze. To her left, the swirling of Sea-Mother's mantle sent waves of emotion through the circle. At any moment now they were going to sweep her away. And still the tension grew.

Light shimmered and thinned and flared again in sight-searing radiance, and Rana blinked at the shape that strode toward her from the north, where the power of Grandmother Grizzly anchored the world. With double vision she saw the beast-shape and the human form within it— the *male* form. Rana felt her own fires burn more sweetly at the realization, and then, through the masks of man and beast and god that veiled him, she recognized Julian.

> *"Fire in the depths, fire in the tree—*
> *Heaven's fire brings you to me."*

The words of her summoning sang in the air. His voice rang like the belling of the stag as he answered her.

> *"Fire in the stone, fire in the star—*
> *Moonfire shows me where you are."*

Bells chimed as Rana began to dance around him. The circle of tree maidens whirled and swayed, moving faster. She saw Lady Madrone's ruddy arms lifting, and the tall shape of the Lord of the Trees. The clearing seemed to have expanded. Beyond the Redwood, all the kindreds were frolicking. Rana blinked, and glimpsed Coyote's grin.

> *"Heartfire burning ever bright,*
> *Spirit's lightning, blinding sight!"*

The King stamped out the rhythm as he turned to face her. A healthy male musk radiated from his fur as she passed. Power crowned him and rayed from his shoulders in mighty wings.

> *"Fire in the loins, fire in the skin,*
> *Fire in the blood that burns within—"*

Rana could feel that fire melting her. She missed a step and stood trembling before the bed of sweet grasses that the tree spirits had made. The Presence of the Lady sparked through her and her human consciousness flared like a leaf caught in the flame. She was the fire, and at the same time she was all that desired the flame.

But she was also the sea, wanting the sun's warmth to waken life in her womb, and the earth, willing the wind to bring her seed. As the King began to move toward her, the radiance of the Lady of Fire shimmered into the shape of the Lady of Westria.

The response was not in Rana's voice, though her lips formed the words.

> *"Fire in the womb, fire in the rod,*
> *Fire when the Goddess joins with the God!"*

Once, an untried boy, Julian had lain with a goddess not knowing. The Master of the Jewels knew the Lady who had blazed before him that morning, but the man within him also recognized the human vehicle through whom that glory shone. He reached out to her on all levels and found no fear. And then the Goddess in her sang to him, and he felt his own human awareness whirling away. A last thought came to him—he had not forced this upon her. It was Rana who had called him here.

"The Jewel Lord seeks the Lady of Westria!" he cried aloud. "The King of Westria has come to claim his Queen!" Another step brought him to her side.

She laughed, and the air shimmered around her. Her scent was the breath of all the orchards of Westria. He warmed his hands at the bright blaze of her hair. Then his fingers were tangling in that silken radiance. Her arms fastened around him. Her breasts brushed his chest and he felt her nipples harden; his own body responded with a vigor that was almost pain.

He was laughing with delight in her beauty and in the same moment groaning with need. The world was a dizzy spiral of stars around them as they fell together onto the sweet-scented hay. A memory of humanity told him, *I am not going to be gentle this time either*, but that didn't matter. The strength that had endured him the first time surged to receive him now.

Now—and now! Julian's own power, unchecked, drove him onward, but however far he fared, she stayed with him. *My life in you! My life for you!* his spirit cried. His frustrated, anxious desire for Rana and the love and terror with which he had served Westria were the same. But now all the channels were clear. All that he had to give was welcomed and returned.

He was the lightning piercing heaven, the whirlwind, the ninth wave, the seed penetrating earth's welcoming womb.

He was Julian.

Consciousness focused. He saw Rana whole and whispered her Name.

She cried out in triumph, and all the land of Westria felt the same pulse of ecstasy. Light exploded within. Then the fire roared through him and seared the last of his enemy's darkness away.

On the Red Mountain, the wood that had been piled for the beacon fire burst spontaneously into flame. As the flames roared upward, another fire sparked across the river on a peak above the battlefield. A beacon sprang to life to the southward as well. As the King and Queen of Westria joined, fire sprang from summit to summit the length of the land as peak proclaimed to peak the triumphant refrain:

The Elements are at war with man no longer, for the Lord and the Lady are at one with the Land.

ACKNOWLEDGMENTS

I'd like to express my gratitude to all of those who have read the various draft versions of the Chronicles of the Jewels since I first discovered Westria in 1971, especially Kelson, Elizabeth Pope, Judy Gerjuoy, Christine Lowentrout, Loren Davidson, and Leigh Ann Hussey. Their enthusiasm and faith gave me the courage to keep exploring. I am indebted to the Guardians of Westria as well for their inspiration, above all to Coyote, who refused to let this book be a tragedy.

For help with *The Jewel of Fire* specifically I want to thank:

—Jon Moriarty of 14 Karats in Berkeley for his information on goldsmithing and for loaning me Herbert Maryon's classic book on metalworking (*Metalwork and Enameling*, Dover, 1971);

—Lynx Crowe, who sped over roads where I would have crawled so that I could see Mount Lassen in the snow;

—Clint Bigglestone, for once more coming to the aid of Westria's armies and working out for me the numbers, arms, and strategies of both sides in the final battle;

—April Stockley for permission to use the invocation to Grandfather Coyote in chapter 9, and to Leigh Ann Hussey for permission to use the chorus from "Harper David" in chapter 15. The whole song is available on her tape *Home Brew*, © 1988, Homebrewed Cassettes.

—and my apologies to the wolf tribe, who are loyal to their own kind and fair to their foes, performing a valuable function in maintaining the balance of nature. Caolin's creation of the Blood Wolves is, of course, a perversion of wolf nature as well as that of humankind.

Those who would like to continue exploring Westria are welcome to write to the Companions of Westria, c/o Loren Davidson, Box 472, Berkeley, CA 94701, which publishes *Westrian Words* and sponsors events and meetings.

FANTASY BESTSELLERS
FROM TOR

☐	55852-9	ARIOSTO	$3.95
☐	55853-7	*Chelsea Quinn Yarbro*	Canada $4.95
☐	53671-1	THE DOOR INTO FIRE	$2.95
☐	53672-X	*Diane Duane*	Canada $3.50
☐	53673-8	THE DOOR INTO SHADOW	$2.95
☐	53674-6	*Diane Duane*	Canada $3.50
☐	55750-6	ECHOES OF VALOR	$2.95
☐	55751-4	*edited by Karl Edward Wagner*	Canada $3.95
☐	51181-6	THE EYE OF THE WORLD	$5.95
☐		*Robert Jordan*	Canada $6.95
☐	53388-7	THE HIDDEN TEMPLE	$3.95
☐	53389-5	*Catherine Cooke*	Canada $4.95
☐	55446-9	MOONSINGER'S FRIENDS	$3.50
☐	55447-7	*edited by Susan Shwartz*	Canada $4.50
☐	55515-5	THE SHATTERED HORSE	$3.95
☐	55516-3	*S.P. Somtow*	Canada $4.95
☐	50249-3	SISTER LIGHT, SISTER DARK	$3.95
☐	50250-7	*Jane Yolen*	Canada $4.95
☐	54348-3	SWORDSPOINT	$3.95
☐	54349-1	*Ellen Kushner*	Canada $4.95
☐	53293-7	THE VAMPIRE TAPESTRY	$2.95
☐	53294-5	*Suzie McKee Charnas*	Canada $3.95

Buy them at your local bookstore or use this handy coupon:
Clip and mail this page with your order.

Publishers Book and Audio Mailing Service
P.O. Box 120159, Staten Island, NY 10312-0004

Please send me the book(s) I have checked above. I am enclosing $ _____
(Please add $1.25 for the first book, and $.25 for each additional book to cover postage and handling.
Send check or money order only—no CODs.)

Name _____
Address _____
City _____ State/Zip _____
Please allow six weeks for delivery. Prices subject to change without notice.